ATTUNED DUNGEON

THE METIER APOCALYPSE
BOOK 2

FRANK G. ALBELO

MOUNTAINDALE
PRESS

ACKNOWLEDGMENTS

I want to thank my family for all the support they have given me with my writing efforts. My wife, for putting up with the random notes left scribbled everywhere and for my son being a constant inspiration with his silly shenanigans. I want to thank all the great people over at MDP for helping my dream of crafting stories for the enjoyment of strangers step into a new, brighter future.

And lastly, but not least, I want to remind everyone that this book is as much mine as the betas, Patrons and readers that helped it reach where it is now. Without their support, I wouldn't be where I am today.

So, I hope all you new readers have a wonderful time delving deeper into the world of Metier!

PROLOGUE

When Ingrid Metier came to, she was not in her husband's office. The world felt heavier, and not only because she suspected she'd been drugged. Something that she couldn't see but felt almost like a membrane pushed in around her, but didn't restrict her movements at all.

While momentarily distracted by the strange phenomena, her son jumped to his feet beside her. He'd already been stirring awake; her lethargic rousing was the push he needed to gain lucidity.

"Mom? What's going on? Where are we?" he asked groggily, spinning around in a slow circle to take in the stone walls, a door with a glass opening, the colored portrait of a field at high noon and the edge of a toilet past an open door. His eyes stopped roving when he spotted a soldier through the small glass on the first door he'd spotted.

He checked to make sure that his mom was okay and strode up to the glass. His insistent taps finally snapped the guard's daydream. When the soldier spotted the frosty, bloodshot eyes of Marcus Metier staring him down, he couldn't help but shiver before approaching the comm on the door.

"Good to see you are awake, sir."

"Where the hell are we? And why did someone spike me and my mother to all hell?" Marcus asked, doing his best to hold his indignation at bay.

"We were ordered to bring you here until you were cleared to join the others, sir," the soldier said, tilting his head in confusion. "Were you not aware?"

"Aware of what?" Marcus asked, pressing his fist against the glass. Even with the barrier between them, the soldier flinched.

"I—"

"I'll take it from here, private." The pristine image of a military man appeared behind the soldier and stared down at Marcus. "You have given us quite the trouble, Mr. Metier. Two of my soldiers were not able to come to this Bunker thanks to the injuries you gave them."

The man's voice was as flat as deflated balloons, but it was one Ingrid recognized. Withdrawing from her own thoughts, the woman strode up beside her son to glare. Just to glare.

"Good to see you in good health, Ingrid. I do hope you will be ready to continue your work soon. Humanity will need your efforts."

"Where is my husband, Starden?" Ingrid demanded without preamble.

"You are an intelligent woman, Ingrid. You should know what it means that you are here and he is not."

"Then you best get me out of this room. He needs me," she said, her voice cracking.

"I'm afraid I cannot do—" Cracks spiderwebbed through the glass as Marcus cracked his knuckles on it. Blood dripped from his fist but the man did not care in the slightest.

"Where is my father?"

Starden had always been a Florida boy. As such, he'd never even been ice skating before. However, when he looked at Marcus, he could only feel like he was skating on thin ice. It was a sensation that infuriated him. To feel it from a man in a cage was more than he could bear.

Before he could dig his grave deeper, a dimpled man strode up to the window. "Might I, sir? I think this won't necessitate your...uniformed charms."

The general threw a frown at the newcomer, then squinted his eyes at the private. It was a silent admonishment if there ever had been one. With the slightest of nods, the two made their way down the hall and out of sight. The dimpled man sighed heavily before looking up at Ingrid and Marcus.

"I'm sorry I wasn't here to greet you first," the man said.

"Elias, don't give me pleasantries. I want to know what's going on. Where is Raph?"

"Ingrid... I don't know how to tell you this, but Raphael is gone. We lost communication with the surface yesterday." He paused as the words caught in his throat. Right before their very eyes, the man aged twenty years. "The crystals... They reached Earth."

CHAPTER ONE

Awkward Introductions

Considering the events of the day, everyone involved was unnaturally silent. After Sarah the orc lady's initial attempt to get an answer as to our origin, and my subsequent silence when their reception proved less than cordial, we'd been cordoned off just at the edge of the wall.

Even with access to the communication feature in our implants, Daniela, Samuel, and I remained silent. No one would hear the conversation happening through our thoughts, but I didn't want to risk reacting to something we discussed. The only thing forcing us to break our stoicism was trying to keep Blobby and Anthony from running off.

Three hours of standing still had even *me* antsy to move, but I refused to crack. My slime companion kept mitosing and merging to pass the time, while Anthony clambered up the wall with ease. Thankfully, Daniela made sure that her fire ant friend didn't climb *over* the side and possibly get shot by the very people we'd tried to save.

When the sun was crashing down past the trees, the first group of the Wild Guard we'd met relieved the others watching us. Oliver, the name of the man who felt the need to keep his gun leveled at me the whole time, and his team of gunslingers had been equally silent and even more restless than we were.

"Are you ready to talk?" Sarah asked, crossing her significant arms across her chest.

"You have our answer. We just want to be friends, but we are not obligated to tell you anything," I said, repeating myself for the umpteenth time.

"I suppose you just expect us to let you go on your merry way, now don't you?"

"That would be lovely actually. Thanks!" I said, taking a step towards the woods.

Oliver, who was already walking toward the town's gate, snapped around to aim his rifle at me. His team trained another group of guns in my direction. While the others on Sarah's team stood at the ready behind her, the orc woman didn't flinch.

"You must think this is a joke."

"It actually wouldn't surprise me. There's not much Ronan takes seriously," Daniela said from over my shoulder. Her teeth clicked in her mouth when she shut it. I sighed at my friend's slip, turning to the orc woman again.

"Ronan, is it? Well, pleased to make the acquaintance of such a powerful Geo." She mocked me with a poor curtsy.

As much as I wasn't bothered by the display, I had to admit she had a way of getting around people's defenses. *Makes sense she would be the leader of the Wild Guard.*

"The pleasure is all mine. Now, if we are done with the formalities, can we go? It's already late and we would much rather not be out in the open during the night." I kept my voice even, and she finally dropped the intentional attempts to rile us up.

"I can't let you do that, Ronan. The Council wants to speak with you. They may even have more questions than I do." *Was that a pleading tone in her voice?*

With my increases in Perception, I'd been able to better deduce reactions in battle. Social nuances, especially of what some might consider a different subspecies of human, not so much.

"What do you guys think?" I communicated through the comm-plant. *Dammit, Danny got that name for it in my head.* I did my best to keep my face blank as I did the next best thing to telepathy with my friends.

"Unless we want to fight a dozen people, probably humans, we should follow along. Maybe figure out how to mold our story without giving everything away. Might as well try to learn something while we are here," Sam said. The blond had helped heal most of the injured and they'd been eager to welcome him. Daniela and I, well, our magical power made us a tad more worrisome for them.

"One night. Should we actually be detained, everyone involved is going to have a bad time. Yes?" I said, turning from her to Oliver.

The man couldn't be more than a few years older than me, but he glared at me like I had kicked his puppy. I had no idea what his problem was.

"I think we can manage that. Tim, get them acquainted with town a bit while I go update the Council heads. Once you are done, feel free to bring them by the office," the orc woman said.

The pink-colored man, evidently Tim, waved our group over. When Blobby and Anthony followed, he held up a hand to stop us. "You can't bring those in the town."

"Why not? They are a part of our group," Daniela said. Her words were punctuated by a little bit of steam released from her heat gills.

"Danny, it's okay. If they aren't used to creatures in the town, then it will be for the best. Sam, we still got those provisions?"

"Got them in the back over by the V-wall," he said, pointing to one of the fortifications I'd created during our fight with the Dreg.

"I assume you lot can feed us for a day?"

"How insolent can you—" Oliver's tirade was cut off by a slicing motion from Sarah.

"We can do that. However, you will have to surrender your weapons while in town."

My fists clenched so hard the knuckles cracked, but Sam placed a placating hand on my shoulder before I could argue the stipulation. His face smiled and nodded our agreement while he spoke to me through the comm-plant. "We *are* weapons, Ron. No sense alienating anyone more than they already are." His gaze landed poignantly on Oliver and his team.

Daniela had no compunctions about protesting. "Oy! You lot already outnumber us and now you want to leave us naked when this gun-toting limp noodle has been waving a barrel in our face the whole time we've been here?"

"I—" Before Sarah could fall into Danny's rousing argument trap, I cut in.

"Danny, it's fine. Take a breath. Sam, go get food for Blobby and Anthony, please. Daniela and I will cordially hand over our weapons," I said, pulling my Infused Pickaxe from my belt strap. I didn't remove my shield, and none of them looked like they intended to take it. Daniela's hands flashed and her Fang Daggers landed in the dirt point down.

"You better not lose those," she added. She and Sarah then proceeded to have a passive aggressive arm crossing competition.

"Since we are waiting for my friend to feed our pets, which will be staying outside in the wild," I said, gesturing at the mess left by our fight, "care to elaborate on your dilemma with the Tendrils? How did that name come about, by the way? We tend to just call them corrupted."

Who would have thought lying through my teeth to people I'd never met would come so easy?

Sarah watched me for a few seconds before she picked up my pickaxe and stuffed the daggers in the back of her utility belt. I noted the half-dozen knives strapped to her leg for the first time.

"Those things have been extracting food from us for years. Not right sure where the name came from, but it stuck. As for this 'dilemma,' I think potato one and potato two explained it as well as anyone. We just can't afford to pay the amount of food demanded to receive their protection anymore. Wildwood is bigger than it has ever been, even with the losses we've had in the last few years."

"So the Tendrils are what? The mafia?" I asked.

"Not sure what that is, but if you mean they keep most of the murderous wildlife from attacking us while we feed them, then yes."

Before I could ask a follow up question, Sam returned with our pack. Thankfully, we'd stashed the majority of our supplies before joining the melee. Sam and I split the food between our two creature companions and asked them to remain close to the walls but on the outside. Anthony appeared more confused than Blobby, but unfortunately the situation didn't allow for much flexibility to spend time teaching the fire ant how to 'stay.'

The Wild Guard watched us intently but thankfully Sarah had already urged Oliver to make his way back to the wall. He and his group proceeded to glare at us from there, which wasn't much better, but at least he wasn't in our faces.

After feeding our creatures, Tim and Sarah walked through the gate with us on their heels. Sarah split off from us to speak with the two dwarves in her team. Thanks to my growing Perception, I was able to overhear her telling them to get Oliver to cool his jets. I was familiar with the phrase thanks to the plethora of media available to us in the Bunker, but I wondered how it'd survived on the surface. *On that thought, how much of our cultural perspective has been retained by people growing up on the surface?*

Two buildings in decent condition flanked the gate and I spotted a pair of guards with pre-Fall bows within. Neither had arrows nocked, but they looked ready to use the weapons if the need arose. A woman with bright yellow skin nodded to Tim and we walked into Wildwood proper. A crooked sign told me we'd just crossed onto Buena Vista Boulevard, which stretched into the distance before bending slightly. Houses and several dozen other people milled about, watching us.

Clearly they were there to observe us, but I watched them right back. Something within me surged, dumping unbridled amounts of adrenaline I hadn't felt before. It wasn't because we were in danger, even if we possibly were, but because we'd found them. Humans.

While only one in five looked purely human, these mostly being the older people I noticed on the streets, the others were a combination of fantasy races. Squat dwarves, towering elves, a number of various-colored individuals, and a fair share of orcs. I even spotted a pair of satyr scramble away with baskets in hand. I almost made a comment about being transported into a video game to my friends, but they were gawking just as badly as me.

"Ronan, how many people is this?" Danny whispered from my right.

"That would be somewhere in the three hundred range. The census was last year and most departments keep their own records on those they are assigned," Tim answered helpfully.

"How? How do you keep this many people fed!?" Sam asked, alarmed. He was pale. I almost reached out to steady him but he plowed on. "The sheer logistics and managerial oversight would be astounding."

Tim laughed at his reaction. "You three sure are strange. I assume you know food grows faster after the Fall. Beyond the wizardry of the House of Commerce, I don't know the specifics. Well, we do have this to supplement our farms." The pink man took a turn south that went past a building covered in half-milled logs. The sight beyond was more water than I'd ever seen. "There are two wetlands within the town we use to trap crayfish and some catfish. This is Lake Miona, and Lake Sumter lies further to the east."

The half-milled logs I'd seen were used as part of a dock

that extended into the lake. Some hundred feet out, men in rafts were hoisting nets onto their crafts. On closer inspection, I realized they were reptilian in nature. Scales of all colors of the rainbow shone in the afternoon light. We stood for a few minutes, gaping as the fishermen worked. My Perception marked several pinpricks in the distant sky, but I brushed that off as something new rose out of the water.

If I'd thought Tim and the other colorful people had strange ears, then what rose out of the water put that concept to shame. Flaps as big as their head flicked like hair before settling flat against their skin. A delicate set of feminine features told me the new arrival had to be a woman. She exchanged some words with the lizardmen on the raft before diving back underwater. I noticed the slight flick of gills on her neck. The next moment, the raft was moving as if on its own. The lizardmen balanced their catch and themselves with practiced ease and were soon offloading on the dock. The merwoman hoisted herself onto shore and I saw the numerous other fins along her body, all flapping flat as if they'd never been there.

"The Reppys are masters of managing the lakes. Without them, we would have starved a long time ago," Tim said, waving at the lizardmen. They waved back, but stuttered in their motion when they spotted our group with him. They didn't dilly-dally, hurrying about their tasks and making it a point not to look in our direction.

"Don't give good impressions, eh?" Daniela said, matching Tim's stride to make conversation.

"Not many people have the Gift, regardless of how much they train. The three of you have already shown more Gifts than anyone in this whole town. Well… all except one, but you need not be concerned about that. The Council heads will want to know how you managed that."

"We killed many ants," Sam said, flatly.

Tim stumbled mid-step, but managed to catch himself. "I see."

The rest of the walk was silent. That was fine by me, as I

gazed upon a living and breathing human community. *Well, mostly human. Until proven otherwise, I am going to assume the fantasy races are humans subject to some magic shenanigans.* Everyone gave us odd looks, probably because we weren't in our forties and still appeared mostly like pre-Fall humans. When we finally made it around the bend of Buena Vista Blvd, my eyes were glued to the main feature of the town.

A three story tall Metier Crystal sat at the heart of it all. I could have been hallucinating from exhaustion, but I swore the air took on a shimmer the closer we got to the otherworldly object. Where there should have been an impact crater to level the entire state was only a slight furrow in the ground. Beyond the crystal, I saw what must have been Lake Sumter. The closer we got to the crystal, the more I realized it was *in* the lake, with a series of bridges and floating docks lining the edges of the crystal. Several people were idly running their hands on it, or just watching its inner iridescent glow like the most magnificent of light features even during the day.

Neither of my friends said anything as we gawked at the crystal. Tim apparently had failed to notice our speechlessness until we turned down another street. When he did, he chuckled awkwardly.

"Sorry, don't tend to give too many tours. Only ever had like three visitors and the last told us never to go south. I'm sure you all know about the Metier Crystals. The catalysts for the end of the world, all that good stuff. Well, that there is why Wildwood still stands."

"How do you mean?" I asked, turning from the crystal to the pink man.

"I'll let the Councilor of New Earth explain that one." He chuckled again before leading us through what I could only call 'downtown' Wildwood.

A few large, concrete buildings that had seen better days were scattered about. Between those buildings were dozens of little wood pavilions with people working on them on a number of things. I even spotted a forge in one of those spaces. The sheer amount of trades showcased all amidst each other distracted me away from the explanations Tim was giving about the concrete buildings.

Acrid, sour smells wafted from the furthest pavilion. Within were a team of elves with masks over their faces, working sets of leather and setting them out to dry. As we passed the forge, the din of steel and the iron taste of metal hung in the air. Two dwarves were hammering away at what looked like scrap metal, forcing it to behave as best they could. The final group of pavilions had a series of orcs cranking a spool as a whole team of elven women managed a loom with expert fingers.

The whole endeavor had me speechless. Not only were a group of people almost as large as the entirety of our Bunker, but they were doing things that I could only dream of doing in the Bunker. The sudden itch to infuse was hard to ignore, but our tour had come to an end.

"And this," Tim gestured with a flourish, "is the Council Office. Not much, I'll admit, but the people inside have done wonders for us. They should be expecting you."

The building in question was yet another block of concrete with, amazingly, two large window panes that had somehow survived the apocalypse in pristine condition. Tim took two steps back as he held the door open for us. A little bell chimed as we stepped into the building. A back door as well as the front windows provided a reasonable amount of light for the three men sitting within. It might have also been better lit than expected as a result of the man who rose immediately to greet us.

"Wonderful! Our visitors have arrived!" A man clearly in his fifties jumped to his feet. His hair flickered with fire, instead of gray as one would expect. Not a strong flame, but just enough for one to notice the light and smoke rising off it. He gave each of us a firm handshake while looking us in the eye. It felt a bit deliberate, but his smile was genuine enough. "I am Councilman Dylan Sage. My daughter must think great things of you if she let you into town. She does have a penchant for violence. As a matter of fact, she wasn't able to stay thanks to that very thing. Organizing a guard rotation, you understand."

Sarah's father, eh? I can see the resemblance. The two had almost no features they shared other than the fire hair, but I was sure that had more to do with the orcish traits of his daughter.

"She has more than enough reason to be cautious. We'd have been long dead if we acted meekly like you want," the second man in the room said.

"Ah, yes, of course. No need to bring these children into our bickering discussion, Kirby," Dylan said.

The man named Kirby huffed while bypassing the fiery-headed councilman. In the light of his companion's hair, I spotted several patches of pink and blue scales hidden just under the collar of his shirt. "Kirby Salem, Councilman of New Earth."

Compared to Dylan's, the handshake he offered us would be called limp fish. I didn't have much experience shaking hands. From a plethora of media, it was said that handshakes can tell you a lot about a person. These two landed straight in the enigma category for me.

"Irwin, wake up. We have guests," Dylan whispered harshly over his shoulder.

"Huh? What?" the third man said as he snapped awake. "Oh, sorry. Was grabbing a little snoozy poo. Welcome to Wildwood. I'm Irwin Bellwick." Unlike his two companions, he just waved meekly at us. At the ends of his hands, I noted wickedly sharp barbs of some kind. They didn't look harmless. No sooner had I seen them, they were tucked behind his back.

"It's good to finally—" Dylan was cut off as a pulse rippled through the room. The people in the room staggered as what I'd come to recognize as a Metier Crystal's pulse flowed over us.

"What in tarnation," Kirby huffed.

I didn't wait for their response, instead rushing outside on the heels of my friends. They'd already been making their way out of the building. With a gasp, I saw what was coming a mile away. The largest swarm of birds I'd ever seen blotted out a quadrant of the sky.

"Incoming! Take defensive positions. Aerial threat!" Dylan shouted as soon as he saw the threat.

"Wild Guard, to arms," Kirby called a moment later.

Patterned bell rings echoed across the town and people streamed in semi-orderly lines as the afternoon sun faded away. Within moments, Oliver and his group were perched on the top of one of the buildings. A swirl of air was picking up around that building and many people rushed for cover. Tim, who'd been close by, stood on top of the wooden pavilions with his machete brandished.

"Sorry, kids. We'll have a talk later, yes?" Irwin said before leaping straight up the side of the nearest building. His hands left furrows on the blocks as he scampered up to the roof.

"We aren't going to sit this out, are we?" Daniela asked, a spell chain already forming around her hand.

"Me and Sam will take defense, you take as many down as you can," I said simply. The woman bounded away with a vicious grin on her face, dodging the rows of people thanks to her incredible mobility attribute.

Within moments, the creatures were in range for me to identify them with my implant. As I roved over the sheer number of them, I grit my teeth.

<Dreg Tendril (Crow)>
<Attunement: Death>
<Refinement: N/A>
<Perceived Metier Quotient: 0>

<Dreg Tendril (Crow)>
<Attunement: Death>
<Refinement: Carrion>
<Perceived Metier Quotient: 1>

This could be even more dangerous than the Tendrils' attack! As soon as the thought crossed my mind, I couldn't help but wonder if our routing of the Tendrils earlier in the day and this surge of crows were connected. I didn't have much time to contemplate as the first of the creatures fell from the sky thanks to a well-placed shot by Oliver. It thudded to the ground, releasing a cloud of miasma and feathers.

Its murder did not go unnoticed as the whole *murder* cawed their indignation and plunged toward the ground with wild abandon.

CHAPTER TWO

Attuned Scavengers

It was pandemonium.

Most of the townspeople sought refuge under the pavilions, but the crows were raining down with abandon. Right before me, most fell from the sky as another pulse from the crystal interrupted their flight. However, the fall wasn't enough and they were able to align their flights and land on the ground. As far as I could tell, at least ten orders of magnitude angrier. Their large wingspans were quite intimidating in the waning sun.

The crack of a whip snapped me out of my thoughts as Sam crushed a Q0 crow with his <Vine Whip>. The ten foot long plant spun as it followed Sam's gestures, smacking another two of the crows before they could even get close to the crafters. When a pair bypassed my friend, I ignored the gunshots and fireballs dealing with the birds in the sky. *Having any aerial-capable weapons or skills is now at the top of my list.*

Regardless, I got directly in front of one of the dog-sized creatures and slapped it away using my chitin shield. The second, I punted away. A glimpse told me that despite most people cowering from the main attack, many finished off any creatures in range of them after I'd downed them. The dwarves I'd seen earlier used their still-hot metal instruments to crush one of the birds' heads, while the mob of orcs were dogpiling the other.

Not nearly as worried about the Wildwoodians anymore, I placed myself as the catcher of diving birds. Any that tried to reach the group, I would intercept with my shield, or a well-placed <Stone Spike>. While my timing wasn't perfect, I always managed to at least clip the bird with the half-powered spear of compressed earth. There was going to be a huge mess to fix up in the work area. I was sure they wouldn't mind as long as they survived.

At fifty percent mana, the stream of birds wasn't letting up, many hopping out of range or behind buildings out of sight. Some of the few Q1 crows were spitting up foul-smelling blobs of flesh. The putrid scent drifted in the air. None of them had reached me or Sam, but the other defenders were coughing up a storm.

"What do they want!?" I shouted over the gunshots and crackling fires. I knew that crows were actually supposed to be intelligent and canny birds. They'd stopped attacking directly as soon as we stemmed their initial attack, waiting us out and using the disgusting blobs to wear us down.

"They are probably here for the bodies," one of the women hiding in the pavilions said.

"What bodies?" I asked, looking over my shoulder to the elf.

A whip cracked, slapping a bird to the ground. Somehow it managed to remain alive, so I stomped on its feathery neck. Thanks to keeping my foot on the creature, it started to crystallize and a meager trickle of Pith flowed from it into Sam and I. The Wildwoodians were stunned for a moment, but at my insistence the woman continued.

"We normally never keep more than one or two bodies in any one part of the town. It attracts too many creatures hungry for the corpses. With the fight we had earlier, and the huge boars the Big Guns brought earlier today, I fear that is what attracted them."

"Point me to them," I said, already doubling down on the plan. I wasn't going to bother asking why the Big Guns sounded like a capitalized phrase.

"I'll take you," she said resolutely. A man in the crowd moved to stop her, but she snatched her arm away. "He is helping us. Bite it, Gareth."

The woman rushed toward one of the concrete block buildings we hadn't passed by on our tour.

"Sam, double down. I have a plan!" The man gave me a grunt as he slapped another frisky crow that got too close.

The crows took notice of the two of us separating away from the bigger group and moved to pick us off.

"Danny, I could use some cover fire," I said through the comm-plant.

In response, three blasts of compressed fire detonated in the air above us. I knew they weren't the strongest of her attacks, but it served to redirect the crows from intercepting us before we entered the building through one of the back doors. They flapped madly, trying to put out the embers that clung to their feathers.

There was a large loading bay folding door just next to a person-sized access. The woman produced a key and unlocked the door. Sure enough, when we stepped inside, there were piles upon piles of bodies. I recognized most of the bodies of the Tendrils we'd fought earlier that day, as well as the three massive boars in the center of the room. My senses had been focused on fighting the crows so much I'd barely registered the stench of fresh death.

"We need to give them this. Now."

"But, how will we eat?"

"We'll figure it out. Live now, eat later."

With that, I lifted the twenty foot loading bay door. Mana trickled into my shield to pump my Strength Attribute. The metal groaned for a second before it started to slide on well-oiled rollers up into the ceiling. Still funneling mana for the strength boost, I tossed body after body out into the open. The woman who'd let me into the building hesitated, but eventually joined me in dragging the boar bodies out. Even with my enhanced strength, the creatures were beasts. As soon as they were in the open, the cawing all around us stopped. The silence was only broken by the occasional gunshot and bird splat, but even those stopped as the silence spread.

Then the entire murder screeched in our direction.

"Shit," I grunted as I tossed one final humanoid tendril body out of the building. "Close the door!" I shouted.

The woman complied, shutting the access door as I leapt up and used my weight to bring the loading dock door down faster. Just in time for the first crow to crash into it. Then another and another. When the metal started to give, I used the remainder of my mana to erect <Stone Spikes> inside the building to brace both doors. The impacts of birds against the giant metal door inside the small loading area felt like someone playing my eardrums as musical instruments.

The woman cried out and coiled into herself as blood poured out of her ears. Not knowing what else to do, I placed my palms over her ears and hoped that would mute the sound somewhat. When my mana had completely run out, and the boost from my infused shield winked out, the constant impacts ruptured my own eardrums. I glanced at my status to see my health ticking down one percent for each gong-like attack.

Thankfully, those did not last much longer. I heard the muffled crack of gunfire before the ground-shaking caws returned. Except, as I listened, the sounds moved further and further away with each second. I slumped to the ground beside the woman. I felt the need to comfort her against the pain somehow, but all I managed was an awkward pat on the shoulder.

Thankfully, Sam and Danny burst through the access door. Literally. With a gout of flames. Danny had used her <Flame Blast>, which nearly reached us before it snuffed out. I nudged

Sam over to the woman first and he tapped her gently with one of his <Health Bumps>. *Don't you worry, Sam, I made note that you don't actually have to slap me to heal me.*

With a heal thrown my way, in forehead slap form, my friends helped us out of the building. The only body that remained was the air-attuned Tendril, all the others we'd managed to get out. While the outside was a mess of multicolored blood and guts, the crows had taken the offering and left us alone.

My eyes tracked the gory trail and I spotted the murder disappearing towards the south. Many were working together to carry the bigger creatures and several were carrying their own dead. Not all of them had been recovered, but there weren't nearly enough crow bodies around for all the ones we'd killed.

The once-neat space within the city was now a disaster. Two of the pavilions had collapsed under the onslaught of the crows, while a third had been hit by that strange goop and was rotting from the outside. The space all around where me and Sam had been defending was a mess of dead plant fibers and stone spike protrusions. Closer to the buildings wasn't any better, as the Carrion Crows had dropped over a dozen of the regurgitated blobs. Some of them had even been lit on fire, surely by the area of effect splash of one of the fire-attuned.

Oliver and his team were working their own magic, trying to keep the acrid smoke and fetid scents from reaching the rest of town.

"Two mass battles on the same day?" Sam asked with a hint of concern. His brow furrowed much more than usual.

"Just be glad we got that three hour break," Daniela said, adjusting her grip on the elven woman. She'd fallen unconscious at some point, but we managed to get her to the man who'd tried to stop her.

Gareth grabbed her close and let out a sob. Regardless of how she'd reacted to his hold, it seemed the man cared for her. The other people congregated around them to give well wishes and lend their shoulders for support. We didn't linger with the other humans, as much as I wanted to ask them a million questions. Instead, the three of us made our way to the impromptu spike and vine jungle we'd created.

"You think they'll need your help with those fires?" I asked, leaning against one of my spikes. At some point I found myself on the ground. My arm muscles twitched with the familiar sensation of overexertion. *Just let more enemies wait until tomorrow, please.* Internal wishes aside, I tilted my head to look at my friends.

"I think orc lady's got it in hand. Plus, I need a break. I probably ran more than you two ever did while in the Bunker," Danny quipped.

"Good to know some carrion didn't dampen your lackluster retorts," I replied.

We let ourselves laugh a little. The last fight had taken the last bit of reservation I had about being in the town, and I was more than a little slaphappy. That didn't mean I planned to reveal everything to the Wildwoodians, but the likelihood that we might be able to cooperate was much higher.

While we caught our breath, Tim rushed over to our group. As politely and pleadingly as he could, he asked for Sam's assistance. The pink-colored man hadn't gotten the whole message out of his mouth before Sam was already urging him to take him to the injured. As the two walked away, I overheard the problem. The strange blobs weren't only corrosive, but were lingering on those who'd inhaled them.

A part of me was interested to test whether our passive regeneration could handle ailments of that sort. Thankfully, the more intelligent part of me told that one to shove off. If we continued to carve out our existence on the surface then there would be more than enough instances for me to get afflicted with all manner of maladies without me seeking them out.

"Sir, is there anything we can do for you?" a voice asked from beside me. I snapped my head around to the voice and the young orc scrambled back a step, but met my eyes. A look at my armor, clothes, and body told me that he had more than enough reason to be intimidated even if that hadn't been my intention.

"Most of our gear we left outside the wall. Would it be possible to get some water and maybe something to rinse… well, my everything?" I said softly. He looked confused for a moment before I gestured at the rest of my body and at Daniela's bloodied clothes. While most of hers had dried and clotted due to the heat she put out, mine was still slick.

"Most certainly, sir. Right away."

"There's no need to call me sir!" I called after the boy, but he'd already turned tail and disappeared amidst the other townsfolk. They immediately noticed my gaze. Most flinched and looked away when I turned, but some offered reserved nods as if in thanks.

"I can't tell if we have fans or not," Danny said, dropping to the ground beside me. She rested her head on my shoulder and let out a deep breath. "Ronan, this is all happening so fast. The Tendrils, the survivors of the Fall. What are we doing here?"

"Surviving. And when we need to ask ourselves that question again, we will be thriving. We'll tell the councilmen that we come from a band of survivors thanks to the Bunker program. Hopefully we'll be able to keep the others back at the camp appraised of what is going on," I said. The plan wasn't clear, or optimal, but it was a start.

"I just get static on the comm-plant. I don't know if we are out of range or," Daniela turned to the colossal Metier Crystal, "if that thing is causing interference somehow."

"We'll have to pay it a visit tomorrow, then. With that size, it should be able to communicate like the Entity back home."

"Are we telling them about the implants? I don't know if that is something we can hide." Daniela used her nail to clink against the metal just at the base of her neck.

"If they ask, they were designed to help us deal with radiation on the surface."

"Hilarious, Ron. Tell them the truth while omitting the

status the Entity granted us?" she said, crossing her arms and looking sideways at me.

"I just don't think we can tru—"

"Here you are, sir!" The orc boy manifested. He wasn't alone. Him, the other orc boy who'd tried to save the older gentleman earlier in the day, and two blue-colored teens carried a number of leaky buckets to us. There was a rough spun pair of rags on the boy's shoulder.

Thanking them for their assistance, I started to give myself a towel shower. It wasn't the first I'd had since coming to the surface and I doubted it would be the last. For the sake of propriety, I kept my undershirt and pants on during the whole ordeal. Daniela did much the same.

The same boy who'd first approached us asked if he could hold my shield. Remembering the look on his face when he'd used it to protect the other orc boy and the man, I nodded. "What are your names? You all have helped us while the others hesitate. Figure we might as well know the names of those lending us a hand."

The orc boy, now holding my shield while making exaggerated poses, told us his name was Lewis. The other orc, who turned out to be a girl to my utter embarrassment, was named Giselle, and the two other boys were Louis and Tristan. After asking about their colored skin, I finally got an answer for what they were. Fae. At least, that was what they'd been called since they started popping up.

"We Fae are really good with plants, so the name came from there apparently. 'Like magic,' they say. I just wish we could do stuff like your other friend, sir," Louis said, staring after Samuel where he was helping a wounded woman with infrequent <Health Bumps>.

I was tempted to ask the youths a bit more about their background and the town of Wildwood. When I moved to retrieve my shield from Lewis, Sarah waved me and Danny over. The orc woman was alone, a grim expression on her face.

She flicked her gaze from me to the group we'd been talking

to before signing. "I suppose it would be a bit paranoid of me to keep you under lock and key."

"Not to mention pointless," Daniela added unhelpfully. However, in that instance, she'd actually beaten me to the punch.

"Right. I'd wager you three are among the top five strongest people in Wildwood. Certainly top ten, based on what I've seen," Sarah said, relaxing her posture.

"While I might be inclined to argue that direct, and purposeful, blow to my pride," I started, "all we want to do is help."

"The Council heads were hesitant to meet you, but with this on display right in town, I'd wager the hesitance is gone," Sarah said. I watched her fist clench before she let out a sigh. "As much as I would love to keep posturing, I could really use a hand."

Nodding at her words, Danny and I agreed to meet with the Council again in the morning. Sarah herself went to fetch us food while Tim brought back a quite loopy Samuel.

"Sam, did you overdo it again?" I questioned him sternly.

"No, no. You see I got right there, though. Or well, I got right there. And then there again. Maybe a third time? Hard to tell after the fourth…" the blond slurred.

"Does he usually, erhm, do this?" Tim asked as he adjusted Sam's arm over his shoulder.

"Side effect of his magic," Danny said. "He'll be good in the morning."

"We'll take you to one of the better vacant houses. Not many visitors to Wildwood, so we don't really have prepared facilities for hosting people."

I lent Tim a hand as we helped Sam into a cute single family home that was missing an entire section of wall and had been patched up with debarked logs of wood. The inside was a little humid, and there was little-to-no air flow to push out the stifling Florida heat, but it was a place to lay down. In fact, the beds had somehow made it through Landfall.

A queen-size memory foam mattress and a regular twin bed were crammed into the cleanest bedroom at the back. Danny and I shared a look before we unceremoniously dumped Sam into the twin bed. You snooze, you lose.

With our friend somewhat situated, Sarah finally handed us dinner and a small animal wax candle to eat by.

Meat. It was *real* meat. From Juan's numerous explanations as to his attempts to mimic the stuff with the Bunker's resources, it was a medium rare prime rib. Or, at the very least, a medium rare slab of protein that led me to forget about Sarah's and Tim's presence entirely.

Danny was not far behind as she started describing the new flavor and her hope to replicate it. She even managed to convince Sarah to let her spend some time with the cooks of Wildwood after our meeting with the Council.

I was distinctly aware that our family back at the Bunker would be worried for us, but I knew they would survive a day without us. Had I not been biting into the salty-with-a-hint-of-crisp goodness of meat, I might have spent more time dwelling on that. Or possibly dwelling on the threat of Tendrils. Or even the realization that if the people of Wildwood had survived twenty-seven years on an Attuned Earth, we might not be so alone in our goal to reclaim Earth.

But those were problems for tomorrow as I tucked into the food and then passed out from sheer exhaustion.

CHAPTER THREE

Laying it on the Table

The following morning came much too soon. Sunlight flickering through the uncovered windows stabbed painful rays into my eye sockets, forcing me to my feet. Daniela groaned in the bed beside me and rolled over in her sleep.

Samuel was sprawled, mouth hanging open and drool on full display, from the edge of his twin bed. I resisted the urge to snort at my friends' antics and left them to their rest. They would never believe that I'd actually woken up earlier than them anyhow.

The town of Wildwood was already stirring. A handful of smoldering campfires showed where guards and work parties had congregated the night before, and a few people were mixing the coals with sand to ward off any potential fires. Off in the distance, I spotted the same group of lizardfolk and merfolk carrying equipment to the lake. They waved in greeting before picking up speed. *I suppose protecting their lives*—again—*has earned us some good will.*

It was during this morning assessment that I spotted something that sent a chill down my spine. That was, until I noticed what they were doing. A demon, since there was no other way of describing the horned, red-black humanoid, was gathering up the rubble of the pavilions. They meticulously separated the salvageable bits from the ruins before getting right back to dismantling. On closer inspection, I noticed three others working alongside them.

One of the demons facing in my direction waved in greeting and my body responded even through the confusion. Unable to stop, I found myself among them.

"Good morning. I don't mean to be rude, but... how did you all...?" I gestured vaguely at their horns and general demeanor.

"You never seen a demon before?" one of them asked before passing me a fallen log. I strained under the surprise weight but moved to place it with the salvaged materials.

"We aren't from around here," I said, returning to the group. Since they apparently wanted assistance for answers, it wouldn't hurt to cooperate.

"Curious." The man seemed to weigh what he was gonna say next. "Bah, I'll wait 'til the council makes an official announcement. We are the dark-aligned Fallen. Nothing more to it. The fire ones look like the orcs from pre-Fall times, the water ones look like fish and lizards, etc." The other people in the group nodded in turn to the man speaking.

Wanting to slap myself, I concentrated on their forms. I didn't know why I hadn't thought to do that with the other humans. It would have clarified our doubts about their origin and given us valuable information. Sure enough, my implant recognized them.

<Demon (Human)>
<Attunement: Death>
<Refinement: N/A>
<Perceived Metier Quotient: 2>

A look around told me that they were all the same Quotient, which was sort of impressive. Something else to keep in mind.

I chatted idly for a while with the crew of demon workers. I'd barely considered it a possibility that I would be able to speak with new people, *ever*, yet there I was. They told me that the demonkin had inherent nightvision, so they mostly worked night shifts and night watch. The first man, Wesley, pointed out several other demonkin that were shuffling off to bed.

Thankfully, before we got to the awkward conversation topic of where I'd come from, Tim returned. He spotted me talking with the demons, greeted them, then pulled me away. "Shall we try the whole 'meeting the council' bit again?" he asked.

"Sounds good to me. Sam and Danny should be getting up by now. Is there any chance to get breakfast?"

The pink man winced at my words. "That would be a 'no.' We usually alternate breakfast days and don't have anything prepared."

"Is it a manpower thing or...?" I left the question open. Based on what I'd already overheard and the result of their broken relationship with the Tendrils, Wildwood wasn't doing too hot in the food department. If they were purposefully rationing, then it was worse than I thought.

"Food. We just don't have the volume for the people we have. After the fields that were destroyed yesterday... I'm hoping we don't lose anyone this fall," he said.

It wasn't hard to tell that the man was trying to keep a steady voice as he talked about his town's plight. Thanks to my conversation with the demons, I now knew why everyone looked like fantasy creatures. The Fallen, as they called those born after the fall of the Metier Crystals, were changed based on their alignment with an element. Thanks to our own crystal benefactor, we knew this was the nature of their Attunement causing changes in their body. Just like the mana changed animals, so did it change humans.

It begged the question of why we, as Bunkerites, hadn't been affected. *Then again, we weren't attuned until we were already grown.* While all sorts of questions and possibilities fluttered through my brain, we arrived at the house we'd been lent. Sure enough, Sam and Danny were groggy and hungry. After I explained the breakfast situation, to Tim's significant embarrassment, Samuel jumped to his feet. The lingering cobwebs of sleep were thoroughly banished.

"Let's get to this meeting. There is no way in hell people are going to go without food if I can help it."

The blond didn't even wait for us and went straight out of the house. His stride was so purposeful and quick, Tim and I were left to jog. Only Daniela was able to keep up with his power walk.

Tim tried to get Sam to slow down a few times, but the man was on a mission. When he strode in, door bell jingling to mark his entrance, he was greeted by an empty room. None of the councilmen were in.

"What I was trying to tell you was that they are in the infirmary. Councilman Irwin hasn't woken from the fight against the blackbirds," Tim said.

"Even more reason we should meet then!" Samuel turned with perfect direction right for the infirmary. Apparently, he'd spent some of his time there helping the wounded. Arriving at one of the few still-standing concrete buildings, the occupants cheered when they saw him. This caught Sam by surprise. Enough surprise for Tim to regain the reins of the group and take us to a small office set into the corner of the building.

A few candles burned in the corners and a cracked window illuminated the three figures within. Irwin laid on the single bed. His hands, and what I realized were both of his arms up to the elbow, were a blend of bark and flesh. Other than the two men arguing loudly over him, he looked like he was just taking a sweet ol' nap.

"—have acquiesced to their demands. This will only be the first of many," Kirby said as we opened the door.

"How could you possibly know that? The crows weren't exactly dropping propaganda fliers, now were they?" the fiery haired man replied. Dylan's hair had taken on a twinge of blue as he stabbed his finger at Kirby's chest.

Tim cleared his throat loudly. "Councilmen. I brought the Gifted as you requested."

Both men stopped themselves mid-retort. It took them a moment to gather themselves, but they both turned to us. Somewhat unified in front. As before, Dylan took the lead.

"We want to apologize for that incident. We have been through some trying times, I'm sure you understand." He paused and looked at Kirby.

"We wanted to extend you a formal welcome to Wildwood. Your... *aid* was invaluable during both of the attacks on our people," Kirby said. There was something strange in his tone of voice, a reluctance of some sort. Regardless, I chalked it up to not wanting outsiders to be responsible for their defensive efforts.

"Yes, very much so. I know that Irwin is indisposed, but we hoped to hear your tale. Your Gifts are some of the strongest we've seen amongst the Fallen," Dylan picked up before anyone could focus too much on Kirby's tone.

"We are actually not familiar with those terms. Had I not spent some time with your people today and yesterday, I would have been even more lost," I said. Sam looked confused, but I had been able to fill in Danny while he marched.

"Curious. If I may, where are you from?" Dylan asked.

"We are Bunker survivors," I said, ripping the 'bandaid' off the whole situation.

Silence hung in the air for several seconds before Dylan and Kirby both broke into laughing fits. The outburst was so surprising, I even noticed Tim taking a step back. He'd been giving us a quizzical look before it turned into one of utter confusion.

When none of us backed down or went along with the joke, the two men slowly lost their sudden mirth. "You aren't kidding?"

"Of course not. This was a serious conversation, and I expected it to be taken that way. If it won't be, we will find someone else that wants our help," I said. My body was already half-turned when Dylan reached out to grab my arm. He didn't get even halfway before Daniela had it held by the wrist.

"How about we all keep our hands to ourselves, deal?" she said sweetly.

Dylan shivered involuntarily as Daniela released him. "Yes, of course. I will act under the impression you are not lying. However, the Bunkers were never populated. The government said they failed and weren't an option for survival."

"Not trying to be crude, but considering where I grew up, it sounds like they lied," Daniela replied.

"Yes. If you three are indeed from a Bunker, then maybe a lot of what we were told were lies," Kirby said. Dylan couldn't see it, but the other councilman was boring holes into his back. *Yet another layer of intrigue.*

"Developments aside," I started. "We want to be of assistance to the people of Wildwood. Since returning to the surface, we've made strides in a number of things. Most center around Samuel and his ability to enhance the growth rate of farms, but we are more than willing to assist in any way we can."

"Before we agree to anything, we would like to know where you hail from," Kirby said. "Just to corroborate your story."

"We don't feel comfortable at this time with that. Suffice to say, we don't mean you ill, nor do we believe *you* intend us ill, but we barely know each other," I said. My words were as flat as possible, but I certainly wasn't enjoying the insinuating tone Councilman Kirby had with us.

"That is more than amicable," Dylan said, taking a step forward and reaching out to shake my hand. "I hope we can help each other reach greater heights."

"Same," a hoarse voice said from behind the two older men. Irwin was slowly sitting up on his bed, turning his head to look.

"My apologies. I checked into the conversation somewhere before Kirby started posturing and Dylan stammered to cover it," he said. The man had deep bags under his eyes, but his smile was unrestrained as it jumped to each of us. His eyes were intense, but kind, as he met mine. "Now, what's this about food?"

The rest of the discussion settled around Samuel's plan for helping Wildwood. There was a plot of farmland that had been cleared within the walls of the city many years ago, but growing anything there had been near impossible. The effort of managing the nearby wetland while also keeping the... well, everything, from being waterlogged after any rain event had led them to create the farms further out from the town. Regardless, after Tim showed us to the spot, Samuel was confident that between him and I, we would be feeding the Wildwoodians by the end of the week.

Irwin had accompanied us while the two other councilmen went about their daily business, in addition to leading the restoration efforts.

"I am going to lay it out on the table for you three," he said, leaning heavily on Tim. "We can't really afford your services or the help you have already given."

"We weren't planning to charge you anything, old man," Danny said, crossing her arms. My face found my palm at the tone she used to address an obviously respected member of their community. Tim's appalled expression certainly corroborated that assessment.

Instead of taking offense, Irwin let out a hearty laugh. The pink fae holding him up struggled to keep him upright but managed it in the end.

"It's been a few years since someone had the stones to talk to a Councilman like that. I welcome it. But no, even if you aren't officially part of Wildwood, we have a system of currency here. Actions like what you have done are considered for the good of the town and remain unpaid. Everything else we hope to give a fair wage for."

"We'll take the minimum. As Daniela said, we aren't doing this for any kind of money," I confirmed. Samuel had been ignoring the conversation entirely and was knee deep in overgrown vegetation half an acre away.

Irwin once again met my eyes before nodding. "I am in charge of the House of Commerce, as insignificant as that is. I am in charge of the crafters, builders, and the like. Should you need anything, feel free to reach out to Tim. He will pass it along, whenever he isn't running around with those hooligan friends of his."

"Grampa, you know we do right by the town. The Wild Guard is very important. Just because you think the House is more important doesn't mean the Guard *isn't*," the pink-colored man said, rolling his eyes as he did. Instead of responding further, he waved off the comment and walked off toward a spread of pavilions. One of them was already in the process of going up.

"I'm sorry about that. He can be kind of dismissive," Irwin said.

"Don't worry. Just be glad you have one," I said, turning to wade through the vegetation after Sam.

For the first time, I cursed my improved perception as I overheard Tim and Daniela talking.

"What happened? Did I say something wrong?" Tim asked.

"No, you are fine. We... don't really have much family. Perks of Bunker life: you live. Cons? Everyone that might have been related to you is probably dead," Daniela replied.

The silence that hung in the air was heavy, but I pushed through it just like the bladed grass I waded through.

CHAPTER FOUR

History Lesson

Thankfully, after agreeing to help immediately with the food efforts of the town, Tim returned our gear. Blobby and Anthony were still a touchy point for being allowed into the town, but we managed to come to an agreement to be able to feed them. I doubted the two wild creatures would starve even without our involvement, but I wanted the council and the Wild Guard to know they were valued members of our group.

With arrangements made for our pets, Samuel insisted that I help him deal with the food situation before I went off asking any of the other questions he knew I had. He managed to convince me by making the very logical argument that if we were going to be spending any length of time in Wildwood, we couldn't be a drain on their resources. Danny, before heading off to who knew where, also added that they would probably be more amicable to answer my questions if they were full of food *we* had grown.

The effort of clearing the space took nearly the entire day. Unfortunately, my Skills didn't help much at all in the initial stages. The thick-bladed grass had roots deeper than a reasonable cast of <Earthen Barrier>'s passive form could flatten.

With consolidating the ground out from under it a bust, I channeled mana into my pickaxe. A flex of thought later, and the crystal trait it contained activated.

Beige-colored crystals grew from the head of the pickaxe and I used my thoughts to direct its shape. Instead of the usual offensive form that I used to extend my reach, I turned it into a makeshift scythe. The crystal crawled down the pointed end of my pick and then flattened. The fact the whole manipulation worked so seamlessly with what my mind pictured was very exciting and once again brought the itch to infuse to the fore. Unfortunately, it wasn't time for that. With my rock-demolishing-turned-grass-demolishing instrument in hand, I mowed down swath after swath.

One of the Wildwoodians had given Sam a machete of his own. With the two of us cutting, the wide field was cleared by sundown. My mana pool and my lower back, however, were more than a bit displeased by the development. Even with occasional <Health Bumps> from Sam to clear away the soreness, there was a bone deep weariness that didn't have anything to do with lactic acid.

As the sky started to shift to orange, Tim returned with jerky and a cask of water for our supper. It looked similar to the steak from before, just dried and tougher.

"Yeah, that's spider steak. They are harder to deal with than the ants, but they are very nutritious. At least, that's what I'm told," the fae said after I asked him.

I stopped mid-chew to contemplate whether or not I was okay eating bugs. However, it wasn't hard to realize that it was just like any other creature. They could be eaten, and it was all that was available. Plus, it still tasted great.

Meals aside, when the world started to lose light, we headed for our borrowed home. Daniela was already snoring up a storm. Samuel and I took turns rinsing ourselves off with a bucket before both of us collapsed in bed. If I knew Samuel, he was not going to let me go until the only work left was what only *he* could do. Tomorrow would be just as hard, if not more.

As I laid back, I pulled up my full Status.

Subject: Ronan Terrigan
Health: 100% (Unafflicted)
Mana: 100%
Metier Quotient: 4 (5%)
Dreg Accumulation: 6%
LPS: Wildwood, FL
Communications
Skills - *(2) Selections Available*
Traits - *(69% Banked)*
Attributes - *Growth Quantified*
Skills:
Offensive - <Stone Spike> / Imbue / Materialize
Defensive - Direct / <Earth Shell> / <Earthen Barrier>
Misc - <Pith Mana Lock>
- <Infusion>
Traits:
Limestone Skin
Unformed (0%)
Attributes:
Strength: 1.52
Mobility: 1.41 >1.42
Perception: 1.63
Refinement: 1.26 > 1.27
Containment: 2.08

The growth I'd experienced since coming to the surface was unprecedented for me. While each Quotient or slight attribute increase was relevant, I pondered how the surface had changed me and my friends within.

As safe as life in the Bunker had been, it was devoid of purpose. Not only that, but the requirements and difficulty with birth made it so that the three of us were the only children. It was a sad existence. Not to say I wanted to have died thanks to the Fall, but life without a goal or even contentment was barely worth living. It was the same as feeling alone in a room full of people.

Now that we knew there were survivors, other humans struggling for *their* own futures, everything had more meaning. The boons and banes of one's actions rippled out to others.

I was determined to make my ripples as positive as I could.

— + —

The next morning while Sam discussed his plans for the new farm, Sarah paid us a visit.

"I come bearing gifts. From what Tim told me, I doubt you three have had this before," she said. There was a closed tray in her hand which she opened to reveal eggs.

We'd never seen them outside of the media downloaded to the Bunker. Danny's father, Juan, could often be heard mumbling about it and bacon after a batch of tofu was made. 'Salmonella be damned!' he would shout at the end. Quite a strange scene.

All of those thoughts were secondary as we dug in. I had no idea where Sarah had gotten the food, or where Tim had gotten the steak from the day before, but I wasn't going to question it. Daniela, on the other hand, did.

"This tastes amazing. Please, tell me there are more. If not, tell me how I can get some more," she said between bites.

Sarah chuckled unbridled. It was a bit hoarse and reverberating thanks to her tusks, but it was full of mirth.

"You know, when Tim told me you were Bunker-born, I thought he was joking. Seeing you lot react to eggs? I think that about confirms it for me."

"You have no idea," she mumbled. "I thought that the hydroponics fish and plants were great until we got this stuff. I need to talk to your cooks!"

"I will let you spend time with them today then." Sarah paused as she turned to regard me and Sam. "I'll say you two are doing the impossible in just a day."

All I could manage was a shrug as I stuffed scrambled and fried versions of the eggs in my mouth.

"Pardon the beasts. They know not what they do," Danny said, smiling at Sarah. There was an egg yoke mustache on her face but no one told her about it.

"I do have to ask… What are those things?" Sarah pointed to the daggers sheathed in Danny's belt as well as my pickaxe.

The question gave me pause and I scrutinized Sarah. Over the last two days, she'd been much nicer than on our arrival. Whether that was deliberate or organic, I couldn't tell. However, we'd already put out one of our biggest secrets as Bunker-born. The Entity would remain a secret, and so would the implants, for now. However, the knowledge to strengthen the people of the surface?

"Come here," I said, wiping my hands on my shirt. It was filthy anyway, but it was the thought that counted.

Sarah looked to my friends for a moment. When they didn't react at all, she took a step to stand less than a foot from me.

I reached up to her forehead and placed my palm on it. Remembering the Entity's directions, I willed the <Infusion>miscellaneous skill to pass to her. My mana pool plunged deep. It wasn't as bad as when I'd given it to the other Bunkerites. Since I'd increased my Quotient and I wasn't giving her the other miscellaneous skill, the transfer was over fairly quickly. One surprising thing that happened was that a prompt appeared at the edge of my vision.

<Memory Canal>

<Knowledge is meant to be passed.>

I didn't know I could form skills myself. Why didn't this happen when I passed the skills to the others in the Bunker? Once again, the skill description was inane and unhelpful. The implications of just what the skill could do, and how I'd managed to make it, ran in the back of my mind as I focused back on the orc woman.

The discomfort of emptying nearly forty percent of my mana passed while Sarah sat back against the wall. Her eyes had a far-away look as she processed the dump truck's worth of information I'd provided. She remained like that for several minutes while we ate.

"Holy crap!" she shouted, jumping to her feet. "How did you do that?"

"Maybe I'll tell you when we are better friends. However, it should let you create stuff like this should you have the correct materials and infusions."

"No, wait. We can do some of what the skill taught me... Why did I just call it a skill and not a Gift?" she asked herself. There was a strange expression on her face; it lay somewhere between horror, wonderment, and confusion. The addition of her tusks made the expression even more complex.

"You all keep using that word, Gift. What does it mean? We sort of just call what we do skills," I asked, finally getting one of my major questions out of the way. I had a sneaking suspicion of what the answer was, but I wanted to hear it from her.

"The sk—Gift. It is what we call the ability to use magic. It comes in different shapes and intensities. First is using alignment cores to give energy to things, this... infusing. That's the most common. Then there are Gifts like my flame hair, similar to my dad. Mom... Well, let's just say she could grab onto something and never let go. As far as I can tell, it's somewhat random, but only the Fallen have them. Those from before the Fall have their mutations. They were the changes that some lady called Ingrid Metier said could happen as a result of exposure. Apparently she discovered the radiation or something."

My tongue caught in my throat at the mention of my grandmother. A grandmother that I hadn't known much about until recently.

"We've heard of her, yes. Most of the people from the Bunker were from before the Fall. As a matter of fact, only us three are what you would consider Fallen," Sam said quickly. I gave the man a weak smile for picking up the conversation before I could reveal something or let suspicious silence linger. My friends had left me to deal with the revelations of my past, and I was glad that they had. Mostly because I'd been ignoring them unless I was talking to my uncle.

Thankfully, Sarah's surprise at his words were enough to keep her from focusing on my reaction. The stoic face that she'd used to greet us returned, as if the revelation that we were the only Fallen meant she could no longer trust us. My perception noted her body language instantly. Relatively speaking, it hadn't increased an insane amount, but since I'd started using it for combat, the subtlest of shifts looked like flailed motions.

"How is that possible?" she asked.

"Since I am the only one still with both of her parents, I'll answer. Their mothers died. In childbirth. The result? They disintegrated into infusions. Suffice it to say, the other fertile people in the Bunker took a big 'No-Babies' approach to life. So, there you go. Happy?" Daniela said, stepping between Sam, me, and Sarah.

The orc woman recoiled from my friend's intensity, but it had the intended effect. Her body relaxed where she was sitting. "I'm sorry. We don't get many new people. Not since I was a child. The ones we have gotten have always been… wrong."

"The Tendrils?" I asked, hoping to change the subject. Her nod was all the answer I needed. "Care to tell us what you know about the Fall? And, particularly, how you came to deal with the Tendrils for protection."

"Direct, aren't you?" When I didn't respond, she shrugged helplessly. "I wasn't around for the early days, but my father has told me plenty. Everyone, really. We hold a festival after the first chill in remembrance of all those lost and losing. Anyhow, the only thing of note about the Fall itself was that the Crystals didn't level the surface of the planet. Scientists all over were expecting the planet to turn into one giant fireball or something. Instead, only some of the crystals impacted like that. The regions that were hit were decimated pretty thoroughly.

"Most of the power was gone within the first year. The animals started to change almost immediately, especially the insects." Sarah paused for a moment to shiver, as if remembering some terrible memory. "I've seen more than any one person should."

"How did you all make it?" Sam asked, clearly caught up in the story.

"Guns. Lots and lots of guns." Sarah pantomimed shooting a pistol with her finger. Had she not had a serious expression on her face, I would have laughed at the visual. "Councilman Kirby told us that the governments of the world focused on dealing with the ocean and mountain creatures. Apparently, they were deadly enough that the country folk had to be left to fend for themselves. When connection with the world finally deteriorated, well, it was every person for themselves. Not the best case scenario when the world ends.

"When travel became too hard between the cities due to the mutated animals, everyone entrenched themselves." She waved vaguely around herself. "That's when they built the palisade. Back before the fuel ran out and the Gifts started to show. At some point, Kirby and my father were able to broker a deal with the Tendrils. We would be their stomach and they would be our shield. Some such nonsense is how they put it."

The entire time she was talking I was trying to corroborate the information with what I knew of the surface. It all matched, and it indicated that for years there had been a higher intelligence than just instinct to guide the Tendrils. Why they attacked now seemed like too much of a coincidence.

"How did these tributes work? Did they just demand too much?"

"They did demand too much, not because it was more food. We could have managed, somehow. They wanted *people*. I made the executive decision to tell Galloway where he could shove that." Her voice grew heated at the reminder.

"Do you think he'll come back?" I asked, watching her expression.

"Oh, I am counting on it. The Guard will be ready this time. The New Hope team should be back tomorrow, and we will personally oversee the west fields. Our battle ruined a lot of crops, but I am hopeful we can recover a fair bit."

"I won't say we will remain indefinitely, but the Tendrils are no friends of ours. We will get you your farm, whatever it takes," I said. My friends nodded in agreement.

"There isn't much I can offer you, but if you can get that field producing food, then that will go a long way to us making it through the winter and having stores if the bastard tries to siege us," Sarah said, smiling.

"We appreciate your time. Knowing that there are humans already staking their claim on the surface is payment enough," I said with a grin. There was a resonance between Sarah and I. It was a connection borne of kindred spirits, of the knowledge that we both would do absolutely anything to keep our people moving forward. The Tendrils were an obstacle of unknown size, but I was confident that Wildwood would stand with us. Plans for improving their lives, and our own back at the Bunker, were already speeding through me.

"Actually, there is one thing I can do for you." The woman's orcish smile almost sent a shiver down my spine, but she was up and at it before I could even process it. "I'll grab the others and give you the private tour."

CHAPTER FIVE

Communing

The world exploded into brilliant colors before dimming to a slightly more saturated version of everything as we crossed the bridge to the Metier Crystal. Crossing that invisible threshold of the Wildwood crystal threw me entirely on my rear. The Big Guns, Sarah's Wild Guard squad, snickered at our antics. Samuel was leaning heavily on the railing and I was sure Daniela had been struck dead. The woman was stiff as a board.

"What in the…?" I whispered as I *watched* a gust of wind blow over the water of Lake Sumter. A gray ripple where things should have been invisible, quickly followed by a gently lapping aquamarine wave that crashed against the wooden construction. Even the bridge had a gentle glow of browns and yellows dancing where it met the waterline.

"We call this the Blessing of Magic," Tim explained, casually leaning over the railing. The man caressed the yellow glow as if it were a physical thing. I did note that the brown avoided his touch, sinking into the bridge out of view.

"I'm sure you've noticed the pulse," one of the dwarves said. They were so similar I had trouble distinguishing between Carl and Karl. The only real difference was how they had their beards braided. Even *that* was hard to tell. When they'd told me their names, I was sure they were joking. They weren't, telling me it was a regular point of contention with their parents.

"Definitely felt that one. Oddly enough, not during the fight with the crows," I said, thinking back to the engagements.

"That's the crystal's defense mechanism. Most of the time, from what we've been able to observe, it keeps creatures away. When it can't, well, they are disrupted by the pulse," the other dwarf said.

"What does that have to do with the Blessing of Magic?" Danny asked.

"Think of it like musical instruments. The crystal strikes all the chords at once, causing the pulse," Tim explained. "The blessing always becomes stronger after the crystal pulses."

It's exerting its influence, I realized. Just like how the Entity back at the camp could pull the Dreg from our bodies, so could this one.

"This is also where we come to train once we discover a Gift. Seeing the alignments helps us get a better hang of them. The ones before the Fall can't see the alignments no matter how hard they try," Tim said, stroking one of the light yellow glows. As if to demonstrate, the glow he touched wrapped around his finger to turn a deep green. Then a spell chain formed. It wasn't as refined or clear as ours, more like a painting than indecipherable writing, before he flicked it towards the shore.

A flat tree trunk sprouted from the ground as if that were the norm. For the first time, I watched energy flow out of Tim, through the spell chain, and then exert its will on the world. It explained a great deal as to how our skills worked, but left me with a hundred more questions. Mostly around the actual specifics of spell chains, the vision of the blessing and what role the crystals played.

"We were hoping to see some of your own magic," Sarah said. "You three are some of the most powerful Fallen we've ever met, outside of the Tendrils. Maybe we could learn something by watching you use your Gift here."

I turned to my friends. Sam shrugged, as did Daniela. It meant the decision was up to me. *How very supportive.* From what I'd seen of the team, none of them had imbue-type spells. It was possible that Sarah's hair skill was related to offensive imbued, but I doubted it. "Danny, can you show them your <Heat Touch>?"

Without fanfare, she called forth her skill. There hadn't been any red glows around us, but the moment her spell chain triggered, it shoved the meandering lights back into the world. The gray of the wind swirled around a red glow coming off her hands, drawn to it somehow.

Instantly, Sarah lit up red. Not in that she was on fire, but glowing with the Fire Attunement. Sarah closed her eyes and focused. The red glow hung in the air for a few seconds before it sunk into her skin.

Then she exploded in a caustic cloud that had us all coughing to clear our throats. The cloud didn't last more than a breath, but she was on her feet, trying to get her bearings. There was a circular soot mark where she'd been standing.

"That's... a new Gift. I understand it..." she whispered.

"Please tell me you have more to show us!" Tim jumped from his spot on the railing and nearly crashed into Sam. There was a desperate look in his eye. I was almost hesitant to proceed because of the sudden mania, but considering his Attunement and the fact that only three people in Wildwood were capable of healing, it was worth the risk the man was vying for power somehow.

"Do you have any other skills we haven't seen?" I asked, prying the fae off my friend.

"No, just my root guard. Clara and that weirdo Dai are the only people with more than one Gift. Eh, not including the use of the creature essences," he added at the end. "A handful of Fallen can get them to mimic really weak Gifts."

"What about you two? Anything other than that joint attack?" I resisted the urge to ask about Clara and Dai. No sense getting sidetracked when we were going to potentially give the group a huge jump in power.

"Nothing but indigestion. That hail is the only thing we can do," the left dwarf said.

"Other than hit hard," his brother added. As if they'd practiced, they thumped chests together. I couldn't help but think of all the football movies and matches I'd been forced to watch by my uncle. Karl and Carl were half-sized linebackers with a facial hair problem. I didn't think even an infused razor could handle those face rugs.

"Right, you guys, give us a minute," I said, pivoting and walking out of the Blessing of Magic area. The moment I did, the world became drab by comparison. Everything looked the same, and in a sense it was true. Without seeing the Attunements around things, they were inert after what I'd just experienced. Regardless, I pushed through. After walking what I determined was a sufficient enough distance that we could see the Big Guns squad but not be overheard, I turned to my friends. "Thoughts?"

"Are these thoughts on what skill to show them, or thoughts on giving them the potential to unlock more skills of their own?" Sam asked.

"Why is this an argument? They could certainly use the help," Daniela argued.

"We can't do this for everyone. Well, at least not right now. A magic school of sorts would be amazing for the long term…" I nearly slapped myself to get back on topic. "No. I want to make an agreement with them."

"Like some kind of alliance?" Sam said.

"Sort of? It would just be with them for now, but the Big Guns have been the only group of mages we've really interacted with."

"There was the Oliver fellow," Danny pointed out.

"I'm not quite sure we are on the best of terms. I can't really get a read on him. Honestly, I feel like my social skills are struggling just dealing with all these new people," I said, admitting my frustrations.

While talking to the kids on the first day had been great for setting my mind at ease, and socializing with the demon night workers had been easy, a whole town's worth of people was a tad much.

"You don't have to do this alone, Ron," Sam said, placing his hand on my shoulder. "Just because we asked you to lead us doesn't mean you'll need to be the best at everything. Let me and Danny help with the social stuff. You figure out how we can get an edge. These," he pointed to Danny's armor harness and his own breastplate, "are game changers. Getting the people of this town a steady source of food? Also game changing. And I am thinking that the game we are playing is already rigged."

"Getting some more magic-slinging friends also couldn't hurt," Danny added.

All the information and plans we had for the future seemed to coalesce in my mind. It wasn't quite crisp, but I had a direction. My ambitions... With the manpower of Wildwood and the support of my friends, it might just be enough to pull them off.

"Ah, see? I told you he just needed to get his head on straight," Danny said, gesturing vaguely at me.

"Damn! Fine, you can have the first crop pick for the next two weeks," Sam said, dejected. The brunette pumped her fist.

"What's all this now?" I asked, focusing on my friends with a frown.

"We made a bet that you would spend the whole first trip here overthinking everything. I put my money on you getting your crazy plan face as soon as we smacked some sense into you," Danny said matter-of-factly. It was delivered in an almost disinterested tone, but I could see the smirk twitch on her lips.

"Good to know I'll always have you two smart alecks, to balance out all these new and far less annoying people," I quipped. My friends couldn't hold back their laughter at that.

"On a more serious note," Sam said, "I think we should let

them see the spell chains. Getting them as strong as possible will be important."

Daniela nodded, the levity of the conversation having passed.

"I will agree, with the caveat that we spend time with the group before showing them anything. I think Sarah is a dedicated and stubborn person, Tim is a whimsical dude with ambitions. The twins, well, I think they are decent people," I said, counting out the members of the Big Guns on my fingers. "If there isn't a pressing need or a redeeming feature, the power we have is dangerous."

Danny nodded grimly at that. "I did a little scouting yesterday. I don't know how, but nearly the entire population is Quotient Level 2. The children are Q1, and the only people Q3 and above are the older Fallen that are in the Wild Guard. Irwin is the only pre-Fall person at Quotient 4."

I ran some quick math in my head and shivered. It was indeed a mind twisting amount of Pith to get that many people leveled. If it took three Q0 creatures to get to Q1, not accounting for the variability of each creature, their Attunement, and the corresponding Attributes of the person taking it in, it was a staggering amount. One that I doubted the Tendrils would hesitate to exploit.

Wildwood was a huge Pith bank. I didn't know where the thought struck from, but it nearly brought me to my knees. The behavior of the Tendrils suddenly made a whole lot more sense. If I was correct, the next step of that would not be good for anyone. It looked like they were ready to cash in their investments.

"Let's get in there. We are going to need to make this official," I said. My friends must have heard the seriousness in my tone, because they just nodded in reply. No quips or ribbing now.

The dwarves hoisted their arms wide. "Finally! I thought you were going to leave us standing here all morning. My knees were starting to hurt."

"I need you to promise you will work with us. What you do with any power you unlock is your business, but if you want our help, it needs to be the business of restoring humanity to the surface," I said to Sarah.

I felt a little guilty being so direct after Carl's lighthearted welcome, but I needed to make my point. If we hadn't been attacked already, that meant we had some time to fortify and grow stronger.

"Don't think small, do you?" Sarah asked, crossing her arms.

As a show of faith, I cast <Earth Shell> on my arm. The imbue-category skill suffused my arm with mana, turning it into stone. Granules condensed and flowed out of my pores before solidifying. As if I'd flipped a switch, umber light shimmered up and down my arm. Carl and Karl blinked with a similar light not a second later. The siblings held on to each other as if they were on a rocking ship. Stone started to materialize around their hands. However, instead of climbing up and along their skin like my own, it bulked their fists up. Two, then three times, it increased in size until the twins had rock hammers for hands.

They didn't affect us like Sarah's cloud, but having individual skills caused the two men to hoot and holler in surprise and joy.

"If this trend continues, I believe Sam will be able to unlock a new skill in Tim. Before he does, I need to know that you stand with us. I have a plan, but it's going to take a fair bit of work," I said, crossing my arms.

Sarah's expression was hard to read. There was the cocky confidence of her position as leader of the Guard, but also the desperation of someone searching for power. A twinge of excitement leaked through as she kept glancing from her own hands to the jabbering twins.

"So long as this does not hurt Wildwood and its people, I will agree to help you," she said, nodding.

A pulse rushed out of the crystal less than twenty feet away. The glows of everything around us brightened again before forming threads in the air. The thin lines were similar to what I was learning to manipulate while infusing, except these danced in the air. Thread after thread wove together into an iridescent one. This glimmering illusion wrapped around Sarah and myself like a snake. An energy pushed out of me—my mana, I quickly realized—and mixed with the partly transparent thread. The brown light of my mana rushed down the thread where it met a red glow from Sarah's. When the two met, sparks flew and the thread was gone.

"What the hell just happened?" Daniela asked. None of us were moving, and other than a slight tingling in my chest, the thread didn't appear to do anything.

"Have you three seen anything like this?" Tim asked, leaning, peering, and examining his squad leader with intent.

"That's a first. And we've seen some stuff..." Sam said, trailing off.

The giant Metier Crystal flared with light, causing everyone but me and Sarah to avert their eyes. Like moths drawn to a flame, our eyes made their way back to it slowly. Warmth and comfort washed through me, and from the pleasant look on Sarah's face, she must've been feeling it too.

The light of the crystal concentrated in front of us before translucent hands reeled us in like human-sized fish. Our bodies were plunged *into* the crystal. Impacting the thing caused small ripples on its surface and felt like running through cobwebs, something barely felt. Thankfully, we didn't break any bones based on the speed we impacted.

A familiar landscape of endless white shimmered faintly all around us as an orb of light ten times the size of the camp Entity manifested above us. Sarah yelped in surprise and fell on her butt.

—You carry piece of family. Why?—

Words floated in the air before me. "Sarah, are you seeing this?" I asked.

"See what? I can't see anything because everything is white!" Sarah said in a panicked voice. She was groping at the air, looking for something to hold. When I offered my hand, she clung to it like driftwood in the ocean. "Ronan, what in Samwise's hell is going on?"

"It appears my attempts to keep some things close to the chest have been foiled by your crystal," I said, turning to address the orb. "Is there some way she can hear us both?" I asked.

—She share not of crystal.—

—Await.—

The giant orb winked out for a second before returning.

—She suffer pain.—

Simple as that, a spear of crystal punched its way into the back of her head. I screamed in horror, but she was still breathing. Her face contorted into one of agony, her grip on my hand actually managing to break my ring finger. Compared to the myriad other injuries I'd taken so far on the surface, that was minor. My focus was on the woman.

When her screams ended, the crystal retracted into the nothing of the whitespace. There was no evidence she'd ever been hurt by the process.

"What did you just do to her?" I asked, alarmed, as she slumped to the ground.

—Create connection.—

—Emulate implant.—

—Convert Dreg Warrior.—

"The Entity Cluster asked for permission. It asked for our input!" I shouted at the glowing light.

—Family superseded humanity. Objection overruled.—

"What does that even mean!?" I asked. Instead of getting a response, five figures winked into existence all around us.

—Companions are linked. Natives must be…—

"Stop!" I said, putting myself between the confused Wildwoodians' necks and, well, wherever the crystal was stabbing them from. "They haven't agreed to this. They don't even know what we know."

—Natives unaware of Entity Cluster objective?—

"Yes! That's right. Only the three of us know," I said, gesturing to my friends. Unfortunately, while I was gesturing, I left Carl's neck slightly exposed. Another spear of crystal punched into the man's head.

"What the hell!" I screamed at the Entity's orb.

"Ronan, I'm not prone to freaking out, but I am kind of blind here, and you are shouting awful loud. Care to explain?" Tim asked weakly. I'd planted my palms on their necks, and apparently that was doing the trick to keep them from being assaulted by the Entity.

"Is this thing friendly or not?" Danny asked, shuffling along the featureless space to take a spot next to me. Samuel checked on the vacant Sarah and Carl.

—Presence is non-hostile.—

"If that were the case, you wouldn't have stabbed our two friends!" I argued. There was a considerable amount of heat in my voice, so I did my best to reel it in. I had a sneaking suspicion that if the Entity wanted us dead, we would have been already.

—Agreement of cooperation provided.—

—New Dreg Warriors required appropriate access to designation: Status.—

A chilling realization came to me. This Entity probably didn't have a personality based around humans. The Cluster back at the camp had been able to interface with us directly, learning and becoming somewhat human. This was pure analytical logic.

"We won't cooperate with you," I said evenly.

The giant orb didn't turn, but I could feel its scrutiny over me. It was a similar sensation to crossing into our crystal's area of influence. That was probably how they sensed things.

—Words do not match dishonesty indicators.—

—Propose alternative.—

"We agreed to assist the Clusters because our goals align. Forcefully conscripting people is not the way to a sustainable relationship. Everything works better if we are cooperating."

—Acknowledge. Allow access to memory matrix?—

"Erm. Yes?" I asked, caught on the backfoot once again.

The new skill I'd created triggered without my prompting. A veritable floodgate of knowledge and information pushed through my neurons and all I could do was hang on. It was gonna be a bumpy ride.

CHAPTER SIX

Gears in Motion

Images of… somewhere flashed through my mind. Vague outlines of humanoid people composed of metal, wood, and rock were dashing around and working on endless tasks. Hammered steel, carved wood, and shaped stone were churned out from their precise work. Hulking stone creatures with preternatural auras lumbered about working on giant crystal structures. When the flash of memory was gone, I was back inside the whitespace.

—Memory is protected.—

—Sufficient data acquired for concept actualization: empathy and collaborative motivation.—

—Entity Cluster requests forgiveness and pledges assistance in exchange for support in Dreg struggle.—

"Are these things those computers the old people talk about?" Carl asked fearfully, having recovered at some point. He was looking straight at the glowing orb, unlike his brother and Tim. They were still looking around in panic. Blind.

—Artificial lattice networks.—

"Not very helpful right now." I turned to the Big Guns Squad. "I certainly didn't know this was going to happen. I hope you all know this. However, it simplifies explaining how we are as strong as we are.

"The Metier Crystals are actually alive once they get to a certain size. We had some smaller ones in our possession that allowed us to make contact with a living one. They call themselves Entity Clusters."

"Wait," Sarah said. The woman still looked out of sorts, but she'd at least been able to rise to her feet. The orc had a half-twisted look of concentration on her face. "We've been to the Blessing of Magic with smaller crystals in tow a bunch of times."

—Neural interface unavailable. Primitive response system implemented for defensive action.—

Sarah's eyes widened as she heard the Entity address her. Those wide eyes turned to regard Samuel, Daniela, and myself. With a sigh, I turned and clinked my finger against the back of my neck. A muted thunk implied where the implant was placed. Even if it had healed over, the implication that there was something connected to me and my friends was clear.

"Is that what—"

—Affirmative. Implant and system specifications have been imported from prime subjects.—

"This is going nowhere. Do you all agree to much more power and a means of protecting your people in exchange for combating the threat of the Dreg?"

Sarah hesitated before asking, "Do we have a choice?" She rubbed the back of her head where the crystal spear had struck.

"I don't know that you do. Tim and Karl may have a chance to avoid it, but if I had to guess, you already have an implant. Or something like it at least," I said.

—Affirmative, design has been constructed from Metier Crystal Category 0.—

"Great. That's fantastic. Is it going to take over my brain or something?" she asked. Carl wasn't even listening, just staring up at the giant orb in wonder. My hands were still clamped around Tim and Karl's necks.

—Negative. Entity Clusters do not interfere with task organisms. Designation humans are the only ones to interact with Entity Clusters.—

I didn't know if I could trust this new Crystal, but the Entity back home had only helped us. "If it works like ours does for us, you'll be able to direct your growth a whole lot more."

"Fine. We need the leg up anyway," Sarah said. I was surprised at the quickness of the response. My expression must have told her as much. "We've been piddling around, unaware of a bigger stage. Well, it's time we joined and made a difference for this town."

"I can get down with that," Carl said, finally joining the conversation.

Karl shouted a "Hell yeah," in reply.

Only Tim hesitated. "Will we be changed somehow?" he asked quietly.

—No mutations outside of trait development can occur in Fallen designation individuals.—

"I... Yes. I'll do it," he said. Instantly, a crystal limb yanked me back and stabbed the two men in the neck.

As violent as the process looked, they were back on their feet within a few seconds.

"Try to say or think 'status,'" I directed them. The four squad members stared off into space as they read over their information.

—Entity Cluster is optimizing growth. You may select your skills here, without need to return. I shall communicate now that their identity signal has been relayed.—

"What did it just—"

<Ronan? Daniela? Samuel?>the somewhat monotonous but accented voice of our home Entity Cluster echoed around us.

"How is this possible?" Sam asked, looking at me in surprise.

—Signal amplification afforded at Category 3.—

<What my less eloquent counterpart is saying is that he can

call me because he is stronger. Since he is stronger, he can also grant you the information for your skills. I would advise against this, as I believe it could have significantly negative impacts to receive knowledge too quickly.>

"We'll trust you on that. Can you let the others know that we are okay? Our comm-plants haven't been working," I said.

—This is likely due to the disruptive force of an area of influence.—

<Yes, I believe that is correct. That would be your area of influence,>our Entity said.

—Affirmative.—

<Cannot believe I am happy to say that my communication matrix was influenced by you three.>

"We love you too, shimmer head. Now, can you get the message to my mom or anyone?" Danny said, snapping the conversation back on track.

<Yes, of course. I will relay it to Alan momentarily. He has not stopped asking questions since you left, despite his aware-ness of my power limitations. I think he expects me to answer them all when I find a break to interact.>

"How *are* you able to communicate with us?" Sam asked.

—The expenditure is being covered on this end.—

"It's like an alien rock payphone," Danny said, snapping her fingers. Everyone, even the Wildwoodians who had been distracted by their statuses, looked at her in confusion.

"I'm gonna cruise past that one. If what the town Entity said is right, then Tim should be able to select a skill. My guess would be that imbue defensive is the most likely to give a skill with some form of healing," I said.

Before I'd even finished talking, a flash of gold-tinged green light flared around the pink fae. When it settled, there was bark and leaves growing out of his hair.

"Sorry, I may have gotten a tad excited. I chose direct defensive and got something called <Regrowth Bolt>," Tim said, scratching the back of his head.

"We need to teach them the passives. We need to get more

people in here, Ronan!" Sam said, jumping to his feet and grabbing me by the shoulders.

"Samuel, we can't just pull people into this," I said, gently removing his hands. "I wouldn't be surprised if the Wild Guard is okay with this arrangement, but we can't subject the people of Wildwood if they aren't willing."

"Unfortunately, I agree with Ronan on this," Sarah said. "Giving everyone access to Gifts would be madness, regardless of their goodwill."

"So we what? Hide this from people and pretend we didn't just get juiced with magic sauce?" Tim asked, brushing leaves from his hair. They disintegrated into the air seconds after.

"For now. As unexpected as this is, it will make my plan that much more feasible. Sarah, is there a group that you think could be trusted with the secret of the Entities and can operate independently like yours?" I asked.

"You've just described New Hope to a T. I can arrange a meeting for tomorrow, but..." she said, suddenly self-conscious for some reason. "How long have we been in here?"

—Approximately 1 hour, 36 minutes and 31...32...33...—

"We got the gist," Sarah snapped at the crystal.

—Seconds.—

The woman sighed. "Can you get us out? But only if there are no people around to see," she added quickly.

—Affirmative. We shall speak soon, Dreg Warriors.—

The world blinked and we were deposited back onto the wooden bridge. The timber groaned at the sudden addition of easily half a ton of humanity. Sarah was the first to extract herself from the pile.

"I've got to meet with my father. I promise you I won't reveal anything, but he needs to know you three have already improved our strength. Kirby has been adamant that strangers in these trying times are just a drain." With that, the orc woman was off.

Heat started to scorch my skin and all of us yelped as we

extracted ourselves from the pile. Daniela was quite literally fuming as Carl or Karl removed his posterior from her head.

"Apolog—" he started.

"Don't. Just don't. *Ever*," she replied coldly.

The dwarves, even the one that hadn't been resting atop my friend, nodded vigorously.

"Okay, we are back. Do you three have time to help us with the farm?" Sam asked after dusting himself off.

"We've got probably an hour before midday patrol," Karl said, eyeing the position of the sun through his fingers.

My blond friend clapped his hands, a devious smile showing the dimples on his face. "You lot are gonna know what work is."

— + —

The next hour was brutal. Samuel put me through the wringer to consolidate the ground while he used his vines to crack the rows into place. Once Tim and the twins were more or less proficient at using the new facets of their abilities, thanks to 'Drill Sergeant' Daniela, we got to the tedious work.

Samuel produced a cutting from his clothes that I wasn't aware he even had. With meticulous channeling of his passive skill, the little plant grew unabated. Once it was at a mature size, he instructed me and Daniela how to plant. He ordered one of the twins to continue expanding the field and the other to use <Rock Hammer> to plow more rows.

While Sam worked the passive materialize form of his skill to aid a swath of ground to sprout, he had Tim focus on individual plants. The man's control over the passive effects of his skill were poor, but growing.

When Sarah came to retrieve her squad, she ran into a small crowd. Many of the children and a good bit of the adults in the town had stopped to watch. Stone trellises formed from my own skill lined the rows, crawling with budding tomato flowers.

When the orc squad leader finally made it to the front, she

could barely get the words out. In fact, she turned on her heel after speaking to Tim for a moment and ran off. The new Dreg Warriors were still for all of two seconds before Sam snapped to.

"These fields aren't going to plant themselves!"

With exacting but repetitive motions, I dug a hole and cast a trellis. Then dug a hole and cast a trellis. And another. The quarter-powered version of my <Stone Spike> still rose up a good two feet, but was only about two inches wide. The drain on my mana pool was much smaller, but the repetitive actions brought a bit of heartburn. The twins had to stop regularly to catch their breath. I smiled to myself when I realized the reduced discomfort was a result of the training and battles I'd made it through.

Daniela wasn't happy to be locked into farm work, but every time she would try to slink off when Sam wasn't looking, a vine would rise out of the ground to catch her. She wasn't even able to use her superior speed for fear of wrecking all the work we'd done. Instead, she grumbled the whole time as she planted the cuttings Sam generated into my preset holes.

"Impossible..." a voice said from the crowd. They quickly parted to reveal the Councilmen and a slack-jawed Kirby.

"This is impressive work," Irwin added, running his fingers down one of the tomato stems that hadn't been there more than a few minutes. "We've only been able to accomplish this with the right essence and someone with the Gift."

"Those with a Life Attunement have what we've called a passive ability. Simply put, enhanced growth. The major draw-back is the effects on the soil. It has to be fairly nutritious and properly hydrated, otherwise the effect will happen but then the plant will just die," Sam said, still channeling his magic. Tim was also working, wholly consumed with getting his assigned plant to shoot and tangle around the trellis.

"When could we expect to harvest?" Irwin asked, taking out a notepad and pencil.

"Right now, if you'd like. Though the entire field is not

quite ready." With a twist of his hand, the materialize spell chain on the ground vanished and formed around his hand. The smaller circle flowed green as Samuel focused his efforts on one plant instead of a dozen.

Before the near-unbelieving eyes of the crowd, tomatoes bloomed on the flowers and then plunked to the ground. For the first time, I watched as the base of the tomato plant expanded out roots and dried out the ground.

Samuel munched on one of the fallen tomatoes and handed the others to the Councilmen and the crowd.

Everyone chewed in silence, thankful for the unexpected snack. It was at that point that Tim let out a cheer of success and hoisted up a small cherry tomato. His face fell when he saw that Sam had already bloomed his—several times—and was feeding the crowd offhand.

"It takes time, Tim. We didn't start perfect and we still aren't. Strive to do better when concentrating your mana, and you'll be the one drowning Samuel in a cornucopia soon," I said, patting the pink man on the shoulder.

"Can I go now? I think I can sneak away without him noticing," Danny said. Indeed, she was correct. Sam was crunching through his mana growing the tomatoes at the edge of the field to maturity. The crowd oohed and ahhed at his antics.

"Yeah, just don't get into too much trouble. Oh, and take some tomatoes for Blobby and Anthony," I said, plucking some that Samuel had grown and tossing them to her.

She nodded and made her way around the crowd, then out of sight. When Samuel started to giggle while using his magic, I knew it was time.

"Thank you, everyone. We hope to have this field fully ready by tomorrow. I best get back to it with my friend, but I appreciate all of your support!" I said to the crowd. It was really the largest crowd I'd ever addressed at once, some thirty people, and I felt I should have been more nervous. Regardless of that introspective moment, I hauled Samuel away from the public eye.

The crowd grumbled a bit but eventually everyone dispersed when Irwin and Dylan ushered them to their respective jobs. Kirby had gone at some point. The two remaining councilmen stood at the edge of the growing field after the crowd was gone. After forcing Sam to sit and take a break to recover his mana, and telling the Big Gun squad to keep at it, the two older men joined me.

"Revolutionary work, Ronan," Dylan said. "And I will admit, you and your friend handled the crowd surprisingly well for someone born in a Bunker."

Ignore the obvious doubt, Ronan. Just talk to the man. "Getting things done is what I focus on. As for Sam, well, he gets carried away."

"I can't imagine the aftereffects of his magic don't compound that issue," Irwin pointed out.

"That too." There was a moment of silence as we looked at each other. It was somewhat stand-offish, but I didn't have anything to say to the men. They had been the ones to approach me.

Dylan cleared his throat and slicked back his smoldering hair. "Right. My daughter has brought it to my attention that you have some sort of plan to help us deal with the threat of the Tendrils. Would you care to share some of the specifics? She was quite eager for us to throw our support behind you, and while I've seen it might well be deserved, we need a bit more to go on. Willy-nilly plans did not get us twenty seven years past the end of the world."

Irwin didn't say anything and just kept his arms folded behind his back.

"How familiar are you two with video games?" I started.

The two looked a bit taken aback, but Dylan was quick to respond. "I'd dabbled before the Fall. That tended to be my brother's territory." Irwin pointed at the head councilman as if in agreement.

"There are a number of ways to look at what happened, most of them negative. However, if you all haven't noticed, there are thresholds for power that each person reaches," I said.

"You are talking about the swells," Irwin clarified.

"Sure, I figured you might have a different name for it. We call those levels. From what I've gathered, ours are higher than most of your population. Should we be able to raise those levels for more individuals than the Guard, or raise the Guards' levels higher, fighting back will be much easier."

"How does that work exactly? Most of us just experience the swells after a few years around town. I, myself, have only felt them twice," Dylan said.

"You all are aware of the dissipating bodies, yes?"

"The essence and the body part," Irwin nodded. "Due to our shortages, the Wild Guard was instructed to make sure the whole creature was brought back."

"I understand. Step one of my plan is already in motion." I pointed over my shoulder at where Tim was trying to rouse a mildly drunk Sam into giving him magic pointers. "If we can mitigate your food problem, then you can absorb Pith. Pith being the stuff that the bodies break down into. This is what helps raise your level. I still haven't figured out why your people leveled without actually killing anything." *I'd bet all the money I don't have that it has something to do with the snob Entity in the middle of town.*

"That makes some sort of sense. I've experienced the dissipation process, and it always looks and feels like I am absorbing something," Irwin conceded.

"How are we going to get enough creatures to really make a difference?" Councilman Dylan asked with a frown. "Our squads already have a hard enough time finding wild game they can survive a fight against."

In response, I threw the two men a Cheshire cat grin. "Are you two familiar with dungeons?"

CHAPTER SEVEN

Bump on the Road

After spending the better part of an hour explaining the concepts of 'dungeon crawls' and 'grinding mobs' to the two older councilmen, they went off to discuss their thoughts on the plan. It worked out perfectly, because by then Sam had mostly recovered. His steps were still a bit unsteady, but he directed us with an iron fist.

When the sky was splashed with orange and purple, he finally released us from our misery. The strain of the day had been so different to the way I usually worked my mana that my Refinement had actually gone up a tic when I checked my Status.

Attributes:
Strength: 1.52
Mobility: 1.42
Perception: 1.63
Refinement: 1.27 > 1.28
Containment: 2.08

Even as worn out as I was, I was tempted to try to speak

with the Town Entity again. Whatever it had done to implant the Big Guns Squad would be invaluable. Not only because finding medical-grade titanium that the printer below ground could use would be hard, but because of the time investment.

If I knew Alan, he was probably scheming some mind-bending shenanigans relating to mana none of us had thought of.

While I didn't get to go to the crystal, I did see a sight for sore eyes. So to speak. Daniela had gone and retrieved Anthony and Blobby. Somehow she'd managed to convince the councilmen that the creatures were essential to our plan. That plan being *my* plan to create dungeon farms.

How she knew I'd spoken with them after she'd gone away, or how she'd managed to convince them to possibly endanger their population, I wouldn't know. Regardless, the green-brown jiggly mass of Blobby took me to the ground as I headed towards our assigned house.

The two small Metier Crystals inside its body clinked as it wrapped itself around me. He wasn't squeezing me, but the slime's gelatinous body was *not* light.

"Blobby, that's enough! It's only been two days and Danny fed you just yesterday," I said while prying the turncoat Tendril off me.

The slime's appendage rose up in the air, patted me on the head twice, then rolled away. As if they'd been waiting for it, a group of children dogpiled on top of its hip-high bulk. I'd never been on a water mattress before, but I figured Blobby was a close comparison. The creature jiggled and wiggled and bobbed under the assault of a dozen kids.

It was a wonder to see people younger than us, especially with the distinct spread of physical features their Attunements provided. The brief encounter with the youths the previous day, the children playing with Blobby, and the sheer freedom of being on the surface almost overwhelmed me.

"We can make a difference, for sure," Sam said, slapping me on the shoulder.

"No need to get sappy on us now, rock brain," Danny added with a jab to my arm.

"Ouch! Improved strength, remember?" I said mockingly, rubbing my arm.

She waved my comment off and rubbed at her stomach. "You think they have any more of that meat? I could certainly do with a few more..." She finally noticed the deadpan stares Sam and I were giving her.

"Danny, these people have been working on rations this whole time. And—don't you even make the argument that so were we—we can make do with the tomatoes I harvested," Sam said.

The woman grumbled something about being tired of vegetables before she looked away. Amazing how a life of the same subset of foods could be fine until you'd tried new things. Our food and companion qualms aside, we spent the rest of the evening discussing the finer details of our plan.

There would need to be another testing phase to figure out how we would approach dungeon runs. The fire ants were the primary target, but with how close those were to the Bunker, I was wary of aggravating them much more for now.

That left the spider den.

Daniela had a pretty good idea of how wide the den extended thanks to her efforts in clearing the road. With the help of a stick, she drew a rough outline of our Local Positioning System. The freeze-framed snapshot of the world denoted the wearer's location as well as updated with each pass through a region.

As the most traveled, Daniela sketched the boundaries of the Wildwood lakes, the general fields around the town, and the path we'd taken to get there from the Bunker. Using tufts of grass and some rocks, Daniela finished a pretty amazing rendition of our general area. A reddish clump of clay was smeared over a large swath of land to the northwest for the Fire Ants, while a bundled up shirt marked the boundaries of where the spiders lived just west and north of the town.

"When did you get a chance to go this far north? I can't say that was a smart decision with all the stuff looking for a slice off our hides," I asked, gesturing to the portion of US 301 Sam and I had definitely not traveled.

"They aren't ready for my Scovilles," she said, huffing and crossing her arms. "What did you think I did all day? Just people watch?"

"Well, you did tell us you got information on most of the people here. How would you have had time?" Sam said, placating the woman. I was fairly sure I saw a small flare of fire coming from her heat gills.

"Samuel, I am over twice as fast as the average person before the Fall. I move quickly. Plus, there were barely any creatures about, except in those areas I highlighted. As soon as I stepped into them?" Daniela splayed her hand out before pouncing on it with the fingers on the other.

"Banana spiders?" I asked. Making sure the tiny bit of hesitation in my voice didn't leak out was difficult. I'd hoped to set up a dungeon camp near the ants, but with the Tendrils an ambiguous threat somewhere to the west, doing so would leave the Bunker more exposed.

"There were a few types. Don't worry. We'll have plenty of time to give you phobias toward the half-dozen other species of arachnid I saw too," Danny said with a laugh.

"Do you think we will need the help of the Wild Guard?" I asked, pushing past a shiver and focusing on the planning task.

The sun set by the time we were done with our impromptu planning session. In the end, we agreed to wait two days so we could meet the other team with prospects for being Dreg Warriors.

— + —

That night was filled with strange dreams of crystals launching like spaceships from the ground of a foreign landscape before disappearing into the very depth of space. Noth-ingness swallowing it.

"Ronan, wake up!" Danny said, shaking me by the shoulder. When I came to my senses, the sun was spilling in through a crack in the plywood that had been used to cover the windows. "Sarah is here and she brought the other team. They are... odd."

"Oy! No one said nothing about odd people. I think *you* are the oddballs!" a voice said from behind our room. It didn't sound close or far, but instead like a whisper right by my ears.

Daniela's mouth clacked and she nearly bit her tongue. *She really needs to watch her mouth.*

The brunette helped me and Sam to our feet. I could feel the soreness immediately, but Sam was quick to follow with a <Health Bump> on me and himself. I needed to talk to Ava, Danny's mom, in the hopes she'd have some insight as to the effects of healing exhaustion. The science side of mana was something that had barely been touched on since coming to the surface.

As I straightened my clothes out and brushed the growing hair out of my face, I looked over my friends. We were due a serious break. Danny's hair was knotted even while in her tight bun. Sam looked like he'd been dragged by the foot through a field, even after rinsing off. While that wasn't too far off from what he did on the daily, I could see the wear on him. I modi-fied the speech I'd prepared for the dungeon farm just a tad.

Standing just outside the house were the Big Guns Squad accompanied by a strange hodgepodge of Fallen. A towering, flat-faced orc man hovered in the back while a merwoman spoke with him animatedly. Beside them, a dwarf and satyr haggled metal coins over something called 'northerner dill.' Standing at the front of the group was a lanky elf glowering in our direction, while a petite demon woman chatted with Sarah. Her horns and claws were so purple, I could have sworn they shone with ultraviolet light.

"Ah, here they are. This is Ronan, Daniela, and Samuel.

They are the Bunker-born we mentioned," Sarah said while sweeping a hand out toward each of us.

"It's a pleasure to meet new people. My name is Clara, and this is the New Hope Squad." The demoness smiled to reveal fangs as she shook my hand.

"It is always wonderful to meet new——" My introduction was cut off as the elf stepped between Clara and me.

"What do you want, outsiders? We've met a few who claim to be from a Bunker and none of you three look like you would. Too social and well-adapted." He crossed his arms.

"What part of 'Bunker-born' implies that there were no other people in the Bunker with us? Though having our identity questioned on a regular basis is starting to grate on me," I said, keeping as pleasant a smile as I could.

"Not buying it."

"Now, Devon, there is no need for——" Clara started before the elf cut her off.

"How many times has your willingness to accept others bit us in the rear, C?" he snapped.

"Now, that's not fair," the demoness said, a frown pulling on her sharp features.

"No one else may have the guts to stand up to these outsiders, but just because they gave us some food, I won't act meek just to walk into another trap."

The other members of the New Hope looked conflicted on where they stood, while Clara looked ready to smack some sense into the Devon character. However, he'd already proceeded to sour my morning and I wasn't about to roll over for a bully.

Uncle, forgive me for choosing violence, I thought to myself.

"Would you like to fight me, or are you just full of hot air?" I asked, crossing my arms and puffing my chest. He wanted to posture, well, two could play at that game.

"You wouldn't stand a chance, Geo. All you Bunker fakes try to lean on that for reputation."

"Ronan, you don't have to do this," Sarah said, stepping between me and Devon.

"I'm sorry, but I believe I do. They seem like a decent group, just from how they are reacting to this idiot's words, but if we are going to work together, we need to be on the same page," I said, looking straight into her eyes.

She only held them for a second before sighing and backing away. "At least move away so you don't wreck anything," she said. I acquiesced immediately and walked to where the fight with the crows had happened.

"You sure this is a smart idea?" Danny asked through the comm-plant. "Not sure if you've looked at their squad, but they are all Quotient Level 4."

Just to appease her, I focused intently on the sneering elf.

<Devon (Human)>

<Attunement: Air>

<Refinement: Gust>

<Perceived Metier Quotient: 4>

If their efforts while caring for the town of Wildwood were to be accounted for, then the New Hope squad would have dealt with many more creatures than my own group. On top of that, I'd never fought an air-attuned human. I hadn't even fought the humanoid Tendrils that rushed the town. However, regardless of how the fight went, the intent was the true victory. I wasn't out to be the strongest, but to show I wasn't a pushover.

"It'll be alright. Plus, worst case scenario, Sam just throws me a heal," I said back.

"That would be Tim. Mine requires touch," the blond added unhelpfully.

I shook those thoughts off and focused on the fight. I'd never gotten into fights outside of the occasional sparring tests Danny's mom put us through, but after punching some creatures in the face, I was at least a bit confident. The fact my skin was partly stone probably helped with that.

"Now, I know you three aren't familiar, but the Wild Guard actually tries to spar together often," Sarah said. "Devon will be strong, and while I don't doubt your abilities, I would like it for both of you braindead knuckle-draggers to make it through the other side. No weapons. No kill shots. I trust you two have enough control of your magic?"

She'd been facing me, but the elf on the other side responded. His voice carried as it had done before. *One of his skills or his traits had to be responsible for how easily he could hear things.* "You know I know the rules. Now let me walk all over this pretender so we can have a real leader in the mix."

I handed my shield and my pickaxe to Danny. Samuel moved to give me a hug, startling me. As his arms wrapped around my shoulders, I felt the soothing effect of his <Health Bump> flush through my body. He gave me a cheeky grin then stepped back. "I hope you know what you are doing."

"When have my decisions ever led to terrible consequences?" I asked.

"I'd rather not answer that," the blond said, stepping back and standing beside Tim. I could overhear him telling the other life-attuned to be ready for anything. *I suppose it should make me happy that they care enough to be ready, but dang, it stings on the doubt front.*

"Ronan, you are going to spar with Devon for the express purpose of being an idiot. Devon, you are going to spar with Ronan for the express purpose of being a hard-headed fool. Are you both agreed to the terms?" Sarah said, deadpan. Apparently she was going to be our 'referee.'

"I just don't intend to be pushed around. I barely know him," I said.

"I'm going to make sure it stays that way. Not sure how you made it past the territories, but you are in for a rude awakening. Wildwood isn't to be messed with," Devon said. The man practically snarled at me.

"Well, whenever you are ready. Start!" she shouted.

CHAPTER EIGHT

Mop Up

"How do you expect to win this, mud boy?" Devon said, spinning around me slowly. His hands were free of any kind of spell chain, but I wasn't about to imagine he wasn't working something in the background.

"<Earth Shell>." Mana seeped out of my arms slowly before coalescing around my fists and forearms like gauntlets. "That would be with me punching the smirk off your face. Preferably more than once, but you do look rather fragile."

I shoved off the ground and rushed toward the man. From the ease of movement with which he dodged, I knew his mobility had to be higher than mine. What he didn't account for was my own Skills. <Earthen Barrier> surged out of the ground to catch me and allow me to redirect my momentum.

"What the—" His words cut off as I tackled him across the chest. Unfortunately, his surprise only lasted enough for him to get touched because a second after, he exploded away in a swirl of air. Without fingers to lock my arms in place, the stone covering me worked against me. My biceps strained, but I didn't have a good enough grip to hang on.

The world spun as his gust of wind flipped me in the air.

Not wanting to be concussed right at the start of battle, I cast <Earth Shell> again. Instead of trying to direct it, I let it cover me whole. I held the spell chain.

My body crashed into the ground with the additional force of my heavy stony exterior, but the tumble was cut short by that same factor. The rock around my joints creaked like it was going to give, but the still-active skill filled the gaps before I dislocated something. The brain rattling was only mildly mitigated.

I dismissed <Earth Shell> and immediately cracked my joints. The rock crumbled almost at my will, but being entombed everywhere but the face still limited my mobility. Thankfully, I was still encased because gut wrenching blows of air hit my shell as soon as I stood. The impacts were mostly mitigated until the debris hit. I fought against the wind to position my arms in an X in front of me. Some of the scattered bits of wood from the collapsed pavilions, and loose rocks in the ground around us, pelted me. We hadn't been through a storm on the surface yet, but if I had to guess, this would be the equivalent of a bad one. I dropped to my knees to dodge a significant piece of wood.

A flare of fire from behind me told me that someone out there was doing their best to keep the fight contained.

My mana was down to about forty percent. The full coverage and repair of my <Earth Shell> had cost me, but I could see it hadn't been for naught.

"You going to fight or just stand there like a coward?" Devon shouted. His voice projected clearly even through the mess of buffeting winds around me.

"Figured I'd just wait 'til you ran out of breath," I said in a normal tone. Raising my voice wasn't necessary if he did have a means of enhancing his hearing. Sure enough, a growl of frustration was all I got. He'd clearly heard me.

When the wind dropped away entirely, I risked looking over my rock-covered arms. A terrifyingly familiar set of motions warned me that Devon was about to dump a whole lot of something on me. Using every bit of practice I'd had while building around the Bunker, I cast <Stone Spikes> with my right hand and <Earthen Barrier> with my left. However, due to my haste, the targets for both were too broad. The layer of stone covering me was included in the mix. Spikes rose up from my body; one from my chest, another from the shell around my head and shoulders, and the last from my legs. The poorly aimed teepee filled in with the <Earthen Barrier>skill. As such, the ground swallowed me a good foot before it hardened.

Ozone hung in the air for a moment before lightning cracked through most of the ground around me. If I hadn't been *literally* grounded, the electric charge would have done a number on everything. As it stood, I watched as my Health dropped from a solid eighty-five percent to just over forty percent. Even entombed as I was, my muscles twitched and fought my rocky armor as they flexed without my direction.

Note—my body jerked—*to self. Air-attuned can make lightning.*

When I was able to string thoughts together, I called forth my spell chain around my body. Not that it took much effort, but the consolidation of the pseudo-fulgurite around me caused it to crumble apart. The rock didn't stand well against the strange pressure my passive skill effect produced on earth.

Less than ten percent of my mana remained before I was able to extract myself from my own protections. My body jerked in spurts as I moved towards Devon. I was fairly sure that if my strength wasn't as high as it was, and if I didn't have Limestone Skin, I wouldn't have been walking at all. The elf in question was panting on the ground. Not the efforts of someone that had just run a marathon or anything like that, but heaving great gulps of air as if there wasn't enough air in the atmosphere.

I wasn't even half way to him when Blobby rolled past me into the middle of the field and started to dissolve some of the crumbled fulgurite. I pushed past the series of questions that left, and dropped on my knees in front of Devon. With the last bit of my mana, and a concerted effort against my muscles' desires to spaz out, I socked the man in the jaw. I never thought the sound of crunching bone could be so sweet, but I indulged in it for as long as I stayed conscious. Which wasn't terribly long.

— ✛ —

A surge of relief flowed through me. It lasted enough for me to curl up into a fetal position. The huge dump of mana of the fight was taking its toll on my everything and it took all I had not to black out again.

"Oh look, numbskull number one is awake," Sarah said dryly. She was standing somewhere behind me, but my mind was too focused on the pain wrecking my body.

"Sam, am I doing this wrong?" Tim asked hesitantly. A whistling sound passed me by before a wet flop followed it. Someone gasped loudly behind me.

"Perhaps it will be best to let him wake naturally. I am not super familiar with air-attuned withdrawals," my blond friend said. Without asking for permission, he pried my head from where it was curled and checked my eyes.

"I'm good... just... need a second," I said through gritted teeth. Samuel patted me on the head before dropping it. A certain gelatinous mass had been ready to catch it, giving it an astounding memory foam feel. *Thanks Blobster.*

"Pyrrhic victory. Truly an exemplary way of making your point, Ron," Danny said.

"I... Ugh... Never said it was a diplomatic flourish," I managed in my defense.

"Rematch!" Devon howled between gasped breaths. A smack resounded from that direction.

"Enough of that. Now, thanks to their efforts, we aren't in a hurry to return to hunting. This will not last if we keep wasting what time we have," Clara said before marking her words by smacking Devon upside the head again. Thankfully I'd gathered myself up enough to see the last strike. It was almost better than the one I'd laid on him.

"But C—"

"Enough, Devon. We've made mistakes in the past, but this is not one. Plus, if they turn on us, we've seen what one of them has to offer. Numbers will be more than enough," she said matter-of-factly. I could hear just a hint of heat in her voice, but it simmered. For some reason, I found that more intimidating than if she'd been screaming at the elf.

"That's about enough of that," Sarah interjected. "Is the pissing contest over?"

When neither Devon nor I responded other than with muted grumbles, she continued.

"Good. Now let's get the introductions properly out of the way. This is Ronan, Daniela, and Samuel, the somewhat mysterious benefactors of Wildwood." She gestured at the other very assorted squad. "This is the New Hope team. They are the only group entrusted with traveling the wilds and making contact with the other survivors. The rest of us mostly deal with local hunts and defense of our fields. Plenty of work there already."

"If you weren't here to protect our family, we wouldn't be able to travel, Sarah," Clara said while smiling up at the orc woman. "You and Oliver stand more than a good chance of making it out there."

"Thanks, but I'll leave that nonsense to you crazies." Sarah chuckled.

"Wait, you have made contact with other towns?" I asked.

"Two so far, and we are the largest of the three. We stay for a week to lend them a hand and help train their people, but times have been tough. Tendrils have been attacking more. I don't remember them ever being this aggressive. They've never attacked a town outright," Clara said, a frown returning to her face.

"I'm sure you heard," Sarah said, pointing to some of the mess around us. It wasn't the aftermath of the fight outside the walls, but we were fairly sure the crows didn't attack Wildwood by coincidence.

"Yes. And to get to the point, Sarah mentioned that you had

a proposition for us. One that would give us a jump in power in exchange for doing what we are already doing," Clara said, turning to me.

For the first time, I noticed some of the glow from her horns and claws had made its way to her eyes. I shivered involuntarily and my thoughts scattered like dust in the wind. Sam placed his arm on my shoulder and relief flowed through me. My thoughts fell back into place.

Apparently there was an argument going on.

" —accident," Clara said.

"Accident, my borking rear end!" Danny shouted. A spell chain hovered around her arms, the threat evident.

Unlike Devon's posturing and his argument with me, the others didn't feel like Daniela would hold back, because the other New Hopers were tense and at the ready.

"Hold on there. I'm alright. Can someone explain before we go blasting our budding allies in the metaphorical foot?" I said. I whispered my thanks to Samuel before stepping forward.

"Some of my magic triggers on eye contact. Usually it's nothing more than a minor distraction, but well, you were spent, Ronan," Clara explained.

"It was deliberate. She was trying to put you on the back foot," Daniela said. More of a growl, really. Samuel stepped up to prevent our hot-blooded friend from jumping the gun.

When I turned back to Clara, I could see that she wasn't meeting my gaze. Instead, she was sheepishly scratching the back of her head.

"Well? And here I thought all I would have to deal with is a windbag," I said.

"I'm sorry, really. It has… become a bad habit of mine to use my fear before negotiations. It really was an accident," Clara said.

I didn't say a whole lot and just watched her and her group for a minute. Other than her appearance, she didn't come across as particularly intimidating. Some of her companions certainly did, but if she had to lead them, it would certainly serve to have an edge in conversation.

"We can continue the discussion. However, I want it to be clear that we are not subservient to anyone. If we move forward, we are on equal terms and everything should be as clear as possible. As we've been doing so far."

"That is understandable. I'm sorry."

"I am sure you all know about the Metier Crystal in the center of your town," I said.

"Of course we do, it's the biggest damn one around," Devon said. He was summarily smacked again before I continued.

"They are living entities." I let my words hang in the air for a moment. The Big Guns weren't surprised and that added to the New Hopers' confusion. They had almost been ready to brush me off. Fisticuffs and attempted manipulation were worth jack when you challenge someone's worldview, I supposed.

"How does that make sense? We've never seen them eat or anything like that," the satyr said. I'd kinda wished I hadn't interrupted their introduction now, but there was nothing to do.

"They are the things that brought mana to us. Their goal is to purge impurities, things they call the Dreg. One of the forms of these impurities seem to concentrate in are the Tendrils you've encountered." When there were no comments, I proceeded. "Dreg seems to overwhelm things in high quantities. With the help of the crystals, we've been able to make a stand against the creatures we've found. However, the more time we spend on the surface, the more we realize we can't do it alone."

"How exactly do you know all of this?" Clara asked, crossing her arms and meeting my eyes. There wasn't the doubt I'd expected, just curiosity and caution.

"If we all care to meet back up at the Blessing of Magic, I can explain better. Sarah, could you cover us while we talk?" I said. The orc woman nodded and started shouting all around her.

It was then that I realized that there was a crowd gathered

around us. Had they been there all along? The fight had been near the center of the town, but I hadn't realized how big of a deal it had been. I must have been really out of it.

Regardless, all of us made it to the town Entity without issue. Many people cheered after seeing that the New Hopers had returned, and Clara took a few minutes here and there to reassure them of their success. Her platitudes were easily pierced by my perception. The strained smile and tightness around her eyes. Whether that was due to what I just explained or the somewhat baseless comfort she was giving, I wasn't sure.

Regardless, we made it to the Blessing of Magic. Just like the first time, I had to pause to marvel at the sheer vibrance of everything. Around Clara was a midnight black haze that flickered in and out of existence wherever she looked. The others had the more common glows of the Attunements I was familiar with. Even Devon paused his incessant grumbling when we entered the Blessing.

"Alright, we are here. What required such secrecy?" Clara said, gesturing to the empty space around us.

Instead of answering, I knocked on the translucent surface of the Crystal. Zips of light shot from the surface of the crystal to Samuel and Daniela. One headed for me, but I held my hand up to pause it. Sure enough, as if it wasn't actually made of light, the beam halted in the air. I offered the beam to the demoness before me.

She squinted her eyes to such a degree I wondered how she'd be able to see, but she closed her hand around it.

—Agreement signaled.—

The town Entity's voice rang out before lances of light touched all of Clara's squad. One final streaked toward me before whiteness overtook me. Hovering in the air were the words, 'Welcome, Dreg Warriors.' Emblazoned in fancy lettering. What I assumed was a private message formed at the edge of my vision.

—Was this entrance more appropriate?—

I gave a nod in response before turning to the slack-jawed Wildwoodians.

"Welcome to the inside of your Entity Cluster. The Metier Crystals, as we know them."

"How the— When the—" Devon stammered.

The orc man had an expression of mild surprise which, considering he hadn't given any indication he was anything but a statue, I took as a good indicator of life. The others ranged from concerned to bewildered.

"Okay. I'll bite. You are serious and it's a serious offer because you somehow just teleported us somewhere. What's the catch?" Clara said, setting serious eyes on me. Her trepidation about using her skill on me was gone because I noticed the purple glow brightened before winking out completely.

—Aggressive action will not be tolerated. Mana induction field activated.—

Just to test it, I tried to call forth a spell chain, but even the thought hurt. *Good to know. Why didn't it have it externally?* After slotting that in my ever growing list of questions, I turned to Clara.

Now it was *her* on the backfoot and she didn't look happy about it. "I'm going to ignore your attempt to magic me into something because I did have you teleported. Or whatever it is the Entity here does. Haven't really had the time to talk about that.

"This is where you make the decision to join us in our effort to retake the surface of Earth. We made contact with the Entity Clusters thanks to implants we received. They gave us access to their magic. You all have already discovered natural means of accessing this magic. You can unlock more, just like Sarah and her group."

Devon looked taken aback and Clara's frown deepened. "What's the catch?"she asked again.

"We fight Dreg, and we collect Dreg. Everything we gather, we bring back to the crystals to purge. It's sort of what you want to do anyways, because if you don't, you'll end up like the

Tendrils," I said evenly. Considering it was my second time giving the recruitment spiel, I thought it went pretty well.

"And what if we say no?" she said.

"Nothing. I just hope you don't go about spilling our secrets. Though considering how much of a splash us three have been making in Wildwood, people are bound to start asking questions."

"Does this have anything to do with this 'plan' we heard about? Something to do with the territories?" the dwarven man asked.

"In part. But I would prefer to keep that between my collaborators until you all have made your choice."

"I don't think we—"

"I'll do it," Devon said.

That caught me by surprise. "Figured you wouldn't trust a word out of my mouth."

"I don't. But, and that's a big but, if you are actually a Bunker-born, then you would have needed something to cheat at a level where you could beat me. So, I'll be the lab rat. Hit me with—"

I should have seen it coming, really. The town Entity had been nothing but trigger happy since I'd met it. So when Devon gave it enough plausible deniability to strike, it did. The crystal pierced the man's neck and held him stiff. If the Entity hadn't also disabled everyone's magic, I was sure me and my friends would have been drowning in more damage than we knew what to do with.

As it stood, everyone was tense until the crystal released Devon.

—Implant complete.—

—Thank you for your cooperation with MetierTech Trademarks.—

"What the?" I whispered. A message printed itself quickly in the corner of my view.

—The implant you carry is stamped by a MetierTech label.

I did not wish to break further norms without including representation of the original hardware.—

I shook my head, realizing that we'd been sponsoring Alan's name for the implants all along. I didn't mind, really. Him and my grandmother's research had come up with the technology that eventually gave us magic, after all, but how he managed to sneak that onto a device the size of my pinky, I wouldn't know.

The aside with the Entity didn't last long. Devon strode forward, holding the back of his neck even though I knew there wouldn't be an injury there. Before he could get a word out, I yelled, "Status!"

My own popped up, but I dismissed it with practiced ease. He, on the other hand, missed a step. Out of politeness, I caught him by the arm so he wouldn't fall. So surprised was he that he didn't pull back. His eyes glanced over with the faraway look of someone looking at the implant information.

"Devon?" the satyr said, holding a hand at the ready. I wasn't sure if it was practice or a nervous twitch, but considering they were the life-attuned of the group, I warranted they were ready to heal.

"It's… a breakdown. A breakdown of everything. It even has the names that I gave my Gifts," he said in a whisper. He blinked then turned to me. "You weren't lying. I never told you this."

"That about covers it. Bit of a major invasion of your privacy, but that officially makes you a Dreg Warrior. And that about covers the commitment for now. Should we encounter Dreg, we purge. Other than that, we work for our own goals. I merely hope that you all will be willing to help us retake some of the surface back for humanity."

"We aren't really humans anymore," the merwoman said, almost quietly enough that I missed it.

"Devon, would you please focus on your friend? I'm sure your perception is high enough," I said, mimicking the command and focusing on the merwoman.

<Lilly (Human)>

<Attunement: Water>
<Refinement: N/A>
<Perceived Metier Quotient: 4>

I hadn't had access to the woman's name before, so I had to assume it came from Devon's knowledge. Or possibly Sarah's. Yet another feature of the implant and the status I wasn't entirely sure about. "Once you have access to the implant, the true nature of things will become clearer. Just because we don't all look the same doesn't mean we are no longer humans. Just because I don't look like a dwarf doesn't mean that I am not earth-attuned. You have all seen it. Why should our humanity be any different?"

After seeing how well everyone in Wildwood got along, and just how different each of the Attunements manifested, I knew that we might be seen as outsiders. Even with my Limestone Skin, Sam's strange nervous feeler things, and Daniela's gills, we were pretty standard pre-Fall-looking humans.

Clara placed a reassuring arm over the merwoman's shoulder. "Might as well get this out of the way. You have more to tell us after we go through this process, don't you?"

I gave the demoness a nod, and she spent a bit of time talking with her people, but eventually they all agreed. With the addition of the New Hopers, the Big Guns, and our own trio, my plan to set up a dungeon farm was a day away.

CHAPTER NINE

Motivations

When I explained the skill acquisition system to the others, the conversation kind of devolved. Kids in a candy store, the saying came to me. Except these were grown men and women floundering about for magic skills. They all shouted in discussion of what they should select and I could barely follow what they each had available. I did find out that the <Fear> was a direct offensive skill from Clara, and the <Lightning Strike> was a materialize offensive skill from Devon.

The elf seemed much more easy going after getting himself a new skill, asking me a flurry of questions about the attributes and their breakdowns. That particular discussion was simple, but ended up taking so long the town Entity actually booted us from its whitespace.

—Conserve resources. Forum safety unnecessary at this time.—

Instead of the planning I'd wanted to get done before setting out the next day, the group headed off to the training area. That was, a training area I wasn't even aware existed. Daniela filled me in on it being the place where they trained the youths who found Gifts in their repertoire. Why Devon and I hadn't fought there turned out to be because they didn't want Devon to wreck the buildings.

I wasn't sure if I wanted to take that as a compliment to pulling the most out of Devon, or them underestimating my abilities. I shook that off as I spotted the group of youths from our first day in Wildwood sitting in a circle, meditating.

Shimmering circles of different mana hovered around them. Some on the ground, some around a limb and some through and into their bodies. With what I knew about skills, I could clearly see they were developing their own direct, imbue, and materialize type skills right before my very eyes.

One young dwarf sat half an inch lower than his companions thanks to the compression of his earth magic. The youngest boy, an orc, had a ring of dried grass around him, and two part-lizard girls hemmed in that grass with a circle of frost. I was fairly sure both were deadly to the poor weeds. A thin mist hovered around the trio as their passive magic met and was canceled.

Again, unlike our own or even the Entity-granted skills the Wildwoodians acquired, the spell chains looked more like abstract paintings, ala Lee Krasner, than rigid symbols. Wavering strokes of multicolored light to mark their Attunements. The passive effects I'd come to note with my perception were being manifested as they worked with their mana.

"Children, you are dismissed. It appears your elders mean to interrupt a lesson," Kirby's voice rang out and I snapped out of my reverie.

As if they hadn't all been deep in their own thoughts, the kids leapt to their feet and ran off giggling. The sheer display of energy made *me* tired. I saw the young orc use his passive skill to help melt some of the ice that had encased the girls before they took him by the hand and joined the others.

Other than a few curious glances, we were thoroughly ignored.

"Can I help you? Did you all not cause enough of a distraction earlier?" Kirby asked, turning from the scattered children to us.

"We are preparing for our expedition. I believe everyone wishes to become more familiar with their abilities before we head out," I said. The scaly man frowned, huffed, and walked away. I heard him call out and Oliver practically materialized beside him.

The two spoke quickly and in hushed tones before disappearing around a building.

"Don't mind the councilman. He is distrustful of those outside the Guard, especially outsiders. He believes we should keep to ourselves and strengthen our numbers to survive. The smaller towns are just a drain on our resources," Sarah said, stepping beside me.

"Sounds more callous than anything," I replied. When she didn't say anything else, I prompted her to say what was on her mind.

"Are things moving too quickly?" the orc woman asked. "How can you just waltz in here, give us all these powers, and then ask that we turn around and help ourselves? Awfully charitable of you. Not to mention we gave you a less than stellar reception," she added, scratching the back of her head.

This elicited a chuckle from me. I watched as Sam and Daniela spoke with the New Hopers and the rest of the Big Guns. They were sharing their own tips for dealing with the less intuitive aspects of Entity-granted skills. Daniela sounded like she had some really good advice thanks to her own training using the Freeform skill she'd unlocked.

Instead of focusing on that discussion, I answered Sarah's question.

"I'm sure you all still have your doubts about our origins. That's fine, I'm not judging," I said, lifting my arms in a placating gesture to keep Sarah from defending herself. "But we were alone. More alone than I really care to describe. The sheer life of this town, of the idea of people, and living on the surface? That's what we've always wanted. Well, maybe me more than my friends, but they share that feeling also."

"That doesn't explain why you'd share this much power freely," Sarah said quietly. This side of the intimidating orc woman was fascinating. She had the strength and will necessary to be ruthless and calculative, but could still be considerate. Meeting more people and learning about them sent a thrill of excitement through me, but I stopped that derailed train of thought there.

"It feels like I could fill a whole book with all the struggles we had gaining the smallest of footholds on the surface. We had the great fortune of stumbling onto our Entity Cluster. We scraped by when, for all intents and purposes, we should have died. This was because we were alone.

"I haven't met these other towns yet, and I would love to, but they rely on you. Not sure what exactly they offer you, but it can't be worth much." Sarah remained silent. "We can offer a little and hope that we can cooperate for the future. Your enemies are our enemies. Doubly so if they are Tendrils."

While we talked, the entire group let out a plethora of skills. Sharp, glinting ice flew from the merwoman's hands. A bed of grass grew out of the ground before wiggling like a caterpillar at the satyr's behest. The orc's arms swelled and I could see veins of red fire highlight his muscles. The dwarf had his hands on the ground where apparently nothing was happening, but I doubted it. Devon was striking the air with measured fists, causing the trees in the distance to rustle.

It was an extraordinary display of magic. Not to mention the swaying vine and floating fire wisp my friends added to the mix while helping the Big Guns get used to their own skills. I was tapped out on the magic for now.

"Do you think your plan will work?" Sarah asked.

"Even if it doesn't work out completely, we all need to stop reacting and start being proactive. If you stayed in the cycle of hunting for survival and not for growth in levels and items, then you'd stagnate. If my guess is right, that life Tendril is at least Quotient 6. That's a huge difference compared to us now. Maybe not our group as a whole, but I doubt it will be alone."

And so, we arrived at the big uncertainty of my plan. The end result. If the Tendrils decided to attack again, then our efforts would be for nil. We had to hope that the other two Wild Guard Squads could defend the town by the time we set up a rotating schedule on the dungeon farm. I could feel time quite literally slipping through my fingers and my sense of urgency retake its grip around my chest.

The surface was not safe.

— + —

The rest of the day ended with almost everyone tapping out due to their mana side effects. Tim, Sam, and the satyr, Dennis, sauntered off to giggle. The orcs and Daniela took a dip in the lake fully clothed, and the merwoman laid lazily out in the sun to thaw.

The dwarves and I took a break on a stone bench I crafted. They were very impressed with my control and utility, since their own skills were based almost entirely on offense. Understandably so. Clara sat off in the distance, sipping water from a mug that looked about as old as all the buildings around us.

The twins and the New Hoper dwarf, Godfrey, argued loudly about what improvements they could potentially give to the bench. Turned out none of them actually disagreed with any of the others suggestions. Instead of joining that echo chamber, I walked over and sat across from the demoness.

Her black skin was paler than I recalled, and she held her mug in a death grip.

"Never seen the after effects of dark alignments? Or, should I say, the death-attuned?"

"Now that I know, either works. I can't expect there to be a uniform nomenclature for things when there isn't instant communication between people. And to answer your question, no. Before the crows and the night shift workers of Wildwood, a skunk was the only death-attuned creature I'd seen," I said.

The sun was starting to set and I could see Blobby pestering Anthony for a bit of food the fire ant had somehow procured. Their bickering reminded me of Daniela and I.

"Nausea is our side effect," Clara continued. "I've been trying for the past thirty minutes not to be ill."

"Suppose I have it simple then, just a bit of a stomach ache," I said, trying to lighten the mood.

"No. None of our side effects should be taken lightly, Ronan. I can tell you have a lot of talent and a cockroach-like survivability—I mean that as a compliment, they are damn near impossible to kill—but the surface is not kind. I've lost more than I care to admit and I am not much older than you."

Ignoring that little age comment, there it was. The reason she was the leader of the New Hopers. A realist that still went out and sought a future.

"I have lost, and missed out, on a lot of life. But I understand. You don't have to worry about me forgetting to let everyone have their self-care. More time for self-care is one of the side effects our strength will provide."

"That was a terrible joke. People usually talk about side effects as negatives!" she said, unable to help from cracking a smile.

"I aim to please, ma'am."

The two of us spoke lightly for a few minutes before I laid out my plan for the following day. It was ambitious and dangerous, but would give us a huge leg up in dealing with future threats. Dreg-related or otherwise.

"Are those things coming along?" Devon asked, scowling at Blobby.

The gelatinous creature was playing with a little pebble. The small stone popped out of the slime's bulk and into the air before Blobby rolled after the pebble, trying to catch it before it touched the ground. It was literally the best pet. Playing fetch with itself! Anthony tracked the pebble with its head but didn't move from his spot beside Daniela.

"Yes. Blobby and Anthony have been huge parts of our survival. They will help here also." I turned to Sarah, who was talking with Oliver on the wall.

The other members of the Big Guns were also standing on the western wall. The previous night, the rest of the Guard had insisted that Sarah's team remain behind to bolster their defenses, even if they were meant to be off the patrol schedule for the day. Councilman Dylan had been on our side of the argument until Kirby pointed out that no one expected the New Hopers to defend; they were gone more often than not. As such, and considering they were a larger number than Sarah's squad, they should be more than sufficient for our 'doomed course of action,' as he put it.

Suffice to say, the Big Guns were not happy when the councilmen overturned their original decision, but I reassured them that it made me feel better about the safety of the town while we executed our plan. The twins, of course, called out that they didn't need more reason for heartburn, while Tim hurriedly asked Sam for more healing tips. Sarah's stonewalled demeanor solidified harder than my own <Earth Shell> as she took her position away from the gate.

We walked down the road fairly early in the morning. Many townsfolk were already tending to the undamaged portions of the field, some even using the stone spikes and barriers I'd created as workspaces for storing tools and water instead of wasting time removing them. A true testament to a people determined to survive.

Before long, we'd left them, and the auxiliary field where I'd saved the Big Guns, behind. US 301 in all its decrepit glory extended north and south of where we stood.

"We've avoided scouting too far to the west, since that is where our 'allies' are housed," Clara said. She put air quotes around the word allies as she continued. "However, the estimates between our maps and what Daniela was able to provide us means that they have to be at least a days' travel west of here. Frequent patrols is how they kept 'order.'"

"Hopefully we don't run into any of those, but the plan is to set up the farm spot then back out. We can come back at full strength once we have somewhere to operate from," I said.

Daniela tapped her temple and everyone but me and Devon glanced at their LPS maps. As the two with the highest perception, we were the designated lookouts. A development that we were both quite thrilled about.

"We are less than a half mile from the rough border of spider territory. Our goal will be to find the most concentrated spot of creatures, take two steps back and dig our heels in," the brunette started. "Ronan will be in charge of the construction together with Godfrey. Sam will work on setting up an outer defense perimeter and the rest of us keep them alive. Simple enough, yes?"

"Except for the part where a bunch of spiders try to eat us," Lilly pointed out.

"That's right. Nothing to be done about that bit. Everyone good on that front?"

Nods around the group and everyone pulled out their weapons of choice.

Funnily enough, Godfrey's weapon was a hammer-shovel combination he called a shommer. A true wordsmith he was. Clara had an axe, as did Rommel, the tall orc. Devon had a bag full of scrap metal junk that made me wish tetanus vaccines were still a thing. Lilly had a pair of hooks, and Dennis had a wooden staff with a flute carved into the top. Not what I would consider practical, but I was swinging a mining tool around, so I couldn't quite complain.

As the tankiest built individuals, Godfrey, Rommel, and myself took the lead while Daniela and Devon spread out to either side. I wouldn't want to race either of those two now that

I'd seen them in action. Anthony melded into the foliage after Daniela, and Blobby rolled along just behind me.

A few spurts of fire alerted me that Daniela had engaged something, but she didn't call out. The rest of us tried to move as slowly and as quietly as possible. I was probably making chameleons jealous with how I split my vision between the forest floor and the canopy overhead.

Webbing of different thicknesses and colors started springing up around the path we took. Clara kept her eyes peeled and made deep notches on the trees as we progressed to mark our path. Something about that tingled in the back of my mind, but I couldn't quite place it.

Regardless of my new trepidations, Rommel took the lead when the webbing became more difficult to circumvent. A spell chain formed around the man's arm and he strode forward unimpeded as the webs withered away. Well, all the webs but a few black-spun ones. My guess was those were from a fire-attuned spider of some kind. Definitely something I wanted to avoid seeing if at all possible.

The world darkened as we made our way deeper under the cover of tree and web. When the hairs on the back of my neck were perpendicular, I called for the group to stop.

"Back. Come back!" I called to Devon and Danny through the comm-plant. I didn't even dwell on the fact that the Entity-created implant the elf had tuned in perfectly to the one in my own body.

"Something is watching us," I said quietly.

"Many somethings…" Rommel said. His eyes were glowing red, bright enough to see from over his shoulder.

"Form up. Godfrey, Rommel, we are going for a triangle. Keep Dennis and Sam in the middle. Do not let anything get the healers," I said, hefting my pickaxe at the ready.

A shift in the webbing marked the arrival of Devon. He was carried on a short burst of wind over a sticky mess of a bush. He looked at the hunkered group for a second before joining the defensive line seamlessly.

"Where is your hot-headed friend?" he asked between pants.

"Daniela?" I said through the comm-plant. Silence.

"Daniela?" I said aloud, hoping that she was nearby and too focused on something to be paying attention to my totally-not-urgent tone.

"Danny!" I called out into the forest. The only response I got was chittering feet and the muted rustle of web-bound leaves.

CHAPTER TEN

Caught in a Web

"Fodder!" yelled Godfrey, before a spray of sand exploded out of the ground. He'd used his shommer to lift a section of the tuft around us before it surged toward the incoming spiders. My eyes focused on one of the larger ones, but most were the size of my foot.

<Twin-Flagged Jumping Spider>

<Attunement: Air>

<Refinement: N/A>

<Perceived Metier Quotient: 1>

If the arachnids hadn't come at us like a tidal wave, I might have plowed through the woods after Daniela.

A spider thunked into my shield hard enough to trigger the material's effects. A weak pulse of heat washed over the smaller spiders, causing them to flinch and reel back. The impact shook me out of my thoughts long enough to remember to never run into the woods halfcocked. Instead, I dug my heels in and summoned three <Earthen Barriers> around us. It wouldn't do much against the nimble spiders, but at least we wouldn't be whacking them from our ankles.

"Devon, give us some room!" Clara shouted from somewhere in our ranks.

The elf inhaled loudly before a burst of wind exploded out from his body. None of us were buffeted by the wind, but it pushed back the spiders and even the loose earth on top of my barriers was blown away. Sam and I took a step back, easily reminded that the New Hopers had been operating together for longer and we were down a member.

"What's the play?" I asked as I cast <Earth Shell> around my torso and legs.

After being singed by my heat and knocked back by the wind, the spiders didn't rush us. Instead, they began to climb around the trees and up the canopy.

"Rommy, clear cut the branches. Lilly, I want an igloo overtop. Funnel them to Ronan's side. We'll go after your friend once we are safe. Can you hold them while we get the igloo up?" Clara said, locking eyes with me briefly before she extended her arms toward the spiders.

A sickly purple fog hovered in the air between the spiders and us. Clara dropped to a knee, steadied by Dennis. A full series of thuds marked the death of a dozen of the smaller spiders.

I was still at the ready when Rommel started to throw discuses of living fire at the trees.A total of four skill casts later, and the orc was steaming just like Daniela, but we had clear sunlight shining down on us. There was also an easy dozen charred spider corpses crackling and popping amidst the burning branches.

The deadly fog still hung in the air, but spiders were already stumbling out of it. Lilly didn't delay much longer. Thin pillars of ice rose up from my <Earthen Barriers> to form a teepee. She stabbed her hook into two of the small barriers and ice started to crackle along the packed earth. It split a little under the expansive force of the freezing water but it held. A moment later, she was breathing a thick white fog that clung to the ice pillars. By the third puff, she had formed semi-translucent walls of smooth water. The spell chain was just barely visible around her neck like a collar.

"Ronan, snap out of it. They're coming!" Devon said, sending one of his new gust fist strikes at the spiders heading towards the one opened section of the igloo.

Sure enough, the spiders that survived the dissipating toxic cloud were heading in our direction. Their movements were more sluggish and not nearly as violent, but there was still a ton of them.

"Sam, hit me and then hang back defensively. It's time to reap some spiders," I said, channeling into my pickaxe. The blond life mage pressed his hand to my lower back and energetic heat flowed through my body.

With now-practiced ease, I pumped more mana to increase the speed of the crystal growing along the metal. Before long, my pick had turned into more of a scythe and then the spiders were upon me. Gouts of wind with chips of metal and swaying vines covered my flanks as I reaped spider after spider.

I saw at least three types of Attunements, but no magic attacks other than their physical differences. My body flickered between hot and cold from the water-attuned spiders that got around my guard and the ones that triggered the effect of my shield. Sweat rolled off me in droves, the condensation in the air making my hands clammy, but thoughts of Daniela kept me swinging.

I wasn't sure how long I was in the kill box, but I'd started roaring at some point. *I'm losing her.* My throat felt raw as I churned most of my mana and extended the reach of my pick-turned-scythe. *She trusted me to lead.* The small boost to my strength was what kept it all together as my muscles began feeling the strain of my carelessly enhanced strikes. *These things are in my way!*

A verdant vine wrapped around my arm and chest before I could finish my next swing. I turned, ready to launch a <Stone Spike> at whatever was holding me in place, but my spell chain stuttered. A look at my mana bar showed it at less than five percent, and a double-take on my target revealed it was Samuel that I had nearly impaled.

The blond was swaying on his feet, but the concern was clear in his eyes. The piercing blue stare finally snapped me out of my fugue. It also unlocked the pain of overusing my mana and I buckled to my knees. If the vine hadn't been holding me, I would have curled up into a ball.

I was vaguely aware of Clara directing her squad while Samuel cradled my head on his lap.

"How is he doing?" the demoness asked.

"I... I think he's doing fine, but I've never seen him like this before," he said.

The demoness remained silent for a beat, before turning to her team. "Hunker down. We wanted to go deeper, but this will have to do. Dennis, I want you talking to these plants. I want them on our side; we want plenty of warning if something is flanking us. Lilly, until we can get Ronan up to fortify the walls, I want you to finish the igloo. Devon, Rommel, you two are on watch."

"Wild!" the group shouted in unison before the frantic scurrying of our team echoed around me. It was oddly soothing and as I focused on the drum of feet through the earth, my aching body relaxed. The pain was still there, tender, but it was manageable.

"I'm alright, Sam. Please, let me help," I eked out.

The blond scowled at me. "What's your mana at, Ron?"

A look at the bar showed that I had maybe recovered twenty percent. When I told him that, he scoffed. "You keep your butt right here." He helped prop me against the growing ice some. Before he turned to leave, he whispered softly in my ear. "We'll get her back."

Thankfully, I wasn't left alone with my thoughts for long. "How much of an idiot are you? And here I thought I was gonna start giving you some respect or something," Devon said. His voice was carrying in the wind. The complete lack of the elf nearby told me that one.

"I'd say I am an above-average idiot," I said, leaning back wearily. Our implants didn't have a clock built in, but I watched the tics of my mana recovering to mark the time. Time that was slipping away with Daniela.

"How is throwing yourself at the problem supposed to help your friend?" he added with a bit of heat in his voice.

"You don't know anything about me," I whispered back. My voice was tight.

"True. Except that you are an idiot. Get your ass together so we can get going. I'm not in the habit of losing my people."

The elf didn't say anything else. He didn't need to. I grit my teeth and hoisted myself to my feet. The whole process was less than steady, but I snatched up my pickaxe from where it had fallen to support me. Sam gave me a look of concern from where he stood knitting a tight web of vines to limit our horizontal access points to two entries. Quite ironic, considering we were in spider territory. I gave him a slight head shake in response before walking to Clara. The woman was hurling off to the side of the encampment.

As if sensing my approach, she held up a finger in a halting motion. She dry heaved a few more times until she was able to gather herself. She raised her hands to her face for a moment, then turned to face me. She was much more put together than I could have ever expected after emptying her lunch.

"Ten minutes and we are rolling. Devon is already scouting ahead. He's found a trail and will keep us posted," she said, her voice only a touch hoarse.

"I'm sorry abo—"

"Don't. We are alive and that's what matters. Focus on recovering what you can before we move. I never thought knowing exactly how much magic I had left would be this helpful, but making that cloud as large as I did would have been impossible before. Hesitation to push the limits and all that life threatening stuff," she said casually.

"That's one I know... Still, I don't know what came over—"

"This thing on?" Devon's voice sounded through the comm-plant. From the jerked surprise in everyone's demeanor, he'd called us all at the same time. "I found the ant with the ridiculous name. Got a few missing legs and several cracks on the old noggin, but it's holding together. Dispatched two larger spiders that were wrangling it in. Could use some heals. Will continue to scout as soon as I have backup. West one hundred meters, then northwest about two hundred." His voice drifted back through the comm-plant after a moment of silence. "Don't worry, bud, help is on the way."

No one commented on the softness of the tone, or the fact that he'd forgotten to cut the connection, but everyone was in gear as soon as we had a target.

"Sam, can you go ahead with Rommel?" I asked after looking at Clara. The demoness nodded, and the two men disappeared to follow Devon's directions.

Just then, I noticed the member of our party I kept losing track of during fights. Blobby rolled after the two men and I could see several crushed spiders within its body. Clearly, the slime had been doing work on the arachnids, but where he had been and how he found enemies we missed I had no clue. But I certainly wasn't going to complain about having a gelatinous silent guardian.

"Does that thing make any noise?" Dennis asked. The satyr had snuck up behind me, very much like Blobby tended to do.

"Only when it's hungry… Or eating." I vaguely recalled the wet squelches and flops of its bulk.

"The trees can't sense it. They only sense a gap. A void that shouldn't be there…" The man drifted off as if he didn't know how to address the fact of what those with the implants knew. That Blobby was a Dreg Tendril.

"Ask me again later and I'll give you my theories," I said, watching my mana tick past the eighty percent mark. "Clara, I'm ready to go."

The demoness gave me a cutting look, but nodded. "Pack it up. We are going hot on the trail."

Lilly, Dennis, and Godfrey snapped to and flanked her. She

motioned and I set the pace as we pushed through the dense undergrowth.

There was tense silence as we left the small clearing Rommel had created. I hadn't realized how much difference the unimpeded sunlight had made in our fight. The gloom, even in the day, had my nerves frayed. Not that I had many nerves left to fray.

The walk was brief with our pace, and soon we came upon a much-scorched battle ground. Smoldering bark on trees, sizzling webs, and blackened patches of ferns and grass. Amidst that mess were Samuel and Anthony. My friend's stoic orcish escort watched the surroundings like a hawk. I almost jumped back when a burning red spell chain formed around his hand. Thankfully, he was well-practiced and instead turned to watch the area not covered by our arrival.

Anthony looked to be mostly healed, but the fire ant was panting where it lay. I didn't even know ants panted.

"Just need a minute. Devon went off further northwest. Something about signs of a struggle," Sam said, placing his hands and releasing his <Health Bump> on Anthony's thorax.

"Is he going to be alright to come with us?" I asked. As if in response, or possibly defiance of being weakened, the ant in question stood on shaky legs.

Sam looked concerned, but he waved it off and instead helped hold the insect up until its limbs were steadier.

"We should follow slowly. If Devon finds something else, he will let us know," Clara said.

She took a moment to reorient our formation with Rommel at the lead and me a step behind. Godfrey and Anthony took the back position. Clara proved ever more capable with each encounter we had. It really drove home why she was the one allowed to lead expeditions far into the wilds.

Less than a minute after starting our trek, Devon contacted us again. Instead of the clear connection of before, however, loud choppy words marked his message. "...Spiders...clearing... dragging...wrapping...come..."

"That's not a good sign," Sam said. "We've never had our comms scrambled quite like that."

"I have a guess as to why, and it has to do with shiny, talking rocks," I said.

"The Crystals? Why would they be trying to help spiders?" Clara asked.

"A few possibilities. Best case, they can't help it and it's a result of their area of influence. Worst case? They are corrupted with Dreg somehow," I said. It was not the kind of comforting answer the New Hopers were wanting to hear, but I was never one to soften the truth.

"Let's get to Devon before this situation scales up a whole other degree of mess," she said quietly, taking the lead herself.

The tension was at an all-time high as we heard air-whispers from Devon. "Stay there, let me get to you."

Like a magically propelled gymnast, the elf flipped over a tree and landed on the ground beside us. The only thing I heard from his approach was a gentle rustling of leaves.

"We are at the edge of what I think is the main, or one of their main, clutches. Daniela was being wrapped when I arrived. She is inside the black, smoldering cocoon," Devon said, pushing our group back and keeping his back to us as he pivoted like a radar disk.

"What are they doing to her?" Lilly asked, clutching her hooks tightly.

"You know spiders, they drink, not eat? Same difference," Dennis provided unhelpfully.

"Why is she in a black cocoon?" Sam asked, pointing to the various shades of grey, white, and silver the webs around us had.

"They tried to hold her but everything was burning away. A huge crab spider came out of nowhere. The implant says it's a Quotient 3 Crab Spider with a fire Attunement. It's the only spider there. Sorta."

"What do you mean sorta?" I asked. I could barely contain the frustration in my voice. Sure enough, a Quotient 3 creature was no joke, but if it was the only one there, then Devon wouldn't have had much difficulty rescuing my friend. That was when the sorta finally clicked into place and I refocused on my companions. Apparently, he'd been waiting for the words to actually reach my brain, because that's when Devon spoke.

"The queen or the king or whatever that nightmare thing is there. And like I said, it's a clutch. Some of the cocoons there might be food but some might be…" The man paused long enough to shudder. "Baby spiders."

That one caused me to shudder as I pictured the swarm I'd managed to cut through, but smaller and more numerous. My skin already crawled.

"Come on. Stay quiet and don't go past me. I've checked all the webs around here. The only ones they are keyed into are the ones right at the border of their lair." The air-attuned crept forward and we moved single file behind him.

Sure enough, he pointed out a series of webs that looked sharper and less downtrodden than all the rest. At the very least, it looked like it would do more than just slow us down. Devon circumvented that strand and pointed out a gap in the trees. Sure enough, there was a flame-scorched trail leading into the clearing. A few spider corpses still smoldered on the ground in the wake of my friend's capture.

What laid before us sent chills down my spine. Dozens upon dozens of cocoons hung up in the trees. I was fairly sure I identified two with the large legs of Fire Ants and another two with parts of an Earth Deer sticking unceremoniously out the sides. My eyes quickly landed on the black cocoon Devon had mentioned. It wasn't actively on fire, but it looked like one of the fire infusions. Perpetual smoldering coal.

The deliberate movement of giant spider legs drew my attention to the figure that was poised above my friend.

<Spiney-Backed Orbweaver>
<Attunement: Fire>
<Refinement: N/A>
<Perceived Metier Quotient: 4>

The thing was a nightmare to behold. At least, that was what I thought when the bull-sized creature shifted in the trees to expose its spiked maroon thorax, hairy limbs, and shifting fangs. Unfortunately, something worse than the Fire Orbweaver was highlighted thanks to my perception. *Thanks for the future lack of sleep, perception.*

<Gray Wall Jumper Monarch (???)>

<Attunement: Air / Pure>

<Refinement: Cluster Bonded???>

<Perceived Metier Quotient: ???>

A mound that I'd thought was cocoon mass and webbing actually turned out to be a spider the size of a small box truck. The thing didn't look like it was moving, but considering the implant picked up on the creature's existence, that meant it was still alive. A concerning fact to have potentially found the boss or maybe the core of the dungeon we were trying to farm. When I saw almost as many question marks in the description as the name, the completeness of how out of our depth we were sobered me. Enough that my brain actually started to consider not just going in guns blazing.

"I see you saw the big mother out there. Now, I can attest to your tankiness, but that thing might shred you if it gets you." Devon spoke directly in my ear.

"How are we going to get to her…?" I whispered.

The elf motioned with his head and our group moved away from the insane creatures in the clearing. "Definitely not going in there swinging. I think we may be able to get away with some kind of extraction," he said.

"Are you thinking the 'slip and pull,' or the 'bash and dash'?" Dennis asked. "Please say 'bash and dash.'"

"I was thinking the slip and pull. With our numbers, it should be very plausible to cover our exit better," Devon said.

"How are you going to break her out? That doesn't look like standard spider silk," Lilly added.

"I could take one of you with me," the elf said.

As if it was practiced, all of the New Hopers crossed their

arms and touched their noses. I didn't recognize the gesture, but it was obviously a version of 'not it.' Even Rommel had done it, as silly as it looked on the tall orc.

Sam and I looked at each other for a second. "I don't care who goes in as long as it is the best person to get her out," Sam said.

"You got any cutting abilities, beanstalk?" Devon asked.

"I'll point out that it may not be good for your health to alienate a healer." Devon gulped at Sam's veiled threat. "To answer your question, no, I don't. Rommel and Ron are the only ones with cutting abilities I've seen. Lilly?"

"Mine would melt before it got much of a chance," she said, shrugging helplessly.

My friend gave the orc a look. "Fire poor against fire," was all he said.

"That leaves Ron. Unless Clara and Godfrey have something up their sleeves?" Both held up their weapons and shook their heads. "Then Ron it is."

Devon tilted his head back in a silent groan until Clara smacked him across the chest. "Get it together. You two need to put your childish rivalry aside. There is a life hanging in the balance."

The elf rubbed at his chest before nodding. The next minute was filled with a flurry of activity. Dennis blew quietly into his flute while Lilly created caltrops out of ice to block off whatever decided to follow us.

Very awkwardly, I clambered onto the elf's back. He grumbled the entire time, but didn't actually buck me. When the rest of the group gave the thumbs up, Sam ran forward and slapped both me and Devon with his <Adrenal Surge> and the world snapped into sharper focus.

With a twitch of his hands, Devon had us rocketing straight through the tree line.

CHAPTER ELEVEN

Slip and Pull

I was not prepared for the speed of Devon's movement skill, or was it an attack skill? Regardless, the world moved much faster than I had ever personally experienced. My perception was able to keep up with the instant acceleration, but only just. However, when we stopped, we were less than ten feet from the cocoon... and the fire spider.

It took the arachnid a second to process the sudden arrival of 'meals.' The delayed reaction gave me enough time to pass mana into my pickaxe. The tool had returned to its more mundane form the moment I'd been knocked out of the first fight. Now, instead of a wasteful scythe, I created the longest single-bladed serrated sword that I could.

Trying to cut my friend out without hurting her would take much too long. With that in mind, I swung at the strands holding the black cocoon to the tree. My first crystal-bladed swing didn't cut all the way through, but the cocoon sagged and a muffled scream could be heard from within. A black limb reached towards me.

"Get her quick!" The hairs all over my body rose up as Devon let loose a <Lightning Strike> aimed at the spider.

The creature twitched back and curled on itself, but remained on the tree. With a fresh dump of adrenaline at seeing how close the nightmare fiend had been to snagging me, I hacked at the webs for all I was worth. The Daniela burrito dropped to the ground unceremoniously. A second <Lightning Strike> singed the air with the smell of ozone and a screech tore out of the Fire Spider.

As soon as I'd lifted up Daniela in a princess carry, Devon wrapped an arm around my chest. The jerk of his skill drove the limb into my gut but I managed to keep hold of Danny.

Two discs of fire cut a trail past us toward the spider. A low buzz reverberated around us and I saw several of the cocoons around us shifting like overstretched water balloons. The source of the buzz then turned to face us and I could have sworn that the world slowed to a crawl.

The creature looked mostly like I expected one of the creepy crawlies to look. Except that what I thought was bushes and grass covering the creature actually turned out to be tiny hairs. Said hairs were crackling like a tesla coil from Ben's super fun science class, except these had an intent. A crackling fang of lightning struck the tree closest to us. Another was getting ready to strike, so I focused my mind long enough to cast one large <Stone Spike> between us and the creature.

Just as I'd hoped, and like had happened with Devon, the stone acted like a lightning rod. The spike itself disintegrated instantly, but we were still alive. The giant spider hissed in frustration, lifting up its massive front legs as if it was ready to jump. The gesture revealed the huge chunk of Metier Crystal that covered the underside of its body like a strange carapace. At least, that was the only thing I thought it could be in the short time it gave me to look. The Fire Ant brought up our rear, interposing itself between us and the monarch as we raced away.

The two creatures had drawn so much of my attention that I barely even noticed the carpet of spiders heading our way. Two small clouds of poisonous fog lingered at the edge of the fires. Most of the spiders that crossed did not make it out the other side.

Then we were in the woods.

Devon panted as he collapsed with us into a dog pile. Clara was quick to pull us off each other, even if she was starting to look a little green around the gills. This was especially concerning since only Lilly and Danny had gills.

"I got' em," Rommel said as he hoisted Daniela and Devon onto his shoulders. The man was *off* before I could even process it.

"Get up, Ronan. We need to at least make it to the igloo for now," Clara managed as she pulled my hand in the right direction.

Godfrey waited until everyone passed him before he launched two sprays of dirt with his shommer out into the clouds of black death. The wind his skill kicked up pushed the spiders back into the fog. He turned tail, covering our back.

An explosion shook the trees as the shockwave reached us. Clara pulled me harder, digging her claws into my forearm. "My <Necrotic Cloud> is flammable. Just keep mov—" the woman paused mid-sentence to hurl as she ran. "Just keep moving." The fact she barely slowed down at all while puking convinced me to just go along with whatever she said.

I sure hope the Tendrils don't have someone like her on their side.

A few minutes later, we were back at the igloo. The mound of spider bodies was still there, but we just jumped over them. I watched Lilly run her hand gently along the outside bodies, letting frost build up around the corpses. Her breath flowed over the blood and viscera to make the nastiest popsicle known to humankind.

"Ronan, can you make some stone caltrops?" Lilly asked as soon as she was done.

"I've never tried, my skill is made for spikes," I said, trying to come up with a way to follow her request.

"You can make them smaller, yes? Well, just make a bunch

of little forward-facing spikes and I'll do the rest," the merwoman said. She was shivering as she spoke.

I cast a glance toward Sam as he tried to cut his way into Danny's cocoon with little to no success. Anthony was trying to bite through the material, but he was having about as much luck.

Focus, Ronan. Spiders are coming! My thoughts were a bit scattered, but I managed to dump half my mana to create foot-tall spikes in a cone in front of us.

"That's good, sit and recover. We are going to need you," she said.

The merwoman started to dance amidst my spikes. Her body flowed with each movement, and her webbed features threw an exotic flair to her arabesque motions. Her leg flicked left and right as she breathed frosty mist right onto the compressed earth. Before my very eyes, wicked pricks of ice formed all along the spikes. The space where she moved tripled in deadliness.

When she returned to the igloo, however, she was shivering to the bone and nearly collapsed. I hauled her closer to Daniela and Anthony, hoping the passive heat of the two would help.

"Incoming!" Devon wheezed. The man was still gulping air, but he stood beside me.

The newborn spiders were the first to make it out into the light. With single-minded purpose, they charged toward us. I made note of the fact that, while they didn't appear to have lightning type techniques, the friction of their swarming over each other was arcing sparks amidst them.

Clara let loose another of her <Necrotic Clouds> to cover the spikes near the ground. That, combined with the rocky and icy death me and Lilly set up, turned the press of bodies into a meat grinder. The press of bodies impaled spider after spider or merely crushed it under its mass. Right as the mass was about to clear the distance, the grass all around us grew almost two feet.

Like a huge net, the grass halted the creatures and caused

them to continue pressing against each other. The skill looked similar to Sam's, but I'd never seen him control that many vines before. A look over my shoulder showed me that Dennis was blowing into his staff-flute. A wiggling spell chain pulsed from him into the ground around us. With a jerk of his fingers on the flute, the net of grass pressed tighter around the <Necrotic Cloud>.

"Take cover! Rommel, light it!" Clara shouted.

The orc in question threw one of his flame disks into the body of spiders. The fire cut easily through the grass net, setting a few of the bound spiders on fire. However, the explosion that followed let a bunch more through. The ones that landed around us were air fried over easy.

On impulse, I fed mana into my pickaxe to create a thin crystal umbrella. Bits of ash and gore rained down around us, but I managed to cover Clara and myself at the front from the worst of it. The others were in the cover of the igloo, fortunately, as it looked like Dennis had fainted for some reason.

I watched the smoke of the fireball dissipate slowly through the semi-translucent crystal. Thankfully, I kept the umbrella up for a beat longer because a glob of black webbing flew right for us.

The impact almost broke my grip on the pick.

Then the webbing went taut and I was pulled off my feet. *Oops.*

The Fire Spider loomed before me through the dissipating smoke. It had oriented itself so that I would be landing directly on its spiked body.

"Oh yeah?" I grit my teeth and focused on thickening the crystal umbrella while keeping an eye on the ground right below the creature's body. Just to double down on my chances of survival, I cast a hasty <Earth Shell> around my upper body. My perception was working overtime. Covering myself in rock in midair to reduce my chances of death was a true stroke of genius. It was really the most intelligent thing I'd ever done.

But this is still gonna hurt, was the only thought I could muster as I crashed into the huge spider. A breath before contact, I cast the largest <Stone Spike> that I could right under the bulk of the creature. Left with less than a quarter of my mana, I landed.

Like the hammer of a god, the impact of my body, crystal, and stone armor drove the spike deep into the spider's under-belly. The creature screeched louder than ever as its flailing pushed the spike deeper. The reinforced rock formed by my skill held for a few seconds, long enough for me to land after I bounced off the creature.

My earth armor struggled to keep together as I landed flat on my butt. My leg was twisted in a *very* wrong direction and the jagged edges of my crystal umbrella had dug into my shin. A bright flash from my implant warned me that I was bleeding.

The ache of my mana expenditure, the broken bones, and the blood were too much for me to think of a snarky retort. Wracked with pain, all I managed was a strangled scream. At least I had the presence of mind to press my hand to the bleeding wounds.

I failed miserably to move out of the way when the spider got over its pain and spotted the source. Its whole body ignited like a furnace as it galloped towards me. Okay, maybe it was more of a hobble, but I was fairly sure all the spider had to do to kill me would be to sit on me.

Like a magnificent raging bull, Rommel bonked the spider off-course. The orc's body was alight with internal fire and I could tell that he was using the new skill he'd acquired. The spider whizzed by me and straight into a tree. It was not happy about the interruption.

Black blobs of webbing formed around the tips of its wide body before shooting towards Rommel. The orc managed to roll out of the way of most, but one snagged him in the leg and another in the chest. The spider's fangs flicked in anticipation as Rommel dug his fingers and heels into the ground to resist the pull.

Using the meager mana I had left, I created a stone spike ahead of where he was being dragged. The orc latched on to it and I watched as his enhanced muscles strained and bulged to keep the creature from devouring him. Unfortunately, the weak link in that equation was my spike. Rommel's body broke through the compressed ground and flew a short distance to the spider.

The delay had been enough for Clara and Godfrey to join the mix. While not nearly as strong as Rommel, the dwarf smacked the single-minded spider so hard in the face that one of its fangs cracked and fell.

Clara pressed her arm directly onto the creature's body and a spell chain formed around it. "<Decaying Clock>!" she shouted. The woman staggered back, but the spell chain remained.

Godfrey sent one last skill, his sand toss, into the Fire Spider's face. The impact wasn't super effective, but combined with whatever Clara had done, the spider was twitching and writhing on the ground.

When a wave of relief flowed through me, I spun to see Samuel was already tending to my wounds. A maroon blur passed me by and Blobby bobbed up and down like a spring. I nearly gave myself whiplash when I turned back to see Daniela stabbing the Fire Spider nonstop. She'd started screaming at some point, then sobbing as her strength faded and the creature died.

Clara and Godfrey helped her walk away from the spider. Before they could get too far, she screamed and stabbed the creature one more time, slowly immolating it into ash and Pith. The New Hopers stared at the shimmering cloud as it swelled then split to strike us all in the chest.

As impressively sized as the cloud was, the strings of Pith that flew to each of us were much reduced.

Metier Quotient: 4 (8%)
Dreg Accumulation: 8%

A quick glance at my status told me that the spider's internal goodies split across so many of us definitely reduced the gains. At least in terms of levels. The thick plate that Rommel pried from the mountain of ash and the cold burning coal of the Q4 infusion were prizes in and of themselves.

When I looked around at the sheer mess of bodies around us, I sighed. It was going to take forever to collect Pith and materials from all of the creatures we had killed.

"It safe, yah think?" Dennis slurred from the ground.

"I think so. If it hasn't gotten here yet, then I don't think it followed us all the way," Clara answered. "Devon, please scout as soon as you catch your breath."

"Wild," the man wheezed.

I turned from the slumped elf back to the demoness. She was holding Daniela close to her chest as the brunette let out quiet sobs. Her daggers were dripping spider ichor where she'd dropped them point down on the ground. Clara gently rubbed her back as the woman let out more of her emotions than I'd seen in a long time.

"Don't. Not now, Ron," Sam said, putting pressure on my leg that caused me to jerk in pain. He was examining my break. The cuts and bruises from my landing had already been closed up. The fight had somehow managed to distract me enough to forget the pain.

"She needs our help," I argued. It was the weakest argument I'd ever made.

"Of course she does, but not now. She's opened up to someone else. Now focus on getting your leg back together."

"What do you me—Gah!" The world turned pitch black and I found myself staring at the sky while spots danced in my vision. Cold stabs of pain and warm surges of relief battled for control of my nervous system. When the warmth was finally able to overcome the stabby-stabby, I felt at the cleaned tracks on my face and wiped my eyes to see through the blurry tears.

The blond was smiling down at me, then gave my leg a comforting pat. I winced involuntarily and glared at him when the pain was absent.

"Just testing reflexes, you know?"

"Oh, if you weren't the healer, Sam," I said, mock strangling the lanky man with my hands. The bastard had the gall to laugh in my face.

Of course, that eventually got me laughing too. Soon enough, the whole group was laughing their slap-happy butts off. Adrenaline highs could do that to you. There was still strain on all their faces, fear and pain and weariness; if they didn't laugh, they might cry. Opting for the better of the two seemed the preferred choice.

Even Daniela let out a few soft chuckles after seeing our ragtag group laughing it up. Blobby and Anthony looked thoroughly confused, even if the slime jiggled up and down to imitate all of our laughing. The comical scene of the two pets set most of us giggling once again, until we heard a rustle in the trees. The New Hopers tried to jump to their feet, but they were just too tired. Instead, Anthony, Blobby, and Sam jumped to action.

The life mage immediately raised one vine that he held at the ready while Anthony covered his flank. Blobby mitosed and rolled away in his smaller forms to complete a semicircle of defense around all of the downed members of the group. Spell chains formed around the hands of those with ranged attacks and we waited with bated breath as the rustling intensified.

A simple rabbit, not even attuned, pranced right into our midst. The poor creature saw the magical death arrayed before it and turned tail immediately. We all remained tense, but when Devon announced that it was gone, there were sighs of relief abound.

"Maybe we need to reel it in for the day," Sam said, dropping his control of the vine.

"I second *and* third that," Dennis said. The satyr was sprawled out on the ground. He'd been the only one unable to even react when the bunny approached. When I gave it some thought, it was probably a good sign we were safely outside the spider's territory if other animals were around. It just wasn't worth pushing that with how exhausted we were.

"Clara, mind if I direct the retreat?" I asked the demoness. She still had an arm around my friend, but she smiled weakly at me.

"Alright, everyone. What are we taking? We need materials and infusions. We brought one set of duffels for each. Expect that whatever we leave won't be there the next time. Devon, can you circle around and get as many of the far out bodies while we focus on the ones here in the igloo?"

The elf waved a hand weakly and slinked into the woods. The rest of us slowly made our way through the throng of bodies scattered about from our latest and earliest fight. Unfortunately, many of the earlier bodies had been Pith-locked by the New Hopers on instinct. The ones that had been charbroiled into ash also didn't seem to have any Pith or loot to give, which was an important bit of information that I filed away. However, the steady trickle of Pith into all of the people spread across the clearing was a good sign of the gains we had available. Unfortunately, if my quick looks at all the infusions were to be correct, the final tally of Pith itself was going to be miniscule.

Tiny plates of spider chitin of various colors, fangs, and twig-like legs started piling up beside the small mountain of air, water, fire and earth infusions. It was the single largest amount of materials I'd ever seen collected by the time we were done. Everyone moved the materials we could into the two duffels, but it quickly turned into an effort to secure the igloo against the other spiders that might find it. Godfrey and I were able to dig a few pits using our orthodox-tools-turned-weapons. We opted against trying to expand and seal the entire half-melted fortification. Instead, we covered the holes with broken sections of my <Stone Spikes>.

While we worked, Blobby rolled through the bodies that we hadn't been able to dissociate and started dissolving them within its bulk. It was almost up to my waist in size when both its Metier Crystals were combined. The gelatinous mass shifted away from the group and settled down. Its strange camouflage ability manifested as its coloration matched the soil and vegetation around it.

"You know, it was the one to bring my daggers," Danny said quietly. I started as the woman practically materialized beside me. "Sorry. Didn't mean to scare you."

"It's alright. The present setting has me a tad jumpy. Though, apparently not Blobby." I turned to look at her. "It freed you?"

"No, that was Sam, but nothing anyone had could cut the spider silk. Your daggers did the trick, and jiggle-body there apparently had them stored inside." She sighed heavily. "I'm sorry, Ron. I messed up. I—"

"Don't. It's not your fault. Take whatever time you need to process what happened. I think even with just this haul, we'll be quite busy outfitting people," I said, motioning to the stuffed-to-the-brim New Hopers. While their clothes didn't have nearly as many pockets as our tactical-oriented gear, the single or double pockets they did have were stuffed.

"Hey, we'll be back for those," I called out.

"Can't just lea—" Dennis started to call out before Devon's air-whispers reached us.

"Water and earth spiders are patrolling. We should leave before they find us. More details later," the elf said. A gust of wind later and he was in our midst.

Note to self, figure out how to deal with insane mobility and enhancing skills. It wasn't the first time something had just fallen right into our laps with barely any warning.

"You heard the man, pack it up!" Clara said. The woman was leaning heavily against a tree as Rommel and Godfrey hoisted the bulging duffle bags. The rest of us, slime and fire ant included, weren't far behind as we hustled out of spider territory.

CHAPTER TWELVE

Turbulent Retreat

Our group didn't take long to exit the spider territory. Daniela led the group out while the tanks covered the rear and Devon ranged out behind us in case the spiders decided to give chase. When we arrived at US 301, everyone let out a sigh of relief. The most surprising thing to me was that it couldn't be later than one in the afternoon. While we'd left really early in the morning, the day had already felt like a month and a half.

"That did not go at all like intended," Devon provided after the elf joined the main group.

"Did you expect it to go well?" Dennis asked while leaning on his staff heavily.

"At least I didn't expect one of us to get kidnapped," he said with a bit of agitation.

"I didn't know you cared about me like that, Devon. I only just met you yesterday!" Daniela put a hand to her face and pretended to faint. Everyone in the group grinned while the lanky, pointed-eared man blushed furiously. It was good to see her somewhat back to her normal self, even though I could tell it was somewhat forced. Her mischievous smile lacked the dimple marks of her full mirth. Regardless, it was a step in the right direction.

"Don't worry, D. We'll make sure that your little sweetheart doesn't get jealous," Lilly added, placing a webbed hand comfortingly on his shoulder. Of course, the mermaid was smirking right along with the rest of us.

The elf stormed off a ways down the road in the direction of Wildwood, grumbling and mumbling to himself all the while. We'd just started to move after him when he stopped again. "Wait, ther—" His voice was cut off by a blast of fire from the opposing tree line. The elf rolled on the ground for several feet before stilling on the ground. The blast had barely missed him, but the explosion left scorch marks along the majority of his body. Most of his shirt was missing.

"Samuel, heals!" I shouted as I focused on the space around Devon. With a surge of mana, the spell chain for <Earthen Barrier> appeared as close to the man as I felt comfortable with. The ground swelled, hiding the Wildwoodian from whatever had attacked him.

"I need eyes and covering fire!" I directed, focusing on the distance between our group and Devon. Three <Stone Spikes> big enough to cover a person sprouted from the ground. I bypassed those and held my shield in front of me as I beelined for the elf.

Another three fireballs manifested out of the tree line before splashing onto the ground. I just barely had enough time to intercept one so that it did not hit Sam. Rommel roared in pain as one hit him on the arm, and the last missed entirely. A look at my mana showed that it was already down to under half. A fast fireball streaked towards my barrier and I was able to deflect it just in time. Samuel was already working on Devon, focusing his efforts on his head instead of his burns, which sent my level of concern climbing rapidly.

Concentrating on the comm-plant during combat was a risk. With what little warning this attack had given us, I was sorely out of ranged options.

"Clara, Daniela! What do we see?" I shouted, channeling mana into my pick to form my defensive umbrella. Before it was even fully formed, I batted another fireball out of the air. Hidden right behind that one was a shard of ice the size of my finger. The bladed frost impacted my Limestone Skin hard enough to punch all the way through my shoulder. The limb went numb, and my pick fell uselessly to the ground. The pain wasn't even that much, numbed by the cold, but I screamed in frustration as I repositioned my shield.

Rommel roared as he let loose one of his fire disks and Lilly added a thin ice wall above my barrier. Chips of ice flew up almost immediately as the ice needles aimed for her and Rommel were stopped in their tracks. The fire disk and ball collided in the air, sending a splash of brow-disintegrating heat over our bodies.

"There are at least four attackers!" Clara shouted as she hid from a fireball behind one of my spikes.

"Make that five!" Dennis shouted from another spike. "I'm fighting for control of the trees!"

"Danny, disrupt with your wisp!" I shouted, trying to spot anyone through the smoke, dust, and steam that covered the space between us and the treeline. The sheer openness of the road had put us entirely on the backfoot. Almost before I was done speaking, a floating ball of flame took to the sky and rained down pellets of fire magic into the woods. In response, a wall of fire rose up to intercept it, taking me by surprise.

Not even the first group of humanoid Tendrils had been that coordinated.

"We've got something else coming from the east!" Danny shouted after lobbing a fireball into the treeline. Her Flame Refined skill pushed through the wall and lit the closest oak on fire. The fire wall winked out instantly, and a burning body highlighted numerous figures hidden in the undergrowth. A quick count of outlines gave me over a dozen. My blood ran cold as I tried to do the combat math. It turned to ice when I saw the thick mist surging from the east to encroach on the trees.

"Deep breaths, Ronan," I told myself as I weighed my mana against the state of our group. Dennis' goat leg hackles were raised as he blew furiously into his flute-staff. Godfrey had managed to make it to the front at some point, and he was using his shommer to build us a trench. The ease with which the ground and asphalt parted around his tool hinted at a skill being used. Rommel and Lilly were still working on blocking the physical and non-physical projectiles that the attackers were sprinkling us with. Sam held Devon's head between his fingers, his passive skill active as he bit his lip. "Crap."

"I've got eyes on someone in the mist!" Daniela shouted with her voice *and* via the comm-plant.

A moment later, a horizontal hail manifested. The shards of ice were wider, but flatter, than the one I'd been hit by. They didn't look any less deadly.

Thankfully, the hail storm flew into the midst of the figures. Pandemonium ensued. I wasn't sure what caused the problem, but the group in the shadows split and ran. The rest huddled together and another spray of skills flew our way.

"I think part of them ran away! The mist didn't attack us!" I called back to the group.

"It's Dai!" Clara shouted, the relief palpable in her voice. "Dennis, push! Lilly, double cast!"

"Wild!" The satyr and merwoman complied immediately. Actual audible notes left Dennis' flute and Lilly exhaled deeply. Her gills fluttered as air bypassed her lungs entirely and flowed out of her mouth like an icy cloud.

The heat of the day and the cold of her skill clashed, throwing wind everywhere. The makeshift cold front she created before collapsing in Rommel's arms roiled and blended with the mist coming from the east.

The mist rolled like an actual charging wall and the enemies faded from view. My perception failed to spot anything except false shadows as the cloud rolled over our little entrenchment.

The cool touch of the mist only sent my senses into hyperdrive. Goosebumps ran along my body as I shuffled closer to Sam and Devon.

"Anyone care to explain?" I asked in a half-whisper. It was more a raspy, low tone, but my voice was the least of my concerns at that point.

"Dai is the strongest individual in Wildwood," Rommel explained. The orc threw up a disk of fire to block a pair of wild fireballs.

"Cool. Great. Suppose that's a relief," I said, glancing back in the direction part of the attackers had vanished. Something still didn't sit well with me, but I wasn't going to complain about another ally in the fight.

"I think this is done," Sam said with a sigh. The blond's hair was stuck to his head from his sweat and the condensation that had manifested around us. Without pausing for a break, he slapped the hole in my shoulder and feeling returned to my arm. I hadn't even been paying attention to how much new blood had covered my shirt.

"Can they deal with all of this?" I asked, risking a peek over the ice wall Lilly had created.

"He's strong, but he is not 'deal with a dozen enemies solo' strong," Clara said as she finally joined us at the trench. She'd managed to drag a now-loopy Dennis all the way to the group.

"Then it's time to charge," I said. "I'm going to provide the cover, you guys follow behind me. Sam, stay with Devon and Dennis. If you can, help with your <Vine Whip>. If not, sit your butt down." My friend wanted to argue, but when I met his over-dilated eyes, he nodded in resignation.

"Clara, does your <Fear> work from here?" I asked.

"I'll need a clear line of sight," she explained.

"You got one more of those disks in you, Rommel?" The tall orc stepped around me and called forth his spell chain. The disk winked into existence before sawing a clear path through the mist. Just the heat alone pushed it out of the way before splashing into the oak that had been burning earlier, reigniting it despite the condensation and mist.

Without waiting for anything else, I crouch-ran towards the treeline. About halfway, I pushed my mana and formed a <Stone Spike> the others could use as cover. When I pushed past the oak, I stepped into pandemonium. Seven humanoids were fighting Daniela, Blobby, Anthony and a tall, blue lizardman toe to toe.

My cursory glance over the Tendrils told me that all but one were Q2. The last one instantly became my target.

<Dreg Tendril (Human)>

<Attunement: Life>

<Refinement: Regeneration>

<Perceived Metier Quotient: 3>

The corrupted human was slinging strings of light into its compatriots, helping them recover from their injuries. The old adage of 'kill the healers first' rang in my mind as a half-powered <Stone Spike> rose out of the ground below the humanoid. Bending in ways that guaranteed it wasn't human any longer, the creature dodged my attack by a hair's breadth. Its featureless face turned to face me and its mouth opened in a silent scream. I would have really rather it didn't, as rows upon rows of miniscule, razor sharp teeth gnashed at the air, giving my imagination ammo it didn't need for the next time I slept.

A lance of white light flew in my direction. I barely had enough time to interpose my shield before it struck. The impact nearly toppled me back and I felt my feet dig into the ground. There was so much energy in that one blow that the heat deflection of my shield singed the ends of my hair. I was thankful the thing hadn't just broken on impact.

The Tendril wobbled unsteadily on its feet, and that was when the rest of the group entered the fray. A barely visible zip of purple-tinged darkness flowed out of Clara to the healer. The eyes of the enemy in question widened, almost comically so, before it fell on its rear. A roar of defiance marked the charge of our orc companion. His weapon flashed as he cleaved a Tendril in half, the inner fire of his newest skill leaving trails in my vision. The lizardman took the opening to launch another spray of thin ice. None of the impacts looked lethal, but the enemies were thoroughly distracted by the rime coating their bodies.

Taking advantage of the distraction, I was finally able to dig myself out of the hole the beam had shoved me in. The other members of our group were launching compressed earth, fire-balls, and frost right at the Tendrils. Without much fanfare, and taking advantage of the continued <Fear> effect, I drove my pick into the life-attuned Tendril's sternum. Its horrifying maw snapped twice at me before slimy green ichor leaked out of its wound and it slumped, dead.

A cursory glance at my mana showed it was somewhere in the twenty percent range, so I grit my teeth and sent two half-powered <Stone Spikes> into the midst of the enemies. They'd already been doing their best to cancel out the fire attacks with their own, and one earth-attuned was using something similar to my <Earth Shell> to deflect and defend against Rommel's frantic strikes. When two Blobbys rose out of the ground on either side of the Tendril in question, a gravelly scream tore out of its throat, as the half slimes encased it completely in seconds.

With Rommel freed up on the front lines, the four remaining Tendrils baked under Anthony's flamethrowing attack and the concussive force of Daniela's <Flame Blast>.

Silence reigned as we all gathered our bearings. A look around told me that no enemies remained, even if everyone was worse for wear.

"Status!" Clara called.

A few 'clears' replied back. Daniela just slumped on the ground beside Anthony. The heat coming off of her and the condensation hanging in the air had manifested her own personal rain cloud. Daniela didn't complain, even tipping her head back to gargle the water before it evaporated off her skin.

Blobby jiggled as it worked on dissolving the Tendril, and I had to look away from that particular sight.

The lizardman, Dai, looked around at all of us before heading back east. He retrieved a five gallon jug, one that you might have seen at an office break room pre-Fall, and slung it over his shoulder. Frost cracked where the jug shifted and the man's skin rippled with goosebumps.

"Well met," he said in a voice like two pieces of paper sliding together. He regarded Clara with double-lidded eyes before giving me a nod. Dai walked back through the woods and his mist trailed him like a loyal dog.

"He is as strange as usual?" A snarky, but weary, elven voice lifted everyone's spirits as Sam helped Devon and Dennis to the battle-formed clearing. It looked more like Devon was keeping the life-attuned duo from stumbling over their steps, but they were all supporting each other like the world's worst tripod.

Wane smiles were all we could muster. The safety of Wildwood or the Bunker called to me, so I pushed myself to give out a last command.

"Let's gather the loot and head back. I could use a break," I said, matching words to action, I pressed my hand to the life Tendril impaled by my pick.

Everyone copied the motion to the closest bodies. For the first time, I watched Clara's death-attuned dissociation. The body took on a strange, pitted texture, turning from the red of the fire Tendril to a mottled gray. The pits grew as the entire thing decayed before my eyes and coalesced into a pool of rot. The drops from the humanoid floated above the pool for a moment, before it sunk into the ground and out of view.

The Pith from all the Tendrils drifted in the air, swirling, before spreading to us all. A wave of nausea and discomfort blurred my vision and I pulled up my status with a grimace. I'd forgotten the Dreg-heavy nature of Pith from the Tendrils. Normally, Pith had an energizing edge, like a little crunch of coffee beans, but the Tendrils had the opposite.

The others around me groaned and sagged as the Dreg settled in their own bodies. Based on the cranked-up sway to

Dennis's steps, I was sure he was close to being overbanked on a trait.

"Danny, can you snatch the loot? We need to get our goaty friend back to the town Entity," I said, using my pickaxe to support me.

The woman didn't say anything, but instead let out a low whine the entire time she worked to cram infusions and materials into her cargo pants. Rommel hobbled back to where we'd first been attacked and recovered the two duffle bags full of drops.

With our goods recovered, everyone headed east along the road with an extra skip in their step. Literally, in the case of Dennis. As I was gathering up the Q3 infusion, and what I was sure was a femur of the Tendril, I spotted a small splatter of blood. My perception immediately zeroed in on the drip pattern that came from the center of the fight to the area where the life-attuned had gone down.

My mind flashed back to the moment when the attackers had split and disappeared. Dai must have gotten one before they were able to completely retreat. Or did he?

What concerned me the most was the color of the blood. Unlike the prismatic mess of ichor that the Tendrils left behind, this was regular, crimson-colored blood. Human, if I had to call it. The implications were not ones I wanted to consider.

"Ronan! You coming?" Daniela called from the back of the group.

I cast a glance at the droplets, trying to place everyone in the battle field and who the blood might belong to if not those who retreated. The weariness in my body screamed to leave it alone. As much as I wanted answers, unless I was willing to tromp through the wilds without any idea what I was actually looking for, it would be futile.

"I'm coming," I said, keeping half an eye on the blood until it vanished from view. My brain spun in overdrive the whole walk back to the wall.

CHAPTER THIRTEEN

Power Greed

Surprisingly, a huge crowd of people was gathered at the gates. Children cheered and their parents smiled as we returned to the town of Wildwood.

"What the heck is that all about?" Daniela asked. She'd beat me to it.

"Sounds like you made an impression on the Big Guns. They must have been watching far for us to return," Clara answered.

"Are they *that* surprised we survived?" Sam asked.

Clara didn't answer, instead pointing to the lizardman standing on the far edge of the wall. As dramatically as possible, Dai turned on his heel and vanished into his lingering mist cloud. Said cloud vanished from the ramparts only a moment later.

"You all did it!" Sarah shouted, hoisting Clara and myself into a huge hug. The orc woman had little trouble lifting us both and adding several new bruises to my list of injuries.

"Oxygen..." I managed.

"Right. Sorry." While the tusks took up a large portion of

her mouth, the smile on her face was unimpeded. "Tell me everything!"

I looked around her to see the other members of the Big Guns trying to keep the crowd from rushing us. The New Hopers appeared used to the whole process, but being around that many people still sent a trill of anxiety through me.

"Maybe when we are in a bit more of a private setting. We need to get Dennis to our mutual friend. If I had to guess, he's about ready for a new trait. Not a good idea to wait on those."

Sarah turned serious for a moment, frowning in the satyr's direction before giving a nod. The ease with which the orc woman flipped into her 'all business' mode still threw me off. She called out to the crowd that we would have a small celebration during the nighttime meal.

There were many boos and foot stomps from the children in the crowd, but a look from the orc was enough to get them moving. I spotted a slight purple glow in Clara's eyes that told me the demoness was lending a hand with crowd control.

Sarah spoke quickly with Tim and the twins before escorting us to the town Entity. We left most of the loot with her as we communed with the giant Metier Crystal. For some reason, the Entity was very brief in its conversation before spitting us back out. Dennis remained, as I'd been correct in correlating the satyr's increased and unabating inebriation with an impending trait. Before ejecting me, the town Entity just left me with a brief message.

—Dreg fluctuations detected within outer area of influence.

—

—Assistance requested. Societal obligations to Cluster Relative cited.—

"Thanks for being as clear and considerate as possible, Tec," I said.

The others gave me quizzical looks until I explained. Lacking a better naming convention, I'd opted to call the giant Wildwood Crystal Tec and the one back home Bec. Town Entity Cluster and

Bunker Entity Cluster, respectively. Not having any suggestions of their own, they went along with it. *I'll probably hear about how terrible I am at naming things from Sam and Danny at some point.*

They hadn't seen what Tec said, and I opted to keep that to myself for the moment. Not that I had much chance to think, because Sarah shoved us off to a meeting with the councilmen as soon as we were outside the iridescent alien rock.

The slight gloom of the councilmen's office encased us as Clara and myself stood before Dylan, Kirby, and Irwin. The three men looked just as they had earlier in the morning, if a bit more disheveled. Irwin had the bag full of materials set out on top of his desk and Dylan was sifting through the infusion one.

"They are back," Kirby provided.

"Thanks, Kirby. That was something I couldn't have possibly deduced with my own eyeballs," Irwin said, clasping his hands behind his back.

"You chil—youths have made a big difference. There isn't much negative that I can say regarding your efforts. Just these two bags represent years of efforts of collected materials. I want you two to know that you will have the full support of the council," Dylan said. He had a placating smile on his face, but I could tell there was more behind his words. There was always more behind the words of people in power.

"Great. This is just one step of the process. Next I'll be working to get those with the Gift, or any inclination to craft gear, so we can turn all of that raw potential into the ace we need," I said.

The fire-headed councilman hesitated and turned to Irwin.

"As Dylan said, we are more than willing to provide support. However, the manpower required for what you are asking is not something we can spare. Our economic balance is tenuous as is," the life-attuned said.

"I can understand. We will continue to help with your food growth efforts, and I hope to enhance the training of your youths. Not to mention the Wild Guard," I said evenly.

"Those are under *my* supervision. I don't feel inclined to

give some person off the street access to the future of this town," Kirby replied.

"The Council of New Earth is in charge of the Guard and the expansion efforts. Per your work so far, Kirby is who you'd report to," Dylan provided.

I did my best to swallow my tongue. The Daniela inside of me nearly snapped at the scaled man. Based on the twitching smirk on his face, that was exactly what he was hoping. Clara was as stiff as a board beside me. Her expression was hard to read, but at the very least, she was not happy with the current treatment of our efforts. That was all the direction I needed.

"Very well. I'll have to take my portion of the loot then," I said, striding forward and grabbing the closest duffle bag.

"What do you think you are doing?" Kirby asked, placing his own clawed hand over the bag.

"*I* do not live here. My *friends* do not live here. We will not be *beholden* to the way you operate. If this is how the 'council' of three old men plans to treat people willing to support them, then we have no place here."

"This is not your property. The Wild Guard—" Kirby started.

"The *Wild Guard* has my respect. You three do not. There was a moment there, when you fought for your people, but that does not cover enough of your flaws."

If I thought Clara was stiff as a board before, now she was a steel rod. The councilmen stammered. In that opening, I snatched both bags of material drops and walked out. Clara was a step behind me.

"You can't leave!" she said in a hurried whisper.

"I can and I will. You all keep doing what you are doing, we won't be gone forever." I hadn't stopped walking, and I was vaguely aware of the councilmen arguing behind me. When I was fairly sure we were out of hearing range, I whispered back to Clara. "Tec told me there is Dreg near Wildwood. I'd hoped to root it out from within, but if we have to do it from without, then so be it."

The demoness remained silent the entire walk back to me and my friends' temporary residence. "What should we do?"

"Go retrieve the rest of the loot. If you have the chance, meet me near the Geode Palm in two days. Well, not near, but you know what I mean."

There was a slight look of confusion on her face until I explained the location on southbound US 301. Recognition sparked and she took a shaky breath but nodded.

"I'll meet you at the Shrapnel Killer."

There was definitely a story behind that one. "If we aren't able to meet in two days, I'll be there on the fourth. Should we not be there for that, assume the worst and try to fortify Wildwood as much as possible."

The demoness did not look happy about the development, but she didn't argue. The two of us walked into the house, killing the somewhat festive mood that had lingered in the air. The New Hopers and my friends were chatting and smiling, retelling the fights we'd survived from their own perspectives. When we called for their attention, all conversation died out.

"We'll be leaving today," I said.

Samuel was about to protest, but Daniela placed a hand on his arm. Sarah, the only person not from our two groups, was frowning hard enough that new folds were forming on her face by the second.

"What about your plan?" she asked. Thankfully she didn't sound accusatory.

"We'll have to slow it down, but I still plan to work on the next part of it. Clara has a time for when we can meet and we'll go from there."

"You know they aren't going to let you go just like that," Clara said, motioning in the general direction of the councilmen's office.

"Let them come. If they want to take any of us, it will be the worst decision they ever made," Daniela said. A hazy circle of fire formed around my friend's throat and arms. It wasn't like her usual spell chains. They were a particular blend of our skills and the spell chains that the Wildwoodians had created on their own. I pushed past the question *that* brought up and calmed her down.

"No one is taking anyone. We are leaving now. Middle of the day. I don't think they have the gall to try to do something while the entire town watches. Not after coming back victorious."

"Would they even allow that?" Sam asked. "They could be trying to surround us already. Or moving people to intercept us on the way west."

"You are all clear," Devon said from his spot in the far corner.

The elf met my gaze but didn't say anything else. I was tempted to thank him, but we didn't quite have that relationship level yet.

"Before I go, I will give you the <Infusion> skill. I can probably only do it once before I am mostly tapped out. Don't want to go out in the wilds half-cocked. Sarah already has it, but anyone want to try to work on infusion crafting?"

Surprisingly, Rommel raised his hand. I nodded at the orc and reached my hand up to his forehead. With an effort of will, I held <Infusion> in the front of my mind while pushing into his. Inadvertently, my <Memory Canal>skill also triggered and the world dropped away.

I stood on a tall tree branch, many, many feet above the ground. Somehow I knew that the branch below me had broken, leaving me stranded way up on the tree. My arms easily pulled me up, but the fall would surely break something. I cried until a small, night-skinned girl appeared at the foot of the tree. She gestured at another person out of view until a lanky child saddled up to her. They argued for a short while, drawing my attention from my fear of falling.

Eventually, the taller boy huffed and wiggled his hands in my direction. Eventually, as if summoned by the motion, a gust of wind blew me off the branch. I screamed in terror until the girl's midnight black fingers tapped my shoulder. I turned to see the tall boy trying his best to hide panting breaths while appearing snooty and the girl's fang-filled smile looking down at me. I'd landed.

The world returned to focus in a spray of color. I staggered a step, but even as unsteady as I knew Rommel had to be after gaining a skill, he gripped my arm like a steel trap. He offered me a small smile before walking over to stand behind Clara.

Still in somewhat of a daze, I dumped out half the infusions into a pile and then half the materials into another. Making use of my increased mobility, I consolidated the split loot back into the bags, putting the other into Clara's hands.

"That should get you started and keep the councilmen off my back a little bit. Quick tips, have water handy for fire infusions because they heat up fast, and air infusions tend to shake and explode. Earth compresses tight; not sure what can happen if it fails, but probably nothing good."

Clara's slight, passive, smile dropped and she paled as she looked down at the bag in her hands.

"Come on, Blobby!" I called out to the slime. Everyone had already forgotten about my gelatinous friend, but it rose from the corner of the room like the world's wettest camo bean bag. Anthony chirped and followed it out the door.

"You all stay safe. I have a feeling things are only going to get more dangerous from here," I said, leaving the Wild Guard inside the room and following my friends out the door.

The people of Wildwood were very confused at seeing us leave the town. I assumed some of that came from the fact that they expected us for a celebration later in the day. However, as much as that prospect excited me, it also filled me with dread. Being around so many people was novel... until it wasn't. The town was invigorating and exhausting at the same time, which didn't help me settle my feelings on the whole endeavor.

The other members of the Big Guns stopped us to ask what was going on. Sam gave them the brief version as I watched the treeline in the distance. There were a few people working the field outside, but many more were working the new field we'd set up inside the town. It would likely flood if there was a strong rain, but thanks to Sam and his directions for Tim, everything in over an acre was already ready to harvest.

With the explanation out of the way, and deep frowns on our new friends' faces, we trekked into the woods. Our first stop was the broken down house where we'd stashed our travel supplies. It would let us spread out some of the loot we'd gained from the dungeon raid, as well as make sure we had supplies after leaving the town abruptly.

The trip to the secondary field further west from town was longer now that we weren't seeking out the Wildwoodians. The corpses of the humanoid Tendrils, along with all their drops and Pith, had been taken by the crows during their attack. It was yet another thing to worry about, just because the sheer mass could make a difference for the humanoids. If they needed food just like us humans, then being able to focus on killing other creatures for Pith instead of their corpses would let them grow stronger.

I guess we'll just have to outpace them. It was a stressful thought, but realistic. There was clearly an extremely intelligent element to the movement of the Tendrils, even if the humanoids themselves didn't appear to be the brightest. A fireball to the chest would still kill anyone. At least, anyone at our level for now.

The entire time I was mulling over this, a gentle breeze blew through the trees as Daniela led us. The Limestone Skin on my left arm rippled with goosebumps. My body stood stock still and I turned to look into the depths of the trees. Branches rustled and my friends' steps crunched behind me. My perception being what it was let me know that there was *something* going on, but nothing definitive.

Part of my thoughts drifted to the possibility of receiving a trait for ears that could pivot in place. The rest was zeroing in on the source of the thermodynamic discomfort. It wasn't natural, but neither did it seem hostile. The latter I deduced because I hadn't noticed the differential right away, so the source was following us for a while or just that good. Maybe both.

"We know you are out there!" I shouted out around us. My friends turned to look at me with eyes the size of saucers.

"Ron, what are you doing? You'll bring the whole forest down on us," Danny said, looking around like crazy. We weren't far from the branch off that led to the Bunker, so I opted for showing that I'd noticed rather than lead them all the way to the Bunker.

A rolling mist floated down by our feet as the lizardman, Dai, practically materialized from the gloomy shadows of the trees. His presence was near invisible, and I wasn't sure if that was the only thing at play. Without the tension of battle, I finally got a chance to give the man a proper look-over. Out of the lizardmen I'd seen, he was the first to have a true tail. It adjusted the position of the large water-filled jug we'd seen on his back before. His face was also much more lizard-like than the others in Wildwood. A true reptilian jaw extended from his face. Other than the blue shade of his body, I would have said that a crocodile had become humanoid and was walking towards us.

"Well met, again. I am impressed you noticed me at all, Ronan," he said. Having obviously seen the man when he revealed himself, my friends had tensed instead of continuing to complain about my loudness. "Worry not, I mean you no harm. Should that have been the case, I would have struck already while I had the advantage. Fighting you five is not something I want to ever do."

"Thanks for the praise, now why were you following us?" Danny snapped.

"Why, that would be a twofold reason. The first being that the Council of New Earth hired me to watch you. The second is that I wished to speak with you all about becoming an agent of your efforts," he said matter-of-factly.

"Let's rewind that a bit. Why would Kirby want us

followed?" I asked, different scenarios already running through my head.

"By my estimate, I don't really need to answer that, do I?" Dai placed his hands on his hips, adjusting a series of straps for the water jug on his back.

"He doesn't trust us, or he wants to find the Bunker," I said, quietly.

"Indeed. While finding it is a matter of time for the other scouting squads of Wildwood now that you three have traveled to us, I figured a warning was in order. I do not intend to follow, unless you are accepting of my other reason."

"What exactly do you think it is we do?" Samuel asked while crossing his arms.

"That would be both a simple and complex answer. The simple being you wish to retake the surface world, or at least initiate the process. The complex one involves your interactions with the things we previously believed to be inert, radiation-producing rocks."

"Close enough. So, you've been watching us. Why?"

For the first time, the cocky lizardman hesitated. "I cannot keep my current existence, I need to understand. What they will tell you in Wildwood is that I am the strongest there. While this is true, it does not mean that I have the support of the Wild Guard. Councilman Kirby arranged for that particular negligence years ago.

"Regardless, the Tendrils pose not only a threat to myself but also to the town. As the only group of people that seem to know what is actually going on, reaching out to you was the most reasonable step. I'm not a fan of not knowing."

"What will you tell the councilman?" I asked, weighing the man and the strength he'd shown so far.

\<Dai (Human)\>

\<Attunement: Water\>

\<Refinement: Mist\>

\<Perceived Metier Quotient: 4\>

"Simply that I lost track of you. He will be moderately

suspicious, but he's seen how capable you are. Well, he's seen the bare minimum, but that is more than enough to convince him."

"We cannot guarantee anything," I said, crossing my arms and keeping my tone steady. I had a feeling we would be alright to trust Dai, similar to what I felt with Sarah. Nonetheless, there was the whole 'friends closer' saying. And someone as sneaky as Dai needed to be kept under close supervision if possible, combat competence aside.

"I understand your mistrust, and I won't try to placate you. Trust, but verify." The lizardman nodded his head and proceeded to dump out the jug on his back. I had limited experience with water-attuned, well, anything. However, it wasn't a stretch to imagine the water made his abilities stronger or easier to use. Dumping it was trying to send a message of either trust or boldness. *I hope I'm not misreading him, because if it's the latter, this could be trouble.*

My friends and I shared a look before they contacted me with the comm-plant.

"It's up to you," Sam said. "He's helped us twice before, no reason to distrust him now."

"Don't recall the first of those, but I am in agreement. Worth a chance, but I'll make sure me or Anthony keep an eye on him," Danny added.

"You can come with us. No sense hiding the path this close, surely you could have found it had you ranged a few days," I said.

All the lizardman did was smile as he matched our stride toward home.

CHAPTER FOURTEEN

Triumphant-ish Return

I never thought that laying my eyes on a dirt road would be so exciting. The fact we were only a few minutes from home crashed through me and I couldn't keep the smile off my face. We'd done it! Partly.

Our excursion had been more than successful. Not only had we discovered humans, and the fact that there were more out there surviving and struggling against the madness that was everything going on on the surface, but we had found allies. While I only counted some of the Wild Guard, and tentatively Dai, as allies, that was more than we started with. That was almost more people than I used to interact with on a regular basis down in the Bunker. Not least of all was the fact that we'd met Tec. The information and options the larger Entity Cluster opened up meant we could reach out and truly get a foothold in the area by having more Dreg Warriors.

Unfortunately, not everything was sunshine and rainbows. The fact that the Dreg Tendrils were much more organized than we'd thought was concerning. I'd suspected some degree of organization since encountering the patrols, but a concerted leadership was almost too much. The fact that they'd come to some sort of arrangement with Wildwood meant they were coordinated and had resources accumulated somewhere. A strong, roving group would have been a problem, but an entrenched enemy would be even worse.

At some point during my reverie, Blobby and Anthony shot forward down the path. Danny and Sam were attentively looking around after the sudden jerk of our pets, but Dai looked positively undisturbed. Since I didn't think he was trying to lure me into a false sense of security, I assumed he hadn't seen any threat himself. He *was* the one more familiar with the threats of the area, after all.

The answer to the tension and our critter friends rushing off was the smell of roasting veggies. I wasn't sure if Blobby even had a nose to smell with, but if it did, then the slime would have ended up salivating like the rest of us. The smell of home was the last nudge we needed to jog up the slight hill and past our torn up training grounds.

I did notice Dai gave them an appreciative look before focusing on the task at hand. The task at hand being the gun pointed at his face.

"Children. It does appear that a lizard followed you home," Ava said. She was as cool as a cucumber—not that I'd ever had one of those—as she leveled her rifle on Dai. A click from behind her showed Ben and my uncle holding pistols out from the rounded front of the vestibule.

They'd flanked whatever Ava was fighting. Smart. As I shook the smile from my face at the tactics of my family, I interposed myself between the guns and the lizardman. Dai seemed to relax a fraction, but I did notice his hands were close to the jug on his back. A combat reflex if I've ever seen it.

"He's with us, Ava. We have got a lot to talk about," I said.

"Why," the woman asked, not removing her finger from the trigger, "in all that is good and bright, would you *not tell us* someone was coming with you!? The thing giving you magical powers *also lets you call ahead!*"

"Uh..." I looked to my friends for support, but they were

slowly edging away from me. Even Dai seemed to notice the implicit venom in the woman's tone. *Traitors.* "We're still getting used to using the comm-plants?"

"I—"

"What the heck is it?" Ben asked from the vestibule wall, thankfully cutting Ava off before she could tear into our tactical blunder. The two old dudes were already holstering their weapons. Ava was a bit less forthcoming, but the barrel of the rifle was at least pointing at our feet instead of center mass.

"I assume these people are related to you? They are just as brusque as you and Daniela," Dai said, reaching his hand out in greeting. "He, not it, sir. Dai Wood. My pleasure."

The three people gaped. Even Ava's gun sagged all the way down in surprise. Ben's mouth opened and closed like he wanted to say something and was failing.

"Not very talkative?" Dai asked, smirking. At least, that was what I thought it was, even if it looked about a hundred times more menacing coming from someone with reptilian features.

"W-welcome!" my uncle said, striding forward. Ever the host and socialite. He clasped Dai's hand in a firm, but not strangling, grip. He'd always emphasized the importance of an introductory handshake.

Ava and Ben were able to snap out of it and greeted the lizardman in a somewhat normal manner. Eventually, Ben shouted in alarm and headed back into the vestibule, disappearing from sight. The slightest smell of burning food told me he'd left the pan on the fire.

"How about we set up for that meal? If you didn't cook enough, I can manage," Daniela said, flicking her hand where it was engulfed in slow-moving fire. A very utilitarian use of her <Heat Touch>skill. Her mother shook her head but grabbed her in a hug before the two disappeared into the vestibule. That meant Sam, Dai, and I stood alone for a bit, awkward as could be.

"Surely you did not forget about me?" Alan practically materialized out of nowhere. He definitely hadn't been two feet behind me and not even my enhanced perception noticed the man. It sent a chill down my spine, but thankfully I wasn't the target of the eccentric scientist's attention.

Alan's hair was wilder than I remembered, but his eyes were as intense as always while he scanned and prodded Dai. For the first time, I saw the lizardman frown and shift around as if trying to keep an eye on Alan while he was inspected. I couldn't deny the slightest pleasure at the smug lizardman's discomfort. Eventually, Sam came to his rescue.

"Come on, Alan. We are all hungry, and we have a *long* story to tell." Samuel placed a hand gently on Alan's shoulder and led the man back to camp. Dai hesitated for a second before following. I chuckled as I followed after them. Dai was in for a treat as the first 'human' the Bunkerites had met since the Fall.

For the rest of the day, we were peppered with a seemingly endless array of questions. From everyone. Even the more reserved Ben asked about the status of the world or anything we could glean. Ava asked mainly about how humans had survived and Alan asked just about everything under the sun. When we mentioned that Tec could speak almost without break, we practically had to restrain him from heading straight to Wildwood. Thankfully, whether to gain favor in our eyes or just to be plain helpful, Dai answered all the questions sent his way. The lizardman spoke in a mix of formal speech and snark that was hard to replicate. Sometimes I felt like I was on the backfoot of the conversation when he was speaking, but he was as coopera-tive as could be.

Pretty much everything the other members of the Wild Guard had said about their corner of Earth checked out with Dai. Humanity struggled, and at some point that no one could really be sure, they started to collaborate with the Tendrils and things turned for the 'better.' What he added next was what really caught my attention.

"They didn't see it at first. Or maybe they did, but refused to accept their lot in the events. My mother and father saw it, but they passed before I was a teen." Dai paused a moment to gather his thoughts while we all remained silent except for the slight jiggle from Blobby and chitter from Anthony. Bec shimmered behind Dai as he sat on another rock bench I'd made, the way the iridescent light danced inside the crystal almost made it look like it was nodding at whatever Dai was alluding. "The Tendrils, they are—were—people from Wildwood."

The words gave everyone pause. While the older Bunkerites hadn't seen the Tendrils, or the others from Wildwood, they knew that there was more to the story.

"Are you sure?" I asked. "We haven't exactly stuck around to ogle the dead Tendrils, but they were pretty much featureless humanoids."

It was a hollow question. I'd already suspected that just like the few animals that were Tendrils, humans should have been able to be corrupted. Blobby was an outlier that I still hadn't figured out. What I really wanted to know was how Dai knew they were Wildwoodians, and if he knew how a regular human went from person to alien horror.

The lizardman nodded his head gravely. His jaw snapped open and shut before he sagged in his seat. "It happened to my mother. Then it happened to my father. The... Dreg... as I've heard you call it, it changed them. Not just like the councilmen or the Fallen or even some of the emergency militia. It was a change that bubbled from within. A voice, my father said, called them to the woods. Instead of succumbing to it, they died in the next wildlife raid that ravaged Wildwood.

"However, I studied and researched and gathered information from where I could. I noticed the change, back when Wildwood had more people and the defensive load was spread out. Someone would disappear here and there, and the wilds were put to blame. When almost half the town was gone, not killed in fights with nature but just gone, the walls went up. The disappearances almost stopped, but conveniently the

Tendrils started to show up and act as our defenders. The tasks were redistributed, and I was pulled into the Wild Guard."

The lizardman stood and started to pace around the vestibule. His tail and scales shimmered in the glow of Bec. Clawed hands swept through the air as he worked to weave a picture of his past and I couldn't help but lean forward as he spoke.

"To say the least, I didn't fit in the best. Something was going on, and I always tried to push everyone too far. Councilman Kirby let me keep training, but they didn't roll me into one of the squads my age. Funny enough, I was meant to take Lilly's place and work with Clara to make the New Hopers the strongest squad. One that could do and defeat anything. Instead, I was shunned by the town thanks to Kirby's inflammatory words.

"The Wild Guard still speak with me, but I no longer live inside the city. When we lost half of two squads, I threw myself into my training. Into my search. I followed Tendrils for days as they wandered, but every time I thought I was making headway, one of the megafauna would show up and push me back to the town."

"Can I stop you right there? Did you say *mega*fauna?" Ben asked, wringing his hands.

"Indeed. I had my suspicions about the crystal and its effects, but after coming here and eavesdropping on your group back in Wildwood... Well, it's been almost guaranteed that they are keeping the bulk of the aggressive creatures away. If you get out further than the immediate territories, the wilds get more... wild. The boundaries between which species dominates aren't as clear, and the strongest amongst them not at the helm of the species just waltz about without a care in the world."

So we were even luckier than we thought that Bec was helping us.

"You are talking about the boss monsters. The ones using Metier Crystals of their own?" Daniela asked in a quiet voice. When I focused on her, I could see her grip tightened around the plastic tray in her hands. Had her strength been any higher, it might have snapped just from her grip alone.

"Yes. It appears that your excursion was much more thorough than I had been able to glean. The 'boss monster,' or species leader as I've been calling them, tend to have a... cadre, for lack of a better word. These creatures tend to range far and wide while growing their personal power."

"How do you know all of that?" Sam asked.

"I told you I live outside the town. Said creatures roam closer to town than many people realize. Most of them, the crystal wards away, some I help frighten away. Never defeat. They are too hard to beat alone. But I try to keep the townsfolk safe when possible; it's not their fault someone twisted my words and is blinded by their station."

"How did you get so... eloquent?" Danny asked, bluntly. I tried to judge her but she was too far away for me not to make it obvious. Thankfully, her mother on the other side had no qualms about correcting her daughter.

"Daniela Vegas! You don't ask people that!" She looked more perturbed by the social faux pas than by the implications that a youth had been pseudo-exiled from his community. Proximity to a problem and all that, most likely.

Instead of being offended, Dai laughed whole-heartedly. The slight shadow that had crossed his reptilian features during his tale was nowhere in sight as he chuckled. It was half-human laugh, half-hiss which caused us all to join in *half*-heartedly. We weren't quite sure where the joke was.

"It is quite alright. I am sure my mannerisms are part of why the townspeople shun me. To put it simply, you might say I am a bit of a scholar. The only *new* scholar, I should add." He coughed to clear his throat and continue his clarification. "I've turned my residence into something of a library. All the books I can acquire—nay, rescue—while I am scouting, I try to add to my collection if only to delay their decay. Paper doesn't have a good track record with a quarter century of nature."

"Wait, why didn't the town try to do that to begin with?"

Sam asked, appalled. We didn't have very many books down in the Bunker, our curriculum was all digital, but it wouldn't be a stretch to say he'd hoarded them. He even had some of Alexia and June's medical reference books. *Suppose it makes his Attunement fit him like even more of a glove.*

"There is no formal schooling in Wildwood," Dai answered, throwing in an indifferent shrug into the mix.

"But you have classes and everything else for your Gifts?" *Oh boy.* Red was creeping up my friend's neck. It was particularly visible on his lighter skin, even after all the tans we'd gotten working on the surface.

"Needs must, after all. Even with the assistance you have rendered the Wild Guard and the House of Commerce, survival will be tight. Children do not wait for the most opportune season to be born, after all."

Even if I'd wanted to ask my question about the births on the surface, it was almost impossible to get a word in. Sam blew his gasket. The exact points of his arguments were lost in his tirade, especially since they weren't aimed at any of the present people, but at the leadership of Wildwood. The gist ran that education was essential in laying the foundations for the future and denying that vital part of their lives meant that people would idle instead of pushing to learn more. Do more. Grow. While I agreed with him wholeheartedly, especially if you added the presence of magic into the mix, there was little we could do about it.

Eventually, my uncle was able to placate the blond into merely simmering instead of boiling over. We shared a look and he picked up the meaning instantly.

"Dai, we can offer you accommodations here in the vestibule, if that is alright. The lobby is just a tad cramped now, but we do have some extra sleeping bags." Dale couldn't help himself from looking at the lizardman's tail. "Everyone has had a long day, and I think it would be in everyone's best interest to rest for the night."

There were mumbled agreements all throughout. I knew if

he had to, my uncle would have pushed harder to call it a day, but at least the others were on board. Alan not included, but Ben gave my uncle a hand in handling the Metier brainiac. The storytelling and the way Dai interacted with my family told me all I hoped to need to know about the man. Not only that, the information he told me checked out with what the Entity Clusters had been telling me so far.

When everyone was on the verge of sleeping, probably sometime around midnight, I stepped out into the vestibule. Unsurprisingly, Dai was staring through the cracks of our shoddy wooden doors instead of asleep in the bed we'd made from nudging my stone benches together and lining them with sleeping bags.

"Ronan. Fine evening," he said, doing a half-turn and nodding to me. Instead of answering, I walked over to Bec. The lizardman turned again, lifting an eyebrow in a silent question.

"Figured I'd present as disarming as I could," I said, settling into the light of the Entity. The crystal hadn't gotten any additional Dreg while we were gone, so its interactions were still sporadic. *I almost wish there was some way of transferring power from Tec to Bec.* Shaking my head to get my thoughts back on track, I met Dai's eyes. "Having us join you would be great. As I explained to the New Hopers and to the Big Guns, it really isn't a strict obligation outside of what you are already doing."

I gestured to Bec with a slight sigh. "Unfortunately, our crystalline benefactor cannot come through for you here. And neither can our mechanical benefactor—that would be the wild-haired Alan, by the way—because we lack the means. The Metier Crystal in Wildwood will be able to give you access to what we call skills and you call Gifts. You can probably get a rough estimate of our power thanks to your experience, but the implant will allow you to inspect and refine your scouting with more information. I don't think I have to tell *you* that knowledge is power."

The lizardman shook his head and sat at one of the free benches. His sharp pupils were slightly off-putting when he stood so close, but considering all the things I'd seen, it only shook me a little. "I can impart skills outside of those dictated by our levels, you can ask Clara and Sarah about those, thanks to my mana pool. It's on my to do list to figure out how to let others do this," I said, raising a hand to placate Dai just as he was ready to ask a question.

"It isn't exactly right for me to ask things of you when you've already come to our aid before. However, I hope that in the spirit of protecting humanity, you would agree to help us. Help me."

"That is a reasonable exchange. Even if our goals did not align, which I assure you they do, the kind of power you speak of would be worth more than a few tasks," Dai said evenly.

"Good. Because I need you to spy on Wildwood."

The directness of my statement seemed to finally put Dai on the back foot. When he asked for clarification, I broke down my suspicions. Considering what he'd told us about his own past and the darker times after Landfall, it really wasn't too much of a stretch. Someone in Wildwood was collaborating with the Tendrils, and with a more intelligent form of the Dreg beyond that. The blood at the Tendril ambush, the poor showing from the Tendril's side during their last attack and then the subsequent lack of a follow-up attack really solidified the theory.

The problem then lay in finding out who would be willingly betraying humanity.

CHAPTER FIFTEEN

Infusion or Intrusion

Dai and I spent another hour hashing out possible theories, but the lizardman really had no idea who might be involved. His efforts had always been focused externally, but with the new information and us to boost the strength of the town overall, he could put his skills to use for a different purpose.

When a grumpy Ben came out of the lobby to tell us to call it a night, we shook hands and went to bed. The man plopped his bulk next to one of the log doors, settling in for the night watch as he peeked into the dark through one of the gaps. There was more to discuss and more plans to make, but keeping clear and rested minds on the problem would also be key. I didn't even insist on being added to the rotation the old crew had been keeping up in our absence.

The motions of the following morning were almost mechanical. Dai was surprised by the amount of food, if not super varied, that we had. Samuel was more than happy to give the lizardman a tour of his farm. Ben, Dale, and a hopeful Alan went along to the farms to the west of camp. I was pretty interested in checking out what Sam had been up to before we traveled to Wildwood, especially when Ben said he'd been making some headway towards milking some of the herd, but there were too many immediate tasks that only I could do. Or, if it was up to my friends, *would* do.

Namely? Sorting, cataloging, and preparing to infuse gear en mass.

Our dungeon farm run had been extremely fruitful. Even with half of the loot going to the Wild Guard, and most of it remaining in our initial shelter, I almost had infusions to spare. Instead of spending time counting and getting a breakdown of the infusions and materials we had, I focused on keeping a tally of our stronger drops. It was just as I was starting this process that Daniela left with her mother. Neither woman commented on where they were going, or what they were planning to do, but I knew they could take care of themselves. The rifle slung over Ava's shoulder, and the Fire Ant following a step behind Danny confirmed it for me.

"Looks like it's just you and me, Blobby."

The ball of slime had the gall to wave a gelatinous limb in my direction as it rolled off into the woods. *Was it bigger than before?* Its two crystal cores clacked against each other as if it were laughing at me the entire time. I knew it was deliberate because they were normally deep in its bulk, silent as I knew the slime could be.

It was in the lone silence, sifting through body parts and tiny, condensed magic blobs, that Bec grabbed my attention.

"I'm quite impressed with the progress you three have made," the crystal said. "Also never expected my sibling to be quite this close."

"We were told that before Landfall, your crystals were struck. It didn't get rid of them, but just fragmented them all over the place," I said, absently rolling the strongest infusion we'd been able to acquire through my fingers. The fire spider that had kidnapped Danny.

"Then it would seem finding more, lower category clusters will be the way moving forward." The light within the crystal pulsed lightly. "My time is not long. Unfortunately, the yields of your adventure were passed on to Tec and not myself. Do you have any pressing questions?"

"Is there any way to share that? And how close are you to being able to replicate implants like Tec? Also, how did you know I was calling the Wildwood Cluster Tec?"

"I'll answer the last one, because it's simple. You already knew that everything within my influence I can sense. Everything within my inner influence I can perceive." The light within dimmed before Bec answered. "As for sharing power, it would be a difficult endeavor. The main problem would be overwriting our guiding sapience structure. Should you, for instance, break a portion of Tec, said portion would hold a part of them that you'd be transplanting onto me. Due to the relative categories in which we are in, he would barely feel my influence while he would likely wipe mine clean off."

"That sounds less than pleasant," I said, thinking about the people with Tec's implants.

"Such is the nature of our intelligence. Highly adaptable, but it makes individualism difficult in the grand scheme of things. Great for interdimensional purging rocks, eh?"

"What about the Wild Guard? They have a piece of Tec as their implant. Could that affect them?"

"Outside of the changes the status system provides, no. Again, the erasure of personality is a result of the way our intelligence is composed. Plus, if you think about it, you already have a chunk of some *other* cluster in your own head, no?"

"Thanks for giving me another source of nightmares," I said flatly.

The crystal didn't laugh, but the rapid pulses of light within told me all I needed to know of its mirth.

"Unfortunately our time grows short, Ronan. I will work to see if there is some way for me to create the implants before reaching category four. Unfortunately, Tec doesn't have the most social personality, and I am beholden to him for long-range communication."

"I'll be here, plugging away. Thanks for watching over us, Bec. Sorry it took so long to actually come up with a name."

"It's simple, and will help identify my siblings with personality in the future. Your efforts do not go unnoticed, Dreg Warrior Terrigan."

With that oddly formal farewell, the crystal dimmed and I felt the slight tickling on my skin as the area of influence of Bec stretched back across the camp. I sat there for a few minutes mulling on the reality that something from beyond had sent the clusters and stirred the Dreg. It was obviously a bad thing for humanity, but I had no way to know how much worse it might have been had the Dreg been left alone longer. That whole scope was way outside my current purview.

Instead of giving myself a further headache, I turned back to my original task. Infusing.

"I'm going to have to ask Ben to help me with this," I said grumpily. There really were too many materials to go through, and even with the surplus, I couldn't bring myself to waste materials. The aspects of quotients I'd discovered during my last crafting sprint flowed through my mind as I considered what to make first. The piles of non-fire infusions called to me too strongly to ignore. Selecting some of the Q1 water, air and earth infusions, I fished out some of the Q0 fire ant chitin plates.

The small, hand-sized plates looked downright boring considering all the other things I'd made. Regardless, they'd served me well and would again for science! *Or was it still science if it had to do with magic?*

Shaking the thoughts from my head, I focused on the plate in my hand. Selecting one of the air infusions, I triggered <Infusion> and watched as the white-gray thread of Pith unspooled from the cotton-like blob. As I directed my will, the thread coiled tightly around the chitin plate, causing it to vibrate and wobble as if it wasn't a material hard enough to withstand getting shot. After several seconds, and the full Q1 infusion covering the plate, the shaking stopped. Thankfully, the plate didn't turn into so much shrapnel, unlike my first attempt at infusing.

The red tone of the chitin had taken on some transparent properties, even if the material itself looked just as strong. I focused on the plate and information about the infused material appeared before my eyes.

<Quotient 1 Infused Chitin Plate>

<Attunement: Air>

<Quotient 1 Density>

"Fairly standard, all things considered," I said. When I moved to drop the material, a rush of hot air displaced into my face. It wasn't enough to hurt me, especially with my Limestone Skin, but it did make me take note. A few faster swings of the chitin told me the effect was similar to the heat dispersion, but probably focused around friction as opposed to impacts. When I rubbed my hand on the material and the effect triggered, I was almost sure of it.

Wanting to see how repeatable the process was, I infused another chitin plate. Sure enough, it had the same nature.

With air out of the way, I churned two of each of the chitin plates using the other elements without any adverse reactions during the infusion. Unsurprisingly, the water infusion caused the chitin to cool excessively and the earth infusion compressed the chitin by a full inch before the thread was fully wrapped around it. The information the system told me about the materials was identical other than the Attunement. The nature of the materials, however, left me dizzy with possibilities.

Originally, I'd thought that the earth-infused plate and the water-infused plate were inert somehow, other than the cracked and snowflake patterns, respectively. After considering that everything else I'd infused had some secondary trait, there *had* to be more. At least an entire hour went into figuring out what those effects were. Funnily enough, the discovery happened when I threw the plates into the haphazard pile of what I'd just infused. There was more than a little bit of frustrated energy in the toss.

The water plate struck one of the air ones. The wave of heat that would have come from the friction vanished on a small plume of mist before dissipating. Like a caveman striking rocks, I rubbed the two chitin plates together. The only thing missing was the grunting and hunched shoulders.

One made heat, the other turned that heat into cold.

The caveman comparison was probably quite apt, considering the behavior of the infused materials broke a few thermodynamic principles. And that was just the ones that I knew of.

"This magic stuff, I tell you," I mumbled to myself.

"Indeed."

My strength sent me straight into the low ceiling of the vestibule and my Limestone Skin actually absorbed enough of the hit not to give me an instant concussion. When I blinked the tears out of my eyes and rubbed the bump on my head, Alan was lurking right over my shoulder.

"Alan, please, announce yourself, man," I said, getting my breath in order.

"Apologies. I really did imagine you'd noticed me. I've been here at least an hour," he said, not looking at me but at the plates I'd been working on. "You gonna use those?"

"Alan, you are welcome to help me figure this out. Before I got too tangled up in upgrading our gear, I wanted to know what I had to work with," I said.

"It appears there is some sort of heat exchange. It's quite possible that the mana of the materials, or even some of the ambient mana is acting as the moderating medium. Though some additional research will be necessary to determine the fluid mechanic properties of mana. If it even has a material state and not an energy state. If it's even energy at all and not some other cosmic trait that humans hadn't discovered about the universe," Alan replied matter-of-factly. The scientist was rubbing the two plates with different levels of force, eliciting different sizes of magical response from the infused chitin.

We discussed the possibilities of what the materials might be doing, but Alan used terminology I wasn't even prepared to handle. I gave him a copy of all the infused chitin I had, which used up all the Q0 earth infusions I had, and made a workstation for him on the opposite side of the vestibule. With that out of the way, I resumed infusing a few more pieces of chitin with each of the elements I had available.

Even without understanding the minutiae of how the effects worked, I already had ideas for what to make. While I'd never combined different materials while infusing, I didn't think there was anything stopping me from doing so. Other than possible explosive side effects. That thought gave me a slight bit of pause, but then I remembered that *someone* had to do it. It also reminded me of how much of a difference our equipment had made against the spiders. *How much stronger would the New Hopers and Big Guns be if they had access to infused gear?*

Rummaging through the duffle bag, I pulled out all the spider parts I had. There were plates from all of the elements I had infusions for, but I wasn't close to ready to catalog that huge pile of combinations. I was still waiting for Alan to figure out what the fire material-earth infusion combination did!

Instead of getting too carried away with testing, I focused on crafting. Without having more... fleshy materials to help bind things together, I would need to get creative. As I let that ruminate on the back of my mind, I turned to the pile of spider bits and our own selection of materials. It had a disturbing amount of human bones in it, but considering who our biggest threat was, it made sense. Prejudices would not help our survival.

So I sifted and separated out the longer pieces. Five fire human radii, two water ulnas, an oversized earth jawbone and the overly large air squirrel skull. The Blaze Ant's stinger was also in the pile, as was a pair of mandibles from some Q2 fire ants. Topping the list was the femur of the life-attuned Tendril that had ambushed us. It was really an impressive display of goods, but it still left me somewhat stumped. Instead of getting too caught up in it, I visualized a hammer that used the squirrel skull as the... head, and the femur as the handle. It was the first time I would be mixing different attunements, so I was more than a little bit curious to see what happened.

After selecting fire as the charging infusion, I manipulated the thread to shave off some of the femur. As if I were trying to sand down steel, the bone sparked and resisted my attempts to shape it, but I persisted. Time ticked by, and infusion after infusion burned up in my hands as I worked the femur. By the end of the process, I'd completely forgotten that the bone had even come from a human. Hesitant to see how it turned out, I set down a last infusion and checked all the edges I'd carved. Smooth as polished stone.

While taking a break from carving the handle, I'd taken a more direct approach to the joint where the skull would set in. The skull in question was about the size of two of my fists put together and had a forward dip before ending on two dulled teeth as thick as my fingers. Using more Pith thread manipulation, I fashioned a groove into the top of the femur that would fit the small cavity that led to the inner parts of the squirrel skull. It wasn't much of a hole, even in the enlarged cranium, but I hoped it would secure the weapon together.

With that out of the way, I placed the femur into the groove and visualized the welding nature of the fire infusion. The bone charred with my passing finger, but they blended together nonetheless. I did make note of the fact that the light yellow coloration of the femur flowed into the skull before overpowering the slight gray tones of it. The series of questions that stirred about the nature of infusions, the quotient of materials, and a whole number of other things, was almost too much to handle. Instead, I finished some final touches smoothing out the hammer before setting it down on my workstation.

"Astounding work. Truly, do you have such command of the essence?" Dai was standing behind me, but not Alan-close behind me, when he addressed me.

"I'm still working on it. My sort of working hypothesis is that different quotients of infusion have different levels of power, which in turn affects how much control I have. Bec didn't want to push my crafting into full items until I was Quotient 4, presumably for that reason. Haven't had the time to really delve into that."

"Is that, perhaps, one of those skills you might share with me?" he asked, taking a step forward.

"Yes, I can." I gave the hammer I was working on a look, but turned to focus on the lizardman. His proposition, and what I'd asked of him, had not gone unnoticed. "Before I do that, I need to ask you to return to Wildwood as soon as you can."

"There isn't more I could do for you all here?"

"Yes, there is. Getting more acquainted with you, and training with you, as a matter of fact, would be an immense boon for us, but I am worried that things are going on behind our backs. As is, we would never know. Your skill set, it changes the game and that's without accounting for your familiarity with Wildwood.

"I need to talk to my friends and figure out what our plan is to return. We'd agreed to meet with the New Hopers tomorrow or in another three days; if we want to get anything done here, we're going to have to extend that. Do you think you could update them on that?"

"As it happens, their squad is one of the few that don't shun me outright." The lizardman rolled his eyes. "I can find Clara to deliver your message."

"This isn't what you wanted to hear, I know. But you are guaranteed an implant, if that is what you are looking for."

"Understandable. I've spent my whole life without access to the system as you describe it, a few more days isn't going to hurt anything," Dai said, inclining his head slightly. Thankfully, I couldn't see anything even close to actual frustration or deception, no matter how hard I strained my perception. The lizardman was a study in poise and steadiness.

"Maybe you can try to talk to Clara or Sarah to take you to Tec," I said, trying to think of some way to give the lizardman a bump in strength before he started his investigation. Spying, really, since we both agreed there had to be a human counterpart to the mix.

"It's quite alright. The town doesn't much enjoy my presence. Even the other water Fallen don't enjoy having me around. As they say, I've gone a bit too 'wild.'" The man twitched his tail so it would come into view before letting it hang behind him. "Apparently, racial criticism in our time starts and ends at having a tail."

The two of us shared a laugh before a gruff throat clear from the other side of the vestibule cut it short. "Apologies, children, but there are some of us trying to get work done."

Alan didn't even turn from where he was typing away on a tablet. Where he'd gotten it and how he'd gotten it to work in the mana- and Dreg-permeated atmosphere was a wonder for me, but I could already see several graphs and charts of data on it. None of it made sense to me, but I was sure they did to him.

"I really need to make some more rooms for us to use," I whispered to Dai. The lizardman chuckled and gave a quiet nod. "Take a seat, I will give you the <Infusion>skill. Maybe you can figure out some other uses for it."

Dai, who was about a head taller than me, adjusted himself and his tail to face me. There was a cool expression on his face and he closed his eyes as I put my hand on his forehead. Head? The flat part of his snout near the top. With a push of will, the information for <Infusion> flowed into him. Just as with Rommel, <Memory Canal> activated of its own accord and I was taken for a ride.

Emotions buffeted me as I tried to get my bearings. Cold, fear, confusion, and more cold. Always the cold. A large group of humans fought off a panther the size of a small house using guns and a number of rudimentary spears. They struggled against the sheer force of the panther, many holding carved wooden shields to rebuff the strikes. Each strike still claimed at least one life.

"Get them out of here!"

A much younger Irwin leapt over the line of men and women before clamping onto the panther's head. His fists struck true a number of times before the creature shook him off. A pair of hands hoisted me and several other children away from the fight and into a nearby building. I could see the beginnings of a wall forming in the distance, but that was all I saw before a woman's face blocked my vision of the fight.

"Listen to me, Dai. I need you to take care of the children. Can you do that? Mommy has to help your dad, okay?" Her voice was even, but tears were streaming down her face. She hugged me, wrapping a tail much longer than the one budding on my own back before rushing out through the door. The wood slammed shut and the sounds of battle grew muted just to be replaced with the crying of children.

Toddlers and youth alike clustered around the open warehouse, a few lanterns having been brought out for the occasion instead of the usual candles. Dai ambled around in search of the youngest ones, hoisting one into his arms before poking the shoulder of one of the older kids. After delivering his charge to the crying child, he repeated the process all throughout the night. Cycling those who were exhausted with those with the energy to cry and mourn. The children didn't know better, and further confusion without reassurance would only serve to traumatize them. At least, that was what his dad told him when the beasts attacked.

When the charge of the lanterns failed them, he finally realized that there were rays of sun streaming through the barricaded windows. All the children except for him were sound asleep in huddles throughout the warehouse. Without thinking, he walked out through the door to the sight of something he'd been trying for too long to forget.

CHAPTER SIXTEEN

Privacy

The world snapped into focus and I plopped down onto the bench next to Dai. The lizardman was blinking his eyes as if he'd been staring directly at the sun. As I'd come to realize, my sneaky-deaky skill was taking me for a little tour whenever I transferred skills. Not exactly the best way to avoid invading your friend's privacy, but it provided insights into the people I didn't even know I wanted. For instance, any lingering doubt I had about Dai was dismissed after that memory.

If I looked at it from an observer's perspective, I might think he had two ways of growing up. Hating everyone or hating himself, which would not have bade well for the future of our interactions. Fortunately, I was in his shoes through the loss and while it was immense, he was determined to keep to his mother's words. The loss I felt was one shared with the exiled Fallen. While I was not my uncle—who would have certainly hugged Dai for all he was worth while tears streamed down his face—I did allow myself to throw a hand on his shoulder.

"Sorry, the transfer takes a lot out of me. How are you doing?" I said, clearing my throat and trying to finish processing the lingering memory.

"It's an astounding amount of knowledge," he said quietly. "I know how to do some of it now, but I feel like I need to really *know* it before I can do more."

"That's a good way to put it. Maybe that's why Bec wanted me to get to a certain level and proficiency, so that I could actually make use of the information trapped in here." I tapped my temple gently.

"Just the possibilities have my mind spinning. I *must* get back to my collection of infusions. If what I've seen of you can be even remotely replicated for my purposes, then I must begin working on it at once!"

"Not even a little broken up about leaving us, eh?" Daniela and Ava stood at the door, both covered in mud. Their clothes were singed to the nines, but they didn't look injured.

"My apologies. As you well know, I intend to join you in your efforts. While that is not possible here, or likely in Wildwood until you return, I feel there is some... preparations needed on my part."

"Cryptic. Would you care to share with the class?" Ava said, setting down her rifle against the wall of the lobby. She patted Alan on the head gently, and I finally noticed the man again. He wasn't even paying attention to the exchange as he worked.

"Ronan and I have discussed at length. I hope that our next meeting will be in less intense circumstances. I would very much love to visit your Bunker. Not much of the old world remains intact," Dai said, gesturing to the lobby door.

"Did you need to restock on anything?" I asked, trying to center the conversation. I felt a tad guilty about the non sequitur, but the memory had injected a whole new source of urgency to my plans. If spying worked at all like the old world recordings, then Dai would need time to work.

"He can leave in the morning, Ronan. If he has agreed to work with us, then we need to make sure rest is an included consideration. For yourself too," Ava said, frowning at me and Dai.

"That is alright. I believe that Samuel wanted to show me a

few more aspects of his farm. I am also quite curious as to how he was able to get a whole herd of cows to cooperate with him. The ones that we've encountered always opted for a 'charge first, ask questions later' type of approach," Dai said, taking the cue. The lizardman gave me a small nod before escorting Ava toward the fields.

As the pair walked away, my perception picked up the start of their own conversation. "So, does your body have different dietary restrictions than the more human ones?"

"She really can't leave it well enough alone," Danny sighed. The brunette plopped down on the bench across from me.

"Nope," Alan said. He didn't even turn from his station.

Ignoring the eccentric scientist, I focused on Danny. "You gonna talk to me about what you were up to?"

"Nope," she answered, tipping until she was laying down on the benches Dai had used as a bed. A few seconds later, she was snoozing gently.

My eyes drifted from my sleeping companion, to the slowly pulsing alien crystal and to the premier scientist on mana that I knew. "Rooms. That's the next step after this hammer," I said, sighing and turning back to my osseous creation.

— + —

The next several days went by in a blur of activity that I was still trying to process. My two main efforts revolved around crafting. Crafting items and crafting a stronger camp overall.

After recognizing that everyone would probably need more work space, since the lobby was acting as our bedroom and kitchen and the vestibule as our work area and dining room, I sketched out a rough plan to work on for the next few days. With daylight still in the sky, I opted to give the rest of the Bunkerites a little surprise.

My increased level made <Stone Spike> reach eight feet on a simple cast. While it still took roughly twenty percent of my mana, the result was still impressive. After a bit of testing, an overcharged cast of it put it at nearly twelve feet and three feet wide at the base. Instead of being mostly silent as it had been, that particular skill use actually caused the ground to rumble and cracks spiderwebbed through the hardened soil I'd worked on before. Daniela grumbled at me the entire way out of the camp's clearing since my skill had shaken her awake.

Not trying to have to deal with too many secondary structural problems, I chose to stick with the regular casting. Using <Stone Spike>, I roughed in one rectangular space on the other side of the Metier Crystal. Bec didn't make any comments as I worked, but I was aware of the light within the crystal shifting to the outside.

"Sorry, friend. Until we figure out how to get some better utilities, I'll be using you as our light source," I told the Entity Cluster. Unsurprisingly, I got no response.

With the space outlined by the pointed pillars, I used my pickaxe to snap the tips off. From there I cast horizontal <Stone Spikes> to create slats for a roof over the space. With all the framework placed, the day had burned away.

The others returned from their various tasks, surprised by the sudden network of connected rock columns. I didn't give any details as we all ate dinner, even at Dai's honest curiosity. He hadn't expected to hear me talk about expanding the camp only to come back that afternoon to see significant change.

The lizardman spoke about his return and his attempts to misdirect other scouting efforts the council had put in place; he didn't feel confident that he'd been convincing enough in his initial dissuasion. He did warn me that Oliver, the sniper we'd met on our first day at Wildwood, was very good at tracking, and it was entirely possible he was also sent after us. The older members of our group discussed the possibility of traveling to Wildwood themselves, but all three of my friends shut them down.

"The less they know, the better," Dai said. "Resources have been scant in Wildwood for years, but the pressure from the Tendrils has only driven people to be more desperate. I'm sure there are already some that want to really explore what benefits a Bunker can give them."

That was a whole other set of concerns I didn't need.

Regardless, Dai left the following morning with a promise to return should he find anything immediately actionable. Us Bunkerites spent some time sharing our thoughts on Dai, but most of it was positive. When Alan exited the conversation without comment, we just took it as a sign to get to work.

A few minutes later, only Alan and I remained. Starting a conversation with Alan about what he might have found could go one of two ways. Quick and easy or torturously slow. The risk wasn't worth it, so I returned to building.

With my mana completely refilled, I cast <Earthen Barrier> to fill in the gaps. The Q4 version of the skill now rose up from the ground with gusto. It only took two casts to compress a wall into existence, the materialize portion of the skill adding soil identical to the surroundings to create the barrier.

While waiting for my mana to regenerate, I headed out to the tree line. Using just my pickaxe, I began to mark a trench along the first wall I'd created what felt like a lifetime ago. The usefulness of the Wildwood palisade as a vantage point and defensive structure had made an impression on me.

The perimeter around the camp wasn't terribly large, but it would still take a long while to create the stone wall I visualized. Thankfully, Daniela had already cut most of the trees right at the edge of the clearing.

Over the next two days, I finished the north, northeast, and northwest portions of the trench while completing the addition to the vestibule. Instead of leaving that added room as one long room, I used half-power casts of <Stone Spikes> alternating from the floor and from the ceiling to split the room in half. In order to access the rooms once I'd sealed it, I excavated two small doorways using my pickaxe. Still lacking the means of making a proper door, I split two logs in half before propping them in front of the openings.

That night, I moved my workstation to the northeast room

and Alan's workstation to the northwest room. Of course, when that was complete, everyone wanted a room of their own. When I pointed out our time constraints, the need for shared space and the fact that Alan and I spent most of our time inside as opposed to the other members of the surface team, the complaints quieted. So, most of the storage stuff got moved to the walls of the vestibule, freeing up a whole lot more room in the lobby for sleeping and the small kitchen setup. It also served the purpose of giving me even more access to all the tools and materials we'd collected.

My new crafting room was smaller than the vestibule. The several breeze holes I'd dug in the walls kept things lit and cool. The main source of light was still the Metier Crystal, but they were helpful. The stone of the walls also helped keep some of the heat out without baking us. I wasn't sure if that was a result of my design, the material composition of the mana-created stone, the presence of Bec, or any other number of magic-related factors. What mattered was that I could focus on crafting again uninterrupted.

That same night, after our dinner meal, I finished the infusion of the hammer. The entire thing was experimental, so throwing more fire-attuned infusions into the mix just seemed like the most sensical thing to do.

"Man, I'm glad the others aren't trying to supervise the nonsense I'm up to," I mumbled to myself before triggering <Infusion> on one of our few Q1 fire infusions and flicking it at the hammer.

The red cord of Pith struck the bone like a lance of fire. The bone charred, blackening almost instantly. The burned surface spread slowly across it, but the material didn't fail as far as I could tell. A few seconds later, the thread of Pith was exhausted.

<Insufficient Pith Enhanced Hammer>
<Attribute: Undetermined>
<Trait: Undetermined>
Running my fingers over the charred bone revealed that it

was actually intact underneath. Or possibly it had healed itself, since it was bound to the regeneration refinement. Yet another thing I didn't know for sure.

As had become a habit, I ignored what I didn't know and focused on what I *did*. I needed more Pith. Over the course of the next hour, I slapped an additional nine Q0 infusions into the hammer. The charred surface was much less prominent with the weaker infusion, but it wiped away all the same. When the final bit of Pith vanished into the weapon, its final information manifested in my vision.

<Quotient 2 Enhanced Hammer>

<Attribute: Mobility>

<Trait: Whistling Health>

It was the first mobility-focused item I'd created, which was noteworthy. Once again, I was fairly unsure of what the trait granted without testing.

"If I knew how, I would call this thing 'the Nutcracker.'" Before I got a chance to chuckle to myself, the information of the weapon changed right before my eyes.

<The Nutcracker (Q2 Hammer)>

<Attribute: Mobility>

<Trait: Whistling Health>

Turning an accusing eye at the Entity Cluster behind me, I set the weapon down. The ability to rename weapons made sense, considering how creatures we knew information about were updated, but I hadn't really intended to name it that. But, it was done and now I could actually label the stuff I created better.

A peek through one of my air holes told me it was way past 'bedtime' at the Bunker camp. Just as I was gathering up my stuff, a knock at my 'door' pulled my attention.

"Come in?" I answered. Knocking had never been much of a thing, even down in the Bunker.

"Hey Ron, you got a second?" Sam moved aside the split boards to enter my workspace. He was carrying one of the rechargeable lanterns in hand, throwing quite a bit of light into the room even with a portion of Bec illuminating it.

Man, I really should have gone to bed a while ago.

"Yeah, man, what's up?" I asked, leaning against my workstation. Since there really wasn't any seating, I used a half-powered <Earthen Barrier> to make a low bench for him to sit. Instead of growing out of the ground, it grew horizontally out of the wall.

"That's new," he said, testing the hardened mound with his hand before sitting.

"Building helps me try out new things. It's how I built the roof," I said, pointing to the smooth ceiling above. "How's the farm going? Sorry I haven't been out there much, but if you need anything, let me know."

Sam waved his hand to dismiss my concerns. "The herd is grazing well where I've boosted the grass. Raymond is more or less tamed now.As far as helping me around the farm, anyhow. These feelers are great for getting an impression of his feelings." Samuel flexed his fingers as the spindly nerve hairs on his hands waved in the air.

"Everything is growing well. I've got it growing staggered so that we can harvest stuff once a week or so without needing my magic to get some blooms. If we had a refrigerator up top, we could keep a bigger stockpile but hauling things down to the Bunker isn't viable. Not while they are sustainable and we are also."

"That's awesome, man. I hadn't even thought to leave things staggered. I suppose that would have been hard to do if you couldn't magically regulate the growth of things."

"Speaking of magical growth…" Sam looked down at the ground and scratched the back of his head awkwardly. It took him several minutes to work up what he was trying to say, but I was in no rush. Samuel was very passionate about certain things, but most of the time, he was as reserved as Alan was eccentric. The fact that he'd jumped in to help the Wildwoodians was both surprising and exactly in character for him.

"I've been working on something." When I didn't say anything and just lifted an eyebrow in curiosity, he continued. "I've been trying to overgrow some of the tomato plants."

"Like, get it to be bigger than normal?" I asked. Considering what I'd seen his empowered <Vine Whip>skill do, it wouldn't surprise me.

"No, not bigger... More like *denser*. Stronger."

"Alright, I sort of follow. What do you need from me?"

"For some reason, since you transferred the <Infusion>skill, something in the back of my mind has been telling me to use it. Not for crafting stuff like you've done, but to change the plants. Somehow. I don't know, it's probably a dumb thought."

"Samuel, I haven't known you to have a dumb thought since I've known you. Danny? Me? Now that's a different story." I moved from the lip of the workstation where I was leaning to sit beside him. The earthen bench protested our combined weight but held all the same. "I've got a little bit of everything except for life and death infusions. The Q3 life infusion is the only one of its type I've got at the moment, but tell me if you think that will work for what you are trying to do."

"I'm not sure. I've got a small section set apart for the plants I've been overgrowing. Do you think you could come by tomorrow, maybe bring some of your infusions?"

"*Our* infusions. We'd be dead without each other. But yeah, I can go over in the morning and we can do some experimenting."

The doors of my work room practically blew off their non-existent hinges. A panting Alan stood in the opening. "Did someone say 'experimenting'?"

After Sam and I were done screaming and reeling our hearts from where they'd leapt up our throats, we explained the idea to Alan. Apparently, it was exactly what he needed for his 'research,' so he promised us he would be there. Neither of us knew what he was going on about, but we knew it would probably help us out in the end.

Just as we were getting ready to leave, Sam picked up a sack. One I couldn't recall him ever having.

The blond explained that with the amount of harvesting stuff he, Ben, and my uncle had been carrying, he'd taken the time to do a little crafting of his own. They were made from woven and knotted vines. The same vines that Samuel summoned to use for Raymond's hitch.

Suddenly, crafting plans I'd been avoiding clicked into place.

"I'll help with your plant experiment, but I'm gonna need your help with something too," I told Sam as we stepped into the lobby. Someone at some point had already moved the wooden slide doors for the vestibule into place.

"You have that 'idea' look on your face, Ron. Is this idea gonna possibly backfire on us?"

"None of my ideas have backfired on us!" I grumped.

"They certainly didn't pan out completely. Just look at what happened to Dan—" Samuel bit his tongue to stop himself. Literally bit it before his mouth could run away from him.

My thoughts of crafting and what we might be able to accomplish crashed to the ground as I was reminded of yet another of my failures.

"Ronan, you know I didn't—"

"It's alright. You're not wrong. I just need to figure out how to do better."

While the night ended on a bit of a sour note, reality couldn't be ignored. Failure—survived— was the best teacher. If all you did was wallow or try to push it away, instead of embracing it and internalizing it, then you'd never learn. Almost losing one of my best friends because of an ambitious idea was much worse than just dying myself.

The night faded into muddied dreams of my faceless father and mother liquefying like I'd seen other water-attuned creatures do. Morning couldn't come soon enough.

CHAPTER SEVENTEEN

Low Hanging Fruit

While my sleep the night before was probably the worst one since arriving at the surface, I knew it would do no good to wallow. The morning had become fairly routine and once everyone was done, we all scattered. Unlike usual, I headed out west with my uncle, Ben, Alan, and Sam. They had a usual round of banter, but I mostly remained to the back of the group with Alan.

I didn't blame Sam, but knowing him, he probably did. The drifting looks he gave me as we walked also highlighted that. I'd preempted that by letting my uncle know he was probably blaming himself for my introspective mood. So, when Dale saw the silent exchange between us, he stepped right in.

The rest of the fifteen minute walk to the pond and farm gave me the time to admire just how much work Samuel had done. Neat rows of tomatoes grew up split wood trellises, and various other veggies dotted the space around the tomatoes. Some short grass in the distance marked where the fence Sam and I made long ago separated the herd from our food supplies. The life-attuned had even cordoned off the different plants using stakes of wood and more of his vines. The scale dwarfed my own work and I couldn't help but feel like I wasn't actually contributing to our group. Even Daniela worked to become an offensive powerhouse all on her own. I was just the one taking the hits.

"Now, I will not be dealing with this issue on two sides," my uncle said, halting our group right at the edge of the herd fence. "I get it, you two have stuff you want to get out. But I will not deal with self-deprecating nonsense and insecure friendships. We have taught you better than that."

"But you don't——" I started to say before Dale tut-tut-tutted at me. He even did the little finger shake in my face.

"We. Taught. You. Better. You are all equal, and so long as you are trying your best and not forcing your ideas on others, the blame is not squarely on your shoulders. I don't know the full picture, but what happened to Daniela was not your fault, Ron. And even if I don't know what you've been up to in that room, I know that you've contributed immensely to our group."

"How did you even know I was thinking that?" I asked, mouth hanging open in surprise.

"Ronan, it really doesn't take a genius," Ben said, making a point of gesturing to Alan, "to see how your expression fell the more you saw of the farm."

"How does anything I make compare to this? To feeding us and even the people down below. He didn't even need me to set up his own fencing." I pointed with indignation at the simple, but sturdy, barriers all around us.

"Ron, why do you think I've been able to focus so much on all of this?" Sam asked, tilting his head.

"Because you are actually super capable and have magic powers over plant growth?" I shot back.

"First of all, not sure if that was a dig or not. Second, it's because you set up somewhere for us to rest. Because you are working on aspects of our infrastructure I didn't even think to work on. You have literally taken fireballs for us while all I do is slap some health on you." Sam's voice went up a notch as he let out his frustrations. "My comment yesterday wasn't meant as a dig at you, Ronan. I just want to make sure you've thought the plan through. More often than not, your nose is so deep in the grindstone you lose sight of what is happening around you!"

If I had expected something to happen during the day, it wasn't being yelled at by Samuel. The blond was actually panting, having grabbed the collar of my shirt at some point. When he saw what he was doing, he let go, looked at Ben and Dale, and power walked as discreetly as he could *away* from the conversation.

"We'll go check on Raymond. Take your time talking with Samuel, Ronny," my uncle said, placing a reassuring hand on my shoulder.

"Wait. Does that mean no experiments?" Alan asked.

"Get over here, numbnuts!" Ben practically hoisted Alan like a sack of potatoes. "Come experiment with some of the other wildlife."

Stuck with indecision, I eventually made my way over to Samuel. He was resting his hands on one of the fences he'd made, looking into a half-dozen tomato plants. Instead of the bright red I'd seen on the other plants, these were a dark shade of maroon. They didn't look unhealthy, in fact the vines looked about as thick as my thumb, but they definitely didn't look like normal tomatoes.

"It took me almost a week to get these fences up," he said.

"They look good," I replied quietly.

"Ha! You could have done this in a day. Maybe two back when your spikes were smaller."

"Doesn't mean it isn't impressive," I said.

"And you think making buildings come out of the ground or creating magical gear is any less impressive?"

"Well, when you put it like that…"

Samuel sighed heavily. "Ronan, we are in this together. You are always the first to remind us. I know you have been putting up an unbreakable front with the people of Wildwood, but you don't need to do that with us. We are your family."

For some reason that probably had to do entirely with what

Sam said, I felt an invisible pressure lift off my shoulders. It wasn't responsibility, because that was still firmly attached no matter how Sam and Dale sliced it, but maybe it was something equally as stifling.

"Suppose I deserve some of my own medicine from time to time," I admitted.

Of course, Samuel had to crack a smirk that reached up to his ears. "Good to know something can get through that rock head of yours."

"Har. Har." I gave the man a half-hug in thanks before pointing at the strange plants before me. Another dose of my own medicine: don't wallow. "These ones?"

"Yep. They haven't changed much after getting like this regardless of how much more mana I use. They fruit, then regrow it, but that's about it. Taste delicious, but nothing more to it."

"You mean you have been eating your experiments?" I asked, eyes widening.

"They are just tomatoes. What's the worst that can happen?"

"You've done it now. Yessiry. We are in for some bullcrap today."

"We both knew that. I have to go deal with Raymond later," Sam said deadpan. That solicited a single chuckle before getting back to business.

"Did you want to give it a crack or did you want me to give it a crack?" I asked, pointing to my cargo pants which were stuffed with infusions.

"I think I'd rather you give it a shot first. I don't have any practice with infusions at all, and I know you at least know how to aim it."

"Big vote of confidence there, friend," I said, but pulled out a Q0 fire infusion nonetheless.

Sam pointed out one of the plants, the one on the closest corner, and I cast <Infusion>. The thread of Pith unspooled and I nabbed it between two invisible fingers with practiced ease. My minute control wasn't astounding yet, but at least I knew the basics of manipulating the thread.

"Fruit, stem, or roots?" I asked, splitting my concentration to ask Sam.

"Might as well try the roots. We can work up from there, if anything," the blond said over my shoulder.

Unsure of what to do, I flicked the red thread in the direction of the tomato plant's base. There was a muted sizzle as it pierced the moist earth and disappeared…somewhere.

"That didn't do much of anything. Is it supposed to do that?" Sam asked, running his hands over the leaves. The feelers on them poked at the leaves but the frown didn't leave his face.

"Well, I've found that each quotient is composed of three of the previous ones. Let me try to throw two more of these and see if it reacts." As soon as Sam had stepped back, I withdrew two identical infusions and flicked them back to back into the plant.

As the third disappeared into the soil, the stem of the plant jerked. Glowing red accents rushed up the stalk, spreading and burning it from the inside. Both Sam and I were speechless as the glow flowed into the leaves and fruit. The tomatoes changed from their maroon back to a bright red highlighted by black edges. The leaves on the plant almost doubled in size and changed color as if they were trees in the fall. With a puff of heat, the last of the thread vanished and information manifested in front of our eyes.

<Cultivated Tomato Sapling>

<Attunement: Fire>

<Refinement: N/A>

<Perceived Metier Quotient: 1>

"Holy… It worked!" Sam said, lifting his arms up in the air and hooting. He grabbed me by the shoulders and shook me with a wide smile on his face. "Ron, we just caused that plant to become attuned! That's what I was so close to."

It was something, to be sure. The first thing that came to mind was if the plant could reproduce and if the offspring would be subject to a life-attuned's passive growing skill. That would let us have a steady stream of infusions without having to fight hordes of creatures.

Before I could stop him, Samuel plucked one of the tomatoes off the plant. The veg in question did *not* like that. A small gout of boiling liquid spat out of the space where the tomato had been. It wasn't particularly strong, but it steamed up where it landed on the ground. The temperature was more than implied, especially considering the attunement.

"Please tell me you aren't going to— Too late." Samuel already had a large mouth of attuned tomato. The juice that ran down his chin steamed gently and soon he was panting with his mouth open to try to cool down the bite.

"Ih hath. An hath. Spazzy," he mumbled with his mouth wide open.

Instead of dignifying that with an answer, I waited for him to finish dealing with his eating situation. Other than the minor discomfort, he didn't appear to be actively dying or anything of the like.

As soon as he finished the bite, a gentle red glow highlighted his head and neck.

"That's definitely new…" I said.

"My affliction status just updated and it now shows Boon of Fire. Not sure what that's about," Sam said when his eyes refocused on me.

"Can you try to concentrate on the words? Maybe Bec can tell us more that way."

Samuel's eyes lost focus again and when he jumped slightly, I knew he'd found something.

"It says, 'Temporarily align your attunement with Fire.' It has a countdown too. Ten seconds left."

"Try to take another bite," I said, already lifting his hand to his mouth for him.

"Hey! What was all that worrying about me tasting the magic fruit?"

"That was before you didn't blow up from eating your experiment."

"*Experiment!?*" Both of us stopped in our tracks as Alan tore through the fields with agility that belied his age. He wasn't out of shape by any means, but that was the most grace he'd ever shown while moving.

"My, Samuel, why do you appear to glow? Also, why do I feel an uninhibited connection to you?" he asked as he scanned the blond from head to toe.

"Uh, Alan, what do you mean?"

"Can you not feel it?" Alan snapped to look at me. At some point, he'd materialized his note tablet.

"No? I can see the glow, but he just feels like standard Samuel," I said, almost defensively. While the man had always been eccentric, his behavior had taken on an extreme edge that I didn't know how to deal with. Not that I dealt with him much better below in the Bunker, but at least I knew what to expect.

"Yes, of course. Working hypothesis correlates to the elemental nature of Metier energy frequency." He sat cross-legged on the ground while he kept typing. "Please outline the parameters of your experimentation efforts, children."

Sam and I stared a lot but eventually I repeated what we'd just done.

"Fascinating. A direct genetic evolution triggered by your increased energy state contributions. Since you provided an energy with the wavelength of fire, then it wouldn't be surprising that the flora retained that element."

"Hey, I think I kind of got that," Sam said while snapping his fingers.

"Please. Elaborate for me," I said.

"The fire infusions gave it fire energy, so when it attuned, it turned into a fire tomato instead of... something else."

"Wouldn't that have been easier to say?" I asked Alan. When he didn't reply and continued to type away, I turned to Samuel. "What's the plan then?"

"Let's attune some more plants! But first, try to attune a

regular plant. I want to know if the effort I was putting into the other ones matters at all," he said. The blond pointed to another row with regular magic-grown tomatoes.

Casting <Infusion> told us that, yes, Samuel had made a difference. The moment the thread of Pith got even close to the plants, they started to wilt and dry out. When I flicked the thread into the roots, the whole thing just caught fire like a gasoline-drowned bush. Samuel and I had to fight off some of the flames that tried to ignite the adjacent plants.

"Okay. Good to know I haven't been wasting my time," Sam said, brushing some ash off his pants. "Do you mind if I try to infuse one of the plants?"

I handed him three of the Q0 fire infusions after a brief discussion. Just like I was hesitant to start mixing up infusions, so was Samuel. He of course added that he was doubly hesitant, as it was his first time using a miscellaneous skill. Recalling the coaching from Bec, I helped Sam get his mind in order, then repeat the process of infusing the plant.

His... flick aim had something to be desired. Instead of the much larger and easier target, his first infusion struck a cluster of leaves on the plant instead of the roots. The leaves in question were turned to ash almost instantly, but the glow still flowed into the base of the plant once it struck the ground. A grimace and two more infusions later, we had another Q1 plant.

"Huh. I wonder why it isn't pushing for a higher quotient?" I asked out loud.

"What do you mean?" Sam asked.

"Well, remember I told you that each quotient is a cumulative mass of three of the previous ones. Three Q0s gives a Q1. When I've crafted Q2 items, it's always taken more before 'changing.' These are stopping at a Q1 baseline."

"It could be surmised that the strength of the materials plays an effect on how high the quotient can be," Alan added, setting his tablet down and joining the conversation. "I've been studying your materials, as well as the items you've created, Ronan. None exceed the level of the materials used. The things you've crafted from 'mundane' materials also have not gotten higher than quotient level one."

Thinking back, Alan was right. The gardening shovel and my own pickaxe weapon were originally regular tools created from non-attuned materials and they'd both only gotten to Q1. The armor I'd been able to craft hadn't used anything higher than Q1 materials and none of it was higher than Q1. The Nutcracker and Daniela's fang daggers both had Q3 components, yet they had stalled out at Q2. There definitely seemed to be some kind of limiting factor in the use of infusions.

"Do you think if you were to start using a higher quotient infusion right from the get-go could you supersede that?" Sam asked.

Alan's eyes were practically twinkling with excitement. "Indeed, it might be possible. I am still familiarizing myself with the 'infusion' process, but perhaps our local expert has an opinion?"

Both men turned to look at me. All I could do was lift my hands up in a shrug. "I've no idea. This is way outside my ballpark. Way outside my sport even, because these plants are still alive."

"What do you think would happen if we overcharge them with an infusion? Alive or not?" Sam said, insisting.

"Well, nothing good, I would guess. You saw what happened when we used a Q0 on a regular tomato. It's sort of what happened to that plastic tray that exploded in my face when I first infused something."

"Could we use the life-attuned infusions?" Sam said, eyes glinting. Alan was practically giving me puppy dog eyes from next to the blond.

"Why are you two pushing? I just said nothing good can come out of this."

"This is the whole point of experimenting, Ronan. Discovery requires risk! You yourself started infusing before you really knew what you were doing. Would you be as far along as you are had you not taken those steps?" Alan stepped around

Sam and grabbed my hands in his. For an older, lower-level man, it hurt. The fire in his eyes caught me off guard. That was because there was *literal fire* in them. Somewhere deep in his pupils was a white flame that flickered. The shock factor was enough to get me to agree.

With some lingering hesitance, I pulled out the Q3 life infusion. I wasn't sure why I'd been holding on to it so much. I'd even left it front and center on my workstation. Maybe it was a reminder that the world was still doing its damnedest to stomp us out. Using the creature's Pith felt a bit cathartic, in all honesty.

My two companions took a step back as I sighted one of the corner plants. It looked no different from the other ones, so I hoped it would be as controlled an experiment as possible. Almost subconsciously, I braced myself for the inevitable explosion. *Should have brought my shield…*

Using <Infusion> on the higher level felt like wrangling an angry fish down in the hydroponics farm. They were *not* happy to get turned into food when their time came. As if the Pith had a mind of its own, it bucked and slid out of my grip. With an exertion of will, and a not-insignificant dip in my mana pool, I managed to get the golden thread of Pith under control. Instead of flicking it like usual and risking it going back out of control, I slowly pushed it into the soil at the base of the plant.

Just as my mana dipped to the forty percent mark with the completion, everything went to hell. Not in an explosion, per se. More like explosive *growth*.

Thick vines unspooled up the stem of the plant while leaves whirled like they had turned into a weedwhacker. The tomatoes all dropped with gentle splats, some getting sliced up by the whirling leaves of the plant. The trellis in the middle snapped as the plant flexed its entire body like a spine. Things got really serious when the roots rose out of the ground and started wiggling like tentacled legs on a starfish.

The System really put it in perspective for us.

<Cultivated Tomato Golem>

<Attunement: Life>

<Refinement: Regeneration>

<Perceived Metier Quotient: 3>

"I told you so!" was all I managed before one of the vines smacked me ten feet back into a row of cabbage.

CHAPTER EIGHTEEN

Farming Foes and Working Woes

Thankfully, the earth was plowed and the cabbages crunchy, because I might have broken something from the impact. As it stood, I shook the dirt out of my hair and looked for the offending vegetable monster.

Alan and Samuel had also been smacked away, but both were recovering much slower than I had. Since it looked like they *were* recovering, I zeroed in on the monster. There was no distinct *face* for me to punch, so I figured doing damage to the stem would be my best bet. I fiddled around with my belt and pulled out my work knife. It was three inches of pure utility, and totally not what you would want to use against a plant that was slowly getting taller than me, but it would have to do.

I charged the tomato golem. Apparently my scream caught the attention of whatever it used for senses, because vines and roots-turned-legs sped in my direction. Thankfully, I still had more bulk than the plant, so my charge overcame its own. My knife cut several of the leafy clusters whipping around it before it got enough leverage to buck me off like a horse. I staggered to my feet only to get slapped across the face three times by passing vines. The force of the impact hurt, but it finally kicked my brain into gear enough to remind me that I had magic. Not a whole lot of mana, but a little knife wasn't my only tool.

"<Earth Shell>," I mumbled, spitting a glob of blood as I blocked a hit from the golem. The rock encasing me, combined with my Limestone Skin, muffled the impact enough that I was able to use my left arm as a makeshift shield.

"Duck, Ron!" Sam yelled. Without questioning my friend, I hit the deck in time to avoid his <Vine Whip> crashing into the golem. It wasn't his fully empowered one, but it was enough to nearly cleave the whole top of the plant off. The broken portion hung there for a moment and the two of us tensed as we waited for a second.

"It's still alive! It's concentrating energy!" Alan shouted from somewhere behind us. A rat-tat-tat marked where the man fired his pistol into the golem. Most of the shots went wide, but some punched holes in the stem.

Before I got a chance to impale the overgrown salad, a pulse of golden light emanated from its body. My body felt very sleepy and I nearly dropped to the ground when a surge of adrenaline jerked me awake.

"It used some kind of skill," Sam said, retracting his hand and pulling me back. "When I saw you sway, I knew something was wrong."

"It's... making... more!" Alan yawned before dropping right into the dirt.

Sure enough, while the stem was still split, the top of the plant was reaching branches into the ground. Now that Alan had pointed it out, my perception screamed a warning as the golem wrapped vines around the two fire-attuned saplings we'd already made. The two plants shivered before their tomatoes exploded in a cloud of steaming juice. The tomatoes grew right back, except now they were cupped by the golem like hand grenades.

"<Stone Spike>, <Stone Spike>!" I raised two half-powered spikes in front of me and dragged Samuel into cover. I pressed my back into the gap between the tips to protect Sam.

The two vegetarian grenades exploded on impact, and I hissed as boiling tomato juice splashed onto the back of my head. My Health flashed a warning as it crossed sixty percent. "How is it doing that!?"

"I don't know, but I might be able to squash them if you can cover me long enough," Sam said, his feelers flexing out of his hands as he ran them through the soil under us.

"You have one minute!" I said, rounding the spikes and heading toward the golem. Even from where I stood, patches of regenerated plant fibers were crawling all over the golem. I was sure that if the creature had a mouth and eyes, it would have hissed at me and glared for all it was worth. Instead, it lobbed more tomatoes at me and I was forced to dodge. *You better hurry your ass up, Sam!*

I used about ten percent of my remaining mana to create an <Earth Shell> along my right shoulder and bicep. The makeshift pauldron slowed me down slightly, but it let me deflect one of the tomatoes that the golem threw my way. When it switched from tossing larger tomatoes with big splash zones to smaller ones but in clusters, I knew I was going to be in trouble. The smelly substance clung to me, and the acrid liquid stung my eyes and nose. Somewhere in the back of my mind, I remembered that tomatoes were acidic, but that was washed away by the burning pain of the juice. It was soaked in my clothes, causing the heat to linger instead of evaporating.

When a large, juicy tomato, hidden amidst smaller ones, splashed against my unprotected shoulder, I dropped to the ground with a scream. I struggled to rip off the shirt I had on, not for lack of strength, but because I was severely disoriented.

A wobbly Alan shaded me as he helped me out of my clothes. Dirt and muck clung to me, my shell having disintegrated into sand at some point during my agony. Or maybe the mad scrambling to get the shirt off.

"Calm down, Ronan. Samuel's got it covered," the researcher said.

When the heat and pain abated, I watched an awesome display of nature versus nature from Samuel.

One giant vine crashed down onto the rightmost sapling. The grasping vines of the golem got utterly pureed along with the smaller attuned plant as the torso-thick <Vine Whip> landed. Samuel jerked his hands in a downward chop. The whip responded, curling back like an octopus before cutting a diagonal opening down the middle of the Q3 creature before pancaking the other sapling.

Samuel swayed, but kept his feet. With unsteady steps, he brandished his own utility knife and made sure the sentient plants were dead. A gentle gold glow flowed over him as the three plant-turned-artilleries dissociated into mulch. A surge of Pith circumvented the blond and splashed into Alan and I.

"That's all of them!" Sam called out.

Alan helped me to my feet, but each motion ached. I could see welt marks all up and down my arms and chest where the burns were swelling up. While my Limestone Skin had made me tougher, apparently it didn't make me as fireproof as I would have liked. Having confirmed the creatures were dead, Sam rushed over to me and slapped a heal on my chest.

The cool relief flowed through me and my legs nearly buckled. Thankfully, Sam and Alan had a good grip on me. When I eventually was able to gather my thoughts, I gestured over to the pile of mulch now feeding the other mundane tomato plants. "Drops?"

Samuel shook his head. "Not sure why, but all I got was Pith from them. No infusion and no materials. Other than the fertilized soil stuff, of course."

"Ah, it appears that one of my hypotheses might be proven quickly," Alan said, almost dropping me so he could retrieve his tablet. The screen of the slick piece of hardware was thoroughly smashed. The scientist looked at it for a second, sighed, and put it away to pull out a notepad from who knew where. "Based on the length of survival of the plant, it wasn't able to garner enough energy to consolidate its form. That is to say, the only energy it had to give was the energy that the infusion provided. If what you've explained of the dissociation process is true, then there was no passive Pith to concentrate into an infusion *or* a material 'drop.'"

The man actually threw in some air quotes there at the end before writing furiously away in his notepad. When he didn't say anything, Sam and I turned to look around at his farm. The prognosis was less than optimistic. There was a diagonal row plowed part way down the cabbages. A whole swath of leafy greens I recognized as rainbow chard was withered and wrinkled from where the tomato explosives had rained down on them. Not to mention the mess of upturned earth all around Sam's dense-grown tomatoes. Bits and pieces of fencing and plant matter sprayed out for at least twenty feet.

"I'm going to say it again. *I told you so*. As such, have fun cleaning this up. I'm gonna take a nap!" I snapped.

The blond stood still with his head hanging as I spotted Ben and Dale rushing down the slope. The two stopped when they saw my topless, burned, and matted self.

"Are you alright?" my uncle asked, gently lifting my arms over my head and examining the mess that I was after the golem fight.

"Doing okay, but I need a shower and a nap. Can you help Sam before he can get too caught up in his own head?"

"Is he injured?" Ben asked with a frown, already moving to walk past me.

"Just his pride, I think, since we all came out alright," I called after him. My uncle leveraged me with a look that said 'tell me what happened?' "What? I didn't do anything!"

"I told you to make up with each other, not to blow up the farm!" Without giving me time to rebut the comment, he also strode past me.

Wasting energy on arguing with my uncle was not a pastime I enjoyed, so I headed up the hill to the Bunker. Those sleeping bags and a change of clothes were calling my name. The rest of the stuff I planned to craft could wait an hour or five.

— + —

"Goddamn!" I yelled, covering my face from the slurry pelting me. The <Earth Shell> on my forearm covered me from what my H-shield missed. The heat emanating from my shield due to the impact was minor, but it was enough to help along the evaporation process of the ice that clung to me. "Note to self. Set up defensive cover for the next infusing session."

Dangers of infusion aside, the item laid there perfectly still amid a corona of half-melted ice. The final piece of the infusion spree I'd done after fighting the golem. Hanging from wooden racks along the shared wall of my work room were three armor pieces and six and a half weapons. The last weapon didn't seem to do anything, other than provide the boost to my strength, no matter how much I tried.

Pushing those thoughts out of mind, I focused on the weapon I'd just created. Its information bloomed as I gripped the cold handle.

<Quotient 1 Spider Shortsword >
<Attribute: Mobility>
<Trait: Frost Step>

I'd used one of the farmed up water infusions to create it and its twin sword, which was already up on the makeshift rack I'd made. The weapons released flurries with each movement made while feeding it mana. There was a big regret in my heart that I hadn't worked on them *first* instead of last. The cooling they would have provided while I tinkered with fire-attuned infusions and materials would have been worth the delay in regenerating my mana pool.

Setting the weapon down, I ran my eyes over the rest of the weapons of monster destruction I'd created. A pair of hatchets made from the fire ant mandibles and Tendril radii infused with fire. One knuckle duster made from the earth-attuned ambusher infused with its own looted infusion.

<Quotient 2 Mandible Hatchets>

\<Attribute: Strength\>
\<Trait: Scorch Touch\>

\<Quotient 2 Jawbone Duster\>
\<Attribute: Strength\>
\<Trait: Ground Snap\>

Those three weapons were on par with the daggers I'd created for Daniela. Unlike hers, which put out oppressive heat that made you want to start chugging water, the hatchets lit with a dark fire. Each strike instantly grilled the section of wood I'd tested them on. It didn't help the poor plank that the mandibles had slight ridges where the ants had used them to grip things. In their new life as weapons, it had given the hatchets some pretty intimidatingly serrated edges.

The jawbone knuckle duster was the result of my collaboration with Samuel. After the little golem incident, he'd been somewhat eager to help. When the farm was restored, he joined me to test out how we could possibly make flexible and workable joints into weapons and armor. We used the life-attuned's\<Vine Whip\> to create some makeshift cordage. Unlike the slapped together one he'd used for the carry satchels and the rigging for the pull board Raymond used, he focused on making it thin but *dense*. The result was a pinky-thin strand of deep moss-green vine. After having worked on the attunement-prepped tomato plants, he actually had a fairly easy time with the exercise. With that major success, we had a means to connect things and still move somewhat!

The vine cordage wrapped around the joints where the jawbone would have connected to a skull. When I infused it, the cordage thinned even more, but became stiff as the jaw shrunk and molded around the binding. It was a tad macabre, since the *knuckle* part of the weapon could clearly be identified as the teeth of the once-human. Nonetheless, it was an impressive weapon that produced shockwaves any time it struck something while fueled with mana.

Next to that smorgasbord of weapons were the three sets of armor I'd made. More or less dwarfing the third set were two of what I named tanker armors.

<Quotient 1 Tanker Armor (Chestplate)>
<Attribute: Strength>
<Trait: Force Dispersal>

Considering the fact both had the same trait as my own shield, as well as Sam and Danny's armors, I was fairly sure the trait had something to do with the fact I'd infused the plates prior to infusing the whole item.

The front and back were composed of those pre-infused Q2 plates I'd gotten from the larger ants. To serve as the shoulder guards and help tie the pieces together were several of the smaller Q0 chitin plates. Each of those I had to meticulously drill using a fire infusion, very nearly wiping out my stock of low level ones. Thanks to the vine cordage, I was able to tie the whole thing together. Unlike with the jawbone duster, the vines weren't covered in the chitin but instead secured in place. My knots weren't the world's best, but the magic of the infusion had smoothed them out. Changing the structure of the vine itself to 'fit' the fact that it was armor. I half-hoped that it would make a buckle on its own, so that it would make adjusting it to the wearer much easier. While the changes to the actual armor were minor, it was the most subtle change that had the most impact. And from the element I least expected not to damage some vines! That all went to show how little I knew about the specifics of infusion crafting.

The last piece of armor was the segmented cowl. It more or less looked like a cowl, except it was made of Q0 plates for a V-shapes front and back. The 'hood' portion of the cowl was made from the few Q1 chitin plates we'd been able to acquire during our fight with the Blaze Ant.

<Quotient 1 Segmented Cowl>
<Attribute: Strength>
<Trait: Haze Cloak>

It wasn't the strongest when compared to the other two

thicker, larger armors but it provided more protection than our bulletproof vests. Tested and guaranteed. Ben grumbled in frustration that the thin armor was actually stronger than pre-Fall tech. From what I'd seen of the surface, it didn't surprise me. Everything post-Fall had a mind to kill you and eat you for jujubes.

And with the few defensive pieces I was able to line up, I arrived at the last set of my creations.

Resting against the corner with almost casual abandon were the strongest weapons I'd made during my frenetic crafting. At least, in theory.

<Quotient 3 Stinger Staff >
<Attribute: Strength>
<Trait: Singe Amplitude>

<Quotient 3 Spider Naginata>
<Attribute: Mobility>
<Trait: Gloss Binding>

The weapons made from the banana spider that had attacked me and from the blaze ant didn't seem to work quite right. Despite non-stop striking and channeling of mana, their effects didn't trigger. The actual weapons provided notable bumps to strength and mobility, thanks to their +0.3 to each attribute, but their traits didn't activate as far as any of us could see.

The staff was meant to be a spear with the stinger set at the very top, but apparently Bec, in his silent observation, did not agree with that assessment. The crystal also hadn't provided any more feedback or comments throughout the week I was working. Instead, we just watched as the wooden rod I'd used for the spear was scorched and hardened. The wood around where I'd set the stinger enclosed it like a tree growing around an intrusive piece of human construction, leaving a tiny tip of the stinger visible and a notable, uneven bulge at the top of the staff.

As for the naginata, its own length of wood and vine cordage took on a shimmery gleam as it wrapped around the spider leg material. Other than that slight change, *and the heart attack it almost gave me shaking like a living earthquake on my workstation*, it appeared fairly standard. Other than the fact the blade was yellow, of course.

I had the owners for all these weapons and armor already in mind. It might seem a bit of favoritism, but they could use the upgrade. Unless Rommel had figured out some good weapons... Regardless of their progress, there would be no chance of there being enough materials and infusions to equip everyone. Our slow climb would have to continue and when the situation in Wildwood stabilized, so would our passing of the information. It was clearer than ever to me after the spider dungeon that we could not hope to retake the Earth alone. It takes a community, as they say.

Except to me, I planned to get the world on the same page.

CHAPTER NINETEEN

Wading Back

"Are you sure you kids are ready to go back?" Ava asked, frowning at the crate we were carrying.

The amount of junk we had stuffed in there, mostly some supplies for us, as well as most of the weapons and the armors, added a significant amount of weight. Thanks to Sam's and my own increased attributes, it wasn't hard to carry at all.

"I'll keep them on their toes, Mama," Daniela said. The brunette made a point of it to flick a little fire cinder at our feet, causing me and Sam to jump before we glared at her. She didn't even try to hide the snickering.

"I know you three are ready, but are you sure you don't want us to come with you?" Ben asked, getting an emphatic nod from over his shoulder by Dale. He'd already given us all a parting hug, but I knew there might well be another one in the chamber.

"Why are you all so obstinate about us not interacting with them? And don't you try to make the argument that we have plenty to do here." I lowered my hand at his read of my rebuttal. "Of course we will always have something to do. There is a time and a place for everything. Also, do you think we don't want to *see* more people? Or, alternatively, kick said people in the rear for messing with forces they couldn't hope to understand while threatening our children?"

There was a surprising amount of heat in my uncle's words, but when Ben, Ava, and even Alan nodded along with his words, I knew we were outnumbered in trying to come up with excuses.

"Alright."

"You can't tell us— Wait, what?" Dale did a double-take. "Did you just agree?"

"I think it would be reasonable. But, not now. When I have time to finish with the wall around the Bunker entrance, or we deal with whatever is going on inside Wildwood. Please. You all can handle yourselves, but you can't even use the weapons or armor that I make. The things out there are *higher level* than the things that have attacked the camp." *Appeal to their logic, while giving them a light at the end of the tunnel. You didn't raise someone incapable of reading the room, Dad.*

I almost missed what my uncle said as my mind internally relabeled him. It didn't upset me, not as much as it had when I'd first found out, but it was still a mental stutter I didn't know how to handle. So it went into the vault of deal-with-you-later-itis.

"How long will those things take?" Dale asked, crossing his arms, squinting at me.

"Do you think I want to keep you all trapped here? That we wouldn't rather have some support while we are out there? Are we not good enough?" *Tell them what they want to hear and then challenge them to rebut something they know they can't say no to.*

"Of course we don't!" Ava said, gesturing at the three of us. "And you three have done more than we could have ever asked of you."

"Then I ask that you listen to us again. Even with Sam's farm in order, there is a lot of work left to do. Any progress you are able to make towards setting up the outer wall will also help when we get back," I added. *Give them something to latch on to.*

"We won't keep insisting," my uncle said, squinting as strong as ever.

"Great, then we will be on our way. We are a few days over what we told the Wildwoodians we would be, but Dai returning was hopefully enough of a heads up to our change of plans."

Me and Sam started walking while Daniela, naginata resting on her shoulder, walked at the front with Anthony and Blobby. I'd almost forgotten about the slime dude simply because when he was around, he tended to be camouflaged and otherwise he was off gallivanting somewhere. Nonetheless, based on what I'd seen the gelatinous mass eat, I knew it was working in our favor.

Just when we'd gotten out of range, my uncle jogged to catch up. He whispered into my ear, "I know what you were doing, Ronny. Don't think you can use your mediation tricks when I'm around. However, I know you are coming from a good place. Stay safe, you hear me? Those of us here in the Bunker got extremely lucky, but not all humans are good. As a matter of fact, they aren't bad either. But humans tend to be notoriously *selfish*. Don't look for bad people, look for those whose selfishness doesn't reach beyond them."

With that cryptic message, my uncle gave me a half-hug before heading back to the line where the other pre-Fall humans stood. They were an odd sight indeed, but I knew they would be alright. Bec was watching over them, and I wouldn't want to mess with the ol' people squad.

— + —

"We've got to be missing something. Why is there always some kind of patrol here?" Danny asked as she returned to us.

The speedy brunette had gone ahead, scouting US 301, when we reached the intersection. Anthony followed after her while Blobby wiggled around us in a wide circle. I'd never seen it do that before, but it looked like it was trying to guard us. When it caught me looking at it, however it was that it sensed things, it waved a little jiggly appendage without stopping its rolling motion. It was while totally distracted by our inhuman companion that Daniela reached out to us on the comm-plant.

"Got two slimes, another hound, and what looks like an earth Tendril," she said. "They are right where we need to turn."

"Do you think we could cut through the woods using the map?" Sam asked, already spaced out while looking at the LPS.

"Possible, but the road offers us the fastest path. Plus, who's to say the woods aren't territory of some other critters? The spiders were already bolder than before." She practically growled that bit. Some had almost gotten in naginata range and paid for it. If I had to guess though, maybe the weapon made from one of their own kin gave even instinctual animals some pause.

"Can we take them?" I asked, already strapping my shield on my offhand.

"I wouldn't have brought it up if I didn't think we could. The hound is the only one I was able to identify without getting spotted, and it was a Q2, but the other two didn't give me that danger feeling that stuff above Q3 gives me."

"So that's not just me?" I asked, getting nods from both my friends. "Good to know I wasn't going crazy or imagining things."

"But how are we going to deal with the slimes? They don't seem to be all that affected by attacks," Sam asked, poking our own gelatinous companion.

"Not precisely true. Blobby loses mass when it attacks, as well as when it takes damage. Though I will say direct magical attacks seem to do the trick better. i.e. You are our slimer, Danny. Well, you and Anthony, since he has that flamethrower breath."

"Sounds good to me. One was a lime green one like Blobby, while the other was a gray one. My guess is air or death, but betting on air."

"Alright. Danny and Anthony with the slimes, me and Sam will deal with the hound and the Tendril. And Blobby..." I turned to look at the slime. It raised an appendage as if curious what my instructions were. "Just do what you usually do, yeah?"

The slime jiggled in excitement and took off in the direction Danny had come from. My first instinct was to call out after it and stop it, but I knew that the haphazard creature was actually quite proficient at stealth.

We carried the crate a bit further north before stashing it at the treeline. With our goods secured, we snuck forward slowly until we spotted the patrol strolling down the road without a care in the world. They were picking through the rubble of the buildings lining the road. The slimes rolled in and amidst the rock and metal debris while the hound sniffed at the edges of the building. The humanoid Tendril was the only one keeping a watchful eye while its three non-human companions looked for... whatever they were looking for.

Daniela and Anthony split off from us as Sam and I got ready to hit the Tendril. I gave the life-attuned a countdown with my fingers before releasing two half-powered <Stone Spikes>towards the Tendril. One punched through its back where its kidney should have been while the creature was able to *catch* the one that came at it from the front.

The stone of the second spike crumbled under its fingers and the Tendril immediately zeroed in on me. Its featureless face still sent a shiver down my spine, but I was ready to make its life even more miserable. Except that Sam took that opportunity to smack the ex-human.

Like a soggy piece of paper, the Tendril fell in two parts when my spike held its lower body in place and Sam's <Vine Whip> removed the torso. The sight caused me to gag, since the insides of the Tendril became the outsides. Fortunately, the hound decided it was time to attack.

The distraction and the ensuing concentration on an <Earthen Barrier> refocused my thoughts. The hound only partially anticipated the ground rising up. Instead of crashing straight into the two foot wall, only its back legs scraped against it as it jumped it like a hurdle. Sam did not let that opportunity go to waste. Thin vines rose up from the ground to catch the hound by the middle. Without giving it a chance to unleash one of its attacks or anything of the sort, I brought my pickaxe down on its head with a sick crunch.

The hound slumped as the vines fell away.

A flash of fire reminded us that Danny was still fighting, so we rushed over to the building. She didn't really need our help.

The brunette had the naginata haft deep in the earth slime Tendril while Anthony was harassing the air slime. Gouts of fire evaporated bits of the slime as the creature leapt great distances with ease. Surely something to do with its type of Attunement.

As we got closer, I noticed thin threads spun around the earth slime, holding its frenetic wiggling in place. The woman then channeled fire up her arms and down through the weapon to slowly evaporate the slime.

When our own slime joined in to assist Anthony, it was all over for the patrol. Like an overinflated bubble, Blobby rose up out of the ground and trapped the air slime within its body. The gray slime bounced around inside the Blobby bubble, causing it to distend, but it slowly closed in. Bits of Blobby blasted away as the other slime used some kind of air attack from within, but the bubble reshaped before it was able to escape. When the Metier Crystals within Blobby crashed down on the air slime, it became still.

The Blobby bubble shrunk and the usual lime green that Blobby was when he wasn't camouflaged had taken on slight gray swirls and the gelatinous mass was a little larger.

"Did you know it could do that...?" Danny asked, holding out a fist-sized Metier Crystal she'd retrieved from her slime. Considering there had been no Pith cloud, there was yet another oddity to add about the slime Tendrils.

"Nope. But I'll just say I am happy that he's on our side," I replied flatly.

"Let's get the loot and get out of here," Sam added, making a beeline for the hound. Danny made it a point to walk over to

Anthony to check him and Blobby over while leaving the last body to me.

I steeled my nerves as I walked to the sheared Tendril. Instead of quickly tapping it and turning away, I gave the body a hard look. It was a reality. At this point, it was almost undeniable that this had been a person and the manner in which we'd killed it was less than pleasant. However, whatever was twisting humans was to blame. Not me. Or at least that was what I told myself as its body crystallized and its Pith flowed into me and my friends.

— + —

An alarm rang through the farm. Unlike the worried looks and screams the first time we'd gone to the city, there was a cheer as we arrived on the western field of Wildwood. Many of the children waved from the fields, as well as the older members of the city that were still working.

With some effort, we made it up to the wall through the small mob. Waiting at the gate was Sarah and the rest of the Big Guns. Once again on the wall was Oliver, glaring down from his perch. I wouldn't be surprised if his own squad was lingering around us somewhere ready to cap us if we did something he didn't like.

"Took you a while!" Sarah said, clapping me on the shoulder before shaking my friends' hands. She even pulled Daniela in for a short hug.

"Was too busy making the stuff that will help Wildwood pierce the heavens!"

Sarah and the others gave me odd looks, and even my friends were groaning at my antics. "Just don't worry about it. The days we've been missing will be worth it. Do you have some time to meet or possibly meet with the New Hopers?"

Sarah was turning but Oliver called out in protest. "Don't you even think about it, Sarah Sage. You've already missed out three rotations that I've filled in. You can indulge the outsiders on your own time. That patrol passed through not too long ago."

"Oh, the one with two slimes, a dog, and a Tendril?" Daniela asked absently before she opened the crate between us. "That hound look something like this?"

The brunette had plucked the pelt out of the crate and was holding it out for all of us to see. All that *I* could see were the veins popping along Oliver's neck. However, for the sake of diplomacy and the improvements we hoped to make in Wildwood, making a boisterous display would be counterproductive.

"I think we can find our way to our accommodations if we are allowed in." I let the words hang in the air until Oliver was forced to give a short nod before doing anything but meeting my eyes by staring into the treeline.

"We'll find Ms. Strant!" one of the two orc youths we'd met the first time called out, jumping to the front of the crowd.

"Well, that would be really appreciated," I said with a nod to them, their older relative, and the rest of the crowd.

We explained to the Big Guns that we had some stuff for them and to meet us when they had a chance. The twin dwarves complained about not being able to go while Tim and Sarah nodded before turning back to their task. I did notice a slight spring in their step. One could only hope it was thanks to our return, but what did that mean about the state they'd been in that three more bodies made such a huge difference?

CHAPTER TWENTY

Wild Toys

"A long time," said a voice from the edge of one of the houses.

Most people in the town waved at us, their excitement easily betrayed, but didn't approach us as we strode with purpose towards our assigned home. The latest Wildwoodian was an exception.

"We had to work on some stuff," I said, spotting Dai leaning against the shadow of the building.

"Fruitful work, I would hope," he said, striding out of the shadows and starting to walk beside us. The large lizardman pointed to the crate and to the naginata held across Danny's back by some of Sam's vine cordage.

"You could say that," I replied with a chuckle.

"Were you able to find anything?" Sam asked nervously.

"Not right now. I will come find you later." The man gave the crate one more look before splitting off from us with a nod.

"What's up with Mr. Moody and Broody over here?" Daniela asked.

"Few things, but likely he wanted to keep our connection a secret for now. He might have been able to sneak that past Councilman Kirby."

"Oh good. I don't really like any of them, but I like him the least."

"Unfortunately, I agree with you, Danny," I said.

We remained quiet for the rest of the walk back. While the people in the town seemed much more upbeat about our presence, I didn't miss the barricaded windows and the many torches that had been set up outside inhabited residences. If an attack came, especially one from within, they wouldn't do much. However, it was the preparation and the mindset that would save the people of Wildwood more than whatever defenses they put in place for a vague threat.

Before long, we were back in our abandoned house. For some reason, it looked much better taken care of then when we'd left. There was a pair of tables in the dining area and there were three platters of food already set up. The answer became obvious not too long after.

"Clara wanted to make sure you got a good impression upon your return," Devon said from where he was lounging and cleaning his nails. He didn't bother to look our way, but I expected no less from the man. "Had me go ahead and deliver this stuff. The others will be coming in a little while."

"Did you eat?" Sam asked, setting down the crate and producing one of his special tomatoes. Knowing the man's penchant for sleight of hand, he just lobbed the tomato without warning. A gentle gust of wind slowed the tomato before Devon plucked it out of the air.

"Did you bake this or something? Why is it so hot?"

Daniela snickered. "Give it a try, pointy ears. Might put some hair on your chest."

Unsurprisingly, he bit into the attuned tomato with a cocky expression. Only to immediately regret it.

Devon was still working his way through his cough when Rommel strode into the room followed by the rest of the New Hopers. Clara took up the rear. She raised one impressively maintained eyebrow up at her squadmate's behavior.

"What happened to him?" she asked.

"Learned a lesson," Danny said, patting the man on the back to 'help' clear his throat.

The New Hopers shared a look, but didn't ask anything else. "I hope you've reconsidered your stance on cooperating with us."

"No, I haven't," I replied. Clara's face fell, but I wasn't done. "My original stance was to work with *you* all. My current thinking is that I might not be able to work with the current leaders of Wildwood."

"They really do mean well, they are just…"

"Numbnuts? Obstinate? Old farts?" Daniela provided.

"…Stuck in their ways," Clara finished.

"Hey, I get it. And if I didn't have bigger fish to fry, I wouldn't care as much, but we need seamless cooperation. I'm not trying to stand above anyone else, but I will take the lead if I have to. You all seem more than capable, and so does Sarah. Unfortunately, I haven't been able to spend as much time with the other squads, but you all do a fine job of keeping this town together.

"My problem is that something external has infiltrated Wildwood and is working against it from within. We need to root that out, and the only people I currently trust are the ones that I've fought side by side with. So in the interest of making said people stronger…"

With as much dramatic flair as I could, I snapped the lid of the crate back. Almost immediately, I watched the eyes of the New Hopers lose focus as they read the information of the items.

"I could barely get one of those spider legs infused…" I heard Rommel whisper. It sounded like a rumble coming from the large orc.

"It takes practice and a lot of close calls," I said with a laugh. "I can try to give you some pointers. After we deal with whatever is going on in this town, I plan to share this knowledge as much as possible. Not only is there so much more to discover, but there is absolutely no way I can outfit more people than I currently am."

"Are all of these for us?" Lilly said, lifting one of the hatchets from the crate.

"Actually, that one or its twin are for you. As for the others, some of them are for you and some are for the Big Guns. I didn't have enough time to really grasp your needs and skills, but I tried to give everyone some kind of upgrade."

"What about you three? You seem to be wearing the same stuff," Godfrey said, poking at one of the chest pieces.

"Well, we can manage for now. I've gotten used to my current gear and want to make some of the same, but better, once I have a chance and the materials," I said, gesturing at my H-shield and the pickaxe leaning against the wall.

"So we are your test subjects?" Devon asked once he was able to stop coughing.

"As much as Danny and Sam are, yes," I said, crossing my arms.

"Alright, well, what's our take of this booty?" Dennis asked, already holding the stinger staff close to his chest.

"Well, I wasn't sure who might want what, but the tanker armors are for Rommel and Sarah. The cowl is for Tim. No offense, Dennis, but I feel like a stiff breeze might knock our pink healer friend dead."

"I won't take offense if you let me have this thing. I don't even know what it does but I want it!"

"Well, if you can figure out what exactly it does, then you can have it."

"You don't know what these do?" Clara asked, stroking her chin as she looked at the staff in Dennis's hand.

"We didn't know what the naginata did until we took care of the patrol on the way here. It attaches binding strands to whatever enemy it hits. Not inanimate objects, we tested that already," Danny said, twirling the weapon in her hand. Where the spider blade scraped the wall of the house, a huge gash opened. "Oops."

"We don't have many of these left, please don't wreck them," Godfrey pleaded.

"Anyways. The distribution. The jawbone duster is for Devon. One of the hatchets for Lilly. It is entirely possible that Daniela won't be letting go of that naginata now. I don't know who would benefit the most from the hammer, maybe the twins?"

"They got that new hammer ability, didn't they?" Godfrey asked. "That and their indigestion is all they care about."

"True, but the hammer heals the user the more they swing it," I said, pointing out the trait we'd discovered. It was more that it felt like Samuel's <Health Bump>, which we then proceeded to test by nicking our fingers and healing it.

"This is almost too much," Lilly said, holding a hatchet and shortsword one in each hand, turning her head to look at each one.

"Well, I know some of you already have weapons. I could try to infuse those instead, and spread these out further."

"How long would that take?" Godfrey had somehow already materialized his shommer and was reaching out with it for me to take.

"Not long, but maybe tomorrow? I want to get these distributed and put on a... little display, so to speak."

"Oh, here we go," Danny groaned.

"I was wondering how long it would take him to come up with a funky plan," Sam added, nodding sagely as if he knew it was inevitable.

"I'm starting to sense a trend here," Rommel rumbled.

We all broke into laughter and discussed the weapons and their effects for a few hours until the Big Guns joined us. When they did, we'd gone full into magic equipment party time. Perfect for my plan.

— + —

"Everyone got a partner?" I asked to double check.

"I've got the twins," Danny called out, spinning the nagi-nata in hand.

"Yer gonna regret it, little lady," Karl said.

"I think *you* are gonna regret it, Carl," she snapped back.

"But *I'm* Carl," his sibling complained.

"Does it matter? You two are in for a beatdown," she said, turning to face the two squat but muscled dwarves. I could have sworn I saw a shiver and a look of uncertainty pass through them.

"Remember, this is just a show match. Try to get as good a feel for your training partner as you can and make use of your equipment," I said, trying to redirect Danny from her battle banter.

The thirteen of us spread out across the training space of the Wild Guard. We'd politely asked the younger trainees to step away and observe if they wanted, which they did with glee. One had even done what I hoped for and gone to fetch more people from the town.

"My eyes are up here, rock-for-brains," a seductive voice called out.

Clara squared up against me, stinger staff in hand. She'd somehow managed to pry the thing from Dennis during the equipment discussions and wanted to see if she could figure out what it did during battle.

"Everyone remember how to—"

"YES!" The Wild Guard and even my friends groaned.

"Geez, I was just trying to—"

"We know how to use the items, Ronan," Devon air-whispered from the other side of the field where he stood across from Dennis.

"Well, in that case... Fight!"

True pandemonium ensued. Even knowing all the different effects that everyone was capable of, adding the equipment into the mix complicated things by yet another layer. I was almost bonked on the head as I tried to keep track of the Daniela-blur streaking towards the twins. Fire trailed up her weapon as her <Heat Touch> seemed to be infused into the naginata.

My perception screamed at me and I hit the deck, focusing on my own fight. The staff whistled over my head. Fortunately, it was just a tad heavy for Clara and that put her off balance. Just as I was getting ready to tackle her, our eyes met and her <Fear> triggered. My breath caught in my throat and I got the sudden urge to dodge, even if there wasn't any attack to dodge. It took a frustrating amount of mental capital to resist the effects of her Gift.

"Boy, I'm glad I'm training against your abilities," I said, adjusting my grip on the spider shortsword. Even if I thought my pickaxe had more utility and strength, mixing it up was good. Plus, the Q2 mobility boost was just *fun*!

Like someone had poured lubricant in my joints, my channeled mana bumped up my attribute. Frost formed up my arms and in the air around me as I took my first step and arrived right in front of Clara. Only to get a mouth full of <Necrotic Cloud>.

I hurled as her own boosted attribute made itself known. *That's a broken rib.* The edge of my vision showed I was down twenty percent of my health and I had something called necrosis in the affliction spot. With every wave of gut roiling nausea that her affliction caused, I saw my health tick down. It wasn't enough to down me outright, and I was sure she knew that, but it made concentrating difficult.

"Remember the fifty percent mark!" the woman called out. I was already closer to the stop point than I wanted, but there was nothing to be done about that. I caught glimpses of Clara from behind her obscuring cloud. Another plus of her skill that I was sure she knew.

Man, I thought we were doing alright. Even with the basic defense training we got in the Bunker, the constant fighting on the surface, and even the benefits the implant gave to knowing how you were doing in the fight, the Wildwoodians had a hell of a lot of experience. *No more holding back.*

An <Earthen Barrier> lifted me up over the cloud and I let loose three half-power <Stone Spikes> when she came in sight. Bracing against the harsh dip in my mana pool, I came down onto Clara. The mobility boost let me easily outmaneuver her swings, but the strength behind the blows was enough to force me to dodge. When a small cloud started to bloom out of the demoness's hands, my perception screamed at me and I rolled out of the way.

The unexpected thing was what happened when her staff streaked through the cloud and ignited the wave with rippling red light, expanding its area of effect enough to reach me.

The necrosis affliction changed to burning decay, and I sagged to the ground as my nerve endings lit up with pain. Stabbing my sword into the ground, I managed to remain on a knee. My health flashed as it crossed the sixty percent mark and continued slowly down. Only marginally faster than necrosis, but oh so much worse.

"Heals!" Clara called.

By the time Samuel was able to extract himself from his own fight, scorched from Sarah's attacks, I was already on my feet. Not well by any stretch, but at least up. My body felt as if someone had ripped my skin off, baked it medium rare, then gave it back after letting it sit in the sun for a few days.

Pain notwithstanding, I thought I figured out what the staff did. I retrieved the weapon from Clara for a moment when the rest of the fights wrapped up. Everyone had been so caught up in their own matchups that they barely even registered my strangled cries. The thing I did next drew eyes from all around.

During the wait, my mana had regenerated almost to full. If I was right about the staff, why not go big? I placed myself in the middle of the training space and asked the Wild Guard to stand back. Inevitably, that caused the audience and trainee Wild Guard to lean *closer*. My mana flowed through me unimpeded as I activated the passive form of my magic. I held it for a few seconds, focusing on the magic as well as channeling into the staff to activate it.

Words materialized in the edge of my vision as I dumped half of my mana into my skill. A smirk cracked my face before the pain doubled me over.

<Stone Spike>

<Infusion Augmentation: Fire>

<Basaltic Lance>

The ground heaved in front of me as a divot was formed before a twelve foot tall, three foot wide spike of rock bloomed out of the ground. Veins of fire provided the whole thing a hellish glow as the material hardened into a pockmarked mess of gray-black stone. Basalt. Sam, Danny and Clara, who'd been standing nearby, gave me looks of concern while the crowd oohed and ahhed. The others in the Wild Guard ranged from stunned to ecstatic in their looks. The kids were talking loudly with each other, clamoring about summoning the 'mythical volcano' with their powers.

Using the staff to support me, I turned to my friends. Their flinch caught me off guard.

"You look just a tad sinister like that, Ron," Sam elaborated on seeing my expression.

"It's the volcano backdrop. Really suits the 'villain' look your beard scruff gives you," Danny added, instantly lightening the mood.

While I explained what I'd done and how Clara's burning decay affliction had changed on the fly, a commotion made its way through the crowd of onlookers.

"What is the meaning of this!?" The man's face was so red I was sure he had to be fire-attuned instead of the water I knew he was.

"Just a little demonstration. We wanted to show the other Wild Guard what investing time in infusing can generate. Plus, with the tension of the last few weeks, everyone benefited from a little stress relief," I said evenly. My stomach was aching more than usual after using the staff, and there was a burning aftereffect I wasn't used to from casting skills, but I did my best to present unbothered.

"You can't just walk on my field and do as you'd like!" Kirby hollered, spittle flying. Parting the crowd of onlookers, Oliver and another man I didn't recognize made their way to the front to stand on either side of Kirby.

"What's the problem, council dude? The veg people all, like, ran off into town. Someone said the Bunker Busters were back or something," the other man I didn't recognize said. He was one of the rainbow-colored fae, an emerald shade of green.

"What happens, Charles, is that this trio of vagrants are turning the teaching of our future guards into a stage show. A mockery of the work we do here!"

"I think it's time that we escort you out of town," Oliver said, a gun materializing in his hand. It was an old world weapon, but I didn't fancy myself bulletproof... yet. A vine coiled its way around the man's leg and a floating ball of flame hovered in the air above his head.

"*I* think you need to put that peashooter away before you bite off more than you can chew," Daniela growled. In the time it took Daniela to make her counterthreat, Samuel had wrapped the gun arm in a vine and snapped it to the ground.

The motion jerked the man to the ground, causing him to drop his gun. Thankfully, I'd been boring holes into Oliver, because he materialized another gun on his left hand and perfectly aimed it at Daniela. My shield interposed itself between them and I stepped forward. The staff still in my hand whacked Oliver in the head hard enough to put out his lights.

"We are done here. Kirby, we will do as we please. We are helping this town whether you like it or not. But if you throw your lapdogs at me one more time, they won't be getting just a concussion!" I flared the last of my mana to produce four half-powered <Stone Spikes> pointing outward from our group, forcing the Councilman to step back.

The man sputtered for words, but Charles interposed himself between us. "It's all mellow, fellow! I've got this, just have yourself a good evening, yah hear?"

The life-attuned pulled Kirby back as he whistled. Several

other people emerged from the crowd to gather up Oliver and help Charles pull the councilman away. I watched the whole exchange with a grimace, digging the staff into the ground with enough force to crack the consolidated stone I'd formed. Just as I was ready to sag from the coiled snake of pain in my abdomen, the youths took up a chant. The rest of the crowd quickly joined in.

"Bunker Busters! Bunker Busters!"

The words sent a surge of adrenaline through me I didn't know I had left in the tank. Goosebumps crawled, walked, then ran all over my body as I felt the cheer wash over me and my friends. When I looked at them, they were a bit uncertain of the new development. Clara was there to explain and warn us.

"Welcome to the ranks of the Guard. Nice squad name," she yelled into my ear, the chant still going strong.

"This is not what I intended!" I called back.

"Rarely do things go like we want them, Ronan. Accept it, and get ready for the shitstorm that will follow," Clara said. "Because Kirby is not one to let dogs lie."

CHAPTER TWENTY-ONE

The Missing

By the time the crowd dispersed enough for us to leave the training field, it was almost night. My mind was a whirl of new information, connections, and questions. I didn't even notice when we made it back to our borrowed living room.

"We need to split for night watch," Clara said. "But I'll have Devon do some loops around to keep you posted on anything going on."

"Why do I have to keep the pot-stirrers informed?" The elf huffed.

"Because I said so, and you nearly cooked Dennis with lightning during that training match."

"I did say I was sorry…" the elf grumbled, walking back outside. The other New Hopers bid their own farewells. Most looked a bit haggard, but they all had lingering smiles.

"We'll be heading out. We have the shift right after Clara's and y'all got me beat. Literally. I appreciate the new gizmo," Sarah thumped her fist on her new armor, releasing a small pulse of heat.

The two squad leaders lingered a bit as their groups filtered out, but they didn't stay long. Before we'd even settled into the meals that had been forgotten during lunch, a stiff mist drifted through the boarded up windows.

"Oh heck no. This is not going to be a working dinner, you workaholics," Danny said between mouthfuls, pointing her spork at me accusingly.

"Did not mean to interrupt your meal. My apologies," Dai said, practically gliding on his mist trail. The lizardman set his weird water barrel contraption down before plopping on the ground. I don't know how he didn't hurt his tail.

"Don't worry. If you hadn't joined us, she would have found something else to complain about," I said, half-turning at the table so as not to give the man my back.

"She's very good at that," Sam added. When the brunette leveled her gaze at him, he resumed eating dutifully.

While I still had some trouble with the lizardman's expressions, I was fairly sure he was smirking at our antics. After a moment, however, his demeanor returned back to a serious one.

"I've made some discoveries that put things in a... concerning light." Dai started. "From what I've been able to gather, people have been going missing for a long time. Founding-of-the-town's-walls type of long time. Nothing strange really, and people have unfortunately become callous to that. Death is the norm."

I grimaced at what he said but nodded. Thankfully we hadn't lost anyone, but we'd had enough close calls that I knew it was a real possibility. One that I knew the Wildwoodians had suffered, along with the rest of humanity. One I planned to do my damnedest to prevent.

"The strange and concerning part is the pattern of disappearances. You wouldn't know this, but we take a census every year. It's not too hard with two-hundred-odd people in the town. Outside of the people killed in monster attacks or while out with the Wild Guard? Twelve gone each year."

"How far back?" I asked, brow furrowing as I tried to put the connection together.

"At least through the decade we've been keeping good

records. Dylan might be a bit obstinate, but he likes his records in order. Irwin pays out the earnings for people, so he benefits from that too."

"The same number each year?" Sam asked, his food now forgotten.

"Twelve each time."

"That's too much of a coincidence. Right? Maybe two years, maybe even two years back to back. But ten?" Danny said.

"Someone must be giving the Tendrils people. That would explain why there are so many of them," I said, thinking about the dozen humanoids we'd fought up to that point. "Do you have any idea who might be responsible? Do you know who it was that advocated for the whole 'tribute to the Tendrils' nonsense?"

Dai shook his head, pressing his clawed hands against his boney brow. "No leads as of yet, but I did notice something strange north of town."

When none of us spoke up, he continued.

"When I came back, I tried to talk to the crystal here. Tec, I think you called it. I noticed some strange changes in the aura around the crystal over the first few days, as if it was being siphoned towards the north. After ranging some ways out, I spotted two groups of Tendrils and the Tendril beasts that they control. Maybe eight to a dozen in each. They were just there, undisturbed.

"I spent the next few days scouting out that entire region. No more Tendrils, but also none of the Wild Guard went that way."

"Don't you guys patrol in quadrants?" Danny asked.

"The Guard does, yes. Except for the north. They leave that to Oliver's team, because they have the best eyesight and ranged capabilities to see stuff from the bridge or across the water," Dai answered.

"I don't like what that implies," I said. "After we get some

stuff situated tomorrow, do you think you could lead us there?"
I asked.

"Yes, of course."

"Good. Then meet us by Tec in the morning. We'll get you
the implant, and you can spend the morning getting used to the
changes. Maybe we'll be able to pick up some more skills
ourselves."

The lizardman bowed his head, eyed our meal before
gesturing at it, and drifted out of our place.

When I looked at our meal, I could see that I wasn't the
only one that had lost their appetite.

"Well, no sense in delaying it. Who's got first watch?"

The next morning, things moved quickly. Word of our little
display the day before had spread like wildfire. When my uncle
had mentioned that small town events got shared fast, I didn't
quite expect what Wildwood had to offer.

A half-dozen of the Wild Guard trainees rushed me down
for commissions of different armor and weapons. They offered
me the meager earnings they had allotted to them, but I refused
them easily. Not because I didn't want to help them *or* take their
money, of which we hadn't received any from the town yet, but
because I didn't have the time.

I promised that I would work with some of their craftsmen
and repairmen. With their hunger somewhat mollified, we
continued toward the building I knew served as one of the Wild
Guard barracks. On the way there, I saw that most of the
crafting areas in the center of town had already been repaired
and people were intermingling. The coins made of pressed
metal sheets exchanged hands for goods and the rest of the
people went about their business. Some felt the need to tell us
all about how they supported our expansion efforts. Some
thanked us for clearing and growing the field like we had. The

few with the Gift and a life attunement had already been pulled to farming duty.

As we got our own dose of small town gossip, we also got a gauge on their general mood. Beyond the initial platitudes and niceties, there was always something for people to complain about.

Most of the complaints were expected. Not enough food. Not enough pay. Not enough fun things to do. The few that we did get to open up were the ones that we cared about.

People who'd lost someone. A sibling, a friend, or even a child in some cases. There was definitely a hidden pressure, and I tried to leverage all the usually obnoxious social skills my uncle had instilled in me. Not that being social was bad, and I wasn't lying when I said I cared about the people we interacted with, but it exhausted me. Early on in this endeavor, we'd split up to get a wider scope of the town. Sam and I spoke with the crafters while Danny talked to the people carrying the goods. My much more introverted blond companion was even forced to join some of the conversations when he noticed how word-worn I was getting.

By late morning, probably an hour or two from noon, we finally stumbled into the Wild Guard housing only to find it empty. Not wanting to waste too much time, we walked to Tec.

The augmented field of magic all around us once again reinvigorated my mood. I just couldn't get bored watching the way the elements danced around each other. As soon as we set foot on the bridge, a shape pulled itself out of the water. Dai. He wore nothing but some trunks with a hole cut in them for his tail, and we watched as he formed a mist from the water that clung to his body. The breeze over the lake quickly made it disappear and he was once again dry.

"How long have you been in there?" Danny asked.

"Since this morning. The bigger aquatic creatures have thankfully been dealt with, but they still need help dealing with them from time to time," the lizardman said. "They usually call me in, but I was already in the area." He gave the giant crystal a meaningful nod.

"Tec, can you bring us in?"

—Justification for whitespace?—

"We have news, questions, and someone else to implant," I said, snappy like Tec was.

—Confirmed.—

Crystal limbs plucked us from the bridge, lizardman companion and all.

"Is this the norm!?" Dai called out, waving his arms around in search of something to grab.

"Yes, here." I lent the man my shoulder to stabilize him. "This might sting."

"What might—"

The crystal punched into the back of his head for only a moment before Dai slumped.

—MetierTech implant complete.—

—Entity requiring clarification on Tec designation and further Dreg information.—

"Oh, I just gave you and your... sibling names. It was odd just calling you both entity this or entity that," I said.

"We'd been talking about giving you all more reasonable names, but he insisted these would work for you," Daniela added, sticking her tongue at me.

—Nomenclature is appropriate.—

—Will petition for future entities to match your proposed naming scheme.—

"Uh... Sure?"

—Information pertaining to the Dreg infiltrating my area of influence?—

"We have a lead on something. People being kidnapped, probably for the Tendrils, if I had to guess."

—Potential justification?—

"They are converting them. To make more Tendrils," Dai said, his eyes focusing back on our conversation.

—Computing possibility of theory.—

Tec was silent for all of two seconds.

—Probability is high.—

"We plan to investigate after leaving. Before we did go, there were a few things I wanted to check with you and Bec. Could you connect us?"

<Currently busy with some— Oh, hey guys. Sorry, some ants got frisky with my area of influence, but your uncle was there to scare them off.>

"Are they alright?" I asked, the desire to head right back to the camp leaping to the fore of my mind.

<They are quite alright. But I will say, since Tec is footing the mana bill for this conversation, that the ants are *not* happy with you. My communication has been even more limited trying to keep them away, but I'm reaching my limits unfortunately.>

"We killed a slime and got their crystal. Hopefully, when we get back, that will help you out," Sam pointed out.

<Thank you, Samuel, yes. Please don't let that strange, unnatural companion of yours snag it. With you three operating with Tec, and your parents working defensively, the Dreg gains have more or less disappeared.>

"We'll bump it up. Like we were telling Tec, we have a lead on someone that may be kidnapping Wildwoodians. Before we try to pursue it, do you think we would be okay unlocking more skills?"

—Query could have been presented to Tec.—

"No offense, Tec, but when we first came here, you started stabbing before we started talking," I pointed out.

<I believe it would be fine. I would recommend that you wait some more, Daniela. Your freeform training is going well, and acquiring a new dump of information could affect that progress.>

"Don't mind me then," she said. "Managing as many skills as I have has been hard enough. Plus, I'll leave the defense to you, rock-for-brains."

"Did you have any recommendations, Bec?" Sam asked.

The voice of our home crystal paused, likely running its own type of computational evaluation.

<I believe that completing your defensive set of skills will be the most beneficial, Samuel. As for Ronan, I believe it would be in your best interest to wait before unlocking your freeform skill.>

"What? Why? Wouldn't that give me more flexibility?"

<Yes and no. Just because you can do more doesn't mean you can do it well. Completing your defensive set might impact your overall offensive development.>

"You do know I have no clue what you are talking about, yes?" I said, my frustration giving way to confusion.

<I've had the beginning of this conversation with you, but I will go ahead and present it to you all. Your skills, or what I help provide the knowledge for, are not something I control. The manifestation outside of the basics of target, intent, and potency are only structured around the template I provide. Your own minds and experiences shape them.>

<If you do not want to be hamstrung offensively, you may want to train with more offensive skills first.>

"Wait. Then why was it okay for me to complete my offensive set?" Daniela asked.

"And why would it be okay for me to complete my defensive one?" Sam added, both of them joining me in frowning at the whitespace around us.

"I am totally lost," Dai said, sitting back and shaking his head.

<The nature of your Attunements and your own personalities.>

<Unlike your other companion, Dennis, whose skills match a more offensive focus of life, you, Sam, are more focused on the recovering or augmenting properties of life. These fall under the defensive set of skills you can manifest. As for Daniela, I don't believe I need to tell you that you are a more 'shoot first, ask questions later' type of person.>

Daniela actually had the wherewithal to blush and look embarrassed while Sam had a contemplative look on his face.

"I actually have a question," Dai said, raising his hand. Considering the deer-in-the-headlights look he had, it felt like he was talking to one of our teachers back when we were doing the equivalent of elementary school. "How many of these 'skills' can we have? If my status is correct, and the trend for gaining one more skill unlocks in the future continues with levels, I will have way more than six skills." *Okay, maybe he isn't as lost as I thought.*

<That is also another topic I have not gotten to discuss. The current system I've worked out is based on the inherent changes that your increased Quotient gives. As for what that entails for you all, it's dumping the equivalent of centuries of magic understanding around one specific subject. Once you have filled out both your offensive and defensive set of skills, you will be able to use the skill points to *advance* your core skills. The freeform skills you will unlock will give you flexibility and utility, but your core skills will always be your strongest and cheapest skills.>

"That's a whole lot to unpack," Sam said, joining Dai on the ground and staring at the whitespace, unfocused.

—Humans appear overwhelmed by the primitive informational breakdown provided.—

<They are just fine, Tec, give them a moment.>

"Okay, so, six core skills and then we can somewhat manipulate our magic using the freeform skill. Once we have acquired all six, then we can upgrade. That's alright, I can deal with that. I will hold off on the *why* for another time, if that's okay..." I said, already trying to consolidate all the information. The gist of it, as it turned out, was simple, but I knew there was probably more to the whole 'upgrade' facet of skills. Nonetheless, Bec's suggestion was one I would follow. The entity hadn't steered us wrong, even through the madness of the surface. "I'll take my materialize offensive skill, Tec. If you please."

Without any warning, my head was placed in a vise.

Metaphorically speaking. Flashes of information, flashes from the lab and man I'd seen before, flew through my mind but my <Memory Canal>skill didn't trigger like before. Several seconds later, information coalesced before me.

<Mineral Strike>

<Release crystalline structures at range.>

"Good to know your system is as vague as possible, whenever possible, Bec."

<I aim to please,>it said with the monotone equivalent of a chuckle. <It is also required since I don't know the specific manifestations or limitations of your skills. Perhaps once I have a more comprehensive list and study of spell-chain-to-human transition, I will be able to provide better descriptions.>

"Huh," I said. It was something I hadn't considered up to that point. Even with all the knowledge that the Entity Clusters had, they were still learning how to interact and deal with having 'Dreg Warriors,' instead of passively waiting for Dreg to be brought to them.

<Would you like for me to give Tec my suggestions for your skills, Samuel and Dai Wood? I really shouldn't fragment my attention for much longer.>

"That's cool with me," Sam said. "I won't deviate from your plan to complete my defensive set anyhow."

"I... Well, I don't know any better, so I will be subject to your wisdom, Mr. Bec." The lizardman actually gave a half-bow from his spot on the ground. A moment later, both him and Sam were twitching from the information being shot straight into their squishy domes.

<You all stay safe. I look forward to that upgrade!>

The voice clicked, as if Bec had hung up a phone. The awkward silence held for about two seconds.

—Justification for whitespace has been fulfilled. Tec requests further information regarding Dreg threat in exchange for whitespace privileges.—

Just as suddenly as we'd arrived, we were ejected. Only me and Danny, who weren't reeling from the skill gains, were able to keep our feet as the bridge appeared under us. The lithe brunette actually rolled out of the way as Samuel crashed on top of Dai and they both toppled into the shallow water. My perception screamed out a warning and I spun, spell chain at the ready. It was a kid, probably no older than ten, standing with a ball in hand. Said ball dropped to the ground as he turned and dashed out of the Blessing of Magic, screaming about the crystal eating people.

"That's going to take some handling," Danny said from her crouch.

"There goes the crystal's secret, more like. That little scoundrel will have told everyone by the time dinner comes around," Dai said, pulling himself out of the water onto the bridge with grace. The scales on his brow were scrunched up, likely due to the situation or possibly the discomfort of having information downloaded straight to his gray matter.

The undecipherable string of words that had shown on my status when Bec had first changed it reformed into a simple word. The source of the message was clear.

—Oops.—

CHAPTER TWENTY-TWO

To 'Scout' or not to 'Scout'

"Is there any way of stopping him?" I asked, watching as the kid turned down one of the many suburban streets west of the crystal.

"I might be able to catch him," Daniela said, scratching the back of her head and starting to crouch into a runner's pose.

"It's no use unless you plan to turn him into a mute. I say this not as an insult, but to point it out, your experience with children is probably limited. They are terrible at keeping secrets," Dai said.

"I could threaten him," the brunette said casually, pulling one of her daggers from her back.

"They are even worse when under duress!" the lizardman said, eyes widening in alarm.

"I was only kidding," Danny mumbled, putting the weapon away.

"What do we do now?" Sam asked.

"I think we need to regroup and try to scope out those camps you mentioned, Dai. If the jig about interacting with the crystal is going to be up, we want to try to keep the upper hand.

I have a sneaking suspicion that the Tendrils and crystals know about each other."

"You're thinking that it will force the traitors in the town to act."

"*Re*act, more like, which is both better for us and also more dangerous. If they do so in the town, then they could endanger the people or even try to snag more while we are distracted."

"We should get help from the Guard. As much as they dislike me, they would never ignore something like this. In that, at least, my reputation serves me well." The lizardman turned to leave, pausing only slightly to look at his bare body. "After some clothes. I don't have *that* kind of reputation."

The three of us stood around a bit lost. While I agreed with Dai, it was no use having us all scramble around town when he was clearly the better choice for finding Wild Guards.

"Let's get geared up. If this scouting mission goes like I think it will, it won't be just scouting," I said, wading through a gentle swirl of gray highlighted by my perception and the Blessing of Magic.

The walk back was silent as we all tried to process the shotgun of information. I'd briefly considered trying to discuss more with Tec, but I wasn't in the mood for the Entity Cluster's nuanced personality. Somewhere along the way, Daniela was unable to resist asking what was on her mind.

"So… What did you guys get?" Danny asked.

"I'm not quite sure of the applications, but my offensive materialize was <Mineral Strike>. It's finally a ranged skill that will *hopefully* let me target things *not* on the ground!" I said, glancing again at the *un*helpful description in my status.

"I don't know how I feel about running combat while unsure of our new skills," Sam said. "My new skill is called <Bush> which, if I'm honest, doesn't inspire me a whole lot."

"Don't be a whiny baby," Daniela countered. She summoned a spell chain in a blink and was cloaked in a simmering haze that dried my eyes out just from looking. It was quite similar to what we'd seen from the Haze Wolf right after selecting our first skills. "Even if I haven't figured out all the bits under the hood, I think <Flare Cloak> will do me just fine. Plus, I think it accentuates my curves!"

"Maybe you'll finally get some then," I mumbled.

Deservedly—but totally worth it—I got a burning punch to the shoulder. Samuel chuckled to himself while dodging as Danny half-heartedly swatted at him too. It was great to know that despite the unknown, I could always rely on my friends to bring it down to earth.

— + —

An hour later, we were standing on the long bridge that crossed Lake Sumter. Blobby and Anthony milled around, prodding and antenna-ing all the things around them while we waited. A sign just before the water's edge told us we were on Morse Boulevard. While we watched, two groups of lizards and mer dove into the lake from one of the rafts I'd seen. I'd picked up in conversation that the lake had been getting deeper each year, and the fish more abundant. The possible implications for that almost managed to distract me, but Dai approaching shook me from my reverie.

"We are on our own for now," he said, scowling over his shoulder.

"Did you tell the Wild Guard?" I asked.

"Yes. Charles said they would meet us there after gathering the others. The other team was posted at the east wall. They were just on their way to the south farms."

"Well, we are just scouting, right?" Daniela asked. "Don't think it will be that much of a problem, if I'm honest."

Dai's scowl didn't dissipate, but he nodded regardless. With our quartet formed, we crossed the bridge to the north of town. The bridge had seen better days, but the major structure was mostly intact. As we approached the north end of town, a question that had been lingering in my mind got an answer.

"That's where all the cars are," I said. Sure enough, stacked at least three deep all along the shore of the lake—and covered in more vines, moss, and mulch than I thought was possible— were the town's vehicles. Probably all the vehicles further out too. Some still had tires filled with air standing out against the rest of the cooked rubber of their companions, but all the cars looked crushed in some fashion or another, and not just from being piled on top of each other.

"Why did you do that?" Danny asked, poking Dai as if he'd personally shifted tons of cars and trucks.

"The gators." The lizardman did not elaborate.

We all took in the sight and arrived at the car-wall. There was a pair of semi-trucks arranged like a square. Dai entered through a gap without hesitation, appearing at the top of them a second later. We followed, finding a small 'office' or rest area with a ladder leading up to the top of the car-wall. A tarp flapped gently, hung from either side of the trucks to act like a roof. There were clear signs of habitation all around us. Someone was posted here regularly. We didn't rummage through anything and just followed Dai up the ladder. Anthony just straight up climbed the side of the truck while Blobby opted to squeeze its bulk through the gaps in the cars. Considering the slime's increased size, it would take a little while.

"The camp is almost a straight shot from here." Dai pointed to an extremely worn road heading north while a street crossed right at the edge of the car-wall. Neither looked viable for vehicles, even if we had them. "The second camp is further to the east, but not much. How did you want to handle this? I am not used to operating with a group," Dai said, gesturing to the rest of us. Including the St. Bernard-sized Fire Ant clambering over the side and causing the semi to squeal on a long-rusted suspension.

"Well, before we get into any kind of fight, we want to try to get at least a good grasp of all our abilities. You've seen all of mine, sans the new one." I pointed to Daniela.

"I've got a fireball I can throw, a wisp that shoots smaller fireballs while flying around, and I can encase my body with flames. I've been able to manipulate fire and spark flames thanks to my freeform skill, but that's about it for now," Danny explained.

"I can heal, boost your body, and slap enemies around with my <Vine Whip>. Trap them too, if that's required. My...uh... new skill lets me grow a bush. Appropriately, the skill is named <Bush>. As for freeform, I haven't even tried to use it," Samuel added. "Hopefully, I can work on some better healing that doesn't require me to slap my allies too."

"You three have seen all of mine, before this last new one. I didn't really have names for them until the implant. <Condensation> is the one that lets me manipulate water around me. I've been using it for misdirection. <Frost Edge> is the one that forms the knives. <Condensation> in conjunction with my <Morning Dew>skill are what lets me obscure so much space around me. The dew skill is the one that lets me make the mist."

The three of them turned to me. "Well, I'll show my fourth if he tells us about his fourth."

The lizardman frowned at his hand. Unlike the spell chains that I'd seen from the Wildwoodians, the primal ones formed from their experience and capabilities with their Attunement, this one was identical to ours except a sky blue in color. The arcane symbols spun and I could have sworn I was able to understand some of the characters before the skill triggered. Water from the air around us coalesced into a small floating blob. Some additional water hovered out of the container on Dai's back, doubling the size of the blob to the size of my own head. The blob became a frosty white, while remaining the same size. Droplets of water drifted off of it, freezing, before drifting back into the pale liquid like it had gravity of its own.

When Dai closed his hand, the blob started to drift in the air, circling our group. Anthony and Blobby were instantly curious, poking at the blob only to flinch back with ice covering the slime and ant.

"It's called <Flurry>. I think I can control it some, or at least direct it."

"Hey, that's like my wisp!" Danny said, smiling as she poked the Flurry. It shivered in the air before resuming its orbit around us. She giggled as the ice turned to liquid within moments of covering her finger.

"Which skill was it, Dai?" I asked.

"According to the status, it was my materialize offensive skill."

"So, the same as Danny huh…" I scratched at my stubble as I mulled over the implications of the parallel skills.

"Oh no, not right now, Ronan. We've got scouting to do. You can work on whatever nonsense you are formulating some other time," Daniela said, tugging me by the arm and practically pushing me off the car-wall. Bringing all of my increases in mobility to bear, I managed to stay on the wall. The group didn't chuckle, but I could see them straining to hold it in.

"Fine, but you are the last person that can say they don't benefit from my experiments!" Just to make a point, I jumped the fifteen feet down to the ground on the other side of the wall. As I fell, I channeled mana into my shield to boost my strength. A small cloud of dust and sand marked my landing, but I extricated myself from the hole with ease. A grin split my face when I saw the flabbergasted looks on my friends' faces. I'd fallen off the vestibule, and a few trees, a number of times during my construction work in the camp. My Limestone Skin and my increases in strength did a real number at mitigating damage. "Come on down, the sand is fine!"

Blobby chose that moment to squeeze its way through the wall, rolling up to me and jiggling in agitation. While I didn't speak slime, I was fairly sure it was upset that I had somehow beaten it to the other side. Dai and Daniela took a series of handholds the lizardman pointed out while Samuel took a page out of my playbook. His <Vine Whip> rose up from the plants growing on the vehicles. It wasn't one of his empowered ones, but it was still as thick as my arm. The vine then wrapped around his wrist and lowered Sam to the ground gently before falling limp. The vine hung over the side like a rope, still firmly attached to the wall.

"You still didn't show us your skill, Ronan," Samuel said, walking over and petting Blobby until its wiggling became more manageable.

"<Mineral Strike>," I said, pushing the mental button of my new skill. A spell chain flickered in the air before my hand, dunking only a tenth of my mana for a base cast. A hunk of what looked like quartz formed in the air before shooting forward. It wasn't as fast as a bullet, but it was faster than I thought I could throw something. I'd join the major leagues if I could throw something like that. The quartz embedded itself in the ground almost a hundred feet away, fragmenting on impact in a way that I knew the mineral wouldn't do. Probably something to do with magic, because the fragments disintegrated a few seconds after.

"Hey! Range attack!" Daniela said with a small cheer. "Now if something flies at us, it won't just be me fighting it."

"That was the hope, yes. All of my magic requires grounded creatures."

"Wonderful. Hopefully, you won't have to use it until you've had more of a chance to familiarize yourself with it. This 'instantly know a skill' thing is throwing my mind for a loop," Dai said, pointing to the woods. "I would like to try to use this... comm-plant moving forward. The silence will aid our scouting, and I would like to become more acquainted with how the system works."

"Works for me," Daniela replied, lips flat as she used the implant.

Dai frowned as he concentrated, but easily replied. "This is a lot more intuitive than I imagined."

"You can thank Alan for that. Well, maybe him and Mayor Elias," I replied. "Let's take it slow. None of us are familiar with the area, and we don't want to be caught unawares."

"A forest is a forest is a forest," Daniela called. She tucked her naginata on a strap Anthony had, courtesy of Samuel. The woman then crouched low and drew her daggers before zipping into the woods. The flashes of red from her armor flashed in my periphery, but other than that, she was pretty much hidden from view.

The rest of us skirted the edge of the road heading north. The asphalt through this section of road was even worse off than on US 301. Entire chunks had been pulverized, while all the trees had upheaved the road several inches. We picked our way carefully through the mess of roots.

Dai took the lead, summoning forth some light mist around me, Sam, and himself. Any of the mist that got near the canopy to our right hissed and evaporated. *I'll have to point that out to Danny.* Before we got too deep into the treeline, I addressed our other stealthy companion. "Blobby, can you split and keep a lookout around us?"

The slime jiggled, waving an appendage in the direction of the car-wall, before splitting into *three* Blobby's. My shock was quickly overcome when I remembered that Blobby had actually swallowed a whole slime by itself. The crystal for the other one was tucked away at the bottom of our gear crate. The third'ed slimes were about the size of Blobby when I'd first encountered it. They each mirrored a wave and split off in a perfect three hundred sixty degree spread around us.

"That thing could split?" Dai asked, his alarm clear through the comm-plant.

"It's a somewhat new development. What I want to keep in mind is the fact that if Blobby can do it, then so will other slime Tendrils," I said.

The three of us tried to keep the conversation light. Unfortunately, my perception highlighted a whole mess of damage all around us. I wasn't an expert tracker or anything of the like, but even a blind person would have been able to follow the trail *something* had been creating. Almost certainly not a simple throng of animals. A few minutes after the marks were persistent, Dai halted next to a particularly abused oak. He had Daniela clamber up the tree to avoid dissipating his mist, and extended the effect. A visible ripple of water reached out wide. "Stay here, I will take a look and we can move closer."

In response, I hoisted my pickaxe at the ready, spinning it in hand. Samuel drew his shortsword and based on the slight shrinking of the mist cloud above us, I was fairly sure Daniela had mana channeled into one of her daggers. The lizardman looked us over, nodded, and disappeared in a swirl of fog.

The anticipation was palpable.

A shrill yip drew my attention to the west. With our position just on the edge of the road, I knew that we would at least get a minor warning from that direction, so I focused on the sound. I strained to see and to hear, doing my best to ignore my other senses. The gloom of the space around us served as the perfect hiding place for the creatures of the forest. Had the things stalking us been creatures of the forest, it was possible I would have missed them. As it was, their information sprung up at the edge of my vision.

<Dreg Tendril (Coyote)>
<Attunement: Earth>
<Refinement: Rumble>
<Perceived Metier Quotient: 1>

Three of the creatures prowled in a loose semicircle with me and my friends at the center. I set my pickaxe down, cracking my knuckles as I started to coordinate with my friends. "Danny, take the left one. Quiet, if you would. Sam and I will take the other two. Give me a <Vine Whip> on both if you can, Sam."

"Got it." The blond didn't need any further prompting as I watched the green spell chain form at the feet of the two left-most coyotes. Anticipating the timing of my friend's attack, I zeroed in on the space right under their torsos. With a grunt, two half-powered <Stone Spikes> rose up to meet the coyotes. They seemed to sense my attack before it even arrived, dodging back enough to only have gashes form on their chests. Their yipping took on a more feverish pitch.

That was when Samuel sealed their fate. The vines had all the time they needed to wrap around the two coyotes and press them back onto my spike. The secondary impact was much more effective. Namely because my stone spike protruded through the back of the coyotes' chests. Daniela quietly dropped down from above. *When did she get all the way over there!?* Her curls barely shifted as she planted both daggers into the coyote. Their ribcage instantly started to shrivel, blood boiling as if it had been lit on fire internally.

Daniela didn't waste time triggering the dissociation of the body, snagging three pelts and three infusions for our trouble. The woman stuffed them in her backpack before climbing back up into a nearby tree. A frenetic Dai rushed back, but his steps slowed when he saw the evidence of our battle and each of us casually resetting our gear.

"Some of the pack split off, but it looks like I was worried for no reason. Thanks to the implant,I was able to get a good gauge of their levels, and only one is Quotient 3, a life humanoid. There is an earth deer and a blend of Quotient 2 fire and water coyotes," the man communicated evenly through the comm-plant even when his body was panting from his rush back.

"Looks like our scouting took the turn I wanted," I said, adjusting my grip on my pickaxe.

"We all knew this is what you wanted, Ronan," Sam said, rolling his eyes. I could practically feel Daniela copying him from the canopy above.

"Let's just go deal with this group. I want to deal with the next one as soon as possible," I grumbled. The others in our group had small smiles on their faces as we followed Dai deeper into the woods.

CHAPTER TWENTY-THREE

Under Our Noses

Just like Dai said, the group milled around a small clearing in the trees. A strange twist of trees that *had* to have been formed by a life-attuned had been hiding the clearing in a thick grove of pines and moss. The whole thing was a nature version of a camp tent with the way the moss hung horizontal over the trees.

We stayed well away so as not to alert the creatures to our presence, but I watched more than one coyote slink through a gap in the trees to sniff around us. When they got close enough to touch Dai's mist, they growled and retreated. The reaction was more aggressive from the fire coyotes, going so far as to snarl at the trees before returning to the clearing.

"Is there something in the water?" Sam asked.

"No, it is just from Lake Sumter. But that's a good idea. I'll have to test that..." The lizardman drifted off, probably contemplating how to get his hands on some poison or another.

"How do we want to do this?" Daniela asked, having instructed Anthony to remain behind, outside of the mist field. She had the naginata in hand.

"We hit them hard and fast. Our biggest issue would be getting pinched, so I am going to plow through and you guys do damage," I said, taking the time to encase most of my upper body that wasn't a joint with <Earth Shell>.

"Sounds like a fun time," Daniela said. "I'll let Anthony know."

The woman disappeared into the mist.

"Are you sure we want to strike now?" The lizardman interposed himself between me and the Tendril camp. "We may be able to glean something from them."

"Not this one. That was my plan for the other. If we try to fight both, we are going to have a bad time, so we take this one down and trap or follow the next one," I said, taking a step to the side to restore my view of the moss walls. *Maybe I can get some of that to grow on the wall around the Bunker camp. Attune it to fire, and have some passive defenses...*

"Done. He'll follow as soon as you punch through the moss wall, Ron." Daniela practically materialized beside us. I spied a gentle red glow from where she was channeling into the naginata.

"On three." I half-turned to meet Dai's eye. "You know your skills best, so I trust you to add whenever you can."

The lizardman gave me a solemn nod.

"One." I channeled mana into my pickaxe, shaping it into a secondary umbrella shield.

"Two." I braced my feet. Samuel tapped me in the back, pushing his <Adrenal Surge>.

"Three!"

If Raymond had a twin brother, then I probably looked like him. The combination of my strength, Sam's boost and a whole lot of momentum took me straight through the moss wall *and* a small tree. The impact knocked my health down by a full ten percent, but the effect was worth it. The deer was pinned by the toppled tree and two coyotes were tossed to the side. My perception did a quick count of the eight enemies within before zeroing in on the humanoid Tendril.

Leaping clear over another of the coyotes, I got halted just short by a wall of stone antlers. The impact with those took another five percent of my health, mostly thanks to the one that managed to get around my chest armor to cut into my abdomen. With my charge stopped, the fight was engaged.

Gouts of fire flowed down onto me from either side. I intercepted both with my shield and pick, but the attacks pinned me in place. Through the heat distortion, I spotted the Tendril forming some kind of spell chain. Twitching due to the rising temperatures, I still let loose a half-powered <Stone Spike> right at its lower body. The creature dodged the skill, but was forced to release their own. A moment later, I lost clear sight of the Tendril as Dai's mist rolled over the space around us. The sting of the fire lessened and the two coyotes on either side opted for a more... mundane form of killing me.

A maw clamped down on my right arm at the same time that the other beast bounced off my shield. While I planned to hack straight into the coyote on my left, the right one yanked me out of line. Its fangs hadn't been able to punch through my <Earth Shell>, but they *had* managed to give it enough grip to ragdoll me. My arm fought to remain attached at the shoulder, so I let out a close range <Mineral Strike> right into its face. The rock that formed that time was more akin to cinnabar, but it hit like a truck regardless. The hunk of red mineral busted the coyote's eye, forcing it to yelp in pain and release my arm.

While that one tried to figure out how to become a pirate, I turned to the one that had struck my shield. The tip of my pick entered, then exited, the coyote's throat. The iron stench of boiling blood hit me like a physical blow as it sprayed me down. Unable to free the weapon, I was forced to give it up, and the boost to my strength, in favor of not getting bogged down. Just as I turned to finish off the other coyote, two ice throwing knives landed with scary precision. One into its still functioning eye, the other into the creature's throat.

The brief reprieve let me evaluate the battlefield.

Daniela had stabbed two of the water coyotes with her naginata, their movements clearly impaired by the trait of her weapon. Most of the other creatures had some combination of ice or vines encasing them as Dai and Samuel hacked into them with their shortswords. Anthony was wrestling with one of the fire coyotes, trying to snap his mandibles around its throat.

With my back covered, I turned back to the two remaining enemies, the deer and the humanoid. The Tendril in question had actually mounted the deer. It was a strange sight, even if the deer's increased size made it more like a horse. Regardless, based on how it was trying to urge it through the trees, the creature was fleeing.

With a flex of my mana, I sent up two <Earthen Barriers> in their path. The deer seemed able to sense the shift, so its own magic created a stone stepping platform that it used to leap over my five foot wall. I knew deer could jump, but with the weight of the Dreg Tendril on its back, it still seemed to be struggling.

"Oh no you don't," I growled, dumping another twenty percent of my mana to create a <Stone Spike> X over the top of my wall.

Since it was already in the air, the deer didn't have time to react, clipping the new stone with its back legs and sending the two of them into a tumble.

I extradited myself from the corpses around me and gave chase. The stone antler wall the deer had created was erratic and difficult to navigate, but eventually I made my way over. The deer was limping away, and I could see the Tendril vanishing into the woods.

"Damn it!" I yelled, turning to look over my shoulder. Daniela was getting ready to engage one of the water coyotes. Dumping the last of my mana, I ripped a column of rock right under the creature. It didn't kill it outright, but I knew the gash in its side would be fatal. Especially with their healer on the run. "Danny, catch the runner!" I said from atop the stone antler mess. She spotted me and the direction I was pointing before taking off. As an afterthought, she released a spell chain and her wisp materialized in the air above.

The creature then rained fiery blasts at anything that got too close. The brunette somersaulted the stone antlers, landing in a perfect crouch that retained most of her momentum. Unfortunately, I lost track of her when one of the water coyotes felt inclined to take a nibble of me while I was focused on the escapees.

My health dropped as the teeth of the creature found purchase in the flesh of my leg, rending it under the weight of its body and dropping me off the antlers. It was a short fall, but I managed to extract my revenge from the bastard.

Leading with my shield arm, I whacked the creature in the chest. The muffled crunch of bone was a satisfying sound. The pulse of heat from the impact caused steam to rise off the water-attuned beast.

Even if my shoulder was dislocated, the creature was dead. Since I couldn't muster the strength to move through the pain in my leg and shoulder, the coyote dissociated right from under me. Pith flowed into me, the nauseating feeling of Dreg overpowering the slight tingle of energy. Then I thudded the last foot to the uneven ground when the energy was through separating into me and my friends.

An 'ouch' was all I managed as I finally spotted the affliction warning in the corner of my vision, along with the low mana warning. For once, the discomfort in my gut had nothing on the pain everywhere else on my body.

"Ronan!" Samuel called out, both through the comm-plant and with his voice.

The blond and Dai rounded the torn up tree and earth that separated us before spotting me. Anthony got to my side first, the fire ant running his antenna all over me. He then looked at the approaching Sam and nodded its big obtuse head. My friend mimicked the motion.

"Did you just talk with Anthony?" I said, half out of it as the ant continued to use its feelers on me while Samuel ran his hands over my injuries. Each prod sent waves of pain through me, but he sighed in relief.

"It's not broken, just hold still." Samuel then proceeded to slap health into my leg while Dai held me. He held the muscles in place with his left hand as his healing mana coursed through me from his right. Samuel plucked a whole fang out of the wound to complete the healing.

As soon as he was finished, there was a wave of relief, the cool restorative feel of his magic alleviating the nerves. My throat was raw and I realized I'd been howling the entire time he worked. My shoulder was also back into place. A cheeky grin from Dai told me that the lizardman had taken the distraction of my pain to put it back in place.

"You know. It won't be long before you are more scar tissue than person, Ron." Samuel had a frown on his face as he channeled some more mana into my leg. I watched as the scars along my leg thinned and *almost* vanished, but not entirely.

"I'll take that if I can keep you all in one piece," I huffed, taking both of the offered hands to rise to my feet. I tested the limb and, other than some next level soreness, it was okay.

"That thing gave you minor frostbite," Samuel said, pointing to some of the gory slush splattered on my pants.

"You're kidding," I said, looking between the pelt material loot and my friend.

"Trust me, I get how terrible that pun is," he said.

"I've fought them before, these are annoyingly resistant. If you don't go for kill shots, they just freeze or burn their wounds and keep coming," Dai provided.

While we gathered ourselves and surveyed the space around us, a thread of Pith flowed into us from the direction Daniela had gone. It was not enough, even split more ways, to account for both the deer and the humanoid. Sure enough, a minute later, Daniela returned.

"That deer was almost as tough as you, Ron," Danny said, hobbling back into the clearing. Blobby of all things rolling behind her.

"It tried to trap me in one of those." She pointed to the stone set of antlers before continuing. "So I speared it with the naginata till I got out. The other one got away…"

"The other camp is about an hour west of here," Dai added. "I don't know where else it might be going."

"It's alright, we'll just have to regroup. Plan's a little busted, but we got some information from this," I said.

"We did?" my friends asked curiously.

"I'm curious about that too," Dai said.

"That's two instances of organized Tendrils with a life-attuned. The person that keeps coming and talking to the town is life-attuned. I'm thinking that their leadership structure might be based around them, either because of their healing abilities or something else we aren't quite sure of, but I know we are close."

Our group mulled over what I said, going around the clearing and gathering up loot and Pith. Even the scaled Dai was looking green around the gills thanks to the huge dump of Dreg into our system. A quick look at my status told me that a few more percent of Dreg would push me right into the 'new trait' territory.

When I told Blobby to go and retrieve the loot from the deer, the slime jiggled and rolled away through the trees, only for it to return a few seconds later from the opposite direction. I was extremely confused until I remembered that it had split itself.

The newcomer slime wasn't idle, it was jiggling in alarm and one of its appendages was undulating before making a popping sound.

"Is it playing charades with us?" Danny asked, tilting her head at the odd behavior.

"I think your stupid pet was trying to warn you we were coming," a voice was punctuated by the click of a gun hammer from the treeline. A pair of others spaced wide echoed the clicks.

"Oliver," I said, placing my shield in front of me. "Cluster up behind me," I added through my comm-plant.

"I have a bone to pick with you, Bunker-born."

"What do you want that needs guns involved? I thought I already kicked your ass!"

"You think just because you've helped this town, we should all bow down to you?" The man strode forward, gun still leveled evenly at my head. *Note to self, helmets are next on the crafting list.*

"I'm not asking anyone to bow down, I'm just asking for some damn cooperation!" I snapped back, unable to keep the heat from my voice.

"Ron, maybe remember that there's a gun pointed at your face?" Samuel added through the comm-plant.

"I don't care that he's got a gun to my face." I half-turned to my friend. I hadn't meant to snap at him, so I quickly turned back to Oliver. "This whole damn planet has a gun pointed at me. *At us.* But you've got your head so far up your butt, you can't see past your colon."

"You don't have any skin in this game. You didn't lose everything you loved and cared about to the wilds!" Oliver screamed, dropping his gun down a fraction and stepping forward. "You have no right to be getting people's hopes up when all you are doing is bringing suicidal plans into our lives. Dungeons, interacting with the damn crystals that put us in this mess in the first place? What are you doing, Ronan!?"

The man's thoroughness caught me off guard. Just before he started up his tirade again, Daniela jumped in.

"We are not trying to be some shiny beacon or any such thing. We didn't even know humanity survived this mess until we crawled our way to the surface. And you don't have any right to criticize our decisions, just as much as we haven't criticized yours for groveling to the Councilmen."

"Those people you are spitting on have kept us safe for over twenty years!" one of the other people in the treeline called out. I never learned their name, but I could tell it was one of Oliver's squadmates. The minor gust of wind now blowing through the trees told me they were probably a Fallen, unlike Oliver.

"This is true, Oliver, but you know as well as I do that things have been happening. I didn't realize just how bad they were until Ronan had me look deeper. Looked where I should have been looking for years, for fear of being even more exiled," Dai added, there was a tension in his voice.

"You were never exiled, Dai. You could have come back to us," Oliver said.

"To what? Be on Kirby's leash? I didn't even live in the town, and he still kept sending the most dangerous jobs to me or to Clara. As altruistic as she is, do you think she wants the New Hopers to have to come back to Wildwood as often as Kirby demands it? Putting their lives on the line as often as they do?" Dai snapped back, causing Oliver to flinch and lower his weapon more.

Something in my head started to click. "Who has the most skin in the game...?"

"What?" Dai and Oliver said, turning to look at me. My friends were also looking at me strangely.

"I mean who has the most skin in the game when it comes to the Dreg Tendrils?" I said louder, mind only half-present as it worked the problem and bits of information we had. "How did you find us, Oliver?"

"What do you mean? You lot stomped all through my guard post. If you hadn't been traveling with Dai, I would have found you before you started this whole mess." He gestured at the destroyed clearing.

"Wait, you mean Charles didn't tell you we wanted assistance with the camps we found?"

"Of course not. I bumped into him as he was headed to train the kids out in the Wild Guard field."

"Oliver, the kids weren't there when we came north," Dai said.

"They weren't in the barracks either," Sam added, recalling our path from that morning.

Taken aback, he checked the sun in the sky barely visible through the trees. "There's no way. You know Marge always brings them lunch. They should have been training with Charles and Councilman Kirby."

Click.

"How long would it take to get to this second camp from the western entrance?" I asked Dai. I couldn't hide the alarm in my voice.

"Maybe forty minutes? There is a road that cuts north towards that one from Buena Vista Boulevard. What are you trying to say, Ronan?" the lizardman replied hesitantly.

"One last question before we sprint our asses to that camp. Who got you all to start trusting the Tendrils to defend you?"

CHAPTER TWENTY-FOUR

Grilled to Deception

Our group, plus Oliver's trio, churned through the woods. There was a tense silence as we plowed our way forward, everyone deep in consideration at what I'd implied.

The hour of travel went by in a blink. We approached a modified wooded clearing identical to the one closer to town. The sun was starting its climb down, but we had plenty of light to see how utterly empty the Dreg Tendril camp was. There were clear signs of habitation and a rushed exit. Mats and chairs in one of the spaces, various piled up mounds of rock, ice, and baked earth in the other. Torn up dirt and claw grooves along the ground, gashes along the western tree wall at antler height.

"They are gone... Why wouldn't they try to fight us?" Oliver asked.

"We need to get back to the town," one of Oliver's squadmates said. His eyes were darting around the space and even with my perception, I could tell the man was ready to leap at shadows.

"Eric, take a bre—"

Oliver's calming arm was slapped away by the man. "Don't you tell me to calm down, Oli! My son was out in that yard!"

The whole group went silent at the man's words. My mind started to spin wildly, scrambling for some plan.

"I'll track them," Daniela said. "I'll push till night time. Without the whole group, I should be able to find something quicker."

"Me too. I'm not as familiar with the north of town, but I don't think going solo is the best thing to do right now," Dai said, stepping back from the group.

"Take Anthony…" I said absently, pulling up my implant's map. The whole section we'd traveled had been updated with a straight shot swath from the first camp. Each time I tried to do the math for how long it would have taken the group to get from the town, out of the way to where we couldn't track them, I was coming up short. The obvious answer was magic, but that just left an unacceptable number of ways that the children might already be gone forever.

It was only when Sam nudged me back south that I realized standing out in the middle of the woods would get us nowhere but dead if one of the stronger roaming creatures stumbled onto us. Oliver and his squadmates argued as quietly as they could while keeping up with the brutal pace I set. The squad leader hadn't said anything more about our gunpoint meeting, and I had no intention to address it. My suspicions were now squarely placed on two individuals.

I'd been so caught up in my own thoughts that I had completely forgotten about our comm-plants. Samuel reminded me as he tested the range to contact any of the Big Guns or New Hoper squads. The disruption of the Entity Cluster's area of influence couldn't have been working against us at a worse time. Nonetheless, we arrived at the west gate in record time. Sure enough, Sarah and Tim were overseeing the last of the farmers leaving the field next to town. My perception easily picked up the strained looks on their faces, and this was before they even saw us blazing our way down the road.

"Ronan! What's going on?" the orc woman called, meeting us halfway down the road.

"We need to put the council on lockdown." She was taken aback by my direct command, taking only long enough to ask why. "The kids, we need to find the kids."

"They left hours ago this way," Tim said, the frown on his face mirrored on every face within earshot.

"Have they ever been out this late?" Samuel asked. *Now's not the time for optimism, Sam!*

"Never. The night creatures are much deadlier, especially since they don't have a perfect hang on their Gifts," Sarah said. "Oliver?"

She finally seemed to register who we'd been dragging along on our heels. Her confusion was clear as her eyes jumped from me to the air-attuned. "Sarah, we need to talk to the council, and I need you to lock down the town. Get everyone accounted for as soon as you can."

"I don't have the authority for that," she said hesitantly.

"Clara does, and the people will listen to you, Sary. Please, we need to figure this out," Oliver said, nudging the orc woman gently. That did the trick. The façade of professionalism snapped into place on the woman. Her shouted orders were barely understandable thanks to the volume with which she projected them, but they served their purpose. The dozen or so people still milling by the gate hustled into town while the rock twins up on the wall shut the gate behind us.

Now that we were properly inside Tec's area of influence, I toggled over to my comm-plant with a thought. The display for my status highlighted who I was speaking to. "Clara. Get everyone to the center of town. Figure out how to run attendance."

The woman's voice snapped into the connection. "What happened? Where have you all been all day? Did you travel with the kids?"

Instead of answering her questions directly, I tried to get her to move. "I'm on my way to talk to the councilmen. Please, help

Sarah round everyone up, but make sure that we've got someone watching the walls. Have Devon double-check the town for the trainees or anyone else unaccounted for."

I ignored the attempt to continue the conversation, opting to stomp to the councilman's office. A strong grip paused my advance just as the building came into view. I was tempted to impale whoever it was with my skill, but I turned calmly.

"You can't be sure of what happened," Oliver said weakly. The bravado with which he'd confronted me had been wearing down steadily by Eric's concern for his child and the snips of evidence I'd provided during our mad dash.

"No, but you can be damn sure I am going to find out. I'm done rolling over just because of the councilman's reputation or to avoid stepping on anyone's toes. The Dreg are a threat and we purge it now before we go find the children. We can't risk leaving enemies behind us while we are looking for *more* enemies."

It took all of my self-control not to kick the door to splinters. Inside, Irwin and Dylan spun in surprise. They'd been talking with their backs to us. I could already see the argument rising to Dylan's lips, but I squashed that with a half-powered <Mineral Strike> to his gut. It was more of a shock to the sturdy survivor of the Fall than an actual attack. The look in his eyes when he was able to gather himself, however, meant he knew I meant business.

"No posturing, we have bigger fish to fry."

Irwin moved to stand between me and Dylan as he caught his breath. The normally sleepy-looking economist was nowhere to be seen. "You made your point, Ronan. What do you want?"

"I am fairly confident that Kirby has been kidnapping people throughout the years to give to the Tendrils, and has now pushed the Wild Guard trainees into the same situation. If I had to guess, at least Charles, the squad leader, is in on it."

Over the next ten minutes, I broke down the realizations I'd come to. While it was all technically speculation, just the fact that Kirby was missing along with the children helped give it a fair bit of credence.

As Oliver had informed me, Kirby had been the one to first make contact with the Tendrils. I was almost sure that Kirby had secured 'protection' from the Tendrils in exchange for the people of the town. There were still holes in that, mainly around how he was able to obscure it for so long, but I was fairly sure it had to do with Charles and his squad. When the people of the town were tired of paying for the Tendrils' protection, whether it was warranted or not, Kirby was forced to deal with the backlash from the Tendrils.

"Us being here was something he didn't anticipate. It had to be the reason he was so adamant about us not engaging with the trainees..." I said, pacing and making more connections as I talked. "Maybe he's trying to get in their good graces again. Maybe he thinks they still need him. So? He has to deal with us... There was blood, regular human blood, at the ambush on our way back from the dungeon mission. I thought maybe I was overthinking things, maybe it was some of ours, but it wasn't in the right place for it. Who knew about the dungeon plans?" It was a rhetorical question. When I looked up, neither of the councilmen could meet my eyes as their frowns deepened.

"It's entirely possible he caught on that Dai was working with us," I said, not pausing the train of thought as the pieces started to fall into place. There was the possibility that everything I was accusing Kirby of was someone else's fault, but his absence and position spoke of means and methods for making the whole mess we found ourselves in possible. "So what does he do? Deal with us, or at least distract us so he can offer up the trainees.

"But he can't do it alone. No, not without making everyone immediately suspicious. So he turns to one of the squads, maybe the one that's been helping him all along."

"The Wild Guard would never betray our people," Oliver shouted, stabbing a finger into my chest.

"Where are the children? Clara, Sarah. What's the status of

getting everyone rounded up?" I asked aloud and through the comm-plant. Oliver and the councilmen looked at me like I was crazy, checking behind me through the doorway as if they'd missed the two squad leaders entering. While they remained confused, I listened to the two women update me. Sarah laid out that they had managed to pull everyone back into town and were working on getting a count. As far as the one count we were looking for, Clara answered that.

"Nowhere. All the trainees are gone! Charles's squad is missing from the roster. Ron, what is going on?" Clara asked. The tension was clear as day.

"The Guard trainees are gone," I said, turning back to the councilmen who Samuel was trying to rein in.

"How do you know that?" Oliver asked, not with distrust anymore but with confusion.

"A side benefit of working with the Metier Crystals is long range communication. As of now, Charles and his squad are missing, and so is Kirby, if he isn't with you two."

"How can we believe anything you are saying?" Dylan asked, the fire on his head shifting shades between red and blue.

"Well, you can't, except that your whole town is being rounded up and accounted for," I said calmly. My thoughts were focused on finding a lead that would take us to the children. The fire on his head flared translucent, the only indication it was still there was a shimmer in the air, before settling on a vivid blue. The councilman then proceeded to put his face in mine.

"On what authority do you—"

I gripped the man by the face, moving to shove him back before <Memory Canal> activated. Instead of the usual times when it had triggered, a rapid fire spurt of memories, emotions and sensations translated through the connection. It was all underlined by a distinct level of heat and pain as my mana practically *vanished*.

Desperation permeated every moment of my life. Deaths piling up at unprecedented rates thanks to declining ammunition and readily available food. Frantic fluctuation in the population. Then, my friend who was slowly growing scales came up with a crazy plan. A group of people that had been entirely transformed by the radiation. Desperation gave way to hope, which gave way to complacency. The arrival of the Bunker-born kids threw everything for a spin. An option outside of the Tendrils. Doubt as to whether the town was strong enough, pouring over the reports of all the people they were losing each year. Befuddlement at the success they brought with their tactics. Meeting after meeting with Kirby and Irwin about how to deal with the group. Increasing agitation and explosive behavior from Kirby. Try to meet him at his office near the training yard only to find it empty every day. The image of the room burned, seared, into my mind.

Sam caught me as I tried to get my bearings. The memories tried to find a place to settle in my mind. Unlike the previous times <Memory Canal> had activated, the transition back into my own body was much harsher. Like I'd been wearing platform shoes for a decade before going barefoot all of a sudden. A wash of refreshing energy flowed through me and my thoughts realigned a bit better.

"I'm—" The energy faded, the dizziness returned and my stomach emptied right onto the floor. "Not okay."

"What the hell was that?" Oliver and Irwin were supporting a dazed Dylan. The man had crumpled to the floor just like me. His once fiery head was now a mess of embers and crispy burnt hairs in a spiky mess. Yet another inconsistency with how the skill had worked before.

"Not really something I want to talk about right this minute," I managed, wiping my mouth of the foul taste.

"What you want to talk about is not my priority," Irwin said, standing and striding over to me. A vine cracked through the ground to wrap around the man's leg. Surprisingly, he was not stopped at all. The plant hissed as if it had touched acid before Irwin hovered over me. Samuel's sword was steadily placed right on his sternum.

"I don't particularly like how you are approaching my friend, sir." The blond's voice was even, and emotionless. *Samuel?* "Whatever he did, he had a reason for. The councilman invaded his personal space, just like you are doing, so I suggest you *back off*."

From where I was slumped on the ground, I couldn't see Irwin's face, not that things had stopped moving in circles for me to tell anything from it anyhow.

"Fine. If your accusations are over, and what you say about the children is true, then what do we do?" Irwin's voice was just as even and cold.

"His office," I coughed, clearing my throat and struggling to my feet. Samuel lowered his sword long enough to lend me an arm.

"If Dai and Danny lost the trail, then I think that might be the next place we should check."

Irwin looked from me to Samuel before coming to some internal decision with a sigh. "Oliver, help them look. If the Guard is done, have them send Devon and Treston. They will be able to help look for... whatever Ronan is looking for. I'll deal with the townspeople."

Oliver hesitated, but laid Dylan down gently and strode out the door. On his way out, he stopped briefly to whisper to us. "You better be right about this, Bunker-born."

"You *are* sure about this, right Ron?" Sam asked quietly as we walked out of the door and watched Irwin and Oliver head toward the middle of town where a bonfire was burning.

"No, Sam, I'm not. But I don't know what else to do for those kids, so I am willing to try..." I said. The fire drifting into the sky was not enough of a distraction from the mess that was my thoughts.

CHAPTER TWENTY-FIVE

Needle in a Haystack

We made the short walk to the training grounds alone. Other than the image of the office, I had no idea where exactly the room actually was, so we were forced to wait for Devon and Treston. The former contacted me via the comm-plant to let me know he was wrapping up handing the reins to Irwin. He also mentioned that hopefully they could find some answers, or the people were going to start devolving into panic. Having your children go missing, even when it wasn't *unusual* after the Fall, was liable to put parents on the razor's edge. The elf was uncharacteristically serious as he arrived at the training yard, trailed by a late teenager demon.

"This is Treston. His Gift lets him see in the dark, as well as grant it to others for a brief while," Devon explained. The demon boy looked distinctly uncomfortable with the entire development, failing to meet anyone's eyes, but he was stoic enough.

"Thank you, Treston, any help is appreciated," Sam said, comforting the teen and shaking his hand with a small smile. That got a nod out of the youth.

"Can you take us to Kirby's office?" I asked, getting us back on track.

"It's the entire second floor here," Devon pointed to a nearby building that looked unassuming other than the balcony overlooking the training field.

Without much more fanfare, we all walked toward the building. Oliver had a lamp in hand, but he left it outside as he motioned to Treston. Even in the fading daylight and flickering lantern light, the blue blush on the youth's gray skin was unmistakable. Treston placed his hands over Devon's eyes and a flash of midnight black fog flowed into the man's face. I heard the slightest whisper under his voice. "Darkvision." Samuel gave him a supportive smile as the demon repeated the process with him. This time, I watched as two tiny spell chains formed right over the iris of my friend's eyes before being engulfed by the black fog. Thankfully, I only flinched slightly as Treston used his skill on me. When the darkness of his mana faded away, everything had been turned into grayscale.

Clear details highlighted things I never even thought had shadows in the fading sunlight. The light of the lantern was like a shining beacon washing everything in white while the dark building was tones of gray. Even when Devon snuffed out his lantern, the gray remained, highlighting everything in stark detail. There were no shadows or hidden cracks we couldn't see, the only thing lost were colors. Admittedly a troublesome side effect, but the benefits of perfect night vision couldn't be under-estimated. The change in my perspective actually had my own perception going crazy. The surprising crispness of all the details had me doing a double take at it all.

"That's a new one," Sam whispered.

"Let's get the search over before I have to rush back and save someone," Devon said, striding into the building.

"How would you save someone?" Treston asked.

"I would knock them out, Tresty. Don't worry about that now, and help us look for anything that's out of place."

Through our comm-plant, Devon asked what exactly we

were looking for. To his increasingly deeper frown, something that looked entirely out of place on the elf's inhumanly pristine skin, I broke down what we knew about Kirby's possible dealings with the Dreg Tendrils. Anything that might solidify that connection, or give a lead toward where the children might be being kept was the goal of the search.

The building was what I would have imagined a pre-Fall dojo might have looked like. Thick mats lined the floor and rough racks were lined with mock weapons of various types. It wasn't a high budget type thing, likely because of the inability to use most of the old world tools, but it looked well taken care of. We spent a few minutes looking through the first floor, but it was barebones. Devon led us up to the second floor while explaining what he knew.

"Kirby usually didn't let people up here other than the other councilmen. Except, thinking back on it, even that was rare. Only if one of us got into big trouble would we be taken here…" Devon said, clearly reminiscing about something as we went up a flight of stairs.

The second floor looked to have once been a housing residence. Part of it was converted into a living, dining, and sleeping area while the other two thirds of the space were cordoned off as one massive office. Sam volunteered to go through the apartment while the rest of us entered the councilman's office. If I had any thought that Kirby was an organized person, that all went out of the window. Papers were strewn about haphazardly, and many just piled up on the ground. A half-dozen hardwood bookshelves lined the back wall with tomes and books of all kinds of subject matter. Intermingled amongst those things and on top of a dozen mismatched sets of tables were various post-Fall drops. The wash of grayscale made it hard to tell colors apart, but the general properties of the items displayed spoke for themselves. Infusions of all the different Attunements, pelts, bones and a number of other different animal bits were pinned and marked with labels in a neat hand like some kind of archeological museum of the world after the apocalypse.

"Good God..." I said, spotting a half-decomposed crow head in the corner. "You said you've been in here before?"

"Well... Yes, but it was never like this..." Devon said. The man was holding his nose as if he could smell something putrid. Other than a staleness to the air, as if the room had been shut and alone for a long time, I couldn't smell anything.

"No sense in waiting. We aren't sure what we are looking for, but anything that looks... Well, more suspicious than all of this already looks," I said. I picked my way gingerly to the desk near the back of the room. There was the smallest path through the mess that looked like it had been deliberately made. I was once again thankful and impressed by the darkvision skill Treston had. There were several candles and lanterns set about the room, but we didn't have to bother with those.

"How long does this last?" I asked the demon youth from across the room.

"About an hour. The effects vary between people, so I'm not sure what yours will be," the youth said with confidence. He was sifting through a pile of infusions and reading through the papers beside them.

We worked in silence for several minutes. Treston remained tense, but he sifted through bits and bobs diligently. Devon used small gusts of wind to push most of the junk he'd sorted through into the corner of the room he and Treston worked through.

For my part, the search of the desk turned up a huge amount of nothing. Most of the drawers were simply filled with various office supplies. The papers scattered about the top of the desk were all reports of the different assignments for the Wild Guard. There were still more papers to process, but all I'd read through were action reports on the New Hopers. After familiarizing myself with Kirby's chaotic organization system, I eventually landed on Charles's squad's stack. Unfortunately, my search companion had things to say.

"This is pointless. How are we supposed to find anything in this mess? We should be out there looking for the trainees!" Devon said, slapping down a stack of papers and yelling loud enough to trigger his air-whispers in a less than optimal volume.

"What exactly do you suppose we do? Even if Treston could give all of the Wild Guard darkvision, would we be able to fight as well in the dark? Would we even find the enemies we are looking for?" I snapped back.

"I don't know, Ronan! Those kids are my family, and I seemed to recall you making a big enough fuss to put us all in danger when yours was in a pinch."

"You think I don't want to charge out there and help? What good would that do but get us killed? I saw reason and I kept my head thanks to you and the others. I'm asking you to do so now," I said, softening my voice as much as I could through the tension of the day.

"Why do you feel the need to take over?" Devon asked, striding through a stack as if the contents were irrelevant.

"How is that even a problem right now?" I asked, caught off guard.

"You just assume that you know better than everyone else in town. I saw you, when Clara was leading. It grated on you. Did you even bother asking the councilmen how to handle the situation?" A gentle breeze flowed through the room even if the windows along the walls were shut.

"It's their fault this is even an issue right now. You might not trust me, but you trust Dai, right? He did the research. Missing people for a decade right under the noses of your 'council.'"

"I don't think we shou—" Treston was interrupted midsentence as Devon's tirade picked up along with the wind in the room. Now it was whipping around, lifting sheets and even some of the lighter trinkets into the air.

"Don't presume to know what you are talking about. While I have given you the benefit of the doubt, unlike Oliver, I won't have you bad mouthing the people of this town!" Devon shouted.

At some point, I'd started to channel my mana into spell chains along both hands. Surprisingly, the brown glow of my mana was highlighted through the darkvision. Thin wisps of the energy drifting off in a particular direction. The shock of the color was enough to snap me out of my own thoughts, particularly as static sparks flittered from Devon's fingers. When I stopped paying attention directly to what he was saying, Devon became even more aggravated. The anger worked in my favor as the man summoned his own primal spell chains. A large, circular one that drifted as a white-gray contrast around his feet. The larger spell chain practically created a video game homing arrow towards the corner of the room with the crow head. The thing all of us in the room had been avoiding, for obvious reasons.

"Devon, stop! Look," I said, snapping my fingers to draw his attention. The man actually growled at me, but I saw his eyes flick down to my wrists and then to the spell chain at his feet. His anger fizzled along with his mana.

"It's never done that before…" he said. The elf walked over to one of the lanterns, pulling a lighter from his pants and lighting it. The white of everything grayscale around us skyrocketed under the light source. "Snuff the darkvision, Tresty."

The demon teen, who'd been cowering back as we squared up, surged into the room. A black haze like midnight, darker than anything giving detail to the room, spun around his hands. With a twitch, the spell chain around his wrists snapped and the world returned to normal color. Everything was immensely dark, and I could have sworn I still saw some grayscale, but the light of the lantern was just enough to go by. Treston's skill had been worth the teen's weight in gold, but none of us were focused on the greatness of the darkvision search. The three of us, plus an alarmed Sam that responded to the electrical racket Devon kicked up, converged on the crow head.

"Why are we all staring at a dead bird?" Sam asked after several seconds of silence and awkward staring. Instead of responding, I summoned a spell chain to my wrist. The normally rigid series of symbols was hazy at best. Closer to the source, the strange distortion was even stronger. I tried to switch to another of my skill spell chains but the effect was the same.

"That's not supposed to happen?" Treston asked, voicing the obvious question.

When all three of us shook our heads, the teen sighed in relief. "Oh good. I thought it was just me."

"Is it the head?" Devon asked, holding his nose but not backing away from the head.

"I'm not sure. I don't suppose you've got some gloves somewhere?" I asked, turning to the elf.

Devon opened his mouth to respond but Samuel beat him to it. He blurted out, "Ihaveanideagivemeasecond." Then he was gone out of the room.

The three of us shared a look of confusion until the life mage returned with a pair of oven mitts of all things.

"How is that supposed to help?" I asked incredulously.

"They cover your hands. And because I got them, I'm not it!"

"Not it!" Devon and Treston parroted my childhood friend and I couldn't help the groan that escaped me.

"The world ended and that childish stuff somehow made it through..." I grumbled under my breath while taking the mitts.

Grimacing the whole way, I grabbed the bowling-ball-sized head off the pedestal. It was much lighter than I expected, but considering the creature was still a bird, its bones were probably hollow. I poked and prodded at the flesh with my mitts but other than the hurl-inducing squelches, nothing happened.

"Maybe there was something behind it?" Treston suggested. Unfortunately there was nothing else on the pedestal or the ground around it. The label only stated 'Death Crow.'

Since there was only one last place to look, I pried the creature's beak open and looked inside. Other than the revolting mess that used to be the crow's tongue, there was a sickly black glow emanating from somewhere in its throat. Without thinking,

I reached into the maw and plucked something that immediately made me feel ill. The dizzying and incomplete information my implant was providing seemed to agree.

<QEunottietnyt 1 ICnlfuusstieorn>

<DDeRaEtGh - CCaorrrriuopntion>

<Integrity: **ERROR**%>

"What the hell is that thing…?" Sam whispered, horrified.

"It looks like… one of the Metier Crystals," Devon said.

The elf was partly correct. It did look like someone had taken a baseball-sized chunk of the Entity Cluster and dipped it in black tar. However, inside I could see what was undeniably an infusion. Taking the creature we'd pulled this from, it made sense that it was a death-attuned one. The part where the implant didn't know what exactly it was had me concerned. Treston was pale, even more than the usual demon, the longer he stared at it.

The fact that it was in Kirby's office and that it had come from one of the crows which had mysteriously disappeared threw a few more answers my way. It was entirely possible that the councilman had been the one involved in bringing the crows down on us.

Nothing conclusive, since there was the possibility that he had just come across this, but the coincidence was too strong.

"It looks a bit like Blobby's core don't you think? Well, if it was black and not green," Sam said. The comparison was obvious once my friend pointed it out. It didn't alleviate my concerns in the least.

"We should bring this thing to Tec," I said, finally setting down the head.

"Who's Tec? What about the trainees?" Treston asked. His gray features were somewhat obscured by the flickering lantern, but the frown on his face was obvious. It was made even more notable by the youth's curling horns.

"Cat's out of the bag now, so I suppose it doesn't matter," I said. A look at the youth, even without all the crisp detail of his darkvision, told me he wasn't familiar with the expression.

Possibly not familiar with what a cat was, if I thought about it. "The Metier Crystals. They have... an intelligence of sorts. They've been able to help us right the bad things on the surface."

"So the rumor was true! You could interact with the Blessing of Magic!" Treston said, concerns momentarily forgotten.

I nodded and the demon teen devolved into a flurry of questions. While I did my best to answer, I communicated to Devon and Samuel through the comm-plant that we should get moving. It might be a tenuous lead, or maybe just incriminating evidence, but I doubted there was much more we could get from the now-mostly-destroyed office. Courtesy of Devon. Almost as an afterthought, while the others were heading toward the exit, I rifled through the desk and found some of the reports I'd been ready to look at. I didn't grab them all because a familiar voice dinged in my head.

"-ing. Testing. Testing." It said every few seconds.

"Daniela!" Unsurprisingly, Samuel and I latched on to the comm-plant call simultaneously.

"Oh thank God, we are finally back in range. We are almost to the town, it's pure madness out there!" she said, sighing in relief.

"Do you need help?" Sam said, I could hear his steps thump in the dojo downstairs.

"We're okay," Dai answered. "But the night creatures are active on a scale I haven't seen in many years."

I spared a look at the revolting crystal in my hand before jogging down the stairs and catching up to our investigating group. "I might have an idea about that..."

CHAPTER TWENTY-SIX

Answers, Questions, and Jukes

Not wanting people to see the unnatural crystal, I turned one of the oven mitts inside out to hide it from sight. Just in case I needed to handle the strange thing, I tucked the other mitt into my back pocket. For some reason, I *really* didn't want to touch the thing with my bare hands. Nonetheless, our little group cut through the town, passing the cluster of bonfires where the townspeople were gathered, until we arrived at the west gate. I leafed through the papers I'd swiped, using the lantern light and the bonfire to light up the pages. The information there wasn't coming together entirely, but it certainly didn't line up with the rotations I knew the other Wild Guard squads had, even the New Hopers with their long-range missions.

Right before we got to the gate, we stopped to talk to Treston. He really wanted to join us, but I insisted that he'd already done more than we'd asked of him. The teen almost pouted as he trudged back towards where the other squads of the Wild Guard were talking with the townspeople. What I didn't want was to include him in a meeting that would almost certainly give nothing but bad news.

To the surprise of no one present, Sarah and Clara were

already present and talking with Danny and Dai. What *did* surprise me was Dylan's presence. The councilman looked to have aged about ten years since the last I'd seen him and considering the man was in his forties, it was actually quite noticeable. He grimaced when he saw me approach.

"Ronan," he said with a nod in my direction. I didn't miss him avert his eyes.

"What do we have?" I asked.

"A whole lot of nothing," Daniela answered with a huff.

"To elaborate, we found traces of a large group but not enough to go by. The night creatures ramped up much earlier than before, and we lost the one lead I thought was good," Dai offered. When I saw how out of breath the lizardman was, and Daniela also breathing heavily, I realized that they'd been pushing themselves.

"You two try to get some rest. Unfortunately, I don't think there is much more we can do today," I said with a sigh. The argument lingering in their eyes was clear, but when Sam entered the conversation, their complaints died in their throat.

"I'll take them to our house spot," Sam said, nodding in the direction of Dylan and Devon. "Behave. You don't have us to back you up if you step in it," the life-attuned added through our comm-plant.

Silence lingered as the Wild Guard and the councilman eyed me. The former with concern and the latter with fearful, flitting looks. The back of my mind told me that I should be bothered by that more than I was, but I pushed that off for later. We still needed to figure out what to do. Thankfully, we had the greatest ice breaker roll up to the scene. Literally.

Blobby's lime green bulk bumped into my calf. Thanks to its increased size, the slime was almost up to my waist and I could see the three crystals orbiting inside it slowly. The slime raised a jiggly appendage and prodded the inside-out mitt in my hand. When Blobby shifted color to a mottled green and *hissed*, I had to do a double take. *I didn't even know it could make sounds like that...* That definitely caught everyone's attention.

"What's in there, Ronan?" Clara asked. Instead of answering, I plucked the strange crystal out using the other glove. The demoness actually swayed from her spot and backed away. Dylan and Sarah didn't look nearly as ill, but they were staring daggers at the crystal. "That's making me sick. What is it?"

"This was inside a crow's head. In Kirby's office."

"Impossible... I was just there last week..." Dylan whispered, but it was audible enough to my improved senses.

"It's not directly incriminating, but this certainly points to him doing something sketchier than anyone here thought. Based on Clara's reaction, I would say it's affecting death-attuned more. I'm currently running on the assumption this is some kind of perverse Metier Crystal with a death infusion at its core. An alignment essence, I think you all call them."

Dylan's jaw worked like a gaping fish. Clara still looked ill, so I put the thing away and she visibly improved. Considering her skin was gray in color, I was amazed how green it got. Sarah was the one with the more cohesive response. "What does that mean for the trainees? If those two couldn't follow the trail and the office was a dead end, what are we supposed to do?"

"We'll have to set up search parties, or scouting squads like Dai and Daniela. Going as far as those two managed today and then pushing further from there will be our best bet."

To Dylan's credit, he didn't try to argue against my plan. "Possible. We might need to call in some people to act as militia in the meantime. The Wild Guard is just simply more effective at keeping patrols around the wall."

"How many do you think we can spare?" My thoughts drifted to the youths still missing and what was occurring in their absence.

Over the next several minutes, we discussed just what the town of Wildwood had at its disposal. The fight against the horde of crows had shown me they were a hardy group, but the free flow of information from the guard leaders and the councilman put things into perspective. There were a few others like Treston that hadn't joined as trainees, but had access to various

Gifts. I also recalled that some of the fishermen groups were also Gifted, just more reliant on existing water. *Probably some kind of direct offensive or direct defensive skill, then.* The thought was irrelevant at that point, but my mind wasn't running on all cylinders.

It almost sputtered to a halt when the gate opened and in walked Charles and two of his squad mates.

The swaggering fae faltered mid-step, apparently not expecting people right at the gate. Him and his goons looked thoroughly trashed. But only *looked*. The relaxed posture and unflinching steps spoke of either healed wounds or faked injuries. The growing confusion and panic on his face had me leaning toward faked.

Something in the combined expressions of Dylan, Sarah, Devon, Clara, and myself must have told the man he was in more trouble than he was willing to deal with, because he turned tail and ran. Fast. Magic-fast.

I caught a glimpse of spell chains around his calves before he left his two companions behind. Clara was already on it.

"Devon!"

The elf didn't even respond, instead opting to blur past the other two men who were still reeling from their less-than-welcoming reception. As the personified wind that was the air-attuned passed them, they finally seemed to snap to.

Before they could do anything, a caustic cloud of black death enshrouded them both before getting dragged away in Devon's tailwind. Sarah's fiery hand manifested a moment later to snag the coughing duo. The woman seemed to struggle, but she hoisted them closer. Under the light of her fire, I saw the demon and fae features of the two men. When the demon started to form a spell chain, I lobbed a <Mineral Strike> at his head. The demon's head lolled to the side like a ragdoll.

The eyes of the peach-colored fae beside him widened and he raised his arms in the sign of 'giving up'.

I kept the skill channeled in hand as Sarah pulled back her fire. She manhandled the pair up against the wall. The armor strapped to her body radiated oppressive heat as she purposefully banged the chest piece. I wasn't sure if that was meant for intimidation or something else, but the fae looked more than sedate after the display.

Clara, stinger staff at the ready, and Sarah kept an eye on the two men while I kept mine out on the darkness beyond. A pair of torches lined the top of the palisade gate cast light out into the fields. The oppressive darkness of the woods yawned beyond the fields.

The councilman joined me at the gate. Dylan had a mundane machete in hand, but with his fiery hair trait, it actually cut an impressive figure as the oiled tool glimmered in the night. "I suppose the world hasn't changed as much as I thought."

All I could do was quirk an eyebrow in his direction. I was doing my best to restrain my nervous energy and not leap after Devon. Not only would it be futile to chase the man with his prodigious speed at this point, but also I had no real way of navigating in the dark.

"People were selfish before the Fall. I suppose surviving just made them hold off a bit longer before relapsing. I... would like to apologize. Life has not been kind, and I've been too preoccupied with the now to see the big picture. Or even where your arrival might fit into that."

"Our intentions are to retake the surface," I started. "When we learned that there might be other survivors, well... I may have been a tad overzealous."

"A little?" Dylan asked.

"Don't push it." The councilman raised his arms up as if to concede that point. "We are just three people and the world is a very big place. We always worked together, in the Bunker, because if the balance broke, then we could all die. I've come to realize it's much the same on the surface. Except the balance here is less about resources and more about egos. Relationships and plans, as opposed to goals and needs."

"There has to be a middle ground. A tolerable medium to the way I am approaching this," I added, mostly to myself. After

all the butting heads, and essentially gallivanting through councilman Dylan's head, I'd realized that maybe I hadn't been
coming across the best. The 'give and take' of our engagements
had been a bit too harsh. For all the trust Clara and Sarah's
teams had towards us, we were still strangers to these people.
Anyone we met moving forward would be the same way.

A flash of light from the treeline snapped me from my
musings. That one was followed by a few more, smaller, flashes.
All of us tensed in anticipation when a figure started to make its
way toward us down the road. They must have seen the spell
chain I almost buried them in because Devon's snide voice
came through the comm-plant a moment later. "It's me, hold
your rocks!"

Releasing my hold on my mana, I walked up to Devon
where he was lugging an unconscious and particularly crispy
Charles in hand. The source of the light flashes was now obvious. The two of us made quick work of hauling the man back
inside the gate, shutting it and barring it from within. The still-
awake fae's eyes widened even further at the sight of their
burned squad leader. Without any ceremony, we dropped the
escapee at Dylan's feet.

"You lot got a jail?" I asked. "I think we ought to have
ourselves a little talk with our traitorous friends here."

Turned out that Wildwood didn't have a proper jail, but the
holding cells at the old sheriff's building on the other side of
Lake Sumter served well enough. All the windows were busted
and there wasn't anything left but broken furniture, the guns
and ammo cleared out years ago. The drunk tank was service-
able enough, but I made some slight modifications. Particularly,
a corona of <Stone Spikes> only inches away from punching
through our captives' torsos, and a heavy dose of chains. The
latter were courtesy of one of the town smiths, whose child was
also missing. He'd insisted on being a part of the interrogation,

but thankfully Dylan and Irwin had been able to calm the man down.

As a matter of fact, both councilmen had to remain with the bulk of the town. When we took Charles and his crew for a little walk, an avalanche of questions was thrown our way. Thankfully, the Bunker Busters had garnered quite a positive reputation, otherwise I almost thought that the group was going to turn into an angry mob just to get some answers. As the two town elders led the way, and the Wild Guard switched guards on the walls, Sam, Devon, and Clara helped me take the men to their cells. Sarah was tasked with organizing all the squads, which was normally Kirby's job, but she promised to send Daniela and Dai as soon as they were awake.

So, it was with bated breath that we waited for the main stooge to wake up. I'd considered having Sam heal the man, just to speed up the process, but I wanted him on the backfoot. It was also why my gelatinous companion was split in three and only inches away from encasing the legs of our captives. A hundred elaborate and arduous possibilities for how one might detain someone with magical powers flowed through my mind, but we hoped that overwhelming force would be enough for now.

"He's not going to tell you anything," the still-conscious fae whispered.

"Shut your trap, Omir. No one wants to hear about how they put you to sleep because you were just a pawn," Devon snapped.

"Are we sure that's all he knows?" Clara asked, rolling her staff in hand.

"I swear! Please, don't kill me!" The man devolved into sobs, eliciting groans from everyone present. As serious as the situation was, none of us were trained interrogators and the man's groveling was grating on our already thin patience.

"Damn right, they won't—Ugh!" The demon companion of the trio tried to surge forward only to push a spike right into his gut. I leveled a <Mineral Strike> right between his horns while Clara put the pointed tip of her staff up to his wound.

"If you don't have anything to share with the class, Oscar, I would suggest you keep your lips sealed. It's better for your health," Clara added, gently.

Man, I know I can come across as brusque, but these two are not far behind. While I thought about how harsh growing up on the surface might be, the star of the show finally stirred. Charles blinked, taking in the two lanterns set behind us, leaving him and his companions staring at our shadowed forms. Unlike Tweedle Dumb, he took in his surroundings quickly before assuming that 'chill' persona I'd seen when I previously met him.

"What seems to be the problem, friends? There's no need for all of these pointy objects in our vicinity."

The four of us shared a look, but Clara affirmed that I should take the lead via the comm-plant. "We want to know where the trainees are, Charles. We want to know where Kirby has been taking people." No sense beating around the bush.

"What would make you think anyone is going anywhere with anyone anyhow?" he said, drawing out each word as if he had all the time in the world.

"I'm not here for any stupid games. If you think you deserve an ounce of mercy for being complicit in this, then you are wrong. Just say the word and I'll let the angry mob of parents in here. I don't even need to get my hands dirty, scumbag," I replied evenly, even if I was white-knuckling my pickaxe. The head was laying on the ground, and I was leaning heavily on it to stop myself from physically lashing out at the man. All the little social handlings I'd seen my uncle do had never included interrogation, but I was fairly certain that when I resorted to physical violence, I lost most of my edge in the conversation. The threat of violence could be more effective than the actual violence.

"You don't even know what you are asking. You don't know *who* you are asking. Get rid of me, and your answers dry up faster than Lake Okeechobee in the summer. This is the part where you give me a D.E.A.L."

"Hey! What about us?" The other fae, Omir, managed to compose himself enough through his sobs to snap at his squad leader. The man had the audacity to shrug, as if it was no big deal to betray his companions.

"You two didn't do a good enough job keeping them busy. As far as I'm concerned, it's your fault we are in this predicament."

"You bastard! After all the things we've don—" the other man shouted before being cut off.

"Nuh-ah-ah. Best keep those to yourself, Oscar. You'll want your own bargaining chips for where all those bodies are buried," Charles's face curled into a sneer as he turned back to me. "So, let's not ask what I can do for the town of Wildwood, but what the town of Wildwood can do for me, yes?"

I was pretty sure you could hear me grinding my teeth all the way from the town proper. The man had embodied all the things I hated most in the shortest amount of time possible. Disloyal, prideful, unscrupulous. If Guinness World Records were still a thing, he would have gotten the award for fastest zero-to-sociopath in the world.

"I'm not going to negotiate with you, Charles. We already know that you were involved in taking the children and distracting us from where they were. That was a brilliant touch, by the way." *Flatter them, in the hopes they lower their guard.* It almost made bile rise up my throat, and the others gave me appalled looks, but I didn't care so long as we got what we needed. "The best I can do is keep you alive."

"I suppose I can't be picky. It is going to get *real* unsafe around here, and fast." The fae eyed us, the precautions we'd set in place and his companions who were stunned silent. "A'ight. The least I can do is tell you where Kirby's got them. After heading out the west gate, we cut north. Not sure how many miles, but it's just off of a road next to a small lake."

I couldn't believe what he was saying. Literally. Even if I

hadn't improved my perception, or even gotten practice reading people with my uncle, I could have spotted the lie. Boisterous as the scum was, he'd actually looked away from me when I met his eyes and had the audacity to shuffle his feet. I was so stunned that he responded and I almost missed it.

"You are lying," I said evenly. My cool tone seemed to draw the man's attention back to me.

"I sure as shit am not!" he said, the pitch of his voice rising.

"We already know for a fact they headed west. Further west, not straight north," I replied, recalling what Dai said. "We don't have time for your games. Deceiving us will get you nowhere."

With my words, I stood and walked closer to the fae. His colored irises were a strange sight from up close, shifty and insecure even as the rest of his body tried to keep cool. After several seconds of staring at each other, he croaked. "They will kill me."

"I'm gonna kill you, you traitor!" Devon said, jumping forward and blasting the man with one of his gust punches. The impact rocked Charles against the back wall before bouncing him back into my spikes. When the man just whimpered once at the blow and avoided my eyes, I knew we weren't getting anywhere with him.

"We don't have time for this…" I repeated. My mind turned to Dylan and the episode we'd had arguing over Kirby.

I'd never actively used the skill, but it had triggered several times up to that point. There hadn't been time to even discuss with either Tec or Bec just what the 'misc' skill category meant. Nonetheless, when I felt around the mental space where I knew the skill knowledge lingered, <Memory Canal> practically flared to be used. Somehow the skill, or my subconscious, knew what I wanted and was simplifying the process.

Since we were way past the point of hesitating, I gripped Charles's head in my palm. The man tried to jerk away, but I channeled some of my mana into my pickaxe to up my strength. He was locked in place.

"What are you doing?" he asked fearfully. He strained

against the pair of handcuffs we'd put on him and I even saw spell chains form around his legs as if he was getting ready to make a break for it. Blobby had none of that. The slime unspooled like a snake to encase the man's legs. The spell chain sputtered as my gelatinous friend put pressure on him.

"Ronan, what *are* you doing?" Sam asked, placing a gentle hand on my arm.

"Whatever I need to do." There hadn't been much time to talk to my friends about the skill, but right then was not it. Before I could get cold feet, I slammed the mental button for the skill. The world swirled into darkness as I plunged into Charles's mind.

CHAPTER TWENTY-SEVEN

Search Parties

Everything was one trigger word away from crumbling to pieces. Decisions, choices, and fighting the inevitable. Kirby's encouraging words, but the weight of survival fought against the crush of guilt. Tens of people left for the Tendrils. I just wanted to live, I—

"Get out of my head!" A thunderous voice shook the walls of a whitespace around us. My body solidified and my other body solidified. Except I realized that the other body wasn't my body. It was Charles. "How are you doing this!?"

The man's voice was married by a bone deep fear of the unknown. Of how I'd somehow managed to get into his mind.

"I need to know where the trainees are." My voice sounded hollow, as if I was talking from a faraway place and not ten feet from Charles.

"This isn't possible..." the man mumbled, true panic cracking the façade of swagger and relaxation he'd put on, even with the sociopathic tendencies to feed it.

Something about the exchange told me that he would not give me what I wanted, so I strode forward and gripped his head again. Unlike outside of the whitespace, the fae was not bound. The moment my fingers touched his head, spell chains formed around his legs. The muscles and everything there swelled and Charles snapped a rib-crushing kick into my side. The brief brush of contact, whether the fingers or the kick, showed me another of the Tendril camps. Bigger than the others, but that was all the information I could drag out.

"You know where they are," I growled, ignoring the pain as <Earth Shell> encased my arms.

"What does it matter!? We are all dead. We only live by their whims," Charles said.

"You don't know that!" I surged the ground below me with a half-powered <Earthen Barrier> and closed the distance between me and the fae. While the man was good in short bursts, his spell chain had already dissipated and was trying to reform by the time I got there. Unfortunately, it wasn't his only attack.

A grotesque contortion of his arm saw it stretch to slap me aside. As his elongated forearm scraped my cheek, I got another flash of memory. The trainees, many I didn't recognize and some that I did, huddled in a dilapidated building. More than a handful looked unconscious and bled from untreated wounds. Then the flash was gone and the pain blossomed on my face.

The blow was nowhere on the strength level of the kick, but it was much faster. Slinging his arm like a whip, Charles rushed forward once his skill modified his legs. With a twist of my wrists, two <Stone Spikes> rose up on either side of me. The elongated arm flopped uselessly after hitting the stone that formed. Hoping that Charles wasn't particularly dexterous while charging forward, I sent a <Mineral Strike> directly in his path. The man was still moving, so it was more like a point blank shot as some kind of obsidian-looking rock formed in my palm and crashed into his sternum. Then I received his charge with a bear hug.

To say the impact hurt would be an understatement, my already-injured chest protesting the motion and leaving me gasping for breath. However, before I got sucked into another memory, I fed <Earth Shell> with the rest of my mana so as to bind my clasped hands to one another. I didn't get a chance to see if it worked because my perspective swapped back to the memory.

"We need to stall them," Kirby said, poring over a rough map. A series of areas were highlighted in red while three were highlighted in green. One large one surrounded by blue ovals, Wildwood, and two smaller ones for the other human towns. Much further beyond the red zone west of Wildwood was a green dot with several question marks around it.

"Sir, how are we supposed to do that? They've probably encountered the bait camps," I said, my voice even, but lacking that swaggering persona I showed the world.

"I need you to take your team back. Pretend you were attacked or something of that ilk. Getting these kids to the Tendrils is our only chance. Your only chance." The scale-splotched man hissed, pointing an accusing finger into my chest. "Ever since those intrusive Bunker-born children started to meddle with my timetable, things have been out of control. Not only that, but the spider has been shaken. Any attempt we make to move through its territory is met with force. We can't risk losing more offerings at this junction. It will take too long to circumvent the known territories…" The councilman mumbled to himself as he focused more closely on the map.

I spared a look over my shoulder at the building just on the edge of the magic-formed camp. Two expressionless earth Tendrils watched over the entryway. I knew the life Tendril was slinking somewhere in the shadows, extracting healing from the small creatures around us. I shivered as I took in the various other Tendrils and their animal companions. The size of this group dwarfed that little display Ronan and his friends had rebutted. The power present around him sent a shiver down his spine because he knew these were not the only Tendrils out there. There were always more Tendrils.

"No use. Even if you can muster a proper distraction, we'll

need to risk turning some of the kids if we want to make it across," Kirby said, snapping me out of my fearful reverie.

"But... sir, that could kill them."

"A price I am willing to pay. The Frond will be happy enough." He turned to rummage through a mound of packs behind him. "It's all I can hope for."

The councilman turned back around as he held up a claw grabber. With a wave of his hand, he gestured one of the Tendrils closer and gave it instructions to retrieve one of the hosts. The humanoid remained perfectly silent as he escorted one of the slimes up to their command area. The cerulean creature shifted gently in place, but Kirby disturbed all that by plunging the grabber into its body. With cold, mechanical precision, he plucked its core and set it on the table.

Before my eyes, the slime staggered, portions of its body sloughing off like melted wax before dissipating into the earth. All that remained was a dark stain in the soil.

"You best get going. You know making these takes a while, and I want to be on the move as soon as possible," Kirby said, waving me off as he got to work.

I watched over my shoulder as the Tendril that had retrieved the slime held the crystal in hand. Oily blue light started to coalesce in the center of the crystal as Kirby spoke into it. Brushing it gently and prodding it, as if directing a macabre concert of corruption.

I beat a quick retreat, rushing to where my squadmates were held unconscious by the other life-attuned Tendril. The creature gave me a flat look as I took its dream meal and hauled them out into the woods.

— + —

The world snapped back into focus before blurring into a mess of lanterns. Arguing could be heard all around me, tightening the vise around my pounding head. My mouth felt like sandpaper. *I suppose it isn't far from being that if my trait extended to—*

Focus! I barely managed to reel thoughts back before the arguing stopped. A gentle rush of energy helped clear my head. As it did, the memories slotted back into place. Unlike before however, I didn't try to talk right away. Sure enough, my body heaved and drool fell from my mouth as the post-magic-heal nausea hit. Thankfully, it had been a long few hours since I'd eaten anything or we would have had a mess to contend with on top of everything else.

Finally the voices took on a more...sensical form. "—is he not responding?" Danny's irritated tone was, of course, the first I heard clearly.

"This is that thing that happened with the councilman, isn't it?" Clara's voice joined the mix.

"Something like this, but he didn't lose consciousness then. And Charles is still unresponsive," Sam said. "Dylan was fine after a little while."

"What do we do with these sorry jokers, then?" Devon asked.

"Why don't we give them to Tec? He might be able to hold on to them while we figure out what to do," Danny said, stepping down and gazing into my face. Her brunette curls only served to highlight the deep frown on her face. "Help me get him to a seat, Sammy."

Daniela and Samuel hoisted me by the armpits until I was propped up in a chair. The world was thankfully not spinning, but my thoughts were still a jumbled mess.

"We..." *Alright, definitely sandpaper.*

"Here, Ron." Sam helped tip my head back and dribbled a little bit of blessed water down my throat. Had I not been wanting to empty the contents of my stomach and curl up into a ball, I would have drained the whole canteen.

"We need... to find them... before it's too late," I rasped.

"Too late for what? And how are we supposed to do that? That was the whole point of this debacle of an interroga—" Devon was cut off by an elbow from Clara.

"Perhaps if you didn't feel the need to run your mouth so

much, you could let the man finish?" she said sweetly. Her eyes, however, spoke volumes. The elf shut his mouth with a clack. *No surprise she has that <Fear>skill. She's already plenty scary.*

I struggled with one of the pockets on my tactical vest before producing the inside-out oven mitt. Even with it still covered, Clara backed up several steps. "More of these... I think use them... to turn people to Tendrils."

The revelation caused several jaws to drop, but I continued talking before my voice failed me.

"There is a camp... somewhere on the northeast of spider territory. Building plus camp like we found," I said, pointing at Danny, Sam, and Dai. The lizardman had remained silent through the whole thing, standing in the far corner. "Spiders stopping them... For now. Not sure how long... kids have."

I met Sam and Danny's concerned eyes. I tried to pass along how much I wanted them to get moving. Urging them to start going without me. Apparently it came across, because Daniela's frown disappeared and Samuel schooled his expression. The blond stood over her shoulder as she started to lay out a search plan. With steady hands, Samuel helped to nudge everyone but Clara out of the room, leaving her and my muddled self to watch over the three prisoners. He promised to return with a wagon or a sled to take the trio to Tec so we could focus on the search.

"Go to sleep, Ronan," Clara said. "Being unconscious is not resting."

"But—"

"No arguments. It's some time past midnight right now. You are not going to rush out anywhere, especially in your condition." After giving me a once-over, she added, "I'll have Devon bring some breakfast."

I wasn't sure when I agreed to resting or when I laid down, but sometime after, the world dissolved into sleep. Garbled, foreign-memory dreams plagued my every moment until the sweet smell of bacon and eggs reached me.

My brain was still sleep-addled as the morning flew by me.

Directions, hauling of materials, and even finishing a rough infusion for Godfrey's shovel-hammer. Only after all of that mess was taken care of did I hear back from my friends and finally acquire the sweet ambrosia of breakfast.

"Tec wasn't happy about it, but he says he can hold those three for now. Something about 'extended mana drain impacting the development of containment and refinement,'" Danny said through a mouthful of tomatoes and eggs.

"Sarah is coordinating the remaining Wild Guard at the west gate and the councilmen are shoring up patrols with the farmers and fishing groups. We've got another brief rest before we head out, and I suggest we make the best of it," Sam added. There were deep bags under my friends' eyes. I hadn't even bothered to look at myself in the mirror or smell my armpits, but I was fairly sure that I was at least deadlier than that skunk we saw on the way to Wildwood.

"Since we are clear of stuff right now… Are you going to tell us just what in the hell you've been doing!?" Daniela snapped, prodding my chest and causing me to drop my fork. To my credit, I only stared at the delicious yolk for two seconds before focusing on my friends.

"Some time ago, after doing the whole miscellaneous skills transfer thing, I *gained* a new skill. It's called <Memory Canal>. It's super vague like all of our other skills, but somehow it's been letting me access people's memories."

"And you didn't think to mention this?" Sam asked incredulously. His own food was forgotten as he gaped at me like a fish.

All I could offer in defense was a weak shrug. "We've been busy, you know?"

"Ron… How can messing around in people's heads possibly be a good thing? I get that we got essential information, but do you even know what that is doing to you or the other person? You were only down for a few seconds with the councilman, but you were down for *hours* when you messed with Charles," Samuel's tone was growing increasingly heated and I could see his finger twitch, ready to wag at me. "While I might have healing magic, I have *no* clue how it works on brain stuff and besides, I'm not even an actual *doctor!*"

"Well, I have a little hypothesis as to why I was out longer. I sort of had to fight Charles in his mind to get the information. I think Dylan *wanted* to share but was just being hesitant or maybe he didn't even realize what was relevant or not."

"You fought in someone's what!?"

Before Samuel could go even more off the handle, Daniela stepped in. Even tanned as he'd gotten, red had worked its way all the way up Sam's forehead from the outburst."Take a breath, Samuel. There's no point blowing up about it now." I was getting ready to thank her before she turned her glare in my direction. "We will be doing the blowing up *later.* Once we've got the kids and you are ready to talk about why you kept us out of this particular crazy plan."

My mouth clacked shut. "Fair."

"Good. Now I'm going to get an hour of sleep, which will probably be less than fifteen minutes because I have to contemplate all the garbage fires burning around me. Including my friend playing psychic. So, good night."

It took all my will to hold back from pointing out it was mid-morning, but I let her walk away.Anthony scurried over to her from where he was resting *inside* the ashes of one of the previous night's fires.

Sam gave me a pointed look before his expression softened. "You need to remember you aren't alone, Ron. Even without knowing how it works, we could have at least been prepared. Please get some rest. Danny's right, we'll deal with this later."

I watched Samuel walk after Danny, except he didn't make it to our borrowed house and instead collapsed onto one of the benches that had been arranged around the fires.

"Those two know how to put someone in their place huh?" I said to myself. I dozed but before I knew it, Dai was shaking me awake.

"They are ready to head out. I think if we wait much longer, the parents are going to revolt and head out there themselves."

"I'm… I'm awake." At some point, a certain gelatinous friend had gotten comfortable beside me. I only noticed because when I tried to get up, my hand sunk into it up to the elbow. Thankfully, Blobby spat me out instead of dissolving me slowly.

"As helpful as it's been," Dai started. "That's kind of gross."

"You get used to it," I said, wiping off some of Blobby's goop and equipping the shield that had been resting in my lap. None of us said anything else as we collected a drooling Samuel and joined the guard up by the gate. Sarah and Daniela were already waiting with a debrief. A small table was strewn with papers, and Sarah looked about ready to keel over, even if her eyes were sharp as they focused on our group.

"I've sent out a squad to secure this location." The orc woman pointed at a map that had been pinned to the bare side of the palisade. Unsettlingly enough, it was an identical copy to the one I'd seen in Charles's memory. When I finally focused on where she was actually pointing, I realized it was where her squad and ours had first met. "There is a building right beside the road that is fairly intact. I want to turn that into a forward operating base. The idea originally was to use it for your dungeon runs, but it will help us out *now*."

"Have we gotten any more information from scouts?" Danny asked.

"What's the plan for the town proper?" Samuel added a second after the brunette.

"Oliver is already at the forward base. I'm sure his squad is already looking in the immediate area, but anything further west has been… tough on solo runs. The spiders have been going nuts even without entering the territory we had marked for them." The woman shook her head in frustration. "As for the town, we'll leave a skeleton crew of the guard here. It's not optimal, but the farmers, crafters, and fishermen are tough. They managed before we were of age, they will manage for a day or two."

"No sense in waiting. What do you need from us?" I asked, adjusting my grip on my shield. The nervous energy of battle was already running through me. Because I knew we would not be getting those kids back without a fight.

"I've split up the New Hopers so there is at least one per squad. Four squads total, five if I count you all. Best bet will be to set out from US 301 north, then cut west in a wide grid. Do you know what the range of your communication implants is?" she said, pointing out some faint lines in pencil she'd drawn.

I grimaced at the question. "No, we know the crystals disrupt it but we haven't tested the range specifically yet."

"That's alright. It's been a crazy few days," Sarah blew out a breath. "We'll work out a minimum range from here to the forward base. Give me a second."

The orc woman pulled out a protractor of all things, marking out the scaled difference between Wildwood and the building she'd signaled out. Then she marked out a radius off the wall, off the base and then staggered radii moving up 301. With a deft hand, she had a search grid set up in no time and was copying it over onto a clear sheet of paper that she handed to Daniela. "You're the fastest, yes?"

"Of us here, yeah."

"Get this to Oliver while I send the rest of the squads over. I'll be letting them know that you and Clara have point on the search," Sarah said, gesturing to me. "Please bring them back."

Sarah's voice cracked at the end, but she crossed her arms and blinked the tears away. There was a time for sorrow and despair, but this was not it. Her emotions were proof enough of her determination and trust. A glance at my friends told me it had come across as clear as day. *And coming from a Bunkerite, that means something.*

Daniela told Anthony to stay with us before taking the spider naginata in hand. With a deep breath, she channeled her mana into the weapon and zipped down the road. Samuel and I shared a look before heading out after her.

We had a traitor to find.

CHAPTER TWENTY-EIGHT

Do It For The Children

The trip went by in a blur. Not only was I stronger than ever before, but the path was now familiar. Not that I was able to recognize individual trees or anything like that, but the woods, the growth and the bumps of the road were no longer something I hesitated on. As my mind drifted through the last few days, I gave my status a good look.

Subject: Ronan Terrigan
Health: 100% (Unafflicted)
Mana: 100%
Metier Quotient: 4 (22%)
Dreg Accumulation: 0%
LPS: Wildwood, FL
Communications
Skills - *(1) Selections Available*
Traits - *(98% Banked)*
Attributes - *Growth Quantified*
Skills:
Offensive - <Stone Spike> / Imbue / <Mineral Strike>
Defensive - Direct / <Earth Shell> / <Earthen Barrier>

Misc
- <Pith Mana Lock>
- <Infusion>
- <Memory Canal>
Traits:
Limestone Skin
Unformed (0%)
Attributes:
Strength: 1.56
Mobility: 1.43
Perception: 1.63 > 1.70
Refinement: 1.28 > 1.29
Containment: 2.08 > 2.11

I did a double take as I saw how ridiculously large my gains had been in the attribute department. I'd noted some gains in strength and mobility after fighting the spiders and the camp of Tendrils, but the jump in my perception was the single largest increase I'd gotten. The obvious root of that would be my intrusive ganders into Dylan's and Charles's minds. Once again, the source of my gains left a bit of a sour taste in my mouth and more questions than I cared to have for Bec.

My considerations were cut short as we were met by one of Oliver's squadmates, the one whose child was taken. "Thank God it's just you. Please, tell me we are getting ready to head out."

"That's the goal as soon as the other squads get here. They are probably less than thirty minutes behind us," I said, motioning off down the road.

The man nodded, leading us the short distance to the building adjacent to US 301. Already, I could see a significant difference between it and the surrounding buildings, even as I watched a familiar satyr working to encase the whole structure in organized vines. Dennis waved with one hand as he kept playing his flute staff. All along the perimeter except for in front of the entrance and the back I could see the short, telltale wood stumps of Tim's skill forming a low wall all around the building. We didn't dawdle, following our guide straight to Oliver.

Much like the watch area north of Wildwood, the building was barebones, but a few sleeping spots had been laid out for people. In the far corner, Oliver stood with Daniela looking over yet another copy of the map of the area. *I need to figure out how to get Alan or Bec to give us a modifiable map. The tactical implications weren't something I even expected when coming to the surface.* The drifting conversation pulled me out of my thoughts again. It was slightly concerning how easily I'd been getting distracted since using <Memory Canal>, but there was nothing for me to do about it at the moment.

"—grid is good. If what you say about the communication system works then the search will be much, much faster," Oliver said before noticing us. His slight smile turned down as his eyes landed on me, but he greeted me positively enough. *Really can't blame him, I've somewhat thrown his whole world into chaos in less than a month.*

"Was just getting Oli here caught up," Daniela said, gesturing to the paper Sarah had sketched. "Once the squads are here, we'll be ready to head out."

We made some small talk, mostly to avoid the awkward silence. Oliver's squadmate told us a bit about his son, waxing on about his ability to fly, albeit slowly and for a short period of time. Anthony and Blobby made sure to poke and prod and... antenna... everything around us while we waited. It wasn't long when the call for arrivals sounded and we gathered in the small area cleared in front of the building.

Sam, Danny, and my own training had been fairly rigorous, if based on simulations and physical training. However, as I watched the might of Wildwood assemble for the task at hand, I knew that we'd been lacking something all along. Something we didn't really experience until the surface pressed down on all our souls. Hardship. I had an innate desire to help those children, to help get them back to their families no matter the cost.

What the people gathered here had was *love, grit,* and *determination.*

It didn't matter that their lines weren't formed up all straight, or that their gear was mismatched and not at all infused. As Clara read out from a note in her hands, the groups shifted with a single glance to line up. Four squads, reformed from their original groups to take advantage of the *gift* we'd been able to offer the surface. *Once this is over, I hope Tec can handle all these people.*

At the head of each of those squads were a pair of New Hopers. One lone squad had just three people to everyone else's four. Two elves and Dai stood off to the side, speaking quietly. After Clara finished off her list, the groups were set and she walked over to me as everyone gathered their gear.

"Good to see you lot are still in one piece," she said, gesturing more to my own head than at my companions.

"Rock-for-brains won't be done in by a little brain slushy. Plus, he doesn't use it most of the time, so he'd be alright without it," Danny said, patting me on the shoulder with a sorrowful expression.

"Not quite sure what a slushy is, but I get your meaning. Before I send everyone off, was there anything else you could tell us about the campsite?"

Clara's question forced me to break off my glare at Daniela. "Nothing other than the fact that it's a much bigger force than what attacked the western wall. I'm not sure how much Kirby was involved—or not—in that particular event, but what he has assembled right now doesn't compare. It would be best not to engage with just one squad if at all possible."

"I'll make sure to pass that along. Here, this is the placement for the Busters." Clara pointed to the outermost line on the grid. "Since you are the only group that will be running together, I hope you'll be able to handle whatever gets stirred up."

"Don't worry, we'll be ready for—"

"You can't tell me to stay here!" A voice cut through the

quiet murmuring around the forward base. Almost everyone turned to look at the source of the commotion. Oliver's squad-mate was less than thrilled about something. "I've been patient, and reasonable, and everything else the whole time. But you aren't going to tell me that after all that you want me to stay *here*. Either put me in a group, or I'll make my own way!"

"Eric, please. You are too…" Oliver's words faltered as he looked at Eric. The man in question was frazzled, hair unkempt and large bags under his eyes. However, his *eyes*, they spoke volumes as to what was going on in his mind.

"Michael is out there! If only—" I hadn't seen him move, but Sam had made it to his side. My perception highlighted the spell chain around his wrist before it sunk into Eric's upper back.

"Now, do you want your son to see you like this when we rescue him?" The spell chain pulsed, light visible through the simple shirt on the man's back. "Oliver, we'll take him with us. We are down a member anyhow, and I imagine holding the fort won't take too much effort. Yes?"

The sharpshooter's eyes narrowed on my friend, but I could see the strain in his expression. With a sigh somewhere between resignation and relief, Oliver gave a simple nod.

"Wonderful." The mana going through my friend pulsed again and I could see him sway slightly. "Blobby, Anthony. If you could give our friend here a ride while he takes a well-deserved nap?"

The slime and fire ant were at the blond's side in moments. I'd never seen either of them react so quickly or with quite so much… precision. What I *did* spot was that Samuel brushed his hands along the two creature's bodies with each command. It was easy to forget his own trait, and I was sure it was coming into play there somehow. How he got them to do it aside, the life-attuned turned the stomach-high slime and hip-tall ant into a makeshift horse and buggy. Except the buggy was a bed of living gelatin and the horse was not a horse at all. The two seemed to struggle under Eric's weight, but they didn't so much as complain. I'd also missed just when the man had fallen asleep, but Samuel gave me a wobbly wink in response.

The rest of the preparations were straightforward. Short meal rations for the day in the form of jerky, lots of water, and then everyone was off.

The first part of the trip was tense just as a result of how boring it was. The whole stretch north, our large group traveled on US 301 and creatures left us alone. I spotted a few spiders and even some hounds in the trees, but nothing was dumb enough to mess with a group as leveled and large as ours. Slowly, about a mile from the forward base, the first group branched. Another mile, another group. The middle group was Dai's group, the lizardman giving us a curt nod before disappearing into the woods with his two elven companions. When we parted with Clara and Devon's group and were left alone, we finally stirred Eric from his sleep.

"Wha—Who—Where?" he mumbled as he shook the last bits of sleep from his head.

"You're alright, Eric. You remember us, yes?" Sam took the lead and gestured to Daniela and myself before pointing to the slime he was laying on. Anthony was already turned around, antenna twitching in the air. That only served to spook the man, but thankfully Danny was quick enough to slap a hand over his mouth before he screamed our location to the entire forest. When he finally made eye contact with the brunette and nodded, she removed her hand.

"How did I get here?" he asked.

"Samuel here intervened on your behalf and put your stubborn ass to sleep," Danny said, pointing a thumb over her shoulder at Sam. Eric turned to look at him, receiving a gentle smile in return. The older man hesitated, still trying to get his bearings, but eventually thanked Samuel.

With the group now more in order, we resumed our northward travel. A mile was a short distance with our increased attributes. While Eric was only Quotient Level 3, he had what he and a few others called an aloof body. Essentially, it made him just as strong but much lighter than someone of his build should be. Other than that, he shared minor versions of Oliver's enhanced sight and Devon's enhanced hearing. The man's main combat potential was in the hatchet at his side and the assault rifle slung over his back.

To pass the time, and probably in an attempt to break the ice and ease his anxiety about the search, Eric told us about his abilities and how Oliver's squad had come about. They were the only group of non-Fallen amongst the Wild Guard, but they were regarded as their long range specialists. As such, they were the only ones with unrestricted access to the town's firearms and ammunition. Apparently, living in the south provided quite the cushion even after a quarter century of shooting mana-mutated creatures.

"Entering the forest now," I reported through our comm-plant.

We received assents from the other teams before everyone focused on moving through the woods. The plan was to cut west from the road, the first team having already encountered spider resistance. Whenever there was strong pushback, they would report through the comm-plants and each group would shift a bit north in their trajectory. The hope was that the drifting grid would catch the new territory border of the spiders and lead them straight to Kirby's camp.

It wasn't long into our trip when we encountered a cluster of banana spiders. Their gossamer threads were spun across the top of the trees, but Daniela burned them down without hesitation. The creatures dropped and our squad descended on them with a fury.

Blobby straight up took two of the spiders out of commission as he swallowed the smaller males. Another found itself pinned to a tree by Daniela's naginata-turned-javelin. Sam used his <Vine Whip> to encase the rest and slow their movements. The larger female spiders were already using their bladed legs to cut and wiggle out of the plants' grip. Anthony and Eric hacked at any spider that got too close, and I drove my pickaxe into any immobile or partially immobile survivors. Within minutes, the creatures were dead.

We checked over our gear, dissociated the bodies, and stashed the loot. Our mission was the kids, not maximizing the bottom line.

We encountered several single spiders that tried to escape us, but a quick blast from Daniela had them cooking in their thoraces. Those sub-Q2 creatures we left alone and just proceeded deeper. By my estimate, we were almost a mile west from the road when the comm-plant came online.

"—peat, this is Team Leader Clara. We've encountered a heavy presence of Tendrils. Please assist. I repeat, this is Team Leader Clara. We've encountered a heavy presence of Tendrils. I repe—"

"Clara! Ron here. What's your status?" I said, calling our group to a halt.

"Ronan! We are about two miles northwest of the road. We haven't been discovered, but Devon says there are at least two groups of Tendrils in the immediate area," the woman said quickly, laying out their information.

"I've got it." Samuel's eyes glazed over as he started to look at the LPS. Out of the corner of my eye I watched him move around in a slow circle until he halted. "That way, about three quarters of a mile."

"Dang, Sam, I'm not even gonna lie, that was impressive," Daniela said. She'd been looking at her map too, but the blond beat her to it.

"Focus, guys. Alright, Clara, we are gonna cut straight to you. As soon as Devon picks up on us, start heading toward us slowly. You've got to be close."

The tension climbed as our group adjusted gear and shot into the woods. As soon as our conversation ended, Clara took up a modified call through the comm-plant. "This is Team Leader Clara. Contact with Tendrils. Possible target acquired. I repe—"

I tuned her out and focused on where we ran. Pines, oaks,

and a few palms that gave me pause flashed around us as we used our enhanced bodies to traverse the forest. The closer we moved to Clara's team, the more signs of unnatural habitation we encountered. Wilted plants in straight sun, broken trees with enormous gashes, and giant piles of scat that made me want to just turn around. *I don't want to meet the creature that dropped that turd.*

Nonetheless, we forged on.

"Stop! Two hundred feet to the east!" Devon's air-whisper fluttered through to us. Apparently the elf had also targeted our creature companions because Blobby rolled forward, but shrunk as it left two copies behind. The Blob-ites instantly stealthed into the undergrowth. Anthony and Danny scurried up a tree as I took center point. Samuel and Eric covered my sides.

A rumble carried through the earth and into my toes. Without thinking, I did a full cast of <Earthen Barrier>, lifting a four foot wall in front of us in a V. It was smaller than if I'd made just a straight line, but I hoped it would break the charge of whatever was coming.

A dull thud, followed by a flurry of others, marked the arrival of our enemy. A second later, a rat crested the wall, bloody ichor leaking from its face. Its information was highlighted, but I slapped it out of the way with a thought.

<Dreg Tendril (Rat)>
<Attunement: Death>
<Refinement: Plague>
<Perceived Metier Quotient: 0>

A pair more crested the wall before Daniela and Anthony unleashed hellish death on the creatures. Through the acrid smoke, I spotted a pair of humanoid shapes in the back. One looked like a molting fruit, while the other was a glowing yellow mess. Their respective information appeared as I cast another <Earthen Barrier>*behind* them to stop them escaping.

<Dreg Tendril (Human)>
<Attunement: Death>
<Refinement: Plague>

<Perceived Metier Quotient: 2>

<Dreg Tendril (Human)>
<Attunement: Life>
<Refinement: Mental>
<Perceived Metier Quotient: 2>

"Sam! Snag them. Eric, keep the rats off of us," I directed, focusing on the two humanoids as creeping vines ran up their legs.

The death Tendril vomited black goo right on the creeping vines. The tar-like substance sizzled as it putrefied my friend's skill. The life Tendril summoned a spell chain around some of the rats at their feet. Their blind charge split, some still trying to drown us in death rats while some climbed the vines and chewed through them about as fast as they were growing.

Eric jumped beside me and hacked through a smoldering ankle-biter that had survived the inferno. I trusted the man to keep them off me as I focused on a <Mineral Strike> in each hand. A quartz and a malachite chunk formed before I lobbed them at the two Tendrils. The blow was just shy, but thankfully the explosion caused the two to stagger back, bleeding multicolored ichor onto the ground. Most of the rats on the life Tendril died to my mineral fragments, which gave Sam enough time to double down and tighten his grip. Just as I was ready to snap another <Mineral Strike>, the death Tendril's head exploded in a gory mess.

Devon, infused knuckle weapon in hand, was panting behind it. A second later, he sent a gust punch at the life Tendril, stealing away the last of its balance as Samuel drowned it in vines. A flickering cloud of black and red washed over the remaining rats, roasting them from the inside while their blood boiled.

We gathered ourselves, looking for any other threats. Devon, Clara, and their two companions joined us in scanning our immediate area. When nothing jumped us and our resident elf gave the all clear, we relaxed. The fight had been quick and we'd managed with only a few scratches, but I'd expended most of my mana, as had Samuel.

The conversation between us was clipped, not out of annoyance but urgency. Eric was practically carving a hole in the ground with his pacing while Devon and Daniela kept watch. The others in the group moved about collecting the loot before stashing it and marking one of the trees. I did my best to stay still and recover as much of my mana as possible.

"We think it's just to the west of here. Other than that horde of rats, there was another scout group with some hounds," Clara said.

"Damn things smell to heck," Devon said, shaking his head as if to clear the smell away. "There are more to the west too."

"So, what, these are like guard shifts?" one of Clara's team asked. I felt slightly bad, but the situation hadn't even allowed me to learn their names.

"That would be my guess. It's just a more tight-knit patrol like what they used to do for you guys," I suggested.

"We need to go maximum creep mode," Daniela added from the tree she was perched on.

All the Wildwoodians looked confused. It even snapped Eric out of his pacing for a moment.

"She means that we need to go slow and be stealthy," Sam clarified.

"Small scale grid. Keep those with the highest mobility, Devon and Danny, at the edges, while everyone else tries to stay within eyesight of the other," I said, glancing at my mana and seeing it tick past sixty percent.

The situation wasn't optimal. However, waiting longer for everyone to regenerate all the way wasn't an option. It was an almost certainty that the dead patrol would be discovered either through absence or the sounds of our battle. And so once everyone was past the fifty percent mark, we spaced out and headed west.

The whole effort to separate was pointless because less than ten minutes later, we were gathering back up. A clearing had come into view and flashes of memory threw me for *waves* of déjà vu. I called everyone back together, and we crept just beside a worn game trail to the edge of the treeline. The worn building in Charles's memory was there. The rusted and twisted hunk of a chain link fence marked the property line that had been overtaken by trees and vines, but in the far distance, I could see the modified space of the Tendrils' camp. The gathering and energies presented in the space before us was what gave me pause.

CHAPTER TWENTY-NINE

Entrenched

"What in the name of all that is holy...?" one of Clara's team whispered.

The rest of us were stunned to silence as we watched what could only be described as some twisted ritual sacrifice.Humanoid Tendrils of each of the Attunements stood around a raised platform. Spell chains were visible around all of them as mana flowed through them into the air. The rainbow of light that I'd seen in the Blessing of Magic around Tec was mimicked on a smaller scale. The central feature of the energy was another of those corrupted crystals held in a familiar scale-patched face

As if passing through the *opposite* of a filter, the energy darkened. Vibrant red turned to a muddy maroon. Clear brown dimmed into a sludge gray. Shimmering gold tarnished into brass. A refreshing blue tainted with slicks of the other colors. The gray of air turning molted, flickering between the once-midnight black turned matte. The six Attunement manas and Dreg versions. I wasn't sure where the connection was forming, but the knowledge flitted through my mind before I suppressed it. There were more horrifying things than the tainting of the mana.

Gathered on the platform, laid out like lambs to the slaughter and hogtied to posts, were the trainees. Not all of them, just a group of ten, but enough to set my blood boiling. No one tied people up to posts without something nefarious as the goal.

"Clara, please tell me you've been able to contact the other teams," I said. My eyes jumped from the ritual to take in the various beasts, an assortment of slimes, and almost a dozen humanoids standing around watching the ritual with rapt attention. It only added to the unnerving scene to see hounds, deer, raccoons, ants, and spiders perfectly still.

"Dai got back to me, but he's still probably fifteen minutes out. The other groups are heading this way, but they are even further away," she replied, whispering quietly for the benefit of the others in the group without implants.

"Then we need to sit tight. There's no way we can take on that many Tendrils," I said through gritted teeth. The mental math of the engagement was not coming up positive. Even the element of surprise would not be enough.

"We need to keep an eye out for that other roving patrol," Devon added, clearing the grass at his feet and drawing a rough map of the area. He used a stick to sketch where we were relative to everything. "I don't hear anything behind us, so it's possible they took this route."

The elf worked to outline and mark the locations of everything he saw, the sketch quickly filling with information. The two other teammates added their own quick suggestions, but the hushed tones fell on deaf ears. Specifically *my* deaf ears, as a single word filled with emotion cracked through my perception.

"Billy…"

I spun. Eric had a nearby tree in a stranglehold. His fingers like claws shredded the bark with his Q3 strength, all while ripping the nails from their place. The man's face was marred with tears and his muscles twitched as he used everything he had not to rush out. Not to rescue his child. I couldn't make out all the details of the children from here, especially with all the distortions from the mana in the air, but that didn't seem to stop Eric.

"Eric, we will get them. We just need to be patient or we'll lose them all," I said, crouching next to the man and placing my palm on his shoulder. *He's not listening...* My words didn't so much as stir the man, and I could feel his coiled muscles even with the gentle touch of my hand. "Eric," I repeated, gripping his shoulder tighter.

Just as it seemed I was going to be able to pull the man from his singular focus, thunder clapped and lightning cracked across the sky. The magic gathering over the platform ballooned as the Tendrils around the platform staggered to their knees. Threads of mana unspooled from the crystal. Like snakes seeking out prey, they drifted along the air. Some prodded at the Tendrils on the ground, bypassing them, before one brushed against one trainee. The boy's throat ripped with a scream as the thread coiled around his leg. Soon enough, other threads surged from the crystal in the trainee's direction. They wrapped around his arms, torso, up along his throat until his head was covered and the screams disappeared.

Now *all* the trainees were screaming.

A kicked-hornet's nest of magical threads snapped onto most of the trainees. Some had slumped in their posts, the strange magical formation ignoring them for the moment. Then my arm bucked.

"*Billy!*" Eric's war cry stirred through us as the man unloaded with his rifle. The clap of bullets beat a staccato against the thunder in the sky. Even enraged as he was, the man's attacks hit their mark. Most, if not all, of the Tendrils responsible for the ritual took bullets to center mass. Kirby, at the head of the platform, seemed to recover only for two bullets to tear a hole where his lung was. The councilman fell out of sight, covered by the platform.

"Charge! Secure the trainees!" I called out as I rushed after Eric.

A zipping green blur shot beside me before splitting three ways. One such blur tangled up Eric just in time to drop him and save his life. A trio of ice shards cleared the space between the line of humanoid Tendrils and the desperate father.

Seeing that a straight run would get us cut down at range, I surged a spell chain right in front of the struggling Eric. An empowered <Earthen Barrier> wedge rose out of the ground, grass and vines clinging to the top. A moment later, I was at the man's side, deflecting a fireball that tried to arc over my wall. I let a trickle of mana flow into my pickaxe, shaping my usual umbrella shield while I waited for the others to charge forward.

A black fog covered the space between my wall and the stage. Taking the small opening that Clara gave me, I peeked around the corner. There was a slew of information scrolling by my eyes, details about the Attunements, refinements, and Quotients of the creatures and humanoids around me but I pushed past that. The time for scouting was over. The Dreg ritual was still ongoing, threads wrapping tighter around the trainees, even as the beasts and Tendrils formed up to the left of the stage. My mind drew a chilling connection between the whole process and the plant infusion experiments back at the Bunker. Nonetheless, it wasn't the time for correlations.

Not bothering to spot where the others were, I sent Daniela a message. "Bombard that crystal above the kids!"

With that, I sent two <Mineral Strikes> into the midst of the Tendrils. My first hunk of quartz missed, but the fragmentation got most of the backline. The second hit a fire-attuned in the chest, shredding its face and chest into fiery spaghetti. This scattered the lines long enough for three concentrated spurts of Daniela's <Flame Burst> to shoot over my head. Flames washed over the trainees, but her aim was unerring.

The twisted balance that had been maintained between the Dreg energies shattered. Crimson and vivid red surged through all of the threads. Where the red touched, Dreg disintegrated into particles of light. The crimson, on the other hand, caused a massive boom that flattened the trainees to the ground, several snapping from their posts completely. An echoing cry shook the clearing before fading into the quiet whining of my injured ears.

By the time my hearing returned, the others had made it to the defensive wall. It was a tight fit, so I sacrificed another twenty percent of my mana to expand it. I left a gap between both of the sections, hopefully to funnel any enemies or divert a charge.

"Let me go, Ronan!" Eric screamed, pointing his gun in my direction. I smacked it back into his face, breaking his nose and snapping him out of it.

"Get it together, Eric! We need you to give us covering fire!" The pain of the injury finally snapped the man from his nonsense, but his determination was not diminished. When I spun, Clara was already meeting my eyes.

"Devon, Garren. You two are on retrieval duty," she said, snapping off commands. The two elves nodded. Before Devon could get too far, I unstrapped my shield and passed it over. He didn't question it, only responding with a nod.

"Daniela, get that wisp up there. Sammy, hit them with your buff, and build up our cover if you—" A boulder the size of my head clipped the top of our wall before deflecting into the air. "Crap!"

A sneaked peek of our enemies showed that a trio of earth-attuned humanoids had jumped to the fore. A berm of earth had risen between our two groups even as fire flickered on the baked soil. Another catapulted rock sought out the gap between our walls and I ducked my head just in time.

"Clara, can you <Fear> them?" The clap of gunfire told me that Eric was in the mix. Wind rustled through my over-grown hair as the retrieval pair vanished toward the trainees.

"I can do you one better." The stinger staff spun in her hand as she stood boldly. Her eyes burned with purple light, but flickering strings of red snapped at the air. "<Smoldering Fear>."

A boulder cracked against my defenses, spraying her with flakes but her gaze didn't falter. I could hear yipping and whimpering as the beasts I'd missed trying to flank us ran for cover.

"<Bush>!" Samuel called out before brambles encased my wall. The growing plants didn't crack the wall like I would have expected, instead they seemed to add a layer of verdant armor to it. The spell chain around my blond friend continued to expand as the growth took root in the unmanipulated earth and shot *up* nearly six feet. Sam staggered, but Clara's other teammate caught him.

"He's overused his Gift!" she announced.

"Give him a minute, he'll pull it together." I said, moving to the part of the wall where the creatures were flanking. A pair of gray blurs appeared and dropped off an unconscious body. The first trainee. "Nine to go!"

"Reloading!" Eric called out. The slide of metal as he exchanged magazines was practiced and smooth. In that brief gap, I pulled Clara down to behind cover.

Even with her darker skin, I could tell she'd gotten close to overdrawing her mana. She was as green as the bushes around us. "Focus on getting us some backup! Get Dai to flank them. I think they are digging in, and so should we. I've only got so much mana, and I bet they have their own limits after that little ritualistic nonsense."

The rat-tat-tat of gunfire started up again and I risked another ten percent mana to lob a <Mineral Strike> at the enemy line. No creatures were moving in the haze of attacks that had formed between us and the Tendrils. Eric's shots petered out as soon as Devon and the other elf returned. There were now four trainees laid out behind us, guarded by an alert Anthony who was chewing on a blindingly white rat. Daniela was leaning against his carapace, taking deep breaths and releasing steaming clouds with each from her mouth and fire gills.

Devon had a number of cuts along his body, and steam was rising from my shield. The impact of some kind of ice projectile was obvious. Garren helped him back and put pressure on one of the larger cuts. The fae that had been looking over Samuel rushed over and channeled green magic into Devon's wounds, halting the bleeding. "They rounded up the others!" Garren said between gulped breaths.

"*You imbecile, infantile, meddling children!*" a voice boomed through the space around us. It was warped, hollow and guttural, but all of us consciously recognized it. Kirby.

"I don't find those things offensive coming from a kidnapping madman!" I called out from behind cover. A few short gestures from Clara, and the recovering Devon and Garren were already scanning the surroundings. Even as their breaths became more ragged, they scanned the forest and shook their heads in the negative.

"This is beyond your comprehension, *Bunker-born,*" he spat. "The business of Wildwood is nothing to you. You should go back to the hole you crawled out of."

"See, I think that's where you are wrong. Everything going on right now is sort of my business. You are the one that's been lobbing rocks at me!" Clara met my eyes, the question clear in them. *What in the hell are you doing?* "Stalling," I said through the comm-plant.

"This is much bigger than this town, child. The world is doomed, and only the strong survive. *I* am the strong. The Wild Guard plays at *my* whim. How else do you think they would have gotten as far? They are but lambs in a slaughter-house, all I can do is lead them back out into fields of green pastures!"

"That metaphor doesn't even make sense..." I shook my head and tried to come up with something else to say to stall further. Fortunately, it seemed the councilman was one to monologue when he got on his massive high horse.

"When I bring the trainees to them, they'll take us back. The whole of Wildwood will be safe, and it will be because of my efforts; not some economic policy Irwin came up with, or some fancy speech Dylan used to 'rally the troops' or 'boost morale.' Survival on the surface is all about power. And I gave us that!"

Stifled cries from the other side told me that the other trainees were *not* having a good time. Eric's grip on his gun was white, but he kept himself from rushing out there. The wild look in his eye told me to do something fast or *he* was going to do something.

"Five minutes out. Group after that is seven minutes out!" Clara told me through the comm-plant.

My mana had only regenerated about halfway, but I could see that my friends and the elf duo were already doing much better. With a deep breath, I jumped up and stood in the gap between my walls.

"I didn't take you for such an egotistical maniac, Kirby! You can't possibly think what you are doing to those kids is a good thing. For God's sake, look at the other Tendrils around you. They aren't really human!" I wasn't sure if that last line was more for me than for him, but I pushed forward regardless. "Your power is borrowed. You are just a scared old man playing with the lives of others."

The scale-patched councilman climbed over the berms with ease, staring me down through our no-man's-land. "You don't even know what you fight. How could you possibly have the right to judge my decisions?"

My eyes drifted to the convulsing trainees on the platform. Two hounds and a life Tendril hovered over them. "That's not living," I said with as much contempt as I could while pointing at the trainees. "Something has gone very wrong if that's the extent you'll go to. Why didn't you do that to yourself, Kirby? Why aren't you leading by example?"

"Minute out!" Clara told me.

My words looked like a physical blow to the councilman, but his expression hardened. The rising red of his human skin paled instantly and his voice deepened again. "I don't have to explain myself to you. You are just a snot-nosed child with delusions of grandeur and power."

"Holding!" Dai's voice reached me directly through the comm-plant.

"As soon as shit hits the fan, you nab Kirby!" I told Dai, keeping a straight face I focused on the comm connection to Devon and Clara. "You guys get to the other trainees. Take Anthony with you!"

"Did you run out of garbage to run your mouth, Ronan? I really expected better!" Kirby called out. I could see the man gesturing to the other Tendrils now that his monologue was over.

"I'm not interested in wasting my time, Kirby. You can let the kids go, or you can rot in a hole somewhere," I spat out. My mana started to gather as the anticipation for the fight climbed once again.

"Your deaths will be a shame. You could have been strong Tendrils indeed. Maybe even retained some of your egos. No matter. Your meager squad cannot stop me. I would have thought people as pampered as Bunker-born would have taken the time to learn arithmetic."

"Maybe not, but we sure as hell are going to try!" I released the mana monstrosity I'd been holding. My voice flowed through all the comm-plants within range. "Go!"

CHAPTER THIRTY

Confronting Madness

In yet another display of her marksmanship, Daniela's <Flame Burst> struck the side of my triple overcharged <Mineral Strike>. The hunk of rock glinted yellow like sulfur, but it was sturdy enough to withstand the impact from my friend's skill. The low arc I'd managed with the torso-sized rock turned into a flat trajectory that landed it just over the Tendrils' berm. The rock shredded and went off like a bomb.

The cries of pain from the Dreg Tendrils were the starting gun for the second act of our fight. Eric remained with the trainees as I surged between my protective walls. Each step saw more <Earth Shell> covering everything but my joints. It took almost all of my remaining mana and left me wanting to coil up in pain, but I had bigger problems.

Namely, the three earth Tendrils who were mighty displeased by my attack. Two were missing bits of their arms and the other was missing a chunk from its torso, yet they stood their ground.

Out of the corner of my eye, I watched mist rolling in from the treeline. Seeing the support, I threw myself at the creatures. Baseball-sized chunks of rock clipped me, bruising even my armored Limestone Skin. Several tried to take my head off, but I held up my pickaxe and formed my crystal umbrella to deflect them.

Torso-hole felt I was close enough to attack personally, so it crashed down on top of me. It was all I could do to interpose my umbrella between us as I dropped to the ground. The Tendril had no business being so fleshy and mobile, yet so heavy. Lacking much mana, I released a quarter-powered <Stone Spike> into the Tendril's side. It was awkward because of how I was pinned, but I managed to use the momentum of my skill and shove the earth-attuned humanoid off of me with my knees. Its weight worked against it there as my spike found purchase in the missing chunk of its chest and sunk almost all the way through.

More rocks rained down on me now that the other Tendril was out of the way. While I struggled to catch my breath from the attack and from dumping so much mana, a caustic cloud of darkness flowed a foot over me.

"Stay low and move forward!" Clara called.

One other rock pinged off my crystal shield before I dismissed it and dropped to my stomach. Even through the torn up earth, it felt natural to crawl forward on my elbows. The vibrations of the battle passed through me, firing senses I didn't even know I had. Unfortunately, the feeling faded as I reached the berm and drove the point of my pick into an afflicted, squirming earth-attuned.

The other must have heard the wet gurgle of its companion passing away, because it fished me off the ground, up into the caustic cloud, before putting me in an one-armed headlock. My breath hitched in my throat as the cloud burned me from within, throwing waves of nausea through me.

The crack of a whip was all I heard before the pressure on my neck disappeared. I heaved on the ground, struggling to catch my breath and keep the contents of my stomach. A warning flashed in the edge of my vision telling me my health had just gone down below fifty percent and I'd been afflicted by Clara's necrotic cloud.

Thankfully, I wasn't alone in the fight. The vine that had saved me reached down and wrapped around my torso. The refreshing energy of healing magic bumped my health by nearly twenty percent and cleared the affliction. A moment later, the zipping energy of <Adrenal Surge> flowed through the same vine.

"Second wind, Ron! Dai needs help!" Sam slurred through the comm-plant.

I didn't even know he could heal like that... My thoughts drifted as I climbed the berm directly to the enemy side. The moment I was clear of the cloud, Clara called through the comm-plant. "Light it!"

Red zips of light were the last things I saw before the explosion pushed me off the berm. Animal bits also flew around me, at least two rats and a coyote, based on the skulls. My perception highlighted this before gravity made itself known once again.

The landing was cake. The damage from the shockwave? Not so much. I coughed out blood even as I tried to orient myself against some enemy.

To the right, at the edge of the platform, Kirby was furiously yelling at a trio of Tendrils lugging a pair of trainees between them. An earth-attuned deer erected a barrier, blocking the group from an onslaught of fireballs from Daniela's wisp. They were heading toward the building.

To my left, Dai and his two companions were flitting around twisting mist. An air Tendril was sending cutting gusts of wind into Dai's cloaking mist. A hard counter to the mist's strength.

Dai's orcish companion seemed to light up like a bonfire, dissipating some of the mist directly into steam, but shooting across the field to tackle the Tendril.

At ground level, I watched a trio of Blobbys fighting the smaller Dreg creatures directly for the first time. Another blinding rat, a few more plague rats, and a raccoon of all things squared up against the split slime. One of the slimes turned in place, acting like a tire spinning out to coat the other creatures in mud. Another of the Blobbys glowed green, causing the mud to harden in the air, turning the mud into ceramic skeets that shredded the other creatures. The white life rat managed to dodge the attack before walking straight into the body of the third waiting Blobby. It struggled, even going so far as to claw at the core within the split slime. The strike caused Blobby to lose some substance, but it rejoined with its two clones before completing its suffocation attack.

This all happened in the few seconds it took me to catch my breath. I could almost feel the <Adrenal Surge> dissipate as my scan of the battlefield ended. While I didn't have a perfect grip on our match up, I had to hope we were at least even now. Our higher Quotient, but exhausted mana pools, against their numerical advantage.

"Ronan, are you alright?" Dai called out from his mist.

"I'm fine! Get to Kirby. I think he's going to where the other trainees are!" The lizardman became visible briefly before he disappeared back into his skill. "Watch out for the deer!"

That was all the time I had as a fire slime and earth slime rolled out in front of me. They were roughly the size of two Blobbys, so when they started to split, I wasn't surprised. Instead, I charged them mid-mitosis. My steel-toed boot connected with their split cores. The satisfying sound of shattering glass reached my ears before the first fire slime lost cohesion. The other fire slime quivered, suddenly trying to stabilize its mass since it hadn't finished separating. The earth slime, however, did get enough time. One latched on to my leg and the other jumped to my arm. Once again, the creatures had no right to be as heavy, because they took me down to the ground before trying to encase me in their gelatinous bodies.

There was a slight burn making its way through my arm and pant leg, but I ignored it as I swirled my hand within the slime. When it landed on the Metier Crystal, I flexed all of my strength to crush it. *That's a nope.* When that didn't work, I flexed all of my strength to rip it out of its body. The creature's insides resisted my tug, particularly the outer skin, but sure enough, the green glowing crystal exited the body and the slime started to liquify. Hand free, I did one of the most important sit ups of my life. Crystal still in hand, which only resulted in my knuckles busting with the impact, I cracked the other earth slime's core.

My teeth ground as I fought against the wave of pain coming from my right hand. Doing my best to ignore my mounting injuries, I focused on the last slime… only for a triple-sized Blobby to consume it whole.

It wasn't clear to me through the lime green exterior of my companion, but the slime fight wasn't over just because Blobby swallowed the other. One of his signature appendages rose up amidst the turbulent shaking within to gesture in the direction of the building. When the appendage shook insistently, I shuffled to my feet. I could hear explosions and grunting beyond the berm, but my eyes zeroed in on the warehouse building.

My hobble-jog was a disgrace, but I wasn't looking to impress anyhow as I collected one of the trainee's broken posts for support and as a makeshift weapon. The four-by-four had seen better days, but it was better than a broken hand. Just in case, I used some of the mana that had recovered to encase my hand with <Earth Shell>, immobilizing and hopefully preventing it from breaking further. *Unlikely with how this fight is going.*

Darker thoughts aside, I followed the drifting mist into the warehouse. The place was dimly illuminated thanks to the numerous holes on its metal roof and the cloudy sky overhead. A flash of black lightning nearly connected with my chest before I got football-tackled to the side by a large orc man. We tumbled behind a few rotted crates as two more zaps lit up the space. My brain registered him as Dai's teammate before I reacted poorly. "Stay down!" he whispered through his tusk.

"*Inept!*" Kirby howled from the other side of the space.

>Failure rests on fleshbag.< A chillingly familiar monotone voiced.

The tone was different, deeper, but reminded me distinctly of Tec.

"Please tell me there isn't some kind of giant evil crystal on the other side of this."

"There isn't some kind of giant evil crystal on the other side of this," the orc said. I let out a sigh of slight relief. "I would say it's a bigger-than-small evil crystal on the other side of this." *Spoke too soon.*

"That thing isn't trying to help you, Kirby!" I shouted, still in cover, but I crawled forward to peer around our defensive debris. I could see Dai bleeding from a few injuries as he and the other person hunkered down. A thin sheet of ice covered his crates, acting as reinforcement for the decaying wood.

"*Be quiet!*" Kirby shouted.

My one-eyed look told me all I needed to know. The trio of Tendrils I'd seen before were hunkered down. One was channeling yellow-green energy into another while a death Tendril kept watch on our two locations. The creature's hand was resting against a crystal the size of a torso, pulsing black energy flowing out of the depths of the crystal, into the Tendril's arm. *That thing is replenishing it if I had to guess.* Beyond them, I could see the trainees chained up. Many of them appeared unconscious, the rest looked on in horror as the Tendrils lobbed attacks to keep us behind cover.

"You say that I don't know what I'm dealing with, Kirby. But how would I know that's a Dreg Entity?" I called out, racking my brain for a plan. With something on the power caliber of one of the entities, I had no idea what to expect. *Well, beyond the souped up skill shots that death bastard is throwing.*

The warehouse got real quiet other than some rustling from the captured trainees and the crackle of the black lightning.

>Earth fleshbag knows.<

"I know a thing or two, you oversized charcoal! Now let these people go, or it's going to get ugly in here."

>Fleshbag has sacrificed much. He would not sacrifice lives for victory. Threaten the captives.< My blood ran cold as I put two and two together.

"I've got <Flurry> up!" Dai said through the comm-plant.

No overthinking! Without trying to weigh anything else, I focused on the space where the cluster of Tendrils and Kirby were. Using the bits of my regenerated mana, I cast <Mineral Strike>. Ironically, another cluster of obsidian formed between my fingers before flying straight at the death-attuned. A bolt of black zipped to meet the attack, causing it to shatter but peppering the defending group in razor shards. Dai's summon flew into the mix. Hardened snowballs pelted the group. The wounded death Tendril zapped the air, missing the flurry. The living snippet of a snowstorm responded with maximum prejudice as it swelled in size.

Out of the corner of my eye, I watched Dai stagger and drop to the ground, shivering. Thankfully, the flurry seemed to have its orders. Columns of misting snow rained down on the Tendrils.

I made a run for Kirby and the corrupted entity. Mist swirled and snapped at the air wherever one of the flurry's attacks landed. Condensation covered my skin and dripped down my hair. Less than three quarters of the way, the earth deer made itself known. Instead of the complex rock weave of horns its male counterpart had, she had power in spades. One massive blunted column struck me and the flurry before blowing me into one of the support columns.

The building and I both groaned in protest at the impact. Thankfully, the doe had hit both me *and* Dai's flurry, because that was the only thing that kept me alive. As it was, my ribs creaked from my injuries and most of my <Earth Shell> armor had crumbled to save me from the impact. My wrist was definitely twisted the wrong way.

Nonetheless, the fight wasn't over.

Dai passed over his infused hatchet and the orc went to town on the deer still recovering from the attack. The man took a black lightning shot to the arm, cleaving it with necrotic death just above the elbow. To my concussed and stunned self, the man's fortitude was incredible. Even having just been maimed, the orc lobbed the axe like a tomahawk. It gave the death Tendril a whole new hair-do.

Kirby screamed out some words and I was faintly aware of the corrupted entity speaking. The words were garbled, and I heard shouts and a scream from somewhere outside. My thoughts swam even as I felt a pair of eyes practically burn a hole in me.

I wasn't sure what prompted me, but I turned my head and saw that I'd landed amidst the captured trainees. They were all staring at me wide-eyed, every one of them looking worse for wear. The one burning holes in me, however, I recognized. *T-something*. When our eyes met, he breathed out a glowing golden mist even as his whole body convulsed violently.

The mist reached me and sweet relief flowed through me. Thoughts and synapses fired as my brain was healed from Lord knows what injuries. The sound came next, almost overwhelming, as the building shrieked in protest of our attacks and all the abuse it had already suffered.

"Take the crystals away!"

My mind relocked on the youth—Tristan—that had healed me, seeing putrid black blood oozing out of his ears and nose. Considering he'd saved my behind, I crawled forward on my good arm and knees. Everything hurt, and even after the heal, I knew I wasn't put together enough to make a difference in a fight. The task the kid gave me, well, that was manageable.

Each of the trainees had one of those corrupted crystals in hand. It was taped to them, on top of the rough knots keeping them bound. Tristan's crystal was glowing with an eerie black light even as the youth sagged. I jiggled my utility knife out and cut him free. The crystal rolled away and color flushed through the blue fae. Another rush of golden light, this time somewhat tarnished with a slick brass, plumed out from his abdomen. "The others!" he managed. More sludge dribbled out of him, but he continued to feed the healing energies that kept me from falling unconscious and recovering the other trainees.

I undid the bindings for an orc, a dwarf, and finally Tristan's twin. The others started to free the rest, and all I could do was slump to the ground. The dwarf manhandled me onto her shoulder and pulled me away from the warehouse wall. Tristan's twin, Louis, hit my arm with a burst of healing before they shot out of sight after the other trainees.

"Thank ye, sir," the dwarf muttered. She was still injured, but her voice was steady. Turning on her shoulder was difficult, but worth it. Not only did I get to see the beaming smile of the dwarf youth, but also the other trainees.

A pillar of rock flipped the life Tendril into the air. While still in the air, four different elemental projectiles struck it. A bolt of light, an ice shard, fireball, and then a boulder. The attacks juggled the Tendril in the air briefly before it ragdolled onto the ground. *Fairly sure they are dead.* It didn't end there, a satyr trainee whistled loudly and the concrete below Kirby and the corrupted entity heaved. A thick pair of vines snapped around the man as he struggled to free himself. A set of vines also wrapped around the entity, but they seemed to decay just as soon as they touched it.

Instead of trying to wrangle the crystal, since it was inert on the ground, the trainees doubled down on Kirby. Another set of vines, frost, and a quicksand pit formed around the councilman. All of his thrashing was meaningless.

"Check on those outside," I wheezed. *Man, my ribs are borked.*

The trainees hobbled, hopped, and stumbled their way out of the groaning warehouse. A neon red fae stopped by to help the tomahawking orc. Dai and his other teammate, a bald-headed satyr, were already tending to the man, but they were swaying. The fae twins and the dwarf stayed with me as she set me down across from Kirby. The councilman in question was waist deep in the ground with both arms pinned in place.

The man's eyes were wild, reptilian slits scanning me and the trainees. The tension between us was palpable. "You don't know what you've done. You've killed Wildwood and everyone near us!" The man howled, even going so far as to snap some of the vines with his struggling. *Seems those scales weren't just for show.*

"I'm too tired for this, Kirby. Ms. Dwarf, could you…?" I gestured vaguely at the man.

A wicked smile split her face. There was a bloody gap there, tooth chipped from some sort of blow, but the emotion behind it was clear. Satisfaction. She threw a haymaker that caught Kirby mid-complaint. His whole body slumped to the ground. Tristan threw in a kick into the man's ribs. Louis was about to join in.

"Enough." I sighed.

"You can't even imagine what he's put us through!" The blue fae got in my face, tears streaking down his face.

"I can't. But I am sure as hell not going to let us beat up an unconscious person. He'll face judgment and he'll be *awake* for it." I tried to inject as much force as I could into my voice. The rest was more of a hiss of pain, but they got the point.

We nursed our wounds in silence after that. The twins offered to start healing my hand more but I waved them off using my left. Having their mana for someone more critical was more important than the pain radiating from my arm. *I wonder if my Limestone Skin numbs that pain some. I feel like I should be rolling on the ground screaming.* It was less than five minutes before people returned. Danny was amongst the group, face blushing red from the use of her mana.

"We're clear." Her expression wasn't one of joy and I felt my heart clench. "The other search teams just got here and the trainees were able to help out, but you're going to want to look at this."

"Tristan, Louis. Can you two please heal me some more?" I asked, struggling to my feet. I was running on fumes as it was. A wash of healing energy coursed through me, refreshing me and sealing up numerous cuts and bruises. Most of the relief focused on my chest, letting me at least draw breath without pain, but as soon as they were done healing, my body wanted to slump to the ground. A notification blipped in my peripheral vision.

<Affliction: Overhealed>

<Exhaustion effects augmented while recovering from injuries.>

The information vanished a second after, but it answered a few questions I had about just how healing worked. Nonetheless, I followed Daniela out. I gave the trainees one final look, eyes roving from them to Kirby before I turned away. A grating monotone echoed in the warehouse.

<Impure fleshbag has been bested.>

CHAPTER THIRTY-ONE

We Are...

To say the clearing was a mess would be an understatement. Scattered bits of burning ice, plant matter, and stone. Limbs and fur and everything in between littered the ground as we exited the warehouse. A hunk of the Tendril's berm had been blown up, leaving a U-shaped depression that Daniela led me through. I could see one of the teams was running around, checking the woods around the clearing and another nearby building for any threats we might have missed. A number of people were propped up against my defensive walls.

While the walk was short, I could still see Clara firing off instructions both in person and through the comm-plant. The telltale staring-into-space look was evident as she coordinated with the New Hopers scattered around. Sam was passed out in the dirt while one of the trainees I'd freed looked after him. Eric was sobbing with his back to me, barely visible on the other side of the wall.

"What—" I started, the words catching in my throat.

"Just take a look," Daniela said as she took us on a wider path so I could see the trainees we'd rescued.

"My God…" We hadn't been able to save them from the grasp of the Dreg, at least not entirely.

In the heat of the fight, I hadn't paid attention to the people Devon and Garren brought back. Now that I could actually count more than bodies, I saw the… changes. While the humanoid Tendrils looked more like colored mannequins than actual humans, what happened to the trainees was much more drastic. The first six we'd been able to rescue had swaths of their bodies transformed by their Attunements. Two orcs had skin that refused to stop smoldering along their upper body. A mermaid had turquoise crystal replacing her arm and most of the left side of her torso. An elf and a satyr looked like their limbs were missing entirely, but upon closer inspection, one could see *air* and limp roots in place of the hand and foot that were missing. The demoness that remained had a pockmarked mess that crawled up her back and partly on her face, visible as she shivered face down.

The remaining four trainees, the first few affected by the Dreg ritual, were over fifty percent changed. The first fae that had been zapped by the Dreg was all but a mess of entwined roots except for the upper right side of their head. Counted among the group of severely afflicted was Eric's son, Billy. The young elf's legs and abdomen were entirely gone, replaced by a thick, misty membrane. Other than being unconscious, they were peacefully laid out next to each other.

"Dreg afflictions…" I whispered. Bec's words from when I'd been attacked by the spiders resonated in my head. Magical mutations of the highest order now put on display for us all to see.

"Is this what the crystal back home warned us about?" Daniela asked, snapping me out of my thoughts.

"I'm not sure, but I wouldn't bet against it."

Clara, with help from Rommel, approached the two of us. "Perimeter is secured, I just sent out one of the fresh groups to start dissociating the bea—"

"No! Stop them!" I called out in alarm, my thoughts zeroing

in on her words. I gave my abbreviated status a sideways look even as I spotted a net of finger-thin Pith drifting toward all of us who'd been involved in the fight.

Subject: Ronan Terrigan
Health: 100% (Unafflicted)
Mana: 100%
Metier Quotient: 4 (22%)
Dreg Accumulation: 0%
LPS: Wildwood, FL
Communications
Skills - *(1) Selections Available*
Traits - *(98% Banked)*
Attributes - *Growth Quantified*

That huge pile of Dreg will put me into Overbanked territory, but what about for those at a lower Quotient? What about the Dreg afflicted? My internal monologue ramped up even as the threads grew closer. Clara was looking at me sideways but she communicated to the groups to stop. *We can't let all that Pith go, it could bring up the trainees and push people to their next trait...*

"If we absorb too much, we will have issues like them," I said, pointing to the afflicted trainees. It was a bit harsh, considering the recency of their injuries and change, but it was the fastest way to get everyone on board. Clara's eyes widened, her mannerisms becoming a tad less composed as she gestured wildly to the teams ambling about. "We will need to leave a team or two here to gather the Pith once we are back near the crystal."

"Is this more of that stuff dealing with our mutual friends?" Devon asked from beside Clara.

"Yes. I know it's already been circulating that we popped out of the crystal, but we'll need to bring everyone into it. I'll also need to talk to Tec and see if we can get everyone a status and proper protection for any trait acquisitions in the future."

While I was talking, the threads started to reach the closest in the group. Most turned some shade of green as the nausea of accumulating Dreg overwhelmed the positive side of the Pith. Knowing the likelihood that absorbing that wouldn't go well, I basically threw myself to the ground. Sure enough, when the energy entered me, my abdomen clenched in protest and the world swayed around me. Clara and Devon grunted, but both remained standing. A look at my Dreg accumulation saw it climb up by almost ten percent. *And that's not all of them...* I grimaced.

Several minutes of groaning and swearing passed before the group felt well enough to move again. My face fell once again as I looked over the afflicted trainees. There was a chance the Entity Clusters might be able to do something for them, but I just didn't know enough about it. With that thought, my eyes roved over to the warehouse. One of the fresh teams had gone over and replaced the trainees, but I still wasn't happy with the situation. Tec would be able to hold Kirby, but I had no clue how to deal with the corrupted entity.

Even with the trainees rescued, I only had more questions and difficulties.

— + —

"Three days. How did it take *three days* to get everything sorted?" Daniela complained.

"It was no use forcing people. We were in no rush," Samuel said evenly.

"Still! We were right out in the open the whole time!"

"With as many earth walls around us as we had, I almost felt safer than in Wildwood," Sam retorted.

Danny let out an incomprehensible sound as she stormed off ahead of us. The moment she crossed the invisible boundary around the Entity Cluster, red wisps of mana peeled off her skin with each huffed breath. The slight smiles on our faces fell off quickly as Tec loomed over us. As comforting as the Blessing of Magic was, what awaited us didn't spark joy.

Even after all the trips to Kirby's hideout, one team still remained to gather the Pith. As soon as we were in range of the crystal, I gave Clara a nod. "You can start, Godfrey."

Everyone that had been present during the fight against the Tendrils tensed. It took several minutes, but eventually the threads of Pith zipped through the town, dodging people before filtering into us. The nausea hit, but thankfully it was short-lived as Tec purified the Dreg. My legs grew heavy and I dropped to a knee. I watched a few others in the group, my friends included, drop also. "You know what to do with the *crystal*," I said to Clara. The woman was grimacing, but she met my eyes and returned the nod. A moment later, crystal hands plucked me into the Entity Cluster.

— + —

It was a whole day later when my mind settled back in Tec's whitespace.

—Ronan trait assimilation complete.—

"Thanks, Tec. How's everything else?"

—Status of Dreg Warriors and prospective implantees is augmented.—

The Entity almost seemed to hesitate.

—Status of Dreg afflicted individuals is inconclusive.—

"It's alright. I know you are trying." A sigh escaped my lips as I looked up at the glowing orb representing Tec. "We'll figure something out."

—Affirmative.—

Unlike usual, Tec didn't rush to push me out of his white-space. Considering I knew that the entities could read our minds to some degree, I didn't dismiss that it was reading my thoughts about what I had to do. Nonetheless, the entity complied instantly. "Bring Kirby, please."

The orb above me winked out before returning a moment later with a person bound in iridescent crystal chains. Two simple chairs formed out of the ground, the ex-councilman of

Wildwood being gently *placed* into one. The landing shook the man conscious as I took a seat across from him.

Kirby took several minutes to fully come around. While the man was distracted and coming to terms with his blindness, I reviewed the changes to my body. I didn't *feel* different, but after reading, the cause became more apparent.

Traits:
Limestone Skin
The surface of your body has taken on some of the strength properties of compacted sediment.
Trait overbanked. Impact forces are minutely dissipated when making contact with soil interfaces.
Quake Osseum
Your skeletal system has taken on some of the strength properties of consolidated aggregates.
Trait overbanked. Minor enhancement to innate earth vibratory organ.

After the mess my ribs and hand were, I guess I can't be surprised that's the trait I got. What's this about a vibratory organ?

"You gonna gloat or just stare off into space?" Kirby scoffed. His voice had lost the hollow and ominous tone. It was more the voice of someone repeatedly kicked while they were down.

"Not blind? Why am I not surprised?"

"What I am used to is more of a black space. You don't know anything. You are just a frog in a well, Ronan. The world is too big for you Fallen lot to understand. How could a Bunker-born twerp possibly understand?"

"Wow. Talk about condescending. You do remember what happened, right? We won the fight." I leaned forward, nearly growling in the man's face. "What I want to know is what sick game you were playing."

"Why should I answer anything? I can deduce a number of things." The man started to flick his fingers as he counted. "You don't intend to kill me, because I am still alive. We are inside the town's crystal. You have no idea what to do next, so you look to your betters for a clue."

"Man, since you talked less than Dylan, I thought you were just a quiet person, but it seems like you were just repressed. Yes, you are alive, but that's because I haven't let the townsfolk loose on you. Hell, I wouldn't even need to set the town loose, all I need is Eric."

Kirby flinched slightly at my words, but quickly composed himself. Thankfully, the motion was as clear as day. *The town's opinion hurts you, does it?*

"What do you know about our struggles? Cushy in your little Bunker, you didn't even survive the early mutations."

"True. But after spending some time with people instead of plotting to turn them into monsters to save my own behind, I got a pretty good idea. Plus, people are generally pretty welcoming when you work alongside them to feed each other."

"I wasn't turning anyone into monsters!" Kirby snapped, straining against his restraints.

"Oh yeah? What were you doing?"

"I was pushing them to *evolve*!"

"Like the monsters of the early days?"

"Yes! Just like—" Kirby stopped mid-sentence, his mind catching up to his mouth.

"You lost your humanity somewhere along the way, Kirby. Did you really think people wanted to live as monsters, possibly attacking their friends and family, instead of just being plain old dead?"

"I..."

"Have you looked at the families that you've broken? I know I haven't, but even the implication that their missing relatives hadn't been taken by the chaos of the surface had them incensed. That even after everyone banded together to survive the Fall, one of their own would betray them."

Kirby fell silent. Somehow, his scales lost some of their shine and the man overall seemed to deflate. I didn't say anything.

Whatever conclusions he came to about his actions wouldn't affect *his* future. All I hoped for was that he would help affect humanity. Correct some of the deviant actions he'd already taken.

Just when I was ready to let the man have the day to come to grips, he spoke up.

"What did you call your plan?"

"Which plan?" I said, turning back to face his seat.

"The one with the spider territory and the ant territory further to the west."

"The dungeon farm?" I asked, confused as to where he was going with the conversation.

"Yes. We are… Well." The man seemed to struggle with the words. "We are *their* dungeon."

I almost dismissed the man's comment as nonsense, but then I started drawing up connections. Connections I didn't like in the least.

"They protect us, so that we can reproduce. The human Tendrils are always stronger than the beast ones, just because they actually coordinate." The words were like sand in my mouth. "Then they send the Tendrils in to either clear us out or pull us into their ranks. Either way, it's a win-win for them."

Kirby nodded slowly. "The attacks in which you intervened were meant to wear us down. Get me to cave to their final demand and upgrade my tribute. Even tell them the location of the other smaller towns."

"And what? You grew a conscience?" I asked, unable to keep the bitterness out of my voice.

"You don't understand what the early days were like. People died by the *hundreds*. It wasn't even the damn crystals that were meant to kill us, but the mutating creatures. And the more they killed us, the stronger they got and the more people they killed. When the sand courier brought the Dreg crystal… It was too tempting not to accept."

"Let's ignore the difficulty of the past and focus the conversation a bit. The sand courier?" I asked, drilling into Kirby with my eyes. He didn't meet them.

"Yes. He... Well, he was more like what the Dreg afflicted were. Part of the alignment, as opposed to changed like we were." Kirby gestured to a patch of scales on his arm.

"Is that what those smaller crystals were for?" I asked, thinking back on the trainees and the ritual overall.

Kirby lifted his gaze for a moment before nodding. "The Dreg...as I understand it, is natural. However, you can have enough that it starts to influence changes in your body." The man gestured to his body once again. "Nothing is static after the Fall. If you accumulate too much or in the wrong place, then you become subject to the commands of the Dreg. But the crystals they...replace and enhance those changes. Make them entirely of Dreg instead of a mutation. Like... Like a tree with a fruit branch grafted on, and all the original limbs pruned."

My mind was spinning with questions. Most relating to how we might possibly reverse some of those changes, others to how those same changes might benefit us. The main question, however, was around what would happen to the trainees changed by the crystal.

"I don't know what will happen to them," Kirby said, as if reading my thoughts. "The crystal was the... swap point. After the people were changed, Tendrils took them off further west. Galloway, the sand courier, and that crystal were the closest I got to a leadership amongst the Dreg. Even then I wasn't told anything."

That's less than helpful! I wanted to scream out in frustration. Even after everything Kirby had done, he was only a dead end. *No. The sand courier is something. By the name, they must be part of an outreach network the Dreg have in place. Plus, I can talk to Tec and Bec about the Dreg entity.*

"If you think of anything, you tell Tec," I said, rising to my feet.

Kirby's head snapped up. "What are you going to do? You can't oppose them. Just my efforts alone were able to feed them over a hundred people. They would have killed us all if I didn't deliver!"

"That's the problem, Kirby. You did it alone. Sure, you pulled Charles into your little net of intrigue, but somewhere deep in that lizard brain of yours, you knew it was wrong. If I wanted to deal with the guilt of killing you right now, I would, but I don't think you are anything more than a narcissist with delusions of grandeur. That led to a whole lot of suffering, and I am going to make sure you never forget it.

"Me and my friends didn't make it on the surface by working alone. The Wild Guard didn't thrive and expand as it did just because you were the head of it. It was the effort of the people beneath you, the community and drive they had, that allowed them to survive. Just like they came together, *without you*, to bring their children home."

As much as I disliked him, and as much as it made me ill to compare myself to the man, I understood the feeling. The need to do it all yourself or see it fail. Thankfully, I had my friends to pluck my head from my ass and keep us chugging forward.

"Wildwood is not alone, and humanity is not alone. The Dreg don't belong, and I'm going to make sure they learn their place."

I turned to the giant orb of light that had been listening in. "Take me out, Tec. We've got work to do."

EPILOGUE

The sand courier's limbs stretched to their limits, snagging a man all the way from the bushes where he hid. The flesh hands covered the man's mouth, stifling the scream of surprise that would have alerted his patrol team.

"Now you listen to me. You'd be dead if I wanted you to be. If you don't tell your leaders to prepare for a monster surge, then you very well will be." The courier waited for several seconds until the man nodded his ascent. "I don't have a lot of time. Here is information on nearby settlements that could use this warning. Pass this off as someone else's information. Do not tell them about me."

The man's nodding shook some of the courier's sand onto the ground. With deliberate motions, he let go of the man. A trio of hooded lanterns rushed through the trees towards the man. One of them had a bow slung on his back and the two other women had a spear and sword respectively.

"George? You alright?" The rays of the lanterns cut through the night and deep into the forest. It was still except for the heavy breathing of the patrol.

"Ye-yeah. I'm fine." The man resisted the urge to dust off

the sand covering his sleeves, but he stood from where he'd been sitting. "Just tripped on the ground."

While being focused on the threats of the night, they missed the tan grains trickling from the man's clothes. George tucked the sheet of paper safely into his back pocket before going to retrieve his own fallen lantern.

"We told you to work on your dexterity, man. You are all right feet and elbows," the spear woman said.

"I think the expression you are looking for is 'klutz,'" the bowman replied.

"That's the one."

"Don't you three have anything better to do?" George shot back. The three were a bit caught off guard by the tone, but brushed it off as embarrassment for his blunder. They checked on George one more time before spreading back to their posts.

"Wellborn, Hawthorne, Wildwood…" The man read aloud from a list of twelve locations. He recognized Hawthorne since that was where his parents came from, but not the others. Geography wasn't the top priority at the Uni.

"How the heck am I supposed to deal with this information?" he mumbled to himself. The sand courier hadn't failed him yet, but keeping his identity a secret was becoming harder and harder. With the strength the Dreg cult was garnering in the city, knowledge of *what* the courier was became common. George debated internally what to do, actual sparks lighting up his hair as if gears were struggling to turn in his head. "Why does he always threaten me, yet always gives me beneficial information?"

The sand courier pushed his limbs to the limit to remove himself from the city and arrive at the meeting point before his tail. He moved towards the location at the edge of town, where he would be giving the same announcement. Instead of a *warning*, the recipients would see it as something to be celebrated. He hoped he'd been able to stall the Dreg for long enough.

ABOUT FRANK G. ALBELO

Frank is a Civil Engineer graduate who rediscovered his passion for writing. The twenty-something year old is happily married and has a toddler who is a cute, but huge, troublemaker. Originally born in Cuba, Frank moved to Costa Rica at a young age and then to Miami, Florida giving him a wonderfully diverse view of the world to draw on for the worlds he creates.

He has been writing stories since he was young and reading them way before that. He hopes to continue to write tales and create wondrous systems to share them with readers. Some of Frank's other hobbies include Magic the Gathering, video gaming, and bugging his wife about buying new bookshelves to accommodate the books that seem to magically appear in their home.

Connect with Frank G. Albelo:
Patreon.com/Falbelo
Facebook.com/FAlbeloWriter
Discord.gg/A6srSxk

ABOUT MOUNTAINDALE PRESS

Dakota and Danielle Krout, a husband and wife team, strive to create as well as publish excellent fantasy and science fiction novels. Self-publishing *The Divine Dungeon: Dungeon Born* in 2016 transformed their careers from Dakota's military and programming background and Danielle's Ph.D. in pharmacology to President and CEO, respectively, of a small press. Their goal is to share their success with other authors and provide captivating fiction to readers with the purpose of solidifying Mountaindale Press as the place 'Where Fantasy Transforms Reality.'

Connect with Mountaindale Press:
MountaindalePress.com
Facebook.com/MountaindalePress
Twitter.com/_Mountaindale
Instagram.com/MountaindalePress

MOUNTAINDALE PRESS TITLES

GameLit and LitRPG

The Completionist Chronicles,
The Divine Dungeon,
Full Murderhobo, and
Year of the Sword by Dakota Krout

Metier Apocalypse by Frank G. Albelo

Arcana Unlocked by Gregory Blackburn

A Touch of Power by Jay Boyce

Red Mage and
Farming Livia by Xander Boyce

Space Seasons by Dawn Chapman

Ether Collapse and
Ether Flows by Ryan DeBruyn

Dr. Druid by Maxwell Farmer

Bloodgames by Christian J. Gilliland

Unbound by Nicoli Gonnella

Threads of Fate by Michael Head

Lion's Lineage by Rohan Hublikar and Dakota Krout

Wolfman Warlock by James Hunter and Dakota Krout

Axe Druid,
Mephisto's Magic Online, and
High Table Hijinks by Christopher Johns

Skeleton in Space by Andries Louws

Dragon Core Chronicles by Lars Machmüller

Chronicles of Ethan by John L. Monk

Pixel Dust and
Necrotic Apocalypse by David Petrie

Viceroy's Pride by Cale Plamann

Henchman by Carl Stubblefield

Artorian's Archives by Dennis Vanderkerken and Dakota Krout

Vaudevillain by Alex Wolf

www.ingramcontent.com/pod-product-compliance
Lightning Source LLC
Chambersburg PA
CBHW020352260626
47156CB00015B/440